ZANE PRESENTS

WHO SAID IT WOULD BE EASY?

A STORY OF FAITH

ALSO BY CHERYL FAYE

Be Careful What You Wish For

ZANE PRESENTS

WHO SAID IT WOULD BE EASY?

A STORY OF FAITH

CHERYL FAYE

SBI

STREBOR BOOKS

NEW YORK LONDON TORONTO SYDNEY

SBI

Strebor Books
P.O. Box 6505
Largo, MD 20792
http://www.streborbooks.com

ISBN 978-1-59309-352-5
ISBN 978-1-4516-0800-7 (ebook)
LCCN 2010940489

First Strebor Books trade paperback edition February 2011

Cover design: www.mariondesigns.com
Cover photograph: © Keith Saunders/Marion Designs

10 9 8 7 6 5 4 3 2 1

Manufactured in the United States of America

For information regarding special discounts for bulk purchases,
please contact Simon & Schuster Special Sales at 1-866-506-1949
or business@simonandschuster.com

The Simon & Schuster Speakers Bureau can bring authors to your live event. For more information or to book an event, contact the Simon & Schuster Speakers Bureau at 1-866-248-3049 or visit our website at www.simonspeakers.com.

*This book is lovingly dedicated to Rev. Dr. LaKeesha Walrond,
Executive Pastor of First Corinthian Baptist Church,
New York, New York. Thank you, Rev. LaKeesha, for your prayers,
love, support, teaching, encouragement and friendship.
You are truly a blessing in my life and the reason
I finally finished this book!*

I love you much.

ACKNOWLEDGMENTS

First and foremost, I give all honor to my Creator. Father, I thank You for my life—the laughter and the tears, the highs and the lows, the pruning and the watering. God, I thank You for eternal life RIGHT NOW, for abundant life RIGHT NOW, for this very second. You are, You are, Lord, You are my Everything!!! I worship and adore You.

To my Immediate Family:

Mommy and Daddy, the late Barbara and James Smith, Sr.— what can I ever say that would express how grateful I am to have been blessed with parents like you? I miss you both so much but truly rejoice in having shared my life with you.

My two precious sons, Michael and Douglas, you are proof that God loves me beyond measure and I love you both so much and am so proud of you. Thank you for being.

My beautiful granddaughter, Mikayla. I love you, Mama, and can't wait to see how you will impact the world with your infectious spirit. You are already a force to be reckoned with.

My siblings, Jacqueline, Mamie, James, Jr. and Stephanie, I love y'all so much and am proud to have shared the best parents in the world with you.

My sister-in-law, Kym—thanks for taking such good care of my one and only brother, and just for being you.

My nieces and nephews, Stacey, Breone, Brittany, Makenzie,

Torian, James III, Brandon, Jovonnie II, and Avery—don't we just have the best family? I love y'all. We must always be sure to keep it tight.

To my dear sister-friends: Sharón Spence, Michele Cordew and Peggy Bailey—what an amazing support system I've been blessed with. I love you very much and truly cherish our friendships.

To Debra Kellman: You are truly blessed. Keep on honoring God with your photography. I love you.

To my FCBC Family: God blessed me with so many sisters and brothers in this Walk and I am eternally grateful. Thank you for the love, support and encouragement. I love you all.

To my fellow FCBC Trustees: I just love y'all. I am honored to be serving God with each one of you. Thanks for the laughter, the dedication and the support.

To Michael A. Walrond, Jr., Sr., Pastor of First Corinthian Baptist Church: thank you for your phenomenal teaching, your amazing transparency, your infectious laugh and great sense of humor, but mostly for your humble obedience. I have grown so much under your tutelage and look forward to where God will lead me and all of FCBC as disciples of Jesus under your unselfish guidance. You are truly one of God's anointed foot soldiers and I'm honored to know you. Creation is waiting...

And last, but most certainly not least, to William Fredrick Cooper: You know I love you and that what we share defies the norm, but God doesn't operate within the boundaries of what our small minds define as normal. So I just want to know, "Who said it would be easy?"

PROLOGUE

"How can you tell me you love me in one breath, and before you even get the words out of your mouth good, you're with someone else?" she asked as tears streamed down her face.

"She doesn't mean anything to me, honey. Nothing," he insisted, moving closer to her.

She took a step back. "I don't mean anything to you, obviously."

"No, Janine. You mean the world to me. I messed up, but please give me another chance. I promise, it'll never happen again."

She shook her head as she walked over to the window. "I don't believe you."

"Why? Why don't you believe me?"

"Because you've lied to me before, Stefan. I'm tired of your empty apologies. If you really loved me as much as you claim, you'd never have to apologize for doing me wrong."

They were in her bedroom at her parents' house. Her mother and father were out at the time and she was home from college on spring break.

"Oh, come on, baby. Don't act like you never make mistakes," he cried.

"I've never cheated on you!" she yelled in frustration.

Knowing he needed to take another approach, Stefan said, "No, you haven't. You've been real good to me and I don't even deserve a woman as good as you, but if you give me one more chance, Janine, I promise things will be different from now on."

She looked across the room at him from where she stood and knew, in this very moment, that he was sincere. He was always sincere at the instant the apology left his mouth. It was when they were apart and he was left to his own devices that things went awry.

He was beautiful; twenty-one years old and already on his way to being the successful businessman he would one day be.

Fresh tears sprang to her eyes and spilled over her lids as she thought about how much she genuinely loved him.

They had been together since right after her senior high prom. Another boy had been her date, but she and Stefan met that night when he defended her girlfriend, Sarah, after Sarah's date had tried to force himself on her in the parking lot.

To her, he had been like something out of a dream. Tall, slim but muscular, and very well-groomed. He and his best friend and running buddy, Julian Walker, had just arrived at the prom when they had come upon Sarah and Oscar.

Seeing Sarah run into the bathroom in tears, she followed and soon discovered what was amiss. Highly agitated, minutes later, she rushed from the ladies' room to confront the jerk who'd hurt her friend and crashed right into Stefan.

"Whoa, baby, slow your roll. You almost knocked me down," he flippantly stated.

"Sorry," she replied, as she collected herself and attempted to continue on her way.

"Wait a minute." He reached for her hand. "Where's your friend?"

Perplexed, she asked, "What?"

"You know, the girl I always see you with. The one who was with that jerk, Oscar."

"Sarah? She's inside," Janine answered as she gestured to the women's restroom.

"Is she okay?" he asked.

"Yeah. I was just going to give Oscar a piece of my mind, if that's okay with you," she snidely commented.

"Oscar's being detained. Principal Davis called the police. I don't think you'll be able to say anything to him for a while."

That surprised her. *How did this guy know so much about what was going on anyway?*

"Who are you?" she finally asked.

"Who am I? You don't know who I am?" he asked, in mock insult.

"Should I know who you are?"

He smiled at her, exposing a solitary dimple in his left cheek. "I'm just messing with you. No, I don't expect that you should know who I am, but I happened to come upon your friend when she was trying to fight that creep off. I took care of him for her. I'm Stefan Cooper. What's your name?"

"Janine Taylor. You said you see me with Sarah all the time. Where?"

"You're a cheerleader for Norman Thomas' basketball team, right?"

"Yes."

"I know. I've seen you at the games."

"You go to Norman Thomas?"

"No, I graduated from there last year, but I was invited to the prom by a friend."

She hadn't had an opportunity to spend much time talking with him that evening because her date had come looking for her, but she managed to give him her telephone number before the night was over, since he'd asked her for it.

When Sarah told her that he had punched Oscar out after he jumped bad when Stefan tried to rescue her, she knew there was more she wanted to know about the fine young defender of her friend's virtue.

But the past two years had been turbulent, to say the least. On one hand, Stefàn treated her like a queen—buying her gifts, taking her out to fancy restaurants, etc. On the other, however, he was an undeniable player. She'd heard people talk about his escapades with other girls and on one occasion had even been confronted by some chick who claimed to be his girlfriend. Stefàn quickly squashed that situation by letting the girl know—right in front of Janine—that Janine was his main squeeze. But that wouldn't be the last time she'd have to deal with another girl and Janine cried each time one of these incidents took place. She couldn't understand, if he claimed to love her, why did he feel the need to be with anyone else?

But she'd had her fill of all that. Janine had finally come to realize that she deserved better than Stefàn. Yes, he was gorgeous, with his meticulous appearance and unabashed self-assurance. He held a black belt in karate and often competed in tournaments, which Janine usually attended along with his parents. In the time they'd been together, she'd witnessed him winning four tournament championships. He was ambitious. Stefàn was not one to sit around waiting for things to happen; he made them happen. He attended classes at Rutgers University, but was also preparing to take the test to get a real estate sales license. He'd told her that he planned to own his own real estate company one day. And she didn't doubt it, because whatever he set his mind to, he accomplished and he would never allow anyone to convince him that he couldn't. His mistake, however, was assuming she needed him so much that she would put up with his lies and unfaithfulness indefinitely.

Looking at him now, as he feebly defended the indefensible once more, and knowing that if she gave in to him, this scene would be replayed again sometime in the future—maybe several times—she couldn't deal with the hurt anymore.

"I'm sorry, Stefan, but I can't do this anymore. I'm done. I really do love you, but I don't want to see you anymore," she tearfully stated.

"What?"

"I want you to go."

"Come on, Janine. I said I was sorry," he replied as he started toward her.

"No, don't come any closer." If she let him touch her, she would give in to him and she could not let him take her love for granted any longer.

"Janine. You can't forgive me?"

She shook her head sadly. "Not right now, no. Maybe after some time, but I can't right now. I don't want to see you anymore. I can't let you hurt me anymore."

Always the tough guy, for the first time since she had known him, Janine saw a chink in Stefan's armor. Tears welled in his eyes as he pleaded with her, "Please, Janine. Look, I messed up bad. I... Come on, baby, just this last time. I swear. I'll never hurt you again. I love you. For real. I love you."

"No," she cried, barely above a whisper. "I can't." She turned her back to him then, shutting him out of her life for good.

Dejected, defeated and demoralized, Stefan stood frozen to the spot for the next several minutes, trying to pull himself together. *She doesn't really mean this. She can't. She's angry right now, and I get that, but she can't be serious that it's over.*

Not willing to accept that this was the end for them, Stefan softly murmured, "All right, J, I'll go now, but I'll call you later so we can talk about this, okay?"

Janine didn't react or respond.

"All right, baby?"

He stood for seconds that seemed like hours, waiting for her to answer. When she didn't, he moved to stand behind her. Without asking permission, he embraced her from behind but immediately felt her body stiffen at his touch. He continued to hold her tightly, before brushing a soft kiss against the nape of her neck. "I love you. I'll call you tonight," he whispered.

When she didn't respond, he released her and left.

His Honda Accord was parked in front of her parents' house, and as he opened the door, a girl that he had flirted with many times called out to him.

"Hey, Stefan," she purred. "I'm still waiting for that dinner you promised me."

The girl was hot, with a body that cried for his attention and a manner that let him know all he had to do was say the word and he could have his way with her. He was about to speak when something told him to look up.

Janine was still standing at her bedroom window, only now she was watching him. Wisely, he ignored the girl, got into his car and drove away.

Later that night, Stefan called Janine. He was hoping she had cooled off and would at least take his call. After two rings, her mother picked up.

"Hello, Mrs. Taylor. This is Stefan. How are you?"

"I'm fine, thank you."

"May I speak to Janine, please?"

"She doesn't want to talk to you, Stefan."

"What?" he asked in disbelief.

"She doesn't want to talk to you," she repeated.

He could hear the indifference in her tone and was momentarily at a loss for words.

"I have to go," Mrs. Taylor said, interrupting the silence. "My dinner's on the table."

Realizing that she was about to hang up, Stefan hurriedly

asked, "Can you please tell Janine that I called and that I'll call her again tomorrow?"

"Okay. Good-bye."

Stefan felt a moment of panic at the sound of the line disconnecting. *Please God, make her forgive me. I won't mess up anymore if she'll just give me another chance.*

At least twice a day, every day for the next week, Stefan called Janine. She never took his calls and the few times she had answered herself, she quickly hung up on him.

Her spring break was almost over and Stefan was no closer to working things out, so he did the only thing he could to get her to talk to him face-to-face—he waited for her after church.

She was laughing as she came out of a side exit with her older brother, Sean, and another dude that he didn't recognize. Stefan got out of his car and waited since they were heading in his direction. Whatever they were discussing must have been hilarious because the sound of Janine's laughter seemed to float in the wind, massaging his ears with its sweet sound.

They were about three yards away when Sean saw him. Noticing that Sean immediately tensed, Stefan tried to be as humble as possible. He didn't want to get into anything with her brother. Stefan liked him, but he needed to speak to Janine and was determined to not let anyone prevent him from doing so.

"Janine," he called to her since she still hadn't seen him.

When she noticed him, the smile immediately fell from her face. Taking a deep breath, she rolled her eyes as they stopped in front of him. "What are you doing here, Stefan?"

"We need to talk."

"I don't have anything to talk to you about. I've already said everything I had to say."

"Well, maybe there are some things I need to say to you."

"I've heard everything I want to hear from you, Stefán. I told you, I don't want to see you anymore," she coldly stated.

Feeling the control of his emotions slipping away from him, he quickly averted his eyes and tried to collect himself. She didn't hesitate to turn and continue on her way with her brother and the other dude. *C'mon, Stefán, don't give up*, his subconscious self screamed. "Janine, please. I love you. Why can't you forgive me?" He probably looked lame standing out in front of the church begging, but at that moment, Stefán didn't care. He refused to let Janine walk out of his life like this and if that meant making a fool of himself, then so be it.

"I already told you. There may come a day when I will, but this ain't that day. Even if I do forgive you, I still don't want anything else to do with you. So please, leave me alone and get on with your life."

Tossing aside the remnants of his guilt, his desperation led to anger. "You're supposed to be a Christian, but that's only when you in there, huh?" He jabbed a finger toward the edifice she had exited. "I thought Christians were supposed to forgive people when they make a mistake. You're nothing but a hypocrite, like all the rest of these holier-than-thou people."

At that, her brother said, "Yo, Stefán, you need to check yourself."

"No! You need to tell your sister to check herself. I might have messed up this time, but I've been good to you, Janine. You can't tell me I didn't treat you right."

Janine was fed up by now. "You call running around with other girls behind my back treating me right? You think just because you spend money on me, you can do whatever the hell you want to do and everything's supposed to be fine? No! I've given you chance after chance and listened to your apologies long enough. You're never gonna change because you think the world revolves around you!" Janine was yelling by now and a small crowd had gathered to witness the spectacle.

"Calm down, J," Sean said to his sister. Taking her arm and attempting to lead her away, he added, "C'mon, let's get out of here."

"Yes, please, let's," she said, shaking her head in disgust.

As they started to walk away, Stefan thought about going after her, but when he looked into the faces of the people who stood staring back at him, he decided against it. Banging his fist on the roof of his car in anger, he yelled, "To hell with you then."

Before he could duck into his car to get away, an older gentleman who had been standing near his rear door, empathically said to him, "Son, if it's God's will for you and that young lady to be together, you'll get her back. But you've got to surrender your will to Him."

"I don't need her and I don't need your God, either!" Stefan yelled at the old man.

Slamming the door as he sat behind the wheel, Stefan immediately started the car and recklessly peeled away from the curb and sped off.

I don't need her! I can have any chick I want. Later for her. Janine's rejection and unforgiveness tore Stefan's heart in two. Realizing too late how much he truly loved her, Stefan, nevertheless, refused to take credit for the demise of their relationship. Yes, he'd made a terrible mistake and had been called to task for it, but the way she completely disregarded his feelings and dismissed his pleas was so wrong. He had never begged anyone for anything, but he had pleaded with her to give them another chance in front of her whole congregation, practically.

I must have looked pathetic to those people, he thought.

Stefan's attempts to assuage his bruised heart and ego were

unsuccessful. He'd reached out to the girl he'd ignored that day outside of Janine's house, as well as several others who had offered themselves to him, and he still hadn't been able to purge Janine from his heart and mind.

When he was alone in his bed—after all the drinking, partying and carousing was done—Janine filled his every waking moment. There were several nights when all he had were his tears for her, but that was something no one knew, not even Julian.

After a month, he made up his mind that it was time to stop crying over Janine and start living. From that day on, Stefan decided that he would spend the rest of his life in pursuit of the best of everything the world could offer, be it fame, fortune or females. The only love he would allow himself to feel was that for his family and maybe a few friends. Women were to be kept at arm's length and never again given an opportunity to get into his heart. He would never expose himself to the pain of rejection again.

CHAPTER 1
AT FIRST SIGHT

I t was a perfect day for a wedding. The temperature may have been in the high-nineties, but there wasn't a cloud to be seen in the cerulean blue sky and the air was free of humidity.

Charisse Ellison was happy about that. She had spent three hours at her best friend's salon yesterday getting a manicure, pedicure and facial, plus a new cut and perm and would have been fit to be tied if she'd had to worry about her style shriveling up.

Standing among the throng at the bottom of the steps of First Canaan A.M.E. Church in Queens, New York, Charisse took in her surroundings. Most of her large family had turned out for the mid-July wedding. Watching them as they all waited for the bride and groom to appear, Charisse realized that the only time they got together nowadays was either for a wedding or a funeral. During her childhood, her parents, uncles and aunts did not need a reason to get their collective families together on a fairly regular basis. Most lived in the New York, New Jersey area, and others were spread out between there and Baltimore, so it was never difficult for them to get together. Sadly, as the elder members of the family got older and died off, the younger generations seemed to be too wrapped up in their own lives to make time for simple family gatherings. That was probably one of the reasons the turnout for Jewel's wedding was so large.

As Jewel and her new husband, Terrance Wilson, emerged from the church, the crowd in front broke into applause. Remembering the conversation she'd had with Jewel the night before, and knowing how happy her cousin was to finally be married to the man of her dreams, Charisse's face was lit by her bright smile.

Still, she couldn't help but feel a twinge of envy because God had yet to send her husband-to-be. Charisse looked forward to the day she would start her own family. Unbeknownst to most of the Ellison clan, Jewel and Terrance were already on their way to becoming parents. Jewel had confided in Charisse at the end of her bridal shower last weekend that she would be three months pregnant this coming week. It didn't matter that she was thirty years old; Jewel's parents were old school and legalistically religious. Aunt Jean was the eldest of Charisse's father's siblings. Charisse and Jewel both knew that she would not have been happy about her daughter being pregnant on her wedding day.

Charisse's thoughts were interrupted by the sound of her mother's voice. "Johnny, why'd you bring your camera if you're not going to use it?"

"I'm getting the pictures, Barb. Besides we've got all afternoon to take pictures of them," her father said.

"But you should at least get a shot of them leaving the church."

Charisse smiled as she watched her parents' playful bickering. Having tied the knot right after high school, they had been married for thirty-eight years. They were both quite youthful looking fifty-six-year-olds and they made an incredibly handsome couple. Childhood sweethearts, the elder Ellisons had met in the ninth grade when John had been assigned as a math tutor to Barbara.

Always thrilled by watching them together, Charisse's heart swelled with pride and joy. Even after all these years, her parents' mutual adoration, admiration and affection were still very evident. She believed their loving playfulness was what kept them so young looking and young-at-heart.

Dressed today in a Christian Dior gown, Barbara presented a striking picture of maturity with her stylishly coiffed silver hair. Looking polished in his Armani tuxedo, John got many second looks from women in the crowd—young and old alike—but he had eyes for no one but his comely wife.

"Mommy, stop picking on Daddy. David's getting the shots. He's right up front," Charisse playfully scolded. Her oldest brother was a professional photographer and, with the help of his crew, was recording the entire event on film and video as a gift to his cousin.

"That's right, Barb, so stop fussing. You know we'll get copies of all the best shots."

John turned to his youngest daughter, placed his arm around her shoulder, and kissed her cheek. "Thanks, baby."

Frowning, Barbara said, "You need to mind your business, Risi."

Sidling up to her mother, Charisse purred, "I love you, too, Mommy," and wrapped her in a quick embrace as she kissed her cheek.

"Get off of me," Barbara said as she smiled and playfully shrugged Charisse off before turning back to the happy couple. "Jewel looks so beautiful."

"Doesn't she?" Charisse agreed as she turned and gazed at her cousin.

"He's quite a handsome fellow," Barbara added.

Cutting her eyes at her mother, Charisse said, "Mommy, brotha's fine."

"Oh, no, I missed the ceremony."

Turning simultaneously when they heard the female voice behind them, Charisse and her parents were joined by her sister.

"I was wondering where you were," Barbara said.

"Joe was late picking up the girls," she replied as she kissed her mother's cheek.

"Hi, Daddy. Hey, Risi," she said and kissed them both in turn.

"Hey, Star," Charisse greeted her older sister.

"Why didn't you bring them?" John asked, referring to his granddaughters.

"Because I want to have a good time. It's so seldom I get to go out. I'm going to enjoy myself today."

"I heard that," Charisse muttered.

Known to family and close friends as Star due to her childhood aspirations of becoming a world famous model and actress, Angelina James was five years older than Charisse and the divorced mother of two young daughters upon whom she had transferred her aspirations. Dressed in a simple, but stylish red tank dress, Star was almost the mirror image of their mother save her long, blond-tinted hair.

Star asked, "Did they start on time?"

"Five minutes late," Barbara answered.

"I was hoping Jewel would have taken her time getting here."

"Jewel was too eager to get married to be late to her own wedding," Charisse stated.

"Hey, Risi!"

Charisse and her family turned at this new voice.

"Hey, girl!" Charisse was thrilled to see her best friend making her way through the crowd. Embracing, the women exchanged pecks on the cheek.

"Ooh, your hair looks great! And I love your dress."

"Thanks," said Charisse.

A portrait of walking elegance, Charisse was wearing a crystal-blue raw silk strapless knee-length dress that flattered her hourglass figure. Her feet were ensconced in ice blue Ferragamo sandals with three-inch heels that exposed her freshly pedicured toes.

"Connie definitely hooked me up, but look at you." Taking her friend's hand, Charisse spun her around as if in a dance.

Almost a full head shorter than Charisse's five feet, six inches, Myra Lopez wore a stunning lime green print halter swing dress—the colors of which blended splendidly with her dark, Mediterranean skin tone—and gold t-strap sandals. Her waist-length hair was styled in loose, flowing curls.

"Hi, Mr. and Mrs. Ellison. Hey, Star." Reaching out, she hugged both of Charisse's parents.

"Hey, Myra," Star answered.

"How you doin', sweetheart?" John asked.

"I'm good. You're looking sharp," she said, gingerly touching his lapel.

"Well, you know, I can't have my children looking better than me," he said smugly.

Everyone laughed.

"Were you inside?" Charisse asked Myra.

"Yeah, I got here right after they started. I was in the back. I saw you when you were leaving the church, but I didn't want to be yelling in there, you know."

Turning back to Jewel and Terrance, who were still standing at the door of the church, Charisse sighed. "Doesn't she look beautiful?"

"She sure does. She looks so happy, too."

"I know."

"I forgot how fine Terry is," Myra said.

"Yeah, isn't he? I was checking out his groomsmen, too. There's some good looking brothas on his line."

"Well, you *know* I was checking them out."

"How're you getting to the reception?" Charisse asked, changing the subject.

"I was hoping to bum a ride with you. Do you have room for me?"

"Of course."

STEFÀN WAS DECKED OUT IN A STEEL BLUE, five-button single-breasted suit, which was accessorized by a pale gray Italian cotton shirt monogrammed with his initials, its French cuffs boasting white gold knotted links. A silver lattice silk tie expertly knotted at his throat, and midnight blue snakeskin shoes completed the ensemble.

Equally eye-catching in a light olive, four button, single-breasted suit with an ecru cotton shirt and olive silk jacquard pattern tie was his best friend, Julian, whose outfit was complemented by brown calfskin oxfords.

Suddenly intoxicated by the smoothness of dual auras, women of varying ages turned to get a better look when the two men entered the reception hall during the cocktail portion of Jewel and Terrance's reception.

Walking with a rhythmic bravado that bellowed as if he was stepping to theme music, Stefàn knew he looked good. He also knew the females were checking him out. They always did. Notoriously vain, the slender six feet, four inches tall, butterscotch complexioned man took great pains to maintain his impeccable appearance. His hair—worn about a quarter inch in length and gradually faded on the sides and back to the hairline—was always freshly cut as he had a standing appointment every Friday with his barber of ten years. Flawless skin and a pencil-thin mustache and goatee complemented his uncommonly handsome face. As the quintessential finishing touch, Stefàn's smile gleamed, exposing a row of perfectly straight white teeth, and brought to light a single dimple in his left cheek.

By contrast, Julian, who was a very handsome man in his own right, but did not possess the "pretty-boy" good looks or self-satisfied demeanor of Stefàn, was quite subdued. One might even say he was slightly bashful. Standing about four inches shorter than Stefàn, but more solidly built, he sported a shiny baldpate and his skin was the color of creamy peanut butter. Julian's only facial hair was a neatly trimmed mustache, but it was considerably thicker than Stefàn's. Whereas Stefàn had a somewhat untouchable countenance, Julian's eyes were warm and very welcoming. An appreciative, playful smile danced across his lips as he slowly scanned the room, taking in the variety of well-dressed female attendees.

Both men were single and enjoyed that status. The difference was that Julian had a respect for the fairer sex, which would not, in good conscience, allow him to be but so much of a Casanova. Having been married once, Julian could actually see himself walking down the aisle a second time, if the right lady came into his life. Stefàn, on the other hand, was a bona fide bachelor and not interested in being yoked to anyone. As an object of desire for numerous members of the opposite sex, he reveled in the fact that he had his pick of so many.

As Stefàn stood checking out his prospects, Julian said, "I'm going to get a drink," before walking away.

Stefàn eyes veered in the direction Julian was headed. Scanning the scene briefly, he was about to turn back when he had to do a double-take.

The woman was stunning. She was laughing at something her friend had just said and although she was too far away for him to hear the sound, he knew it would be music to his ears. He could not have been happier when he noticed that Julian had paused right near them.

CHARISSE AND MYRA WERE STANDING AT THE BAR, sipping their drinks and chatting when they were interrupted by a stranger.

"Excuse me, ladies. Could one of you get the bartender's attention for me?" he asked kindly.

Turning and quickly giving him the once-over, the girls gave him a silent stamp of approval before facing the bar again to summon the bartender.

Charisse suddenly turned back to the man. "What are you drinking?"

"Remy Martin," he said with a smile.

Myra waved the bartender over to their end of the bar.

"What can I get you ladies?"

"Remy Martin, please," Myra stated.

Charisse then asked the stranger, "Straight?"

"On the rocks," he replied.

"On the rocks," she added.

Smiling, the man said, "Thank you."

"You're welcome," Charisse replied in a preoccupied tone as her attention was directed beyond the gentleman at the gorgeous man whose dark eyes were locked on hers. As he moved toward them—in slow motion, it seemed—Charisse suddenly and inexplicably felt butterflies in her stomach.

"Good afternoon, ladies." His smooth baritone voice was accompanied by an interested gaze that lingered on Charisse a moment longer than was necessary.

"Good afternoon," they chorused.

"You're both looking quite lovely this afternoon."

In unison again, "Thank you."

"Are either of you related to the bride or groom?"

"Jewel is my cousin," Charisse answered.

Nodding, he replied, "Now that you mention it, I do see a bit of resemblance around the eyes. I'm Stefan Cooper." Offering his hand, he asked, "And you are...."

"Charisse Ellison."

Extending her right hand, a quiver ran up Charisse's spine as Stefan firmly but tenderly grasped and softly kissed it, without breaking eye contact.

"Pleased to meet you, Charisse," he seductively whispered. Turning then to Myra, he again offered his hand.

"Myra Lopez."

He kissed her hand as well, but not nearly as demonstratively. *What a smooth operator*, Charisse thought.

"I see you've already met my man, Julian."

"Actually, we haven't been formally introduced. We were just helping him order a drink," Charisse stated.

"Well, I can understand that. I'm sure Brother behind the bar is more apt to notice two beautiful ladies like you before this guy," Stefan commented as he tilted his head toward his friend.

"Julian Walker, and thank you again for your assistance," he said softly, shaking both of their hands.

"Are you guys friends of Terry's or family?" Charisse asked.

"Friends," Stefan answered.

"We play ball together," Julian added.

"Here you go, partner," the bartender said as he placed Julian's drink on the bar.

"Can I get a Ketel One shot with a 7-Up chaser, please?" Stefan asked.

"You got it."

"Thanks." Addressing the women, Stefan asked, "Do you ladies live in the city?"

"I live in Brooklyn," Myra answered.

"I live in New Jersey," Charisse said.

"Where about?" asked Stefan.

"Englewood."

Apparently amazed, Stefân responded, "Oh, yeah? We're in Teaneck."

"Small world," said Charisse.

"No doubt," Stefân murmured with that seductive glint still flickering in his eyes.

"You guys live together?" Myra asked.

An emphatic "No!" issued from both men's mouths.

"We're just good friends," Stefân stated.

"Been hangin' since junior high school," Julian added.

"Oh, okay," Myra said.

The bartender returned with Stefân's drink, which he placed on the bar. "Thank you." Reaching for the shot glass, he said, "So, Charisse, I guess your whole family's here, huh?"

"Pretty much." Pointing to the photographer who was going around the room taking pictures of the guests, she said, "That's my brother right there."

"I'm guessing," said Stefân, "since neither of you are wearing wedding bands, that you're both single."

"You guessed correctly," Charisse said with a coy smile.

"And I don't have to worry about anyone running up on me if I stand too close to you, do I?" Stefân asked. As he put the shot glass to his lips and downed the clear liquid in one swallow, he looked at Charisse in a manner that indicated he wanted to get even closer.

Feeling suddenly anxious about Stefân's suggestive words and mannerisms, she nevertheless answered, "No, you don't."

"Charisse, don't believe a word he says to you."

Turning at this audible intrusion, the quartet was joined by the best man, Don Wilson, who had, at one time, tried to get close to Charisse.

Smiling patiently, Charisse said, "Hi, Don."

Reaching behind Charisse and placing the shot glass back on the bar, Stefan retrieved his soda. Then, flicking his thumb in Don's direction, he mockingly asked, "You know this guy?"

"Yeah, she knows me but she doesn't wanna know you, so leave the lady alone," Don jokingly instructed.

Exchanging a soulful handshake with the newcomer, Stefan asked, "Whassup, dog?"

"You, man." Turning to Julian, who he likewise greeted, Don said, "Whassup, Dub?"

"How you been, man? We haven't seen you on the courts in a while. Don't tell me we scared your behind off the last time you were out?" Julian teased.

"Yeah, right, you wish. I've been out of town on business. Just got back in yesterday morning," Don said. Turning his attention away from the men, he then asked, "So how have you been, Charisse?" as he leaned in and kissed her cheek.

"I've been great. Did you ever meet my girlfriend, Myra?"

"No, I haven't. How are you?" Don asked, extending his hand to her.

Myra gently shook it. "I'm fine, thank you."

"This is Terry's brother, Myra."

"Yeah, I was gonna say. You look a lot like him. Are you older or younger?" she asked.

"Older."

"Are they about to make an appearance?" Julian then asked Don.

"Yeah, I just came in to tell everyone to head on into the banquet hall. The party's about to begin."

Shaking Don's hand once again, Stefan said, "All right, Bro, we'll see you inside."

"No doubt."

As Don walked away from them, Stefan asked, "So, Charisse, will you promise to save a dance for me?"

"I guess so, but don't expect me to come looking for you," she smugly answered to cover the unease he caused in her.

The corner of his mouth turned up in a sly smile. "Oh, don't you worry about that. I'll be keeping my eyes on you," he provocatively stated as his pupils bore through her.

CHAPTER 2
AN OFFER SHE COULDN'T REFUSE

Two hours later, the wedding reception was in full swing. Jewel had tossed her bouquet to the throng of enthusiastic bachelorettes, and Charisse had earnestly tried to catch it.

Choosing not to participate in that portion of the festivities, Myra, who had no desire to marry or have children, remained at their table and watched. She was soured to the institution of marriage due to her parents' failed union. Having watched her mother struggle to raise seven children on her own after their father had left them, Myra refused to be put in a similar situation.

To their guests' delight, immediately following the tossing of the bouquet, Terrance made quite a show of retrieving Jewel's garter. Eager, excited, eligible bachelors lined up to catch the meager adornment. Julian, a successful litigation attorney at an up-and-coming firm in New York City, however, was the lucky gent who had the pleasure of sliding the frilly lace up the shapely leg of the woman who'd caught Jewel's arrangement. Considering how suggestively he had performed the ritual, Charisse was glad she hadn't caught her cousin's bouquet.

Thoroughly enjoying Julian's show, Stefan, like Myra, sat out this event as he, too, had no desire to give up his freedom.

After dinner was served and the wedding cake had been cut, the skillful deejay set out to entertain the revelers with music that kept them on the floor for almost every song. Myra and Charisse had no shortage of dance partners, and Julian was also enjoying himself on the floor. Stefàn, however, danced only a few times, opting instead, to watch from the sidelines.

Although numerous women at the festivities had made no secret of their desire to become better acquainted with Stefàn and he pretended to welcome their advances, he was inexplicably captivated by Charisse and repeatedly found his eyes drawn to her. Something about her attracted him like a magnet. As beautiful and alluring as she was, there was a deeper influence he could not readily explain. Understanding that her obvious comfort at this celebration was probably due to the presence of her family, Stefàn noticed—as he watched her dance and laugh and flit around the hall—that she was something of a flirt. He was tickled because she was actually quite cute with it. He could tell she wasn't trying to be a tease; she was simply enjoying the attention she was receiving from the male guests.

Stefàn chuckled as he watched the best man coming on to her. Grinning up at Don, who was nearly as tall as Stefàn, Charisse whispered something close to his ear, then turned and walked away. Seemingly unable to move for quite a while after she had left him, it was obvious that Don was affected by whatever she'd said, as well as by her naturally sensuous strut.

In the next few minutes, the deejay slowed the music down. That was when Stefàn rose from his seat. Slowly making his way across the room in Charisse's direction, he watched as another man approached her for a dance. Never hesitating in his advance, instinct told him that Charisse was the type of women who didn't make a habit of dancing slow with men she didn't know. His ego, however, had him convinced she would dance with him.

As expected, Charisse turned the guy down but seemingly in a manner which did no major damage to the guy's self-esteem. Stefàn liked that.

Continuing toward her, Stefàn saw that she was talking with an older gentleman who was seated at her table. Stefàn acknowledged the man with a nod, before he interrupted them.

"Excuse me, Miss Ellison."

Turning, Charisse looked up.

He extended his hand and asked, "May I have this dance?"

"Stefàn, I...."

"You promised," he reminded her before she could refuse him completely.

His piercing gaze held her captive as it had earlier, and she was momentarily enthralled. "Yes, I did, didn't I?"

"Yes, you did."

"Well, since I try not to break my promises, I guess you may." Turning to her table mate, she said, "Excuse me, Daddy."

"Oh, Mr. Ellison." Immediately offering his hand to her father, he introduced himself. "I'm Stefàn Cooper. It's nice to meet you, sir. Do you mind if I borrow your daughter for a dance?"

Smiling, Mr. Ellison shook Stefàn's hand as he said, "Not if she doesn't."

Again offering Charisse his hand—which she took—Stefàn led her to a place on the floor in the midst of the many couples already there, yet strangely, they were alone in a world exclusively constructed for the two of them.

Pulling her into his arms, Stefàn was cautious about holding her too close. Aside from the fact that he was slightly aroused by her closeness, the protective eyes of her father were watching them.

Charisse's own heart was racing. The excitement this man inspired was brand new to her. *Mmm, he smells so good. What is that he's wearing?* she wondered.

Her head came right up to his chin, and what she didn't know was that he delighted in the clean, citrusy scent of her hair. Decoding her tentativeness while perceiving her tension, he figured some friendly conversation would relax her. "You thought I forgot about you, didn't you?"

She looked up at him, and when he met her eyes—the most beautiful fiery brown eyes he had ever gazed into—something inside of him changed. A sudden and quite uncommon sense of uncertainty washed over him.

"No, I figured it was a line you used all the time," she said with a coolness she in no way felt. "I didn't take you very seriously."

"Ouch," he intoned. Stunned by her candor, he felt as if he had been slapped. Not expecting such a cold response from her, he was also surprised at how much her words actually stung. "Why would you think that when you don't even know me?"

"Well, you have a way about you. You seem to be…quite sure of yourself."

"Is that a crime?"

"No, but…. I don't know, it's like you expect people—women, that is—to 'ooh' and 'aah' when you walk into a room."

Immediately transported back to his childhood, Stefan recalled the original Batman television series. Whenever the Dynamic Duo were embroiled in a fight with the evil villain, words like *POW* and *BAM* would flash across the screen with every blow. That was the image that went through Stefan's mind with Charisse's words. "Boy, you don't believe in pulling your punches, do you?"

Diffidently, she remarked, "If I'm wrong, please feel free to correct me." *Let me be wrong, God.*

What am I supposed to say to that? he simultaneously wondered. On more occasions than not, he had noticed women stop their conversations to gawk at him when he walked by. It had happened so often in the past that he *had* come to expect it, so he couldn't refute what she said without lying to himself. With less confidence, he insisted, "I'm not as self-centered as you make me sound."

"No?"

"No." Having never been at a loss for words in the presence of a beautiful woman, Stefàn found himself swimming uncharted waters, defending himself in a manner he had never had to before. "I may come off as... I'm really a regular guy trying to make it in this dog-eat-dog world like everyone else."

Looking up at him cynically, Charisse asked, "Are you really a regular guy?"

Knowing she was baiting him now, he decided to play her game. "No, I'm not. I'm anything but, if you want to know the truth," he stated with an air of arrogance that belied his still uncharacteristic unease.

"I didn't think so," she derisively murmured. *He has one dimple*, she noticed as her racing pulse betrayed her outward calm.

Defensively, he continued, "You see me as some Casanova Brown-type dude, but think about it. What makes a man like that, a man like that?" Giving her only a moment to consider his question, he quickly answered, "Women!" He paused. "Can I ask you something?"

"Sure."

"Why do women make it so easy for us, then complain when we take what they're throwing at us?"

Oh, no his fine behind didn't! Relinquishing all cool, she stated without hesitation, "First of all, you won't ever find me complaining, because I don't throw myself at anyone. Why other women do what they do, I can't say. But you talk about dog eat dog... There are a lot more single women out there than there are single men, and, sadly, a whole lot of women who don't feel complete without a man, will do just about anything to get one."

"But you won't."

"Of course not! I don't need a man. I mean, it would be nice to have someone special who I could share my life with, but I don't *need* a man to be happy or to feel complete. I have everything I need 'cause God loves me and I love Him. I can go where I want, when I want, with whom I want. I've been blessed with a great career. I own my own home. I'm about to buy myself a new car for my birthday."

"Oh, yeah? When's your birthday?" Realizing he had met his match but was unprepared to deal with the reality of that meeting, he immediately steered the conversation to less volatile territory at the opening she unwittingly provided.

Unprepared for the abrupt change of subject, Charisse hesitated a moment before answering. "August sixth."

"Aah, Leo." *That explains her fiery attitude.*

"Yeah, Leo, so?"

"Nothing," he replied with a smirk. "What kind of car are you buying?"

"A Corvette."

He was surprised, but with her spirited temperament, he shouldn't have been. It fit perfectly with her demeanor. "You like fast cars?"

"Yes, I do. I collect them."

"You collect fast cars?" he asked with raised eyebrows.

Laughing now, Charisse replied, "Yeah, I wish. I collect miniatures of fast cars and high end cars. Rolls Royces, Bentleys, Jaguars, et cetera."

"Really?"

"Yup."

"How'd you get into that?"

"My father used to participate in drag races when he was younger and used to take my brothers to the races all the time. I had to beg him to take me with them 'cause that was their guy thing, but once I went, I was hooked. I love fast cars. I couldn't wait to learn how to drive."

"You don't drag, do you?"

Cutting her eyes at him, she chuckled. "No, I'm not that daring."

Stefan laughed.

Looking down at her as they continued their dance, Stefan marveled at her uniqueness. Charisse's conversation was delightfully refreshing—once he had gotten through her attack unscathed, that is. She piqued his curiosity. *Is she a church girl?* he wondered. *She did say something about God, didn't she?* Knowing he would undoubtedly enjoy getting physical with her, talking to her only cemented his interest. Combined with her stunning beauty, her wit and whimsy were unlike anything he had ever encountered from the opposite sex.

In the next seconds, the deejay changed the tempo of the music, bringing an end to their dance. Charisse's arms fell away from him and she took a step back.

"Well, it was nice chatting with you," she nonchalantly stated and started away without the slightest hesitation. *Whew! That was close.*

"Charisse."

"Oh, no," she grumbled under her breath. *Be cool, girl.* Stopping in her tracks, she turned back to him. "Yes?"

Feeling a strange and uncomfortable sense of apprehension in his gut, he drank in her beauty for a long moment before he asked, "Have you ever ridden on a motorcycle?"

"No, but I've thought about taking lessons to learn how to drive one," she admitted with a bright smile. "Myra thinks I'm crazy." *Why's he asking me about motorcycles?* she wondered.

"What are you doing tomorrow?"

"Going to church."

Taking a step to close the distance between them, he asked, "What time do you get out of church?"

Looking up at him questioningly, she answered, "About eleven o'clock. Why?"

"I'm going to a cycler's get-together tomorrow in Connecticut. There'll be live music, plenty of great food and good folks. Why don't you take a ride with me?"

"You have a motorcycle?"

"Yeah. A few years ago a couple of my friends and I made a bet over some beers that we'd all buy bikes, learn how to ride them and start a little club, you know?"

"Doing that macho thing, huh?"

Laughing, he had to agree. "Anyway, only Dub and I and one other dude actually followed through."

"Who's Dub?"

"Oh, that's Julian. Dub is short for the W in his last name."

"Oh."

"So, what d'you say? Want to take a ride to Connecticut with me?"

"I don't know, Stefan," she hedged.

"You'll be perfectly safe," he assured her as they slowly strolled back to her table.

Stefan volunteered information about his motorcycle driving safety record, the proposed rendezvous time and the company they would be joining on this excursion. When he informed her that he was originally planning to go alone, despite his friends all bringing a companion, she inquired as to why.

"Well, honestly, because it's a pretty diverse crowd that attends these gatherings and I don't want to have to listen to anyone moaning and groaning about the people there. You strike me as an open-minded sister, and I think you'd enjoy the diversity of this type of get-together."

"Thank you, but I'm probably more conservative than you think," she told him. After pausing momentarily, she continued, "But you know what? I think I will join you. I've always wanted to ride on a motorcycle and, well, something about you gives me the sense that you're as safe a driver as you say you are."

"I am," he responded.

An awkward silence fell over them momentarily as they stood near Charisse's table. Her father was no longer seated there.

"I like talking to you," Stefan suddenly admitted.

"Yeah, you seem pretty cool to talk to, too," she off-handedly remarked.

Chuckling stoically, he said, "You're something else."

"Yes, I am."

"So do you want to give me your number now or later?"

"Why don't you give me your information and I'll meet you at your place."

Trying to determine if she was playing with him or not, he gazed into warm brown pupils that unabashedly challenged him. Another involuntary chill coursed through his body as they stared each other down.

Finally raising his hands in surrender, Stefan declared, "You win." Reaching into the inner breast pocket of his jacket, he removed a business card holder and flipped it open. Taking out one of his cards, he asked, "Would you have a pen, by any chance?"

"Yes, I do."

She reached for her pocketbook on the table and removed a pen and handed it to him.

"I'll put my address on the back."

She sat down at the table and he sat across from her in the empty chair. As he proceeded to write his information, he asked, "Do you know Teaneck?"

"Somewhat."

When he'd finished, he handed her the card. Looking at the address he had written down, she responded, "Oh, I know this street." Turning the card over, Charisse read the information there. "You sell houses, huh?"

"Yup."

"Are you any good?"

"I'm very good," he answered in what she perceived to be a sensuous tone.

"I meant at selling houses."

"I did, too."

Charisse blushed and lowered her eyes.

Smiling at her reaction, he asked, "What do you do for a living?"

"I'm a CPA."

"Really?" He was impressed.

"Yup."

He nodded in admiration.

"What should I wear tomorrow?"

"Well, for the ride up, you should probably wear jeans and a sweater or lightweight jacket. It can get cool on the bike. You might want to carry a pair of shorts, though, for once we're up there, 'cause it's supposed to be pretty hot tomorrow."

"Okay, so I'll be at your house at about noon."

"Yeah, that's good."

Smiling sweetly, Charisse said, "Okay, so…I'll see you to-morrow."

Reaching across the table for her hand, Stefan gazed into her eyes as he gently pressed his lips to the back of her hand before whispering, "I look forward to continuing our discussion."

Blushing, Charisse replied, "Me, too."

He rose from his seat. "I'll let you get back to your family," he said before he turned and walked back across the room.

Returning to their table seconds after Stefan had walked away, Barbara took the seat he had vacated and asked, "Who was that, Charisse?" Star was right behind her and took the seat next to Charisse.

"Stefan Cooper," Charisse said, reading his card aloud. "Certified Residential Specialist and Licensed Real Estate Broker. He's a friend of Terry's."

"He's cute," Barbara said.

"No, Mommy. Brotha man is fine!" Star stated.

"That he is," Charisse agreed with a smile as she nudged her big sister.

"And what's his story? I saw him talking to a couple of different women in here tonight, including your cousin, Debbie."

"So did I."

"So...."

"So, what?"

"What's up with him? I saw him giving you his card, but I didn't see you give him yours," Barbara added.

"That's 'cause I didn't."

"I hope you're not going to be chasing that man. He looks like he gets plenty of exercise as it is."

Laughing at her mother's play on words, Charisse assured her, "No, Mommy. I'm not going to be chasing him, but I'm thinking about going riding with him tomorrow."

"Riding? What? On horseback?" Star asked.

"No, on his motorcycle."

"What?" Catching the tail-end of their conversation, Barbara's query was echoed by Myra, who had walked over and sat down.

"What? What's so wrong with that?" Charisse asked.

"You don't know that man. How you gonna be riding on his motorcycle?" Barbara said.

"Mommy, I'll be fine."

"She'll be fine, Mommy," Star concurred.

"Shut up, Star," Barbara snapped before turning back to Charisse. "Where are you supposed to be going?"

With a bright smile, she answered, "To Connecticut for a biker's cookout."

"Go 'head, girl," Star cheered.

Shaking her head, Myra said, "You're crazy."

Waving Myra's comment off, Charisse replied, "That's what you always say."

"Yeah, and she's got a point this time, Charisse," Barbara stated.

"Look, I'll be fine. Don't worry. I trust him."

"You don't even know him!" Barbara emphatically reminded her.

"I trust him not to let me get hurt on his bike."

Still shaking her head, Myra hummed, "Mmm, mmm."

Star leaned in and conspiratorially whispered, "Don't pay them no mind, Risi. They're jealous."

As THEY LEFT THE RECEPTION HALL TOGETHER later that evening, Julian asked Stefan, "So did you get her digits?"

"No, but she's riding with us tomorrow."

That news stopped Julian in his tracks. "What?"

Without slowing his pace, Stefan stated over his shoulder, "You heard me."

"You don't ever take anyone to these functions. Matter of fact, you've never even let anyone on your bike," Julian pointed out when he caught up with Stefàn.

"I like her."

"That's never been enough criteria before. You like a lot of women."

"Nah, Dub, I *like* her." Chuckling as he recalled Charisse's first words to him during their dance, Stefàn said, "You know what she said to me? She said I act like I expect women to 'ooh' and 'aah' when I walk into a room."

"You do!"

Laughing, Stefàn added, "Yeah, but I've never been called on it before."

"Oh, so what? You think she's going to be more of a challenge, huh?"

"Nah, it's not like that. She's cool. I mean, she's about something, you know. I could have talked to her all night, man." After a brief pause, Stefàn added, "I think she's a church girl."

"A church girl, huh?"

"Yeah, but she's very high-spirited, if you know what I mean. She's getting ready to buy herself a Corvette for her birthday."

"Word?"

"Word, man. She collects cars. High-end miniatures."

"Well, she definitely sounds different."

Looking over at his friend, he declared, "Exactly!"

"So what time you wanna pull out tomorrow?" Julian asked.

"Well, she doesn't get out of church until about eleven, so maybe I should meet y'all."

"All right, call the cell when you get there."

"All right, bro." They touched fists. "Mañana," Stefàn said.

"Peace out."

Before heading home that evening, Stefan made a stop at the bike shop he frequented in his old neighborhood in Queens, where he usually purchased his biking accessories.

"Hey, Coop. Lookin' sharp, dude," the proprietor said when he entered.

"What's up, D? Yeah, I just came from a wedding."

"You just caught me. I was about to close up."

"I'm not going to keep you. I only need to pick up a lady's helmet."

As Charisse drove her home later that night, Myra asked, "You're really going to go riding with him tomorrow?"

"Yeah."

"You're not going to church?"

"Of course, I'm going to church. I'm going to need extra protection tomorrow."

Myra let out a sigh. "Yeah, really. You'd better be careful, girl."

"I will."

"I'm not just talking about on that bike. That brother's way too fine. I don't know if I'd want to mess with anyone that pretty."

Laughing, Charisse said, "Well, he knows I've already got his card read."

"Oh yeah? And how does he know that?"

"'Cause I told him."

Myra sucked her teeth.

"Look, I'm sure women are regularly pushin' up on him and I'm pretty sure he laps it right up. I saw him and them. But I'm not trying to get hooked up with him. I just want to ride on his bike. I've got his number. He doesn't have mine."

"All right, now. I know you know he's not the settling down

type."

With a frown, Charisse replied, "Oh, please, girl, like I would set myself up like that."

Silence ensued for the next few minutes until Myra cried with a shake of her head, "Brother sure is fine, though. Dang!"

Laughing, Charisse agreed. "Ain't he gorgeous?"

"And that suit. He was wearing that suit."

"Yes, my man was too clean."

"Dang! He looks like something off the cover of *GQ*," Myra said again. "What does he do?"

"He's a real estate broker."

"Teaneck's not that far from you, is it?"

"It's the next town over."

"Yeah, well, I still say, you watch yourself with that pretty boy. He'll fool around and break your heart."

"He can only do that if I give it to him, and I'm not that careless with my vital organs."

DURING HER DRIVE HOME AFTER DROPPING MYRA OFF, Charisse pondered her hasty decision to go riding with Stefan. Like her mother had stated, she didn't know him. Matter of fact, the only thing she knew about him was that he sold houses for a living. Star seemed to think she should go for it, but ever since her divorce, Charisse had noticed that her older sister had let her hair down and showed no signs of putting it back up. There was something about Stefan, though, that attracted her in a way no man ever had. Granted, like Myra had said, he was fine, but that was really an understatement. Stefan's looks were like something out of a romance novel. His face rivaled that of a sculpture—chiseled, flawless; dark brown eyes that pierced through to her very soul; lips that looked as inviting as a cool drink on a hot day; and a smile that made her insides quiver. The electrical surges she had felt in his powerful yet tender embrace when they danced told her that he would protect her from all harm; that is, if she let him.

"Father, did I speak too quickly?" she softly questioned over the low volume of the Richard Smallwood CD playing on her car stereo.

Charisse was new in Christ. She had only been baptized four months ago. In January, a co-worker had invited her to attend a retreat, which the women's ministry of her church sponsored yearly. Several other sisters from the accounting firm they worked for were also attending, so Charisse decided to go as well. She hadn't attended church on a regular basis since she'd gotten out of high school and even then, hadn't fully understood what it meant to give one's self to Christ.

That weekend, however, changed Charisse's life. She had never experienced anything as powerful as the fellowship of the Christian women participating in the retreat. She could honestly say she felt God's presence among them as never before.

Upon her return, Charisse joined the woman who had invited her to the retreat at the Sunday service at her church. After three weeks of listening to the powerful sermons delivered by the pastor of the New Covenant Baptist Church, Charisse felt as if she had found the place she was supposed to be. She went up during the invitational on that fourth Sunday, giving her hand to the preacher, but giving her heart to God.

Gradually, her views began to change and the way she had been living didn't feel right anymore. She hadn't really dated anyone in over six months, but made the decision that when she did start to date again, the rules would be entirely different.

Charisse made a conscious effort to study the Bible, reading a chapter or two every day, and she also began to read inspirational literature to help her in her Walk.

Her gut told her that Stefan wasn't saved, so she didn't understand why this man had made such an impression upon her. The few hours of his behavior she had witnessed at the reception was evidence of her assumption, but she didn't want to judge him, either. That was not her place.

By the time she arrived at her house that evening, she'd decided that first thing tomorrow, she would call Stefan and apologize, but she couldn't go riding with him. He was too much of a temptation and she was not sure she was strong enough to resist him.

CHAPTER 3
CHANGES OF HEART

C hurch let out Sunday morning at ten-forty. As soon as she got into her car, Charisse reached for her cell phone and the business card Stefàn had given her the day before.

She took a deep breath before dialing his home number and sent up an prayer to the Lord to guide her in the way she should go. Then she dialed his number.

He picked up on the third ring. "Good morning." The baritone voice that came through the line was cheerful, confident and as smooth as thick, dark chocolate. It warmed her immediately.

"Good morning. Stefàn?"

"Yes."

"This is Charisse Ellison."

"Hello, Charisse."

"Hi. How are you?" she nervously inquired.

"I'm well, thank you. How are you?"

"Not too good," she admitted.

"I'm sorry to hear that. What's wrong?"

"Well, I've been thinking and…I spoke too soon yesterday when I said I would go riding with you. I can't go."

Silence filled the line. Charisse held her breath the entire time.

He finally said, "I'm guessing there's an underlying reason why you suddenly can't go, so may I ask why you've changed your mind?" His tone was different. No longer did he sound like the confident man who had answered her call. She now sensed his disappointment.

"I...um. I don't want to give you the wrong idea about me," she replied.

"What idea would that be?" he asked.

"Well...," she hedged. "I think we... You strike me as the kind of man who...well, who has...who likes a lot of women and...I don't want to get involved with anyone like that."

She waited for his reply.

"Stefan? Hello?" Charisse called when he didn't respond.

"You're judging me and you don't even know me. You did that yesterday, too."

"No. I'm not judging you."

"Yes, you are. You're assuming things about me and you're making decisions based on things you don't even know."

"I..." Charisse paused, looking for the right words.

Before she could collect her thoughts, he asked with a definite edge in his tone, "What is it you think I want from you?"

"I don't know," she answered honestly. She felt his irritation through the line and was uneasy about having caused it.

"You said you'd never ridden on a motorcycle, but you'd always wanted to. Aside from the company of some decent people, good music and food, that's all I was offering. But if you don't want to go, that's cool. I'm sorry if I offended you in any way because that was never my intent," he magnanimously stated.

"No, you didn't offend me." Charisse sighed. She couldn't tell him how much he excited her. He could never know that she found him so appealing. "I'm sorry," she muttered.

"Listen, I thought we could get to know each other, but if I'm not the type of person you want to know, well.... You have a good life."

The line went dead in her ear.

Stunned and stung by his abrupt dismissal, Charisse felt as if the air had gone out of her lungs. "Oh, God, what did I do?" Feeling a desperate need to reclaim her connection to him, she pressed the redial button on her phone.

After two rings, he picked up. "Yes?"

"Stefan, I'm sorry. I didn't mean... You took that the wrong way."

"I took it the way you said it," he coolly stated.

She sighed in defeat. "I... Look, it's not that I think you have some ulterior motive or anything...."

"So what is it, then?" he wanted to know.

"Connecticut is pretty far. I've never been on a bike before and... we'd have to ride on the highway, right?"

"Yup."

Sighing again, she continued. "I'm nervous about riding so far. The first time." She closed her eyes, hoping he would not see through her falsehood.

"Is that it?"

"Yes." *Forgive me, Lord.*

"So why don't we ride right here in New Jersey. I know a little park that's only fifteen minutes from here and doesn't require getting on the highway to get to." She didn't respond right away, prompting him to ask, "Is that okay with you?"

"But what about your friends? Weren't you all planning to go together?"

"No, I was going to meet them there," he said.

"But won't they be looking for you?"

"My not being there won't affect their good time. Besides, I can call Dub and let him know I'm not coming."

"I don't want to ruin your plans."

"Look, Charisse. Keep it real. Do you want to ride with me or not?"

Well, there it was. All that was required of her was a straight yes or no. He had made it very simple. It was apparent he was finished playing with her.

"Yes," she uttered, barely loud enough to be heard. Her heart was pounding so hard, she wondered if its beating resonated through the line.

"Do you want to check out the park I was telling you about?"

"Okay."

"Where are you?"

"In my car. I just got out of church."

"So, this is your cell phone number on my caller ID?"

"Yes."

"Do you still want to meet me here?" he asked.

"Yes."

"What time should I expect you?"

She looked at the watch on her slender wrist. "I can be there at twelve."

"So, I'll see you then?"

"Okay."

The line went dead again. Taking a deep breath, she whispered, "Lord, what am I doing?"

WHEN HE HUNG UP THE PHONE the second time that morning after speaking to Charisse, Stefan felt relief. It was only minutes ago that sadness had descended on him with lightning swiftness. Hearing her say he was not the type of person she wanted to get involved with was like a knife in his heart.

Why is this woman so important to me? Why is what she thinks of me so relevant? Never before had he given much credence to other people's opinions of him. Aside from his family—whom he was very close to—and Julian, who'd been his best friend since they were kids, Stefan placed little value on anyone's views of how he lived because, for all intents and purposes, he was a decent guy.

He sensed the reason for her initial change of heart was not due to her conceit or even egotism. Although she'd said he wasn't the type of person she wanted to be involved with, he assumed she was referring more to what she believed was his lifestyle than her own self-righteousness. The vibe he felt when he first introduced himself to her was one of mutual affection. Truthfully, although she had captured his attention when she and her friend were assisting Julian yesterday, it was her eyes locked with his as he approached them that most intrigued him. There was confidence in her gaze, as well as mutual curiosity. She had acted nonchalant about their interaction, but he knew she felt it, too—this connection between them. Maybe that scared her. It certainly gave him pause, but he needed to find out if his intuition was as astute as it had always been. Stefan could not ignore the genuine yearning he felt to get closer to her.

CHAPTER 4
A DREAM COME TRUE

Pulling up to Stefan's house at five minutes after twelve that afternoon, Charisse admired his contemporary, split-level home with an attached two-car garage. The front lawn was freshly manicured and it appeared to Charisse from the variety of colorful blossoms adorning the yard, that Stefan either had quite a green thumb or an expert landscaper.

She walked to the door of his house but as she reached out to ring the bell, the front door swung open. "Good afternoon," he said.

Charisse stepped inside. "Hi." Her intention had been to comment on his lawn, but seeing him again—looking even better than he had yesterday—caused her initial thought to evaporate. Her doubts about the decision to spend the day with him were immediately renewed.

"I heard your car when you pulled up," he told her.

"I'm not late, am I?"

"No, you're right on time. Have you eaten?"

"I had a little something before I left."

"Can I get you something to drink?"

"Yes, thank you."

"What would you like? Orange juice, cranberry...."

"Orange juice, please," she answered before he finished naming her choices.

"Come on in the kitchen."

She wanted to tell him she'd wait in the foyer, but quickly realized how ridiculous that would seem to him. He had invited her into his kitchen, not his bedroom. *Why are you tripping?* she asked herself. It wasn't as if she feared he would do anything threatening, but her intense attraction to him made her wonder if she might be giving him unintentional signals he could interpret as a come-on.

As she followed him into his kitchen, she was unable to ignore his tight gluts, muscular thighs, small waist and broad shoulders. *Even in his own home, he walks with a bit of a swagger*, she thought. Busy studying his body movements in the black jeans he wore, watching his muscles flex and relax with each stride, Charisse didn't even notice the layout of his house. The cream colored, sleeveless body-hugging muscle shirt, which covered his well-defined torso, seemed as if it was painted on. Mindful of his vanity, she figured Stefan worked out regularly; his sculpted torso and biceps were evidence of his diligence. Wondering if sweat looked like dew on his chiseled frame, it frightened her to think that with the way he was affecting her now, if she had met him six months ago, she would have been open to any seduction efforts he put forward and more than likely would have initiated her own form of temptation. *Thank you, God, for Your amazing timing.*

Trying to appear at ease, Charisse took a seat at his kitchen table. As he opened the refrigerator door and bent over to remove the juice container from one of the lower shelves, she shook her head and exhaled. *This man is too fine*, she thought. *What am I doing here with him?*

"Are you already sorry you changed your mind again?" Stefan suddenly asked as he handed her a glass of juice.

"No," she answered too readily. To her dismay, he'd recognized her apprehension for what it was.

He smiled and asked, "You're sure?"

Reasoning that she might as well stop acting so silly and immature, she told herself, *I'm a grown woman. I can hold a conversation with him without imagining him as some type of hedonist deity.*

"This is a nice house," she quickly stated and took a sip of her drink.

"Thank you," he answered with a smirk, but thought, *Avoidance. That's cute.*

"How long have you been here?" Charisse asked.

"Three years."

"How long have you been selling houses?"

As he leaned against the sink and folded his arms across his chest, he responded, "Oh, about twelve years, now."

"Wow! How old are you?"

"Thirty-three."

"You look a lot younger than that."

"Thank you. You know we age well."

"True, true."

"How old are you?" he asked.

"I'll be twenty-nine on my birthday."

"You're not offended that I asked your age?" he queried, eyeing her sardonically.

"Why should I be? I asked you how old you are."

He snickered and faintly shrugged before asking, "Was it always your dream to be a CPA?"

"No, but I took some accounting classes in high school and did so well I decided why not take it all the way?"

"I heard that. You like number crunching, huh?"

Shrugging modestly, she said, "Yeah, but more than that, I like knowing where my money is and what it's doing. Since I've always excelled in math, I figured I might as well take advantage of that edge."

With an appreciative nod, he said, "That's smart."

"How'd you get into selling?"

"I've been selling stuff all my life," he admitted with a laugh.

Charisse frowned slightly.

"Always legal," he emphasized.

"Well, that's good."

"Remember when you were in school and they'd have those candy drives?"

"Uh-huh."

"I always got top prize for the most sales. I'm relentless."

Chuckling mischievously, she couldn't resist saying, "I bet that's a characteristic that comes in handy in more ways than one, huh?"

Briefly glancing skyward, Stefan said, "Okay, there she is."

"There who is?"

"The woman I met yesterday. I don't know who I was talking to this morning."

Charisse made a face at him.

He chuckled and said, "I'll be right back."

Stefan left the room and Charisse took a deep breath. She decided that when they got back after this ride, she would sever all contact with him because he was too tempting, way too dangerous, and impure thoughts of him were consuming her. Unsure if she could resist his charms for too long, Charisse resolved, however, to have a good time in the meantime. *What harm can come from taking a ride on his motorcycle?*

Stefan returned to the kitchen with a helmet in his hand. "Why don't you try this on and see how it fits."

Taking the helmet from him, she studied the exterior design closely. It was basically black but muted gold streaks ran through it. "Your girlfriend won't mind me wearing her helmet?"

"I don't have a girlfriend. I'm a free agent."

"Well, your friend."

"Charisse, the helmet belongs to me."

Smirking, she replied, "Yeah, but I'm sure it's been used by several of your lady friends."

She noticed his jaw clench before he tersely stated, "For your information, Miss Ellison, the helmet has never been worn. It's brand new. I bought it last night so you could wear it today."

Feeling two inches small at that moment, Charisse pursed her lips before she mumbled, "Sorry."

"Now, would you like to try it on?"

Without another word, she put the helmet on her head.

"How does it feel?" he asked, seeming to have put her assault of seconds ago out of his mind.

Thoroughly humbled, Charisse replied, "Fine."

"It's not too tight?"

"No, it feels fine."

"Good. You're not going to get all bent out of shape if your 'do gets smashed, will you?"

With a mock grin, she said, "No."

The doorbell rang. "Excuse me a minute," he said and went to answer the door.

Removing the helmet from her head, Charisse placed it on her lap, then finger-combed her hair back into place. She felt foolish about her assumption that he had given her a helmet that had been used by every Tonya, Liz and Jane he'd ever known, especially when, upon closer inspection, she saw that the security sticker was still on the inside of the helmet.

Returning to the kitchen moments later, Stefan explained, "That was my neighbor trying to sell me some male grooming products."

"A woman?"

"Yeah."

"Well, she sees you're well-groomed and probably figured you'd be an easy sell."

"No, she probably saw you when you pulled up and being the nosey person she is, was looking for a way inside to see who you are 'cause she already knows I'm not going to buy any of her products."

Really? Charisse thought. She wondered if there was some history between Stefan and his neighbor and was tempted to ask, but he quickly quieted her inquisitive mind by asking, "You about ready to pull out?"

Forced to let the neighbor go for now, she took a deep breath and said, "As I'll ever be."

"Don't be nervous."

That's easy for you to say. Charisse finished off her juice and walked over to the sink. She was about to rinse her cup out when Stefan said, "Leave that. I'll take care of it later."

He opened a door in his kitchen that led to the garage. When Charisse followed him through the exit, she took note of the shelving, which lined the walls and housed various tools, reminding her of a hardware store. A dark blue BMW 535xi was parked next to a beautiful blue BMW motorcycle.

Charisse murmured, "Nice bike," as she eyed the large machine cautiously.

Noticing the anxiety she tried to stifle, Stefan smiled. "Climb on up."

Taking a deep breath, she proceeded to mount the bike.

"Put your foot on the stirrup, here," he guided.

Dressed in jeans and sneakers, Charisse wore a white tank top beneath her denim jacket. A fanny pack was fastened around her waist and contained her shades, wallet, keys, and a few other incidental items. Twisting it so the pouch was at her back, she climbed onto the bike and settled herself on the soft seat.

"You okay?" he asked.

Her heart thumped in her chest as she nodded. "Uh-huh."

"I want to give you a couple of pointers about riding, okay? Most important is to relax. I won't go too fast. I'm no daredevil, so don't worry about that."

She chuckled nervously.

"You can hold me around my waist if you want, or you can hold on to my jacket. Whatever's more comfortable for you. But if you hold me around my waist, try not to hold too tight, because I need to be able to move freely to control the bike, all right?"

She nodded.

"When we're making a turn, you have to—and this is very important—you have to lean into the turn with me, 'cause if you don't, we could both fall on our butts, and that's something we don't want to do, right?"

"Right."

Smiling tenderly, Stefàn lightly touched her shoulder. "You're gonna be fine, Charisse. I give you my word."

"Okay."

She hadn't noticed it before, but there was a lightweight black leather jacket hanging from a hook on the rear wall of the garage. Stefàn reached for it and put it on. His helmet was hanging on the handlebar by the chinstrap. He unfastened it and climbed on the bike in front of Charisse.

"Do you have shades?" he asked as he straddled the bike and turned back to face her.

"Yes."

"If you don't want to use the visor on the helmet, you might want to put them on."

Twisting her fanny pack back to the front, she reached into it and removed a pair of Ray Bans. She put them on, then pulled on her helmet. Noticing that she was having trouble fastening the chinstrap, Stefan did it for her.

"You okay?" he asked.

"I think so."

His face broke into a broad smile. *I'm glad you changed your mind*, he thought before facing forward on the bike. Stefan pulled a pair of shades from the upper pocket of his jacket. He put them on before pulling his own helmet on and fastening the clasp. That was when Charisse noticed they had matching head gear.

As he started the engine, he must have also activated the garage door opener because the door suddenly began to rise in front of them.

The engine roared to life. Immediately feeling the smooth vibrations caused by the bike's motor, Charisse's heartbeat picked up its pace in conjunction with it. Seconds later, however, it seemed to settle down and the roar became a purr.

"Ready?" Stefan turned back and asked.

"Yes."

"I'm making a left turn out of here, so lean with me, okay?"

"Okay."

Reaching back, Stefan gently patted her thigh before putting his hands on the controls and slowly moving out of the garage. Charisse's hands were securely wrapped around his waist, and although she tried to relax when he turned off of his property, she felt incredibly tense.

When they reached the end of his block, Stefan pulled up to the light on the corner and stopped.

Charisse's heart was racing. Although she was nervous about riding on the motorcycle, she was also excited. This was something she had always wanted to experience and now she was. The fact that this intriguing man was the catalyst to her living out this small dream served to excite her all the more.

Attentively watching the signal, Charisse saw the light turn green and felt Stefan rev the gas a split second before he accelerated into traffic. When they pulled up to another light at a busy intersection, she noticed he had put on his left turn signal.

Lean into the turn with him, she told herself over and over. *Relax, girl.*

When the light changed, Stefan followed the traffic through the intersection and into the turn. There were no lights or congestion on this road so the bike picked up speed, but Charisse made an effort not to hold Stefan any tighter than she already was.

Minutes later, he stopped the bike across from a junction at Route 4 and turned back to her. "I can get to the park through the streets or I can jump on Route 4 and get there faster. What do you want me to do?"

She breathed deeply. "Take Route 4."

"You're sure?"

Chuckling nervously, she said, "Yes."

"Okay," he replied with a smile.

As he merged onto the highway seconds later, Charisse knew he had no choice but to move with the flow. She drove this roadway on a regular basis so she knew the average vehicle speed was fifty-five to sixty miles per hour, despite the posted fifty miles per hour limit. Many times she had even topped those speeds when she was behind the wheel of her own car.

Moving steadily with the flow, Charisse noticed that Stefan seemed to be a very relaxed and skilled driver. Weaving between the vehicles, shifting from one lane to the next with ease, his mastery was comforting and calmed her to the point where she felt like she'd been riding with him forever. She loved the freedom of being in the open air, zooming past the cars on the road and the scenery that lined the smoothly paved highway.

I could definitely get used to this, she thought.

Thinking of Myra briefly, she was momentarily saddened by the fact that the combination of her friend's cynicism and fear of adventure would most likely keep her from ever experiencing a thrill such as this. She thought, too, about her mother and her words yesterday, emphasizing how much she didn't know Stefan. *Well, that certainly was true*, she thought as they sped along. The simple fact that he had taken the time to purchase the helmet she was wearing only last night so she could ride with him today was proof. What if she hadn't changed her mind again, she wondered. Would he have taken the helmet back? *Probably not*, she reasoned. *He could always use it for one of his other women friends.* In fact, she decided that was what he would most likely do since she wouldn't be riding with him anymore after today.

All things being equal though, she could not deny she liked his style. She liked the way he looked, the way he walked and even the way he talked. Aside from which, he'd floored her when he told her to have a good life and hung up the phone when she first told him she couldn't ride with him. Thinking about it earlier as she prepared to meet him, she was forced to acknowledge she had unfairly judged him. She'd seen him flirting with several different women at Jewel and Terry's wedding yesterday, but she had done her own share of flirting, too. Regardless of what he said, though, she was still certain he was the type of guy to play the field as regularly as possible.

Why did I agree to come with him? Because you like him, that's why. But there's no future for me with him. You're riding on his motorcycle, not making love with him. There's nothing wrong with getting to know him, at least until he shows you otherwise. Charisse went back and forth in her mind trying to justify her wishy-washy behavior. With her new life, she'd known there would be challenges sometimes when it came to staunching old habits, but then who'd said it would be easy?

STEFÀN HAD A VERY PERSONAL RELATIONSHIP with his motorcycle. When he and his friends had decided to buy and learn to ride them, he had always treated it as a very serious matter and attacked the endeavor with the same zeal he used when selling houses. Julian and a couple of other guys sometimes teased him about his unyielding tenacity. And, unlike his crew, Stefàn had never invited any of his women friends to participate in any of their biking events. He had never ridden any of them on his bike, either. Not even the ones who had asked. He'd always used the excuse that he didn't have an extra helmet.

Stefàn surprised himself when he invited Charisse to ride with him yesterday. He'd used his bike in an effort to keep her from walking away from him and out of his life. That's why when she called this morning and told him she couldn't ride with him, he'd felt more than disappointment. He'd been genuinely saddened. He had spent most of last night imagining their day together. It was seldom Stefàn swooned over a woman. Plenty of them had swooned over him, but even the most physically beautiful ones he'd hung out with had never affected him the way Charisse did. It hurt when she insinuated he was not the type of person she wanted to associate with. *I'm not such a bad guy*, he'd told himself. Yes, he dated several women, but he was a single man. He never led anyone on with promises of a future or any such thing. He didn't allow them to get too close to him because he was not interested in anything permanent. He wanted to have fun. There would be time for all that other nonsense later.

He was intrigued by Charisse, however. Yesterday, she had seemed unaffected by his suave demeanor and debonair looks. This morning, it was as if that self-assured, straight-talking woman had been a figment of his imagination. As beautiful as she was, too, she was so much more than her outward appearance. Her free spirit and uncanny sense of adventure piqued his curiosity.

He wondered what had happened to cause the change in her this morning. Maybe someone had told her something about him. She didn't strike him as the type to listen to anyone's nay-saying if her mind was already made up.

Cruising along the familiar roadway now with her holding him comfortably around his waist, Stefan smiled. In spite of her erratic behavior this morning, he liked this woman behind him. Her personality was as refreshing as the cool wind that blew in his face as he raced along the highway. Despite the feelings he struggled to suppress, he longed to romantically pursue this new passion that jolted his senses. Knowing she had her guards up, he looked forward to the work he would have to put in to bring them down. Although he had no desire to change his lifestyle or give up his freedom, Stefan, uncharacteristically, wanted to get to know her in a way that would also allow him to let his own guards down.

CHAPTER 5

WHERE DO WE GO FROM HERE?

Less than thirty minutes after leaving his house, Stefân drove his motorcycle into the lot of Hamilton Park in Saddle River. Parking the bike in a space at the far end, he wasted no time dismounting. Turning to Charisse, he immediately asked, "So, what do you think?"

Charisse couldn't help but smile. "I liked it."

"You liked it, huh?"

"Yeah. That was off the hook."

With a laugh, he said, "Oh, you liked it that much?"

"Yeah, now I kinda wish we had gone to Connecticut."

"Well, there's always next year," he nonchalantly stated.

Next year, she thought. *Boy, he sure is optimistic.*

Cool and intense all at once, Stefân watched her closely for a reaction to his comment. Although she tried to remain nonchalant, he'd picked up on her surprise. *She's going to be fun. I can see that already.*

When Charisse moved to dismount, Stefân offered his hand in assistance. Standing before him, she looked up at him and said, "You probably think I'm a flake after the way I acted this morning, but I really appreciate you not holding that against me."

"So do you want to tell me what that was about?"

She paused momentarily to consider how much to tell him. After a few seconds, she said, "I wasn't sure if your intentions were...pure. I saw several women grinning in your face yesterday—one of them was my cousin—and I saw you reacting to them. I wasn't interested in being one of your groupies."

Stefan chuckled at her description. "Well, I knew after your scathing commentary yesterday that you weren't the groupie type."

"I wasn't trying to be mean by what I said. It was an observation I had made."

"Oh, so you were checking me out, too?"

"No. Well...."

He gave her a look which implied, *tell the truth*.

"I wasn't just sitting there watching you."

"But you were checking me out," he smugly repeated.

"No more than anybody else," she fibbed.

"Yeah, okay," he murmured glibly.

Unlike the clear sunny skies of yesterday, today was partly cloudy and quite muggy. Nonetheless, the park was alive with the smell of charcoal and barbecue, and the noise of people talking, laughing, playing and enjoying the day.

"You wanna take a walk?" Stefan asked.

"Sure."

They left the parking area and started down the path that led to the lake. As they walked, Charisse removed her jacket and tied the sleeves around her waist so as to leave her one free hand unencumbered since they were carrying their helmets.

"I've never been to this park before," she suddenly said. "Do you come here a lot?"

"Not really. I play ball here sometimes, but other than that, no."

"Why'd you decide to come here today?" she asked.

"Well, I figured it wasn't too far, since you were nervous about riding, but by the same token, it was far enough for you to appreciate the experience."

They strolled along in silence for the next several minutes. As they passed a playground with children running, jumping and swinging on the different apparatuses, Charisse noticed an ice cream truck.

As she turned to mention it, Stefàn asked, "Would you like some ice cream?"

She smiled. "I was about to ask you the same thing."

"Great minds think alike," he lightly replied.

Turning in that direction, Stefàn led her to the queue formed at the side window.

"What would you like?" he asked as they stepped behind the folks ahead of them.

"A vanilla-chocolate cone. What are you getting?"

"I think I'll have a sundae," he answered.

When they reached the front of the line, Stefàn tucked his helmet under his arm as he pulled his wallet from his back pocket.

To assist him, Charisse reached for his helmet. "Let me hold that for you."

"Thanks."

"You're welcome."

Her unselfish nature touched his heart, prompting Stefàn's lips to curl in a sideways grin.

Once he had purchased their frozen treats, he suggested they sit down at a vacant picnic table nearby to eat them. While Charisse took a seat on the wooden bench, Stefàn stepped up on the bench and took a seat on the table top.

After a few seconds of shared silence as they enjoyed their desserts, Charisse said, "This is really hitting the spot," and licked the ice cream running down the side of her sugar cone.

He chuckled. "Yeah, it is."

They resumed their quietude for the next few minutes as they enjoyed their ice cream.

Breaking the silence, Stefàn asked, "Do you go to church every Sunday?"

"Unless I'm sick or not in town," she answered. "Do you go at all?"

"No, it's been years…. Well, with the exception of weddings and funerals, I haven't been to church in years. It would probably go up in flames if I walked in on a Sunday," he stated.

"Don't say that. That's the great thing about God. He forgives everyone who asks."

Stefàn glanced down at her with a slight smile. "You've been a church girl all your life, huh?"

"Oh, no. I'm a baby Christian. I've only recently begun to grow my relationship with Him."

Finding that information surprising, he inquired, "What happened?"

"You mean to cause my change?"

"Yes."

Charisse had finished her ice cream by now and rose from the bench to sit next to Stefàn on the table. "Well, at the beginning of the year I joined a co-worker on a spiritual retreat and over the course of those three days, something in me changed. I can't even tell you specifically what caused it, but being with so many God-fearing sisters and experiencing the love and fellowship I did, let me see there was something missing from my life. I came back and went to Sunday service the following week with my friend, and a month or so later, I joined her church. Before that, I hadn't been in church since I'd stopped going to Sunday school when I got out of high school. And it wasn't that I was ever living…you know, like…loose or anything. But things I did before my change, I'm making a conscious effort not to do anymore."

"Like what?"

"Like using foul language, drinking—"

"You weren't drinking yesterday?" he interrupted to ask.

"I had two glasses of wine at the reception, but that was it. I used to drink hard liquor—margaritas, screwdrivers or Long Island iced tea—until I was tore up. I can't do that anymore. And those two glasses of wine I had yesterday, I didn't even finish the second one. My taste for alcohol has diminished."

He nodded his understanding. "What other things have you given up?"

"I don't listen to certain types of music anymore. It's funny, but things that just a year ago didn't bother me at all, I find offensive now. I guess it's because now I realize my true worth. I finally know who I am and Whose I am."

"So I guess you can quote me Scripture and everything, huh?"

Charisse chuckled and said, "Not really. I mean, there are a couple of verses I know by heart, but that's because they have a special meaning to me. Like, 'I can do all things through Christ who strengthens me.' That's Philippians, chapter 4, verse 13."

"I can understand why that would be memorable," he noted.

"Yeah, but I don't know the Bible yet. I'm only just reading it in its entirety for the first time."

"Is it hard? I mean, the changes you've made?"

"Yeah, it is. Well, I should say, some things are harder than others. It hasn't been difficult for me to stop swearing. I made the decision that as a child of God, I can't talk like I live in the gutter anymore. I'm trying to live as a reflection of Him." Charisse paused momentarily before adding, "The hardest change will involve my sexuality."

"What do you mean?"

"Well, I've made the decision that I won't be intimate with a man again until I'm married."

"Whoa, really?"

"Yeah."

"When you say you won't be intimate, what exactly do you mean? I mean, besides intercourse?"

"Well, there's a lot that can be done before a couple ever gets to the intercourse stage," she said with a sidewise glance at him. "But basically, unless he'll be my husband, I won't leave myself open to the possibility of anything more than a kiss happening. And I'm not talking about French kissing, either. And it's easy to say I'm going to do that right now, since I'm not seeing anyone, but that's going to be a struggle because I'm very affectionate when I truly care about a man. I'll have to stay in prayer about that," she candidly admitted.

"Why do you have to give up sex?"

"Because fornication is a sin. And I'm not about to tell you I'm not a sinner, 'cause we all are, but I'm trying to be more Christ-like in the way I live. And when you willfully do something that goes against His principles, then ask for forgiveness… that's hypocritical, and that's something I've always tried not to be. Even before I became a follower of Christ."

Stefan was thoughtful, digesting what she had said. "Sounds like you have quite a struggle ahead of you."

"The funny thing is, I feel more at peace within myself than I ever have before. I don't worry about things I can't control anymore. God is to going bless me as long as I'm trying to live right. But really not just 'cause of me but by His grace. The things I need, He will give me. When the time comes for me to settle down and get married, He will put that special man in my life. I feel a sense of joy like I never have before because He's going to take care of me."

Stefan smiled thoughtfully. What she revealed about her faith and her feelings were very personal, but she didn't seem to have a problem sharing. The glimpse of her he'd gotten yesterday let him know she was not like the women he was used to associating with, but today, witnessing this very spiritual side of her solidified his earlier opinion. He felt at peace just sitting with her.

"I'm talking too much, right?" she said, interrupting his thoughts.

"Huh? No! No, I was thinking about what you were saying. I admire you. It's great you feel the way you do."

"Can I ask you a personal question?" she suddenly said.

"Sure."

"Do you believe in Jesus Christ?"

"You mean, that He died on the cross and rose from the dead?" he asked.

"Yeah."

Stefan pondered her question for a few seconds before saying, "Yeah, I can believe that."

"Do you believe He died to save you?"

His mouth turned up in one corner for a brief moment. "I don't know. I've never really thought about it like that."

"He did, you know?"

Stefan smiled but didn't comment.

"Okay, I'm done," Charisse said as she playfully nudged his shoulder with her own. "What about you? What do you like to do?"

"It's funny you asked me that. My favorite thing to do in all the world is ride my motorcycle. In truth, I've always felt very close to God when I'm riding. Probably because one wrong move and I could be standing before Him in the blink of an eye. But I could get on my bike and ride for hours. I love the freedom and peace it affords me." After a brief pause he continued, "Truth be told, you're the only person I've ever ridden on my bike."

Stunned by that revelation, Charisse asked, "Why?"

"Because riding my bike is something I consider very personal and private, and I don't let many people get close to me."

"But why me?"

He shrugged. "I don't know." After a moment he admitted, "When you started to walk away from me on the dance floor yesterday, I had to think of something quick to stop you. I had to be different, at least as far as keeping your attention." With a chuckle he added, "My usual smooth-talking wasn't going to fly with you and since you'd already told me you liked fast cars, the first thing that came to mind was my bike." He couldn't tell her he felt that if he'd let her get away yesterday, he would have regretted it for the rest of his life.

"So you wouldn't ordinarily have done this?"

"No, but I'm not sorry I did. I'm glad I asked you and I'm glad you reconsidered."

"You scared me," she conceded.

That surprised him. "Why?"

"You have a lot of sex appeal. I don't need to tell you that, but I've never been one to hold my tongue, which I'm sure you realize by now. But I felt this…attraction to you that made me think…. I don't know."

"I felt it, too, Charisse," he softly intoned.

"More than just physical, though," she clarified.

"Yes, it is."

"What do you think that is?"

In the same tender tone he said, "Maybe it's our destiny to be friends or something. They say everything happens for a reason and that people are put in your life for a purpose. Who knows?"

"God does," she softly uttered.

With her beauty, charisma and honesty sending explosive sensations through his body, Stefan's heart skipped a beat as he affectionately glanced at her. *What is this I'm feeling?*

Charisse had been able to discern upon meeting Stefán yesterday that he was something of a fitness buff. The way his suit had framed his tall, slender physique accented his broad shoulders and slim waistline. Seeing him today with his muscle shirt defining the exquisite musculature of his arms and torso hammered her assumption home. She asked him about it and he admitted he was steadfast in his routine.

"I work out every day in some way. If nothing else, I do one hundred and fifty crunches and push-ups every morning as soon as I get out of bed. I work with weights, either at home or at the gym, but that's usually with my friends. I play basketball on a regular basis, and I box. I'm also a black belt in karate."

"How long have you been studying martial arts?" she asked.

"Since I was a kid. My father made all of us study. It kept us out of trouble."

"Do you participate in tournaments?"

"Not anymore. My brother, Devin, and I were an awesome team in our day," he said proudly.

"Is he older than you?"

"No. Two years younger."

"Is it just the two of you?"

"No, we have a sister. Nikki. She's the baby. What about you? Do you work out?"

"Yeah, but not as regularly as you. I have to admit, I'm a little vain. Got to keep the girlish figure tight, you know," she said with a chuckle as she nudged his shoulder again.

Grinning slyly, he said, "There's nothing girlish about your figure, Charisse. You've got the woman thing down pat."

Blushing, she murmured, "Thank you." Continuing, she added, "I go to a health club, but not all the time. I love to swim, too. Sometimes, I'll go to the gym just to swim."

The sun had broken through the clouds, but played hide and

seek for the remainder of the afternoon. After a while, they retrieved their helmets and continued their stroll through the park. Further on, they stopped near the lake. Taking a seat on a bench overlooking the body of water centered in the park, they watched as people of all ages passed by in rowboats and paddle-boats. Their conversation continued with the same easy flow. They shared stories of their childhoods and the neighborhoods where they'd each grown up. Stefan admitted he used to intentionally intimidate his younger sister's male suitors, and Charisse revealed her own agitation regarding her older brothers' overprotective tactics. They exchanged information about their likes and dislikes, hobbies and such and discovered they both had a fondness for fine clothes, fancy restaurants, music and traveling.

There was a mutual comfort they felt conversing with one another and unlike Charisse, who was always outspoken, Stefan found himself opening up to her in a manner he never did with a woman he didn't know extremely well. He had to check himself because the desire to stop and stare at her in amazement over-came him several times that afternoon. The combination of her spirituality and candidness was intoxicating to him. Additionally, he found her to be incredibly sexy. The jeans she wore were molded to her curvaceous frame although she had plenty of room in them. Her tank top was loose fitting, but did nothing to cover her natural shape. With her denim jacket tied casually around her waist, she seemed almost juvenile, even tomboyish, but cute as she wanted to be. Her white Nikes added a slight spring to her step. When she had removed her helmet after they arrived at the park, she had run her fingers through her hair to fluff it, but hadn't made a big deal about it the way some women might have. Yesterday, at the wedding, her face had been fully made up, but today, aside from a neutral shade of lip color, she was makeup free. Stefàn was trying to decide if he liked her better with or without the makeup. Either way, he reasoned, she was beautiful—inside and out.

It was close to four-thirty and they had just about circled the park and were coming back toward the playground where they had been seated to eat their ice cream when the first drop fell on them.

"Was that rain I felt?" Charisse asked as she held her free hand out.

"I think it was," Stefàn replied as several big drops began to fall on them.

The sun was peeking through the clouds overhead, but the flow persisted.

"I didn't hear anything about rain in the forecast today," Charisse said.

"Neither did I."

As they picked up their pace, Charisse asked Stefàn, "Do you ever ride in the rain?"

"If I get caught in it like this."

"Race you back to the parking lot," Charisse then challenged. "Last one there's a rotten egg."

"What?" He thought he was hearing things.

"Race you back."

Stefàn laughed. "Yeah, right."

"Oh, what? You scared?" she taunted.

"You're serious, aren't you?"

"Yes. Are you scared?" she asked again.

"I don't think so."

"So let's do it. Last one back is a rotten egg," and with that she took off running, untying the jacket from her waist with one hand and carrying the helmet in her other hand.

Stefàn was taken aback and was slow to follow her, but he soon recovered and started after her. Because of his longer legs and stride, he easily caught up to her, but she gave him a run for his money. Charisse was only inches behind him when he passed through the entrance of the parking lot.

"I guess that would be you I'm smelling," Stefan haughtily stated as he stopped to catch his breath.

"That's all right. You won this one. I had too much stuff in my hands, anyway."

Holding up his helmet and jacket, he said, "Don't make excuses, lady."

"Your legs are longer than mine. That's the only reason you won," Charisse said.

"Where'd you learn to run like that, anyway?" he asked.

Charisse laughed through her rapid breathing. "I was a sprinter in high school and college."

"Oh, so you're a cheater. See, you didn't tell me that."

"I can't give away all of my secrets," she said with a big smile.

"If I had known I was going to be racing you, I would have worn the proper foot gear." Stefan had on the black boots he always wore when he rode his motorcycle.

"Boy, it's really coming down," Charisse said as she put her arms in her jacket.

Stefan followed suit. "Put your helmet on," he told her as they hurried toward his bike. "I have a poncho in the storage compartment on the bike." Retrieving it, he unfolded the large plastic covering and proceeded to put it on her.

"What about you?" she asked.

"I'll be all right."

"You don't think we could both fit in here?" The poncho hung on her almost to the ground.

He smiled and said, "That's a nice idea, but I don't think so."

Blushing, "I didn't mean it like that."

"I know. I'm teasing you."

"Is it safe to ride in the rain?" she asked.

"Oh, yeah. I have good tread on my tires. Besides, I'm going to stay on the streets. I'm not going to get back on the highway."

"I can't believe the sun is still shining."

"Yeah, right. It probably won't rain too much longer," Stefan replied.

He wiped down the seat of his motorcycle, then helped Charisse mount it. He climbed on immediately and started the engine.

Turning back to her, he asked, "You okay?"

"Oh yeah. I'm good to go now," she answered easily.

"Glad to hear it."

They took off without further comment. After riding about fifteen blocks from the park, they realized they'd driven right out of the shower. Stefan drove a few yards further, then pulled the bike over.

"It looks like it didn't even rain here," Charisse noticed.

"Yeah, how about that. You want to take that off?"

"Okay." They both climbed off the bike and Stefan helped her pull the poncho over her head.

After shaking it out, he folded it down to a six inch bundle and replaced it in his saddle bag.

"Are you soaked through?" she asked with concern.

"It's all right. I won't melt right away," he answered with a smile.

"Since it's stopped raining, do you want to take the highway now?" Charisse asked.

"No, I'm in no hurry," he answered. "Unless you are."

"Oh no, I'm not."

"Are you hungry?" he asked. "You want to stop and get something to eat?"

"No, thanks. I have some work at home that I have to do before it gets too late. There's a movie coming on tonight that I want to see."

"Okay," he said, making every effort to hide his disappointment. He didn't want this time with her to end.

Climbing back on the bike, they resumed their ride.

Reflecting on the day's events during the return trip, Charisse surmised that despite her earlier trepidation, it had been a perfect day. In addition to loving the experience of riding a motorcycle and being close to him, she had utterly enjoyed their conversation and appreciated his openness. Her attraction to him yesterday, as much as she'd tried to fight it and ignore it, had grown due to their time together today. She sensed he seldom let his guard down, but felt he had revealed more about himself to her that afternoon than he normally would have to anyone he barely knew. She was glad he felt so comfortable with her because she was quite at ease with their rapport. Those few hours had given her a new perspective of Stefan Cooper. He was a genuinely sweet man and she got the impression he was probably a lot more sensitive than he cared to admit.

When all was said and done, she admitted her intrigue: she wanted to know more about him. In order to do that, however, she would have to change her mind once more because now she wanted them to be friends.

AS THEY RODE THE STREETS OF THE TOWNS they passed through, Stefan's thoughts were very similar to Charisse's. *What a perfect day it turned out to be.*

He was tripping, though, on the conversation they'd had during their stay at the park. He was surprised at how open he had been with her, but found he could be no other way in the face of her unabashed honesty. *How I'd love to make love to her*. With her confession earlier about her decision to abstain from physical intimacy until she was married, he realized his desire was in vain. His body hardened, nevertheless, at the mere thought of laying with her. At this particular time, there was nothing more un-comfortable, but Charisse had awakened something in him by giving him a peek into her heart. There was no doubt he enjoyed the time he normally spent with his lady friends, but Charisse was so much more enchanting. Her spirituality—her faith— actually enhanced his affection. Truth be told, although her physical persona was sexually appealing, it was her inner beauty that really bowled him over.

She would never be counted among his harem, though. Charisse was far too extraordinary for that. He realized suddenly that he had enormous respect for her; more than he had for any woman, next to his mother and sister.

That train of thought brought to mind, for the first time in years, his one and only love, Janine, and he was briefly saddened when recalling that painful time. It was his selfishness that had pushed that beautiful lady out of his life. He had been an immature man-child then, but he couldn't use that excuse anymore. His eyes wide open and his senses awakened, he now knew the value of a good woman's love and he had vowed to never squander or take such a precious gift for granted ever again.

Love. That was an emotion he hadn't felt, used or connected to any of the women who'd been in his life in well over ten years. Why now? *I don't even know her*. But he wanted to. He wanted to know everything about her—what made her laugh so he could tell her jokes; what made her cry so he could comfort her with a loving embrace; what were the things that frightened her so he could protect and shield her with his strength. He wanted to know what she looked like when she was asleep, and what she looked like first thing in the morning.

As quickly as the vulnerability of his soul involuntarily emerged, the cold waters of reality washed over him. *Whoa! Slow your roll, dude! You're sounding soft. You already know she's not going to put up with your player ways. But I can feel how she's grooving on me. Why would she be holding me this way, if not?* Stefan knew she was no longer nervous about being on the bike with him and he had expected her hold to relax or loosen as a result of that. But the opposite was true. Not that she was holding him tightly; no, that wasn't it at all. Her hold was possessive. Charisse's arms were wrapped around him in such a way as to make him feel like she had already claimed him as hers. Funny thing was, he was perfectly okay with that. Stefan could feel the impression of her very feminine physique against his back and the sensation did nothing to calm his already heightened libido. But what he was experiencing was not entirely inspired by lust.

Stefan wrestled with himself for the remainder of the ride back to his house. Charisse would never agree to see him on a regular basis as long as he was seeing other women. But he wanted to see her—on a regular basis. At the same time, he was reluctant to relinquish his player card. He enjoyed living the single life; seeing different women whenever he wanted. But he felt an inexplicable urgency to be with Charisse.

Stefan had lived so much of his life driven by physical and material needs and desires that the deeper, more ethereal bond he felt with Charisse was strange to him. But it was exciting, exhilarating and enthralling, too. *I could ride off into the sunset with her.* That thought caused him to chuckle.

"What's so funny?" he heard her ask.

Turning back briefly, he replied, "Nothing."

Yeah, I could see myself with her. Being with her now feels right.

Fifteen minutes after those thoughts floated through his head, Stefan turned the bike onto his block. Activating the automatic garage door opener when they were a couple of doors away, he drove right into the space beside his sedan. When he turned off the engine, he removed his helmet and stepped off the bike. Charisse removed her helmet as well, but momentarily stayed in her seat. They stared at one another for a few moments without saying a word.

Finally, Charisse smiled. "This was a perfect day," she said.

Stefan smiled as his heart fluttered off-beat. "I'm glad you enjoyed it so much."

"Oh, I really did. Thank you."

"Thank you for sharing it with me."

"Believe me," she said, "it was my pleasure."

She moved to get off the bike.

"So, are you thinking about taking bike lessons, now?" he asked.

Laughing, she replied, "No, I like riding shotgun better."

It was his turn to laugh.

"Will you take me out again sometime?" she asked shyly.

"No doubt," he easily responded.

When Charisse stepped away from the bike, Stefan moved over and leaned against it. He folded his arms across his chest.

"Well, I'd better start home." She reached into her fanny pack and removed her car keys. "Oh, here's your helmet," she said as she handed it to him.

"You keep it. I bought it for you."

Charisse blushed as her heart fluttered. "Thank you."

After an awkward few seconds of silence, Charisse said, "Well, I'll talk to you soon."

Stefan nodded his head.

As she started out of his garage, he wondered, *Will she call me? I hope so. She's so beautiful. Do I want to take the chance that she won't call? I have her cell number on the caller ID box. What if she doesn't want me to call her, though? Only one way to find out.* Deciding not to leave his fate to the mercy of the four winds, he spoke her name. "Charisse."

She was at the door when she turned back to him. "Yes?"

Gazing at her hopefully for a few seconds, he took a deep breath and asked, "Can I call you?"

She'd figured he would ask this of her before the day was over. *God, I need a sign.*

Stefan saw her contemplating his request and hoped she would not turn him down.

"I need to ask you a favor," she suddenly said.

"Sure."

"You have to promise me something."

His arms fell to his side and a frown creased his brow briefly before he asked, "What?"

Taking a few steps toward him, she asked, "Will you promise to never lie to me?"

Paralyzed for a moment by the honesty and sheer simplicity of her request, he realized that was the last thing he had expected her to ask of him. When he thought about it though, he had to acknowledge that he had been honest with her from the start and it had been effortless, as if she were already his best friend. Something about her made him want to tell her nothing but the truth. "Yes," he finally said.

"Say it."

"I promise to never lie to you, Charisse," he said softly.

Stepping closer still, she looked up into his eyes. "Thank you."

"Will you promise me the same?" he then asked her.

Holding his gaze, she responded, "Yes." Reaching into her fanny pack, she removed her wallet. Taking one of her business cards from it, she proceeded to write her home number on the back. Stefan, studying her cocoa brown countenance as she did this, felt warmth permeate his being as he took in her beauty.

When she handed him the card, he breathed, "Thank you."

Directing a tender smile his way, Charisse took his hand and squeezed it ever-so-gently. Then she turned and walked away.

Stefan's eyes followed her fluidity as she slowly strutted to her car, got in, started the engine and pulled off. Unable to move from his spot, he stood there, delightfully dazed. When she was no longer in sight, he looked down at the card in his hand.

"Charisse Marie Ellison," he reverently muttered, then smiled, shook his head and walked into his house.

CHAPTER 6

A REASON, A SEASON OR A LIFETIME?

As part of Charisse's efforts to grow in her faith, she had begun journaling. She didn't write in it every day; usually only when something significant happened. That evening when she arrived back at her townhouse, she headed straight to her bedroom and started writing.

July 17th

All praise and glory to God through our Lord and Savior, Jesus Christ. Thank You, God, for another day of Your awesome grace and tender mercies.

I spent the most enjoyable afternoon with an amazing man. Stefan Cooper.

Recounting her feelings upon their meeting, then their conversation that morning when she got out of church, she also wrote about their day together and how her earlier feelings had changed dramatically by the time Stefan rode them back to his house.

She ended the entry with a query.

God, why did You bring us together? What are Your plans for us? I pray that You will reveal Your plans for us. If I continue to look to You for guidance, Your plans will be made clear. I don't mean to be impatient, but he makes my heart flutter. I wanted to kiss him today when we parted.

I need to calm down, but he excites me.

GET A GRIP, CHARISSE.
Lord, help me, please.

LATER THAT EVENING, Charisse was stepping out of the shower when her telephone rang. Wrapping a towel around her still-wet body, she hurried into her bedroom to get the call before her answering machine clicked into action.

"Hello!"

"Oh, I was about to hang up," Myra said on the other end.

"I just got out the shower."

"Did you go riding with him?"

"Yeah, but not where we originally planned to go."

"What do you mean?" Myra asked.

"After I dropped you off last night, I was thinking about what you and Mommy were saying about him, and I decided not to go."

"For real?"

"Yeah, so this morning when I got out of church, I called him and told him I wasn't going."

"What did he say?"

"He told me to have a nice life and hung up on me."

"What!"

"Humph, you think you're shocked? Myra, I panicked. I called him back and apologized to him."

"What did you have to apologize for? If you didn't want to go that was your choice. He didn't have to be so rude," Myra indignantly stated.

"That wasn't why he hung up." Charisse told Myra of her first conversation with Stefan that morning. "When I actually admitted to myself that he was right, that I had judged him without really knowing him, I had to apologize."

"So where'd you go riding?"

"Right here in Bergen County."

"Well, how was it?"

"It was great. You've got to take a ride on a motorcycle, Myra. It's the bomb!" Charisse said excitedly.

"You weren't scared?"

As she removed her towel and continued to dry herself, she said, "At first, I was, but he told me what to do before we started and after a while, I was fine. By the time we got to the park, I wanted to do it again." She chuckled.

"So how was he?"

Charisse sighed. "He was wonderful."

"Wonderful?"

"Yes, Myra. He was wonderful. He was a perfect gentleman the entire time. He was really a lot of fun."

"You sure he wasn't putting up a front?"

"No, he wasn't. Everything between us was so natural. It was as if we'd known each other forever."

"So are you going to see him again?" Myra asked after a while.

"If he calls me, I probably will."

"You gave him your number, huh?"

"Yeah, but only after he promised not to lie to me."

"Charisse, is he saved?"

"He believes in Jesus."

"How do you know?"

"I asked him, and even though he doesn't go to church or have a real relationship with Christ, I believe he'll keep his word."

Myra sighed. "Do you really?"

"Yes, I do." Sensing Myra's skepticism, she continued, "I like him. I'm comfortable with him, but I'm not trying to get physical with him. I've already told him that I wouldn't go there with any man I wasn't married to. But I'd like us to be friends."

"Are you sure you know what you're doing, Risi?" Myra said

softly. "He doesn't strike me as the kind of guy who would want to be just friends with you. I saw the way he was looking at you and it wasn't in a friendly manner, if you know what I mean."

"I understand your doubts, Myra, and honestly, I have some of my own, but there's something about him that I can't ignore. There's a reason God put him in my way. Maybe I'm supposed to bring him to God. Maybe he's supposed to help me learn discipline. I have to admit he excites me and that scares me, but trials come to make us stronger. That's what it says in the Bible, Myra. Maybe he's a vehicle for my growth in Christ."

"I don't want to see you get hurt by this guy, Risi, and you sound like you've already got your nose open for him."

Charisse snickered at her friend's words, but deep inside she trembled, for the truth of them hit very close to home. "I'm going to keep my hand in God's hand, Myra. That way, no matter what, I can't go wrong."

IT WAS NINE FORTY-FIVE THAT SUNDAY NIGHT, and Stefan was still flying from his afternoon with Charisse.

After she left him, he went straight upstairs to remove the wet jeans he was wearing. Changing into a pair of sweats and sneakers, he moved to his spare room. Furnished with exercise equipment, including free weights, a weight bench and a Bowflex System, he dove right into his workout. Pent up tension, both identifiable and not, had to be relieved.

Charisse had gotten under his skin today. Taking him on a roller coaster ride of emotions in less than six hours, she left his spirit soaring high, riding on a cloud of pure bliss and he wasn't sure when or if he would ever come down.

He'd exhausted himself during his workout for the sole purpose of banishing her from his mind, but it had been an exercise in futility. The moment he spied her business card, which he had placed on the dresser in his bedroom, everything they'd shared was brought back to the forefront of his memory. The woman thrilled him to no end. Maybe it was because she was basically untouchable. He couldn't seduce her; his conscience wouldn't let him. The last thing he wanted to do was compromise her. She'd been big enough to admit that her decision to abstain from sexual activity would be something of a struggle, and he admired her truthfulness. He felt certain the physical yearning he felt for her was reciprocal. He was no biblical scholar—not by any stretch of the imagination—but he was pretty sure that anyone intentionally leading someone in Christ astray would surely go to hell. He was probably on his way there as it was, but he definitely wasn't trying to hasten the trip.

What is it about her? he wondered. *Why has she captured my attention so completely?* It wasn't like she was the most beautiful woman he had ever seen. She wasn't even the sexiest woman he'd ever known. *What made her so special?* The chemistry he felt between them was undeniable. Recognizing it the moment he touched her hand yesterday when they met, her eyes pulled him in like quicksand, and it seemed, just like that natural phenomenon, the more he tried to resist, the deeper he sank.

Showering in mostly cold water to anesthetize his senses, Stefàn, nevertheless, felt a rising warmth just by thinking of her.

After his shower, he went downstairs and retrieved an ice cold Corona from his refrigerator. Taking the brew back up to his bedroom, he placed it on the nightstand next to his king-sized bed. Stacking the pillows behind him so he could sit up in bed and watch ESPN for the day's sports highlights, he reached for the remote control next to his beer and brought the flat-screen television on the wall across from him to life.

At the same moment, his telephone rang.

Pressing the MUTE button on the remote, he picked up the handset of his cordless phone.

"Hello."

"What happened to you?"

"Hey, Dub." Stefan chuckled. "You'll never believe it."

"Try me."

"I got bit today, man," Stefan simply said.

"By what?" Julian wanted to know.

"By a bug named Charisse Marie Ellison."

He proceeded to tell Julian about his day, from Charisse's early morning phone call until they returned from their ride. Stefan also divulged his anxiety over his uncommon attraction to her.

"She left here around six o'clock, but she's been with me all night. I can't shake this, Dub. This woman's got me sprung and I haven't even kissed her," Stefan admitted.

"Well, she is fine."

"It's got nothing to do with her looks, man. The lady is.... I've never met anyone like her. I mean, I don't even know why she's got me so caught up."

"Is she a church girl like you thought?"

"Yeah, but just since a couple months ago. She even told me she's made the decision not to have sex again until she's married."

Julian cracked up laughing. "Well, that's all she wrote for you."

"No, Dub, it's not. I want to see her. Right now."

He paused, obviously stunned. "Damn, she's got you like that?"

"Yes," Stefan said with a sigh. "I never thought I would say this, Julian, but I think...I think she's the woman I'm gonna marry."

"Really? Now, that's deep, especially coming from you," Julian noted.

"Yeah, how 'bout that? But that's how she's got me. I can't stop thinking about her. I feel like...." Abruptly halting his love-driven declaration, he stated, "Never mind."

"What?"

Shaking his head, Stefan said, "It'll sound stupid."

Sensing how strongly Stefan was feeling, Julian—who had a genuine appreciation for true love—compassionately replied, "This is me, Coop."

Stefan sighed deeply and in a tone filled with emotion said, "I feel like I'm high, man. Like I've taken some kind of drug or something. She's got my heart racing. We got back over three hours ago and it's like she's still here."

"Hey, man," Julian said with understanding, "maybe she is the one. They say there's someone for everyone. Maybe she is the one for you."

"But we're living such different lives, Dub. I mean, it's not like I don't believe in God. I do, but we both know I'm far from being a saint. She was talking to me about her faith and I felt so much admiration for her."

"Maybe you should go to church with her," Julian suggested.

"And have it burn down around us," Stefan said laughing. "I don't think so."

Julian laughed, too. "Hey, Coop, man, I go to church every now and then with Michele and L'il Jay. There've been times when I didn't even wait for her to call and ask if I was going; I called her. There's something to it. I don't understand it all, but there's definitely something to believing in an omni-potent God. I've been thinking about going to the Bible study at Shelly's church, too."

"But, Dub, I don't even know this woman. I mean we talked a lot today, about a lot of different things, but I don't even know her and she's got me feeling like this."

"Well, maybe you need to work at rectifying that. I'm sure she was put in your life for a reason, with you feeling as strongly as you do already. There's gotta be a reason."

"Yeah, I guess. I need to chill for a minute, though. I don't want to play myself."

"So take your time and let nature take its course," Julian suggested. "If y'all are meant to be together, there's nothing in the world that can keep y'all apart."

CHAPTER 7

YOU CAN'T FIGHT LOVE

Over the next couple of days, Charisse, reestablishing boundaries of control, intentionally refrained from contacting Stefan. Busying herself at work on Monday and Tuesday, she didn't leave her office either night until very late. His image had taken up permanent residence in her mind. Shamefully, not all her thoughts of him were entirely pure. As she'd told him, he had a magnetic appeal. Being honest with herself, she had to admit sensuality oozed from his pores. Even though he had been the perfect gentleman when they were together Sunday, she had no doubts if she were the type of woman to proposition him, he would not have refused her. And in spite of her spiritual renewal, her natural desires and instincts had not waned. That being the case, she made every effort to concentrate on her Bible studies when she had free time so she would not daydream about him.

Stefan, whose office hours were much more liberal, chose to work late Monday and Tuesday for much the same reason as Charisse. Purposely making appointments with clients for late in the day gave him plenty to do so when he finally got home, he basically fell out from exhaustion.

Although he could have easily occupied his time with one or another of the several women he frequently called on for companionship, surprisingly he opted for solitude. When he'd arrived home Sunday evening after spending the afternoon with

Charisse, and before he started his workout to exorcise her from his mind, he listened to the messages on his answering machine. There had been three of them, each from a different woman trying to log some very up close and personal time with him.

He still couldn't believe he'd actually told Julian he thought Charisse was the woman he would one day marry. Before Saturday, the thought of marrying anyone was so far removed from his vision of his future that he would have readily insisted he'd be a bachelor for life. Being the somewhat libidinous man he had always been, even the idea of not making love to a woman he was involved with was foreign to him, but she was serious about her decision. Knowing he wouldn't be able to get physical with her until they were married, if that even happened, in no way diminished his longing for her or his desire to be with her. In fact, the opposite was the case.

The sentiments she awakened in him were frightening to a degree. Like the thunder before a storm, the depth of his passion for her was intense. Sending sensational shockwaves through him, no woman had ever sparked such emotional chaos in his heart and soul. At the same time, the thought of her inspired dreams of their future together. Stefan found himself daydreaming about her whenever he had a spare moment. Several times a day, he would pull out her business card and gaze at her name.

He'd always considered himself a player so he didn't want to start acting like a weak-minded little boy with a crush, but that was exactly how Charisse made him feel. Try as he might to ignore his yearning, when Wednesday rolled around, Stefan's resolve crumbled and he called Charisse at work early in the afternoon. He had an irresistible urge to stare into her beautiful brown eyes, hear her lovely voice, or merely touch her hand.

Rising from his desk chair, he closed the door to his office for privacy. Everyone there knew of his many and varied female admirers, and had heard him woo them with his smooth talk on numerous occasions. His feelings for Charisse, however, were no game and certainly nothing to be taken lightly.

He dialed her number and was grateful that the call was answered after one ring. "Good afternoon, Miss Ellison's office. May I help you?"

"Good afternoon. May I speak to her, please?"

"Who's calling?"

"Mr. Cooper."

"One moment." Stefan's call was put on hold.

Charisse was working on a client's spreadsheet when her assistant paged her. "Yeah, Lynn?"

"There's a Mr. Cooper on the line for you."

"Is that the guy from Bennett's office?" Charisse asked.

"I don't think so. It doesn't sound like him."

"Would you find out for sure? If it is, I'm not available. If it's a personal call, I'll take it," Charisse said. She was ducking a business caller by the name of Cooper because she didn't yet have the information he was calling for.

"Okay." Lynn took Stefan's call off hold and said, "I'm sorry, Miss Ellison is not available. May I ask what your call is in reference to? Maybe someone else could help you."

"No, it's personal. Just tell her…"

"Oh, wait," Lynn hurriedly said, "she just hung up. Hold on a minute."

Lynn paged Charisse again. "Hi. It's a personal call."

"Okay, thanks. I'll take it." She picked up the line. "Mr. Cooper," she said with a smile in her voice.

"Miss Ellison. Nice ploy. Screening your calls, huh?"

In those few short days, she'd forgotten how the timbre of his voice over the phone could send shockwaves through her system. His melodious baritone voice sounded every bit as smooth as he was. As nonchalantly as possible, she replied, "Yeah, there's this guy named Cooper I'm ducking until I can get the information he wants. He's been calling every couple of hours."

"Relentless, huh?"

"Yes. Sounds familiar, doesn't it?" she said with a chuckle.

"Must be something in the name."

"I wonder."

"So how have you been?" Stefan affectionately asked.

"I've been good. Busy, but good. I haven't gotten out of work once this week before nine."

"Really?"

"Yup. I'm in the midst of an audit."

"Well, I hope tonight will be the exception, because I'd like to have you for dinner, I mean, take you to dinner," he quickly corrected with a snicker.

Charisse chuckled at his gaffe and wondered briefly if he was playing with her or had made an honest slip of the lip. She had a feeling the former was the case. "That was cute," she replied, "but I can't tonight, Stefan. I won't be getting out of here before ten, and I have to stay because I'm leaving early tomorrow to pick up my car."

"I'm sorry to hear that," he said. Then quickly added, "Not about your car, of course. About dinner."

"Me, too. I would have enjoyed seeing you tonight."

"Likewise. You've been on my mind, but I've been busy, too, the last couple of days."

"I can imagine." *Have you been fighting this feeling like I've been?* she wondered.

"So you're picking up your baby tomorrow, huh?"

"Yes. I'm really excited about that."

"I bet you are. What color d'you get?" he asked.

"Black-on-black leather. Fully loaded. Convertible, of course."

"Of course."

"Ooh, I'm so psyched!" Her excitement was evident in her voice.

"I don't blame you. That's a monster machine. I can see you now, flying down the highway with the top down, shades on, running from the cops," he said with a laugh.

She laughed heartily at his verbal picture.

"Well, listen, are you busy Friday? No, what are you doing Saturday afternoon?"

"Myra and I were planning to go to the movies, but that's about it. Why? What's up?"

"I remember you telling me how much you love to swim, and a friend of mine is having a pool party this Saturday in North Brunswick. It's going to be quite an event. I was hoping you could join me there."

"Oh, but Myra and I already made plans," Charisse said in a disappointed tone.

"She's more than welcomed to join us. Why don't you ask her?"

"Okay, I will. What time is it?"

"Well, I'm sure they'll be starting sometime around noon, but I have to work Saturday morning and probably won't be leaving my office until about one, so I figured about three o'clock. They're going to be there all night anyway. As a matter of fact, the second shift will be coming in at about six or seven," Stefan added.

"Second shift?"

"Yeah, it's a pretty big function. This guy's home is enormous and he and his wife always have a full house for these parties."

"They do this often?"

"Well, this particular party is a yearly thing. You might even meet a couple of celebrities."

"Really? Who is he?"

"Just a very gifted businessman with a lot of powerful connections. This party is actually an excellent place to network so you should bring some of your business cards."

"It's like that?"

"Yeah. It can get pretty outrageous sometimes, too, but it's always fun, so make sure you ask Myra if she'd like to come."

"All right, I will. What time will you be home tonight?"

"Around eight-ish."

"Okay, I'll call you then and let you know."

"Good enough."

"Let me get back to this mountain of work I have in front of me. Thanks for calling, Stefàn. It was nice hearing from you," she said softly.

"It was nice hearing your voice," he said in like tones.

Not as nice as it is to hear yours, Charisse thought.

STEFÀN'S DISAPPOINTMENT AT NOT BEING ABLE TO SEE CHARISSE that evening lingered for the remainder of the day. He had been looking forward to sitting across from her and gazing into those deep jewels that were her eyes and being captivated by her infectious laugh and witty conversation.

Julian had called not long after he had spoken to Charisse and told him a few of the fellas were going to be meeting at the gym later that evening to work out. Stefàn briefly thought about hooking up with them. He always enjoyed working out with the guys, but for some reason, he knew tonight would be a waste of time for him if he went. His mind wasn't there.

He was at the office until six-thirty that evening but had gotten little done since his earlier conversation with Charisse. He couldn't get her off his mind. When he left, he got into his car and headed straight to New York City instead of going home like he had earlier decided. He was a gambling man, so he decided to roll the dice and see if they turned up lucky seven.

CHARISSE HAD JUST FINALIZED THE FINANCIAL REPORT her boss had been waiting for when her telephone rang. She glanced at the clock on the wall to her left before she answered. *Seven-thirty.* She sighed and reached for the receiver. Her stomach growled with hunger as she announced, "Charisse Ellison."

"Are you hungry yet?"

"Stefan?"

"The one and only."

My God, he sounds so good on the phone. "Hi." She smiled and leaned back in her chair as, once again, pulses of electricity seemed to run through her body as she listened to his gentle, yet self-assured tone.

"Are you hungry?" he asked again.

"I'm starving. My stomach growled at the same time I answered the phone."

"Do you like Chinese food?" he asked.

"Yes, I do."

"I've got dinner for you, then. Do you want to come downstairs and get it? I don't believe these good gentlemen down here are going to let me up."

Quickly sitting up in her chair, she asked, "You're in the lobby?"

"Yes, ma'am."

A broad smile appeared on Charisse's face as she told him, "I'll be right down," then hung up the phone. *How thoughtful of him. How sweet and what perfect timing.*

When she reached the lobby, she immediately noticed Stefan standing near the building's entrance with a shopping bag at his feet. Wearing a tailored gray suit, a white collarless shirt opened at the neck, and black shoes polished to a high gloss, he looked fantastic.

"Hi," she called as she approached.

"Hey, beautiful," he said with a big smile.

"C'mon. Let me sign you in," Charisse said as she reached for his hand.

He took her hand, but as she led him over to the information desk, he asked, "It's okay for me to come up with you?"

"Sure." She stopped suddenly and turned back to him. "Unless you don't want to."

"Of course I want to."

"Good." Turning back to the guards at the desk, "Hey guys, this is my friend. Could I get a pass for him, please?" she asked as she signed the guest log on the desk.

"I don't know, Charisse," one of the men said. "It doesn't look like there's enough food in there for us."

"Oh, I left yours in the car. Let me take this up and I'll be right back down to get it," Stefan said, playing along with the man.

Everyone laughed as the ringleader said, "Yeah, right."

A few seconds later, Charisse and Stefan were on the elevator going back up to her office.

"I can't believe you did this. You must have been reading my mind or something; I was just about to order dinner."

"See, I knew you'd be hungry about now. That's why I timed it this way," Stefan joked.

"Well, your timing is impeccable. I really appreciate this."

"I wanted to see you tonight," he said tenderly.

"You did say you were relentless."

"I promised I wouldn't lie," he said with a grin.

Charisse laughed.

When they reached her office, she led Stefan inside and closed the door. "Come on in and sit down. Let me clear some of this stuff off my desk." She started moving papers from her desk to the credenza behind it in an attempt to clear enough space for them to eat. "You brought enough food for yourself, right?" she asked him suddenly.

"No doubt." Removing his jacket, he added, "I figured you'd probably not want to eat alone."

She grinned at him. "How insightful of you."

"Yeah, I know," he said in a smug fashion. "You like lobster, don't you?"

"I love it."

"Good. There's lobster Cantonese, General Tso's Chicken with extra broccoli, a couple of egg rolls and brown rice. I hope you like brown rice. It's healthier for you, you know?"

"I know, and I do like brown rice. As a matter of fact, you've managed to order all of my favorites."

"See, women aren't the only ones who have intuition."

"Would you like to bless the food or should I?" Charisse asked as he placed the containers on her desk.

"You do it this time. I'll take care of it the next time," he replied with a smile.

"Okay."

As Charisse prayed over their dinner, Stefan studied her adoringly. When he echoed her "Amen," it signaled a different type of thanks for him.

He stayed with her until approximately eight-forty-five. As they ate, they talked about their jobs—Stefan gave her the low down on a couple of recent sales transactions he had initiated and commissions he was working on, and Charisse talked about the promotion she was striving for. They talked about their families with Stefan sharing a funny story about his first karate tournament where he got beat up by a girl.

Charisse thoroughly enjoyed sharing dinner and conversation with Stefan. She found that despite his cool demeanor and laid back persona, he was quite entertaining. Aside from the activities he seemed to involve himself in during his free time, that is, the various sports he played, as well as the dating scene, he was also a very hardworking man. She learned that in addition to his real estate sales job, he also owned a six-unit apartment building in Queens.

When they finished eating and Stefan looked at his watch, he said, "Wow, I've been taking up all your time and you could have been busy working so you could get out of here before tomorrow."

She laughed. "That's okay. I needed this break. I'm really happy you came by. It's been good seeing you."

"It's been my pleasure, Charisse. I decided to take a chance to see if I could convince you to make a little time for me."

"Well, as you can see, I wouldn't have been able to leave, but I am glad you came. Dinner was excellent."

"The company was excellent, too."

When she blushed and looked away from him, he asked, "Did you get a chance to speak to Myra about Saturday?"

"Oh yeah; she said she'd love to come."

"Great! Tell her there will be plenty of single men in attendance, in case she's interested."

Laughing lightly, Charisse replied, "I'll let her know that."

Stefan took the emptied food containers and placed them back in the shopping bag. "I'll take this down with me."

"Oh, you don't have to do that. We can dump them in the pantry. C'mon, I'll show you where it is on the way out."

After discarding their trash, Charisse walked him back to the reception area. Since there was so little activity in the building due to the late hour, the elevator arrived only seconds after they rang for it. "You know, it never comes that quick when I want to leave," Charisse noticed.

"Well, it's obviously trying to tell me that my time is up," Stefan joked.

"Ya' know." She smiled up at him, then grabbed his arm as she tiptoed to kiss his cheek. "Thanks for coming by, Stefan, and for dinner. I really enjoyed your company."

"You're more than welcome, Charisse. I've enjoyed you as well," he said with a warm smile. "Good luck tomorrow."

"Thank you. Ooh, I can't wait," she suddenly screeched.

Stefan let out a laugh. "I can't wait to see you in it, either."

"Yeah, I'm going to tear up those streets now."

"Uh, oh, let me know when and where you'll be, and I'll make sure I'm nowhere around," he teased.

"That's all right. See, I was going to take you for a ride in my new car; now I'll have to reconsider," she said.

"Well, don't reconsider too hard. You're going to need some-one daring like me to keep up with you." He winked at her after stepping onto the elevator. "Get home safe, sweet face."

"You, too," she said demurely.

Introspective smiles covered each of their faces as they stood in each other's sights until the elevator doors closed.

When the doors opened on the ground floor, Stefan was still smiling.

CHAPTER 8
A PERSONAL INVITATION

C harisse left her office at four-thirty Thursday afternoon, and headed directly to the car dealership. It was close to six-thirty by the time all of her paperwork had been completed and she was handed the keys to her brand new Corvette. When she got into the car and started it up, tears of joy began to flow from her eyes. "Thank You, Father. Thank You."

Aside from her townhouse, which she had purchased three years ago with funds she'd saved from two consecutive Christmas bonuses and her 401k, this was the biggest purchase she had ever made. In addition to a significant down-payment—which she saved exclusively for this purchase—she used her Camry as a trade-in. That being the case, she was sure she'd have no problem making the monthly five hundred-dollar note.

She sat in the car for almost twenty minutes, checking out all of the instrumentation on the dashboard. For the ride home she had brought a Donnie McClurkin CD, which she popped in the multi-disc system. Activating the convertible top controls, she lowered the roof, shifted into reverse and eased her Corvette out of the lot. Since it was still rush hour, she was unable to do anything but creep along the highway toward Englewood. She really wanted to open it up on a vast stretch of roadway and put her new toy to the test.

When she finally got to her house, instead of pulling into the garage, Charisse parked in her driveway. Retrieving her mail from the box as she rushed inside, she took no time to scan it; even briefly. Instead, she dropped her pocketbook and keys on one of her living room end tables and headed up to her bedroom. Quickly removing her office attire and carelessly tossing it on her bed, she grabbed a pair of jeans from the closet and hurriedly pulled them on. She took a polo shirt from her dresser, and ignoring the creases in it, put it on, but put a lightweight jacket on over it. She slipped her feet into a pair of brown leather thongs, then darted out of her bedroom and back downstairs. She grabbed two more CDs from the rack, snatched her keys, cell phone and purse and raced back out the door.

Practically running back to the Corvette, Charisse hopped behind the wheel, started the car up and took off. Eager to head for the hills so she could drive somewhere where there would be a minimal amount of traffic and she could really open the car up, she realized, however, that she didn't want to take this ride alone.

Stefan had just stepped out of the shower. A towel was wrapped around his waist as he headed for the kitchen to grab a beer. As he reached the refrigerator, his telephone rang.

He grabbed the cordless extension off the wall. "Hello."

"Hey, you busy?"

"Charisse?"

"Yeah."

"No, I just got out of the shower. I was about to grab myself a beer and chill. What's up? Did you pick up your car?"

"I certainly d-id," she sang.

He laughed at the tone of her voice.

"Wanna go for a ride?" she quickly asked.

Stefan was taken aback by her invitation, but he smiled as he answered, "Sure, I'd love to. How long will it take you to get here?"

"I'm outside," she sheepishly answered.

"You're outside right now?" Stefan walked into the living room and pulled aside one of the slats of his blinds to look out.

Charisse waved.

"You're outside," he said softly. His heart fluttered and his stomach turned over with nervous excitement.

"Yeah."

"I'll be right out."

Stefan hurried up to his bedroom, taking the stairs two at a time, removing the towel from around his waist as he went. Throwing it on his bed, he grabbed a pair of boxers from the drawer. Stepping into them as he hopped over to the closet and opened it, he quickly took a pair of jeans and a print short-sleeved shirt down, hastily donning both. He started to grab a pair of socks from his drawer but decided that would take him too long. *She came to get me to ride with her in her new 'Vette.* Thrilled that she had thought of him, he knew she couldn't have been home for too long, especially if she had just picked it up this afternoon. *She probably hasn't even ridden anyone else in it yet.* That thought caused a trembling in his gut. Hurriedly slipping his bare feet into a pair of loafers, he grabbed his wallet and keys off his dresser, clipped his cell phone to his belt and headed back downstairs.

When Stefan stepped out of his house and started toward Charisse in her shiny black Corvette, he was smiling from ear to ear, as was she as she sat behind the wheel.

"Wait a minute," he called, stopping in his tracks. "I'll be right back." He disappeared back inside and quickly returned, this time with his face hidden behind a digital camera. "There she is. Pose for me, baby," he called to her.

More than happy to oblige, Charisse threw her arms wide and smiled glowingly for the camera. She opened the car door and stepped out, then went through a number of exaggerated poses as Stefân clicked away.

"Damn, girl, that's a fly ride you've got there," he said as he stepped up to the car and reverently touched the exterior.

"Isn't she beautiful?" Charisse said with a cheesy grin.

He turned to her and a warmth suddenly filled his heart as he witnessed the unadulterated joy pouring from her. *Yes, you are beautiful.* He reached out to hug her. Charisse grabbed him and held him tight. "Congratulations," he softly said.

"Thank you, Stefân. I'm just so... Oh my goodness, I can't even tell you how happy I am. C'mon, hop in. Let's take her for a spin."

It took every ounce of strength in Stefân's long, lean, two hundred and five pound body to sit beside Charisse as she sped confidently along, and not gawk at her like some silly, inexperienced, love-struck little boy. *My God, how she thrills me!* Everything about her made his nerve endings tingle. *And she's even more beautiful than normal when she's happily excited about something. What is she doing to me?*

They rode for almost forty-five minutes in relative silence, but there was nothing awkward about it. Stefân thoroughly enjoyed the simplicity of sitting beside her as she drove through the night in her awesome vehicle. The evening was warm and they welcomed the breeze that fanned them from the open top. The car stereo was blasting Yolanda Adams' latest song and although he didn't regularly listen to gospel music, he enjoyed the sounds coming from the stereo.

Stefan was happy to see that Charisse had a sense of adventure. A woman after his own heart, she liked excitement, but was by no means reckless; she was self-assured without being conceited; and she was independent, but confident enough to know that it's okay to need someone else. He knew she drew her strength from her spiritual beliefs. Having made that clear from the start, he realized he could take lessons from her. In concert with her spirituality, she was vibrant, fun-loving, intelligent and extremely sensual. He was in awe of her. *Is this what loving someone feels like?*

Over the years, Stefan had known women with whom he had become smitten for one reason or another, but never so quickly or intensely. *I haven't even kissed her*, he kept telling himself. Charisse was probably the most unpretentious person he had ever met, too. He didn't think she had a phony bone in her body. Her personality hit you head on and never faltered, but there was nothing calculated about her. That was just the way she lived. She seemed to have a zest for life and it showed in everything she did. Her positive attitude was infectious and quite endearing.

Suddenly, her sweet voice broke into his reverie. "Are you hungry?"

"A little."

They had been zooming up I-87, a part of the New York State Thruway system that had a normal speed limit of sixty-five miles per hour but Charisse, like most of the drivers on this stretch of road, had surpassed the limit.

"We passed a cute little Italian restaurant a while back on 17. Can I buy you dinner?"

That surprised him, and it obviously showed on his face because she asked, "What? Haven't you ever had a woman offer to buy you dinner before?"

"Yeah, sure, but…."

"What?"

"I just wasn't expecting you to, that's all."

"Well, do you mind?"

He smiled and said, "As long as you promise not to take advantage of me afterward, I don't."

"Ha, ha. I don't think you have anything to fear there."

"What are you saying? Aren't I handsome enough that you might want to take advantage of me?" he facetiously asked.

Charisse fixed her mouth to respond, but he quickly added, "I mean, if you hadn't already taken a vow of celibacy?"

"Yes, but I have taken a vow of *abstinence*," she emphasized.

"Okay, abstinence, but…so, is that yes, that you would want to take advantage of me?"

"No. How did we get here from talking about getting something to eat?" Charisse suddenly asked with a frown.

"Well, you started talking about buying me dinner. I just wanted to make sure your intentions were pure," he said with a mischievous smile, sounding remarkably like she had a couple of days ago.

"You're a funny guy, you know?"

Turning the car around at the next exit, she headed back to the restaurant. When she pulled into a space in the parking lot twenty minutes later, she waited a moment before turning off the ignition. When she finally cut it off, she sat behind the wheel a while longer, her head bowed.

Unsure of whether to disturb her, Stefán finally asked, "Charisse, you okay?"

When she raised her head and looked over at him, he was surprised to see tears. "What's wrong?" he tenderly inquired.

She shook her head, "Nothing. I'm just happy."

Stefán felt his heart swell at her show of sensitivity. He reached over and gently wiped away a tear. "You should be. You did good."

Charisse chuckled through her tears. "Do you know how long I've wanted this car? Ever since I was a little girl. This has always been my dream car. I remember the first time I ever saw one. We were down in Baltimore at my grandparents' house. An older cousin had a boyfriend who came by to see her. I was outside playing with my other cousins when he pulled up. His was black on black, too. I stopped playing and said to him, 'Wow, that's a really nice car.' He said, 'Wanna take her for a spin?' Of course, I thought he was crazy and he laughed at my reaction, but he let me sit behind the wheel and pretend I was driving. He even drove me around the block in it, much to my cousin's dismay, but that's when I decided I was going to get one of my own."

"How old were you?"

"About ten or eleven."

"That young?"

"Yup. I still have the first model Corvette my father ever gave me, too." She sighed with pleasure. "I've always wanted the first car I bought to be a Corvette."

"Well, second's not too bad," Stefan said.

"No, this *is* my first car. My parents bought my Camry as a gift when I graduated from college."

"Then you already know if you want something bad enough, there's nothing to stop you from getting it if you put in the necessary work. Congratulations, Charisse."

"You know, I've come to realize that if you put your faith in God, He will bless you in more ways than you could ever believe."

"Do you really think God is responsible for you getting this car?"

"Absolutely."

"But you worked for it," he stated.

"Yes, I did. But you have to work for some of your blessings. God is not just going to indiscriminately bless you if you don't first recognize who He is. You have to first acknowledge that He is the head of your life. He wants to be in relationship with us. He wants us to worship Him. His word says, if you love Him and worship Him, He will bless you abundantly."

"I believe in God, Charisse, but…. I've accomplished things in my life without worshipping him."

"Yes, but it's through God's grace that you've accomplished all you have. Whether you realize it or not. The first step is believing in Him. You just said you did. Now, granted, the devil is a great imitator. He will have you believing you don't need God, that you can make it in this life without His grace and mercy. But all that's good is from God, Stefàn," she said with conviction.

He smiled and said, "You make me feel very…unworthy."

"Oh, no, I'm not trying to—"

"I know you're not. Your faith is strong. I admire you for your convictions. Maybe one day I'll come to understand it the way you do," he told her.

"I hope so."

There was a moment of silence between them for an extended period before Stefàn said, "I know we haven't known each other long, and I don't know if it even matters to you but…I'm very proud of you."

She couldn't explain why, but hearing those words from Stefàn meant more than she would have ever imagined. "Thank you."

Seated beside him was a woman who knew who she was, knew what she wanted and was steadfast in her beliefs without being self-righteous. *She's a credit to black women everywhere, and I'm proud to be the man she chose to share her accomplishment with.*

"Charisse, can I ask you a question?"

"Sure."

"Why'd you call me?"

"When, today?"

"Yeah, after you picked up the car. I'm guessing you got home not too long before you came to get me. I was just wondering why you called me to ride with you."

He noticed her blush and she briefly turned her head away. But just as quickly, she turned back and defiantly met his eyes with her own. "I called you because I knew you would be able to appreciate what I was feeling about having this car."

"Is that the only reason?"

She hesitated for a moment. "No," she softly admitted.

He waited for her to continue. When she was not immediately forthcoming he asked, "Care to elaborate?"

She took a deep breath then confessed, "I called you because I like you, more than I wish I did considering we just met, and I wanted you to ride with me. Now, have I stroked your ego enough?"

She appeared angry, as if he had forced her to reveal more of herself than she wanted to, but he could identify with what she was feeling. "I didn't ask because I wanted my ego stroked, Charisse," he said affectionately. "I asked because I was curious to know if you…well…if you were fighting the same battle I am."

She was momentarily taken aback by his phraseology. That was exactly how she felt, but she challenged him nonetheless. "And what battle would that be?"

His gaze appeared to soften as he said, "The one between my head and my heart."

His words gave her pause. *Is he really feeling like that or is this just another of the lines he uses to get what he wants?* "Which one's winning?" she asked.

He chuckled. "Now if I told you, what would you do with that information?"

"I really can't say. But you know what? I think we're both experiencing something we probably never have before. I mean, I could be wrong, but I'm sure you're used to having your way with the women in your life whenever and however you like."

Stefàn didn't respond verbally, but his left eyebrow twitched.

"And you've probably never met a woman who, to use your words, doesn't pull her punches and pretty much tells you exactly what's on her mind," she continued.

"Not often and not with such...finesse," he said with a smirk.

"Well, I told you I'm not like other women."

"Yes, you did. And no, you're not. And you're right, it has been a long time since I've met anyone who challenges or intrigues me the way you do, but I know it's not just me. At first I thought you had a grudge against the way I live my life, but I see that's not it at all. You're on guard, just like I am." He paused momentarily. "There's something about you, Charisse Ellison, that makes me want to put my guard down, but I'm hesitant to do so. You see, I like you, too, a lot more than I'm comfortable with considering our lives seem to be worlds apart." He paused again for a few seconds. "But make no mistake, I'm glad you called and I'm even happier that I was there when you came by because I would have been bummed if I had missed you. I know you've got an opinion about me and the way you think I'm living, and that's cool. I made a promise I would never tell you a lie and I don't intend to start now. I'd like to get to know more about you, Charisse, and I want you to get to know me. I think you'll find that with all of my...faults, I'm not too bad a person to have as a friend."

Charisse sighed and said, "Neither am I."

Stefàn smiled at her and reached over to caress her cheek.

In the next breath she said, "C'mon, let's go eat. All that driving has worked up my appetite."

As they emerged from the car, Stefàn said, "You seem to handle her very well."

"She responds extremely well, too. Here..." She tossed him the keys. "You can drive back."

CHAPTER 9
THAT'S WHAT FRIENDS ARE FOR

Myra Lopez lived alone in a two-bedroom co-op apartment in Brooklyn, New York. She and Charisse had
met when they were both students at Baruch College
and had become fast friends. She had worked to put herself through
school and graduated magna cum laude with a degree in Business
Administration. Myra currently owned and operated two very
successful beauty salons in her old neighborhood in the Bronx—
one near Tremont Avenue and One Hundred Eighty-third Street
and the other on Southern Boulevard, across town—although
she had no training as a beautician or stylist. Her two cousins,
Consuela and Carmen, both worked magic with a comb and super-
vised the cosmetological end of her businesses. Myra handled the
money and the management, and, if necessary, she washed hair,
swept floors and took appointments.

The youngest of six, Myra had come a long way from the
tenement apartment she had grown up in with her siblings and
their mother. Although her father was still alive, she didn't count
him in the equation because he'd left when she was still in
elementary school, despite the fact that he managed to make an
appearance in their home every six months or so to take advantage
of her mother.

Mrs. Lopez had died of congestive heart failure three days after
Myra's college graduation. Knowing the type of stress she had
lived with every day, Myra often thought her mother had hung

on just long enough to see her graduate. She could remember watching her mother struggle to hold two jobs and still be home every evening to cook dinner for her children. Each time one of her four brothers got into trouble—which was more often than not—her mother had aged a few years, but she had always been there to bail them out. When her sisters got pregnant, Mrs. Lopez took on the responsibility of caring for still more children because her sisters were so trifling.

After watching the way her father and siblings had abused their mother's kindness and trust, cynicism and skepticism enveloped Myra, so much so that she vowed to never love a man so much she would give up her name for his and consent to be his slave for the rest of her life. Harboring quite a bit of anger and hostility toward her family when her mother died, she was able to let most of it go with the help of a capable and caring therapist, but because of her upbringing, she still had an unhealthy distrust of men in general.

Thanks to her incredibly gifted accountant, who also happened to be her best friend, Myra had a nice little nest egg, but she often wished she was more like Charisse. Even though it was only recently that Charisse had found Christ, she still had a hearty sense of adventure. Charisse was outgoing and audacious. Myra, to put it plainly, was a coward. She had always handled her business with aplomb, and she managed her father's affairs equally as well. He was now an invalid and a permanent resident at a nursing home. Despite his parental failings, Myra still loved him and was the only one of her six siblings who even took the time to visit him.

She had always been very good at taking care of other people's issues, but when it came to her own, Myra was running scared; cautious almost to the point of inactivity. She loved to dance, especially to the salsa rhythms of Hector Lavoe and Tito Puenté, but seldom had the opportunity to do so. That was one of the reasons she had enjoyed herself so much at Jewel and Terry's wedding. She detested the club scene since every time she had ever ventured into one, some rude man had tried to accost her on the dance floor. She liked to go to the movies and the theater but was too afraid to go by herself. About the only thing she felt comfortable enough to do alone was shop, although she seldom had to because Charisse was as much a shop-aholic as she was.

Unfortunately, Charisse lived in New Jersey and Myra didn't own a car, nor did she know how to drive, so her world was somewhat limited. Charisse frequently tried to convince her to loosen up and do something wild and crazy. Myra envied her friend's boldness. She knew she could never have agreed to take a ride on a motorcycle with a man she didn't know like Charisse had done with that guy, Stefan. She couldn't even see herself on a motorcycle with a man she'd known her entire life. Even the way Charisse had embraced her religion was typical of how she had always undertaken anything new. She put her whole heart into it. Several times Charisse had tried to get Myra to attend services with her, but there was still too much pain. In some ways, Myra felt God had abandoned her mother, who had been a staunch Catholic, so she was unwilling to trust Him either.

Despite Charisse's protestations to the contrary, Myra noticed she was getting quite caught up with that Stefan character. She knew Charisse was looking to settle down with a man who shared the same spiritual beliefs she did. Following Jewel's bridal shower and during their drive home after the wedding, Charisse had told her just that, but Myra had already known. Charisse had come from a stable family. Her parents were still together and from what she had seen, still very much in love.

That guy Stefan was a player. Myra knew it, Mrs. Ellison knew it, and Charisse did, too. *So why does she want to hang out with him so much?* Charisse had called her earlier in the week to invite her to a pool party he had invited them to at some rich guy's house in New Jersey. Although they had already made plans to go to the movies that afternoon, Myra could tell Charisse really wanted to go with Stefán. The only reason Myra agreed to go with them was to keep an eye on him and make sure he did not try to take advantage of her friend. Charisse was already too blind to really see him for what he was—despite all of her big talk—so Myra felt it was her responsibility to watch her girl's back.

OUT EARLY SATURDAY MORNING, Julian drove to his ex-wife's house on the other side of Teaneck to pick up his seven-year-old son, Julian II, better known as L'il Jay, for little league practice. Julian adored his son and was very happy he and his son's mother, Michele, had such a good relationship.

Having somewhat old-fashioned values, when Michele became pregnant nine years ago, Julian had felt it was his duty to marry her. Sadly, a month after they had wed, Michele miscarried. Devastated by the loss, the couple wasted no time trying to conceive once again to assuage the pain of the void left by their misfortune.

Julian believed strongly in family, but when L'il Jay was eighteen months old, Michele gave him the shock of his life. Asking for a divorce, she told him that although she appreciated what a good father he was and what a good husband he had always been, she was not in love with him and felt if they stayed together, their lives would be miserable. Despite being comfortable in their marriage, Julian could not honestly tell her he was in love with her either. His main concern regarding their breakup had been whether it would affect how much time he could spend with his son.

Michele and Julian grew to be extremely close friends after their marriage ended. Always diligent with his child support and alimony payments, Julian was never denied the right to see his son. In fact, Michele regularly included him in any special activities L'il Jay took part in and had always kept the lines of communication open in his regard. They had a great respect for one another and because of that, there was nothing Julian wouldn't do for his ex-wife.

Later that same afternoon, when Julian returned to his house after dropping L'il Jay back with Michele, he called Stefan.

"What's up, man?" he asked when the call was answered.

"Same ol', same ol', Dub. You're going to Dre's party, right?"

"Yeah. What time are you heading over there?"

"About three o'clock. Charisse and her friend, Myra, are coming with me."

"Cool. Did Charisse pick up her car?"

"Yeah, we went riding the night she got it."

"You've been in it?"

"Yeah, she picked me up to ride right after she got home with it, and let me drive it, too."

"Word?"

"Yeah, man."

"So what's up? You still think she's the one?"

"I don't know." He released a long sigh. "You know I'm nowhere near ready to be settling down, but I like this lady a lot!"

"What you gonna do?"

"I don't know. Just hang with her, see where it goes. She makes me laugh. She also makes my nature rise, but that's another story."

Julian laughed and said, "Well, you already know that's a waste."

"I know, right? But I like spending time with her."

"You think she'll want to get hooked up with someone who's not in the church?" Julian asked.

"Probably not," Stefan solemnly stated.

"Look, Coop, I know you think if you stepped into a church it would burn down, but maybe she's a harbinger of change in your life. It's obvious there's something she feels for you, too, or you wouldn't have been driving her car the other night."

"I took dinner to her on her job on Wednesday."

"Oh, so you've seen her a couple of times this week."

"Yeah." Stefan sighed again. "You know I got a call from Candi last night, but I blew her off. She wasn't too happy about it, either, but I felt like I'd be cheating on Charisse if I had hooked up with her."

"Damn, man, she's really got you sprung, huh?"

"No kidding."

"Well, I'ma tell you something. I'm glad you're feeling like this. For a long time I was worried you might never take the chance again. I know how what happened with Janine hurt you, but I'm glad Charisse seems to have the power to expel your demons."

"Yeah, but if it turns out this is all just my fantasy and she's not interested in being anything more than my buddy…what then?"

"Listen, don't speculate on what might or might not happen. Just take it one day at a time. And you know anytime you need to talk about it, I'm here."

"Yeah, I know, Dub. Thanks."

"So, listen, I'll see you at Dre's."

"A'ight. Peace out," said Stefan.

"Peace."

CHAPTER 10

POOL PARTY ANIMAL, ENOUGH IS ENOUGH!

Charisse and Myra arrived at Stefan's house at a few minutes after three that Saturday afternoon.

"Nice house," Myra off-handedly stated as they pulled up. "You been inside?"

"Yeah, when we went riding last weekend, remember? I picked him up," Charisse reminded her.

"That's his car?" Myra asked with a sideways glance as they walked past the freshly washed BMW parked in the driveway.

"Yup."

"Humph," she huffed.

"Be nice, now," Charisse scolded.

"What?" she asked innocently.

All too aware of Myra's blatant displeasure regarding her attraction to Stefan, Charisse wanted Myra to see what she had learned about him—that he wasn't as bad a guy as she had originally assumed. That was the main reason she had wanted Myra to come with them today. She also acknowledged that having Myra by her side—along with all of her skepticism— would help keep her own vision a little clearer. However, she didn't want Stefan to pick up on Myra's distrust so before ringing the doorbell, Charisse cautioned, "Now Myra, I don't want you going in there startin' no stuff with him."

She folded her arms indignantly. "I'm not going to be starting anything."

"No, but we both know you have a way of making these little biting remarks."

"Oh, and you don't?" Myra said as she looked up at Charisse over the top of her shades.

"Yeah, but he's used to my smart mouth," she said with a smile, then rang the bell.

Stefan opened the door a few seconds later. "Good afternoon, ladies."

"Hi, Stefan," Charisse cooed with an affectionate smile. "You remember my girlfriend, Myra, don't you?"

"Of course. How are you, Myra?" He offered his hand.

Myra shook it. "I'm fine, thanks. How're you?"

"Great." Appreciative eyes turned back to Charisse. Stefan thought she looked angelic in her gauzy white sundress and sandals. "And how are you, gorgeous?"

With a blush, she answered, "I'm fine, thank you."

"Come on in," he offered.

As Charisse and Myra entered his house, he asked, "Did you remember to bring your bathing suits?"

"Of course. It's a pool party, right?" Charisse replied.

"Just checking."

Stefan's living room was a large, airy space with a bay window accented by ivory vertical blinds that were currently positioned so the sunlight streamed into the room, bathing the numerous leafy green plants situated there. His furniture was purely masculine in flavor but tastefully laid out. His color scheme was earthy, with rich brown, tan and cream hues. Cherry coffee, end tables and bookcases complemented the lush leather seating arrangement. A connoisseur of fine art, several eye-catching pieces were hung on the walls, rounding out the decor.

"You've got a nice place."

"Thank you, Myra," he replied magnanimously.

Sporting summer weight cream linen pants and a matching short sleeved shirt, Stefan also wore light brown leather sandals and looked as good as he did comfortable. Charisse considered telling him her thoughts but refrained for the sake of his ego.

"Is your friend, Julian, going to be there?" Charisse asked.

"Yeah, he's coming. So listen, do you want to follow me, or do you want to leave your car here and ride with me?"

Charisse smiled affably and said, "Nothing personal, but...."

"That's okay, I was just kidding anyway. And believe me, I'd feel the same way," he said with an engaging smile. "We can pull out whenever you're ready."

"I'm ready. You ready, Myra?" Charisse asked.

"Yup."

"Which way are we going?"

"Down the turnpike, to exit nine. If you get there before me in your speed buggy, wait for me, will ya'?"

Charisse laughed heartily. "I'm not going to leave you in my dust."

"So you say, but I've seen you drive, remember?" he responded as he picked up his keys and wallet from the console table against the wall.

"I don't know where we're going."

"Yeah, but I'm sure you know how to get to exit nine."

"I'm going to follow you," she said innocently. Before Stefan could get another word out, Charisse added, "As long as you don't drive too slow."

About forty-five minutes later, Charisse followed Stefan into the expansive cul-de-sac that encompassed a stately Colonial home in North Brunswick where several cars were already parked. The front of the house was beautifully landscaped with blossoms of varying colors and some of the most lush green trees and shrubbery she had ever seen in a private residence. The lawn, which wrapped around on both sides of the house to the back, looked rich and naturally plush.

"Whoa! So who is it that lives here?" Myra asked Charisse as she gaped at the house in awe.

"I don't know. One of Stefàn's friends. Nice, huh?"

"To put it mildly."

As Charisse and Myra stepped out of the Corvette, Julian pulled up behind them in a dark green Volvo S70. He quickly opened his door and jumped out. "Woo-wee! Now *that's* a fly ride. Can I borrow it?"

Recognizing Stefàn's handsome buddy, Charisse laughed as she said, "Sure, in about ten years."

Myra, along with Julian's lady friend, who had just stepped out of the Volvo, laughed.

"Damn, girl," Julian reverently exclaimed as he walked up to it and lovingly caressed the vehicle's body. "Damn!"

"Hi, I'm Charisse," she said in greeting to Julian's companion.

"I'm Robin. How are you?"

The women shook hands.

"I'm sorry, I got a little caught up," Julian said when he noticed that they had introduced themselves.

"That's okay," they chorused.

Introductions were then made between Myra and Robin and greetings exchanged as Stefàn walked back to where they were all congregated around Charisse's Corvette.

"Charisse, this is a beautiful car," Julian said in sincere admiration.

"I know," she answered with a smug smile.

"Did you just get this?" Robin asked.

"Yes. It was my birthday present to myself," Charisse told her.

"I heard that! Congratulations!" Robin enthusiastically offered.

"Thank you," Charisse replied with a warm smile.

"How's she handle?" Julian asked.

"Like a dream," Stefan answered.

"Nobody asked you!" Julian said with a playful smirk.

"Don't playa hate, man. It doesn't become you."

"You've driven it?" Robin asked incredulously.

"Of course." Stefan put an arm around Charisse's shoulder. "My girl let me drive it the night she picked it up."

"Stop bragging," Julian said.

"Stop hatin', Dub," Stefan scolded with a shake of his finger. The girls laughed.

"Why'd you let him drive this baby, Charisse?" Julian asked.

"'Cause he's my buddy," she answered as she put her arm around his waist and snuggled closer to him.

Stefan had a smug look on his face, but was thinking, *I wish I could keep you snuggled next to me like this for the rest of the day.*

Julian then asked, "Has she let you drive it, Myra?"

"No, but I don't know how to drive."

"Oh, well, I probably wouldn't let you drive mine, either, then," he quipped.

Everyone laughed.

"No, but seriously, this is beautiful. Congratulations, Charisse. Enjoy it."

"Thanks, Julian," she said warmly.

"Hey, let's go on back. It sounds like there's a party going on," Stefan stated.

"Lead the way," said Charisse.

Several people were already in attendance in the enormous back-yard of the magnificent home. Charisse immediately zeroed in on the kidney-shaped in-ground swimming pool at the center of the expansive yard. With the temperature being what it was, she couldn't wait to jump into it. Guests wearing swim suits and/or street clothes lounged comfortably or stood around talking, laughing, eating, drinking and apparently having an all-around good time. Mary J. Blige's latest hit rocked from speakers that were unseen, and a buffet table on the deck directly outside the back door of the house was laden with what looked like a wide array of foods. In two separate areas of the yard were attended bars that had lines in front of them as partygoers waited to be served.

Soon after their arrival, Stefan and his group were greeted by their host and hostess, Andre and Marsha Williams, an extremely attractive and statuesque couple in their early fifties. The Williamses, both dressed in white linen, were quite stylish, gracious and effortlessly engaging. Charisse liked them right off. After exchanging introductions and cordialities, Marsha went about making sure they all knew where to change for the pool, satisfy their palettes and quench their thirsts. Additionally, she pointed out to the girls that there was an abundance of single male guests for their viewing and wooing pleasure, much to Stefan's and Julian's chagrin. When Charisse complimented the couple on their fabulous residence, Marsha informed her that Stefan was their realtor. Impressed by that information, Charisse noticed Stefan blush at Marsha's revelation, prompting a bit of teasing from Marsha and Charisse until Andre came to his rescue.

Fifty minutes after their arrival, Charisse, Myra and Robin had all changed into their swimsuits and had made themselves comfortable in the lounge chairs alongside the pool. They sipped beverages as they perused and exchanged opinions about the numerous and varied attractive, and like Marsha had stated, apparently single male guests.

Since Stefan and Julian were acquainted with many of the partygoers present, they had spent a good bit of time since their arrival, mingling. Charisse, in particular, made note of the many different women who flirtatiously greeted Stefan. She also noticed his pleasure with the attention these women paid him. To her it seemed as if they were drawn to him by some strange, erotic, pheromonal mist. She tried hard to ignore him and focus her attention elsewhere, but like a needle to the northern-most point on a compass, her pupils repeatedly returned to him. To her dismay, there was usually a woman nearby, clinging to him like she was his Siamese twin.

Suddenly, Charisse rose from her chair.

"Where you going?" Myra asked.

"To take a dip."

The micro-mini white cover-up she had donned over her bathing suit was removed without circumstance, revealing a shimmering gold maillot that dipped very low in back and was accented by sheer finely-woven gold mesh across the waistline in front. As she moved toward the diving board, numerous pairs of eyes, male and female alike, followed her sure-footed stride. It was hard to ignore her feminine allure even though her suit only exposed her back and a minimal amount of cleavage, but her hourglass figure struck envy in the hearts of several women present, and desire in even more men.

Stefan, who at the time was in the midst of a conversation with another female guest, noticed Charisse, too, as she moved to the side of the pool. Her appearance in the gold suit—which actually reflected the rays of the sun—struck him speechless, and he completely lost his train of thought.

Quickly dismissing their dialogue as irrelevant, he stated, "Excuse me. I've gotta do something," and summarily turned away from the woman without another word.

As Charisse stepped onto the diving board and prepared to

take the plunge, a man approached and asked, "Are you taking prisoners?"

She acted as though she hadn't heard him and skillfully dove into the pool.

In the meantime, Stefan had made his way to where Robin and Myra were still seated and hurriedly proceeded to remove his shirt and pants, carelessly tossing each onto the lounger Charisse had just vacated.

In a teasing manner, Robin asked, "What's the matter, Coop? Did somebody light a fire under your butt?"

"Did you see that suit she has on?" he asked as he nodded in Charisse's direction.

"Yeah, it's great, isn't it?" Robin said as she continued to taunt him.

"Myra, how could you let her come out in something like that?" he teasingly asked.

"Excuse me, but Charisse is a grown woman. A grown, *single* woman, and she can pretty much do what she likes. Just like *you*!"

Stefan was surprised by the antagonism in her tone but gave it little thought at the time, and continued to discard his clothing.

"What's wrong with her suit?" Robin asked.

"It's attracting way too much attention," he admitted.

"Wow, it even attracted you, huh?" Myra derisively commented.

Stefan didn't hear her, so distracted was he by Charisse's appearance.

Clearly annoyed about Stefan's behavior since their arrival— that is, basically ignoring Charisse for the attention of all the women who'd been grinning up in his face—Myra, however, was immediately taken aback when she fully caught sight of his exquisite physique.

When he moved away from them and jumped into the pool

behind Charisse, Robin said, "It don't make no sense for a man to be that fine *and* have a body like that on top of it."

"It sure don't," Myra couldn't help but agree. "No wonder these women are all over him. I just wish he'd leave Charisse alone 'cause I can see my girl falling for his player behind and getting her heart broken."

"Maybe," Robin said thoughtfully, "but from what Julian tells me, Stefan's got it pretty bad for her."

"Yeah, well, he sure has a good way of hiding it," Myra indicated.

"He's probably scared."

"Scared or not, I still don't trust him. Charisse puts up a good front like she's tough, but she's really very sensitive and she's showing all the signs of falling for him—way too fast. They just met last week."

"So I heard. I think she was supposed to come riding with us last Sunday. Humph, the fact that Stefan was even going to bring her along is a big deal, Myra, because he doesn't let anyone on his bike," Robin informed her. After a few seconds of quiet contemplation, she added, "Maybe Charisse is the one to straighten his fine behind out."

Myra didn't comment because she couldn't seriously put any faith in that happening.

Meanwhile in the pool, Stefan swam to where Charisse was floating casually on her back. "You think your suit is attracting enough attention?"

Glancing over at him without a word, Charisse flipped over backward and went below the surface. She swam away from him, but he followed her. When she resurfaced a few feet away, he was right beside her.

"Why are you running from me?" he asked.

"I'm not running from you. I'm swimming," she snidely answered as she tried to appear unaffected by the symmetry of his sculpted torso.

A little green monster prompted him to say, "Your suit is attracting quite a bit of attention, with the way it's reflecting the sun and all."

"Oh really? Has it attracted your attention?"

"Mine and every other man's here." If it were up to him, she would be wearing one of those striped numbers they wore back in the dark ages with a high neck and long legs.

"Is that a problem for you?" she asked while derisively eyeing him.

He was used to her sharp tongue, but this was different. He sensed a bit of hostility from her, too, and that surprised him more than Myra. Unlike with Myra, though, he couldn't ignore this. "What's the matter, Charisse?"

"What do you mean, what's the matter?"

"You seem upset about something."

"Well, I'm not. I'm just chillin'."

As he stared into glorious brown eyes that dared him to refute her words, she nonchalantly stated, "I think I'll do some laps."

"Mind if I swim with you?"

"Do what you want. It's a free country." With that she swam away from him.

Something's wrong. This wasn't his Charisse. He had come to enjoy her pointed barbs, but he now sensed quite a bit of antipathy from her and that troubled him. *What is she upset about?*

He followed her to the other end of the pool. Since he was such a strong swimmer, and she appeared not to be putting forth much effort as she glided through the water, he easily caught up to her. When he did, he grabbed her arm, which forced her to stop and direct her attention to him. "Charisse, you can't tell me nothing is bothering you. I can feel it as sure as I can feel your arm in my grip."

"You must be imagining things, Stefan. Or maybe you have a guilty conscience."

"What do I have to feel guilty about? I haven't done anything wrong."

"So what makes you think I'm upset with you?"

"I feel this vibe from you I've never felt before."

"Maybe you should take it easy. You're probably worn out from all the flirting you've been doing since we got here," she said flippantly, before swimming away from him again.

She's jealous. That reality hit him like a brick and for a short time he was unable to move. Watching as she flowed away from him, he wasn't entirely sure how to handle this revelation, so for the moment he chose not to. Eventually, he swam to the edge of the pool and climbed out. Looking back at Charisse, he tried hard to ignore the anxiousness he felt in his gut. *Admit it, man, you're jealous, too, that all these brothers are checking her out in that beautiful suit she's wearing.* Stefan was so unaccustomed to the feelings that engulfed him when he was in her presence that to hide his unease, he shrugged as if unfazed and started across the yard to get a drink.

As he turned away from the bar sipping an Absolut and 7-Up, Marsha Williams and a very attractive woman who appeared about her same age, approached him. "Stefan, sweetheart, I've been looking all over for you. I want you to meet my dear friend, Jeannette Lucas. Jeannette, this is the man I was telling you about, Stefan Cooper."

Trying to put Charisse's unpleasant disposition out of his mind, Stefan immediately turned on the charm as he greeted Marsha's friend. "Miss Lucas, pleased to meet you," he said as he took her hand and kissed it.

"Please don't insult me by calling me Miss Lucas. My name is Jeannette," she stated boldly, and with a look that let him know, in no uncertain terms, she found him quite attractive with his torso exposed and dripping wet.

"Forgive me. I didn't mean to insult you, Jeannette."

"Well, my forgiveness depends on what you can do for me."

Stefan's curiosity was instantly piqued. "And what might that be?"

"Marsha told me you're the genius who sold her and Andre this exquisite house. I happen to be in the market for a new home, but all of the agents I've met with so far have been totally incompetent or racist."

"Oh, well, I don't mean to toot my own horn, but you've definitely come to the right place. I'm your man," he said with a bright smile.

"You know, some women would take that literally coming from a man as fine as you are," Jeannette said. "Good thing, I'm sharper than most, huh?"

Stefan could only laugh. "So where exactly are you looking to buy?" he asked to draw attention away from himself. The manner in which she was ogling him made him feel like a piece of meat. He suddenly wished he had his shirt nearby to throw on.

"Englewood Cliffs and the vicinity."

"Oh, that's perfect. That's my main territory. I have some beautiful homes in that area. What are you looking to spend?" he asked her.

"Excuse me, you two. I'm going to go check on my man. Too many of these little young things are getting too familiar for my comfort," Marsha broke in.

"Go handle your business, girl," Jeannette said to her. Then, without pause, she returned her attention to Stefan. "Now back to you. How much am I looking to spend? Price is no object."

"Well, that gives us plenty to work with. When are you available?"

"My calendar is quite free. Can we get together tomorrow?"

"Sure."

"I put my purse in the house, but before I leave here today, we must exchange numbers."

"Definitely," said Stefàn.

CHARISSE SURREPTITIOUSLY WATCHED STEFÀN as he engaged the woman Marsha had introduced him to. She openly flirted with him, seemingly with no regard for the fact that Marsha was standing right next to them, and Stefàn didn't appear too upset about it either. *He's got a lot of nerve, talking to me about how much attention my bathing suit is attracting. At least I'm not running behind these men here like a dog in heat the way these women are with him.* He'd acted like she had committed a crime against him because she had worn this suit. *He's got a lot of nerve, especially now that he's got this chick who looks like she's old enough to be his mother grinning in his face, and he's probably lapping it up.* She huffed before she dove beneath the water and continued the laps she had begun earlier. *Why do I even care*, she thought, hoping the water she swam in would douse the fires of jealousy raging in her heart. *He's not even the type of man I want to be with.*

LATER, AFTER THEY HAD ALL CHANGED back into their street clothes, Charisse, Myra and Robin conversed with some male guests near the deck of Andre's and Marsha's home. After a few minutes, Julian and Stefàn joined them.

Immediately upon their approach, Stefàn walked directly to where Charisse was seated and squatted next to her. He had been watching her covertly ever since their encounter in the pool, purposely keeping his distance so as to maintain his cool. But enough was enough. "You've been ignoring me all day," he said for her ears only.

She frowned and said, "No, I haven't. You've been preoccupied all day."

"Oh really? Well, I'm not preoccupied now. Do you mind if I join you, or would I be cramping your style?"

"What do you think?" Charisse asked with a sarcastic edge.

"I don't know. The brother in the red shirt just shot me a look like he wanted to do me harm for stepping to you," Stefan said with a smirk.

"He did not."

"You obviously didn't see him."

"Well, that's probably because he thought I came here alone." Again, her beautiful brown eyes challenged him. "Especially since you've been grinning up in all these different females' faces."

"I was not!" Stefan pretended to be offended.

"That's what it looked like to me. But it's cool. You owe me no allegiance."

Stefan grinned at her for a moment. The look on her face was one of utter indifference, but her tone expressed an entirely different emotion. As he sat gazing at her, his heartbeat seemed to triple its rhythm. *There it is again. Why on earth would she be jealous of the females here?* He had to admit the idea of her actually being resentful of any attention he might have paid to another woman there was quite flattering. *But not a single one of these chicks can hold a candle to her*, he thought. *She is an exceptionally beautiful woman. I can see why that brother would be trying to get next to her. Especially if he saw her in that shimmering gold suit she had on earlier. That thing was off the hook! If she was my woman, though, I don't know if I'd want her wearing anything that attracted so much attention in public. But she's not your woman*, he silently conceded with a sinking heart. *She's her own woman and there's nothing you can do about that 'cause you know you are not the man she's looking for.*

As Stefàn was submersed in his musings, Charisse suddenly began to rise from her chair.

"Hey, where you going?" he asked as he hastily rose to his feet.

"To get a drink."

"Stay there. I'll get it. What're you drinking?"

"7-Up."

"I'll be right back," he said with a wink. Before walking away, Stefàn turned to face the guy with the red shirt who had been talking to Charisse. "What's up, brotha?"

"Yeah, whassup," the guy muttered with a cynical look.

As Stefàn moved away from them, the man's dagger-filled eyes followed him. When he turned back to Charisse seconds later and after Stefàn was out of earshot, he deridingly asked, "Is that your man?"

"He's a friend."

"Oh, because I noticed that he seemed quite friendly with a number of the women here and I was wondering if you didn't have a problem with him disrespecting you like that."

Charisse smiled and said, "Well, he's not my man, and like I said, we're just friends so what he does is his business."

"He stepped to you like he was staking a claim."

She laughed. "He invited me. He was making sure I was all right; that's all."

Stefàn returned rather quickly with Charisse's drink and after he handed it to her, he turned to the young man in the red shirt and introduced himself. "Hey, I'm Stefàn. How you doin', man?" He offered his hand.

"I'm Bruce."

"Hey, Bruce. You friends with Dre and Marsha?"

"No, I went to school with their son, AJ."

"Oh, okay. You've met Charisse, I gather," Stefàn said magnanimously as he turned and gestured in her direction.

"Not formally, no."

"Oh, well, this is my good friend, Charisse Ellison. Risi, this is Bruce."

Charisse smirked at Stefàn, then rolled her eyes. She was surprised to hear him refer to her by her nickname. "Hi, Bruce," she said and offered her hand.

"Hi."

"You enjoying yourself?" Stefàn then asked Bruce.

"Yeah."

"Nice looking crowd, huh?"

"Yeah."

"Oh, this is my man, Julian," Stefàn said as he turned to him. "Dub, this is Bruce. And these ladies are Myra and Robin."

"What's up, Bruce?" said Julian as he offered his hand.

"Hey," Bruce replied as he weakly shook Julian's hand.

"You live nearby, Bruce?" Stefàn then asked.

"Not too far."

"Dre and Marsha give a slamming party, don't they?"

"Yeah, they do."

"You still in school?"

"No."

"What do you do for living?"

Charisse, meanwhile, looked over at Myra and Robin, before she turned her eyes to Julian, who wore an ambiguous smile. She knew Stefàn was patronizing this young guy simply because he had been talking to her.

"I'm a financial planner," Bruce answered with a self-satisfied air.

"Really? Hey, Risi, that's along the same lines of what you do, right? Charisse is a CPA."

"Oh yeah?" Bruce muttered.

"Yeah."

"What do you do?" Bruce challenged Stefàn.

"I'm in real estate. As a matter of fact, I sold Dre and Marsha this house."

"Oh yeah?" The look of disdain he gave Stefàn was unmistakable.

Stefàn noticed but continued speaking in the same supercilious manner. "Yeah. If you're looking to buy some property, I can give you my card. I've got the inside track on quite a few very fine parcels all over New Jersey."

"Thanks, but I'm not interested."

"Okay, but if you change your mind, AJ's parents know how to get in touch with me."

"I'll keep that in mind."

Stefàn then turned to Charisse and openly winked at her.

Bruce said, "It was nice to meet you, Charisse. Excuse me." He immediately walked away from them.

Charisse shook her head and said to Stefàn, "You're a piece of work."

"What?" he asked with a shrug of his shoulders and a blameless look on his face.

"Yeah, what?"

Julian and Stefàn then slapped each other five as they shared a conspiratorial laugh.

"So, Stefàn, are you going to chase away all the men who try to talk to Charisse the way you did that one?" Robin asked facetiously.

"I didn't chase him away. I thought we were holding a conversation. It's not my fault if the brother feels threatened by me."

"Oh please," Robin said as she rolled her eyes.

Myra, too, looked skyward at his words.

"Yeah, like you really wanted to know what he did for a living," Charisse said.

"I was curious. I wanted to see if he was up to speed for you. He looked kind of young. You need a man who can take of you; at least better than you can take care of yourself," Stefàn said to Charisse.

"Yes, I'm sure that's of great concern to you."

"Hey, you're my friend. I always try to look out for my friends."

"What would I ever do without you?" she sarcastically questioned.

"Let's hope we never have to find out."

The five of them spent the next hour or so together, laughing and poking fun at each other and at some of the guests; basically, enjoying the atmosphere of the gathering. Charisse felt considerably more at ease because Stefàn had since given her his practically undivided attention, although she would have never admitted that his earlier neglect had bothered her at all. Stefàn, too, felt better since he didn't have to wonder where Charisse was or who she was talking to. Besides, her smile was back and directed at him, and that made all the difference in his world.

Fate being as it may, however, Charisse's and Stefàn's momentary bliss quickly came to an end when Jeannette Lucas crashed their private assembly.

Unceremoniously walking up to Stefàn and grabbing him from behind, she wrapped her arms around his waist in a possessive manner and lustfully stuck her tongue in his ear.

Jerking away from her as if he'd been burned, Stefàn shot her a look that questioned her sanity as he wiped her saliva off his lobe.

"I didn't mean to startle you so, but I've been trying to get your attention for the last ten minutes. I figured if I kissed you on your ear, you'd notice me."

"Ya think?" Stefan caustically replied.

Charisse and Myra exchanged a look of disapproval.

"I wanted to give you my number and get yours so we could get together tomorrow."

"There are several other ways you could have gotten my attention. You could have used my name, for instance," he said.

"I know. I'm sorry," she said demurely. "Forgive me folks, I didn't mean to interrupt, but I'm trying to buy a house, and from what I understand, this is the man to see."

No one said a word.

"So, cutie, do you have a pen?" she asked Stefan as if Charisse, Myra, Robin and Julian had suddenly vanished into thin air.

"No, I don't." He turned to the girls and asked, "Do any of you have a pen?"

After a pregnant pause, Robin muttered, "I do."

With a look that attested to everything she felt about Stefan, Myra said to Charisse, "You ready to go?"

"Oh yeah."

Robin handed Stefan a pen just as Charisse and Myra rose from their seats. "Nice meeting you, Robin," Charisse muttered before she started away from them. "Bye, Julian."

"Do you have one of your cards?" Jeannette asked Stefan.

"Yeah." He reached into his back pocket for his wallet as Charisse and Myra began to walk away. When Stefan noticed that they were headed out of the yard, he called, "Charisse!"

Stopping in her tracks, she reluctantly turned back to him. Her face was devoid of emotion.

"Where you going?"

"Home," she replied and continued out of the yard.

"Wait up." He turned back to Jeannette and said, "Excuse me a minute." He hurried to catch up with Charisse.

She was at the front of the house when he caught up with her. "Why are you leaving?"

Looking up at him with a resolute frown, she stated, "Because it's time."

"So, you're just gonna walk out and not say anything to me?"

"What do you want me to say, Stefan?" Shaking her head, she sighed in exasperation. "I don't even know why I came here with you."

"I thought because you wanted to."

"Yeah, I did. And I didn't know what to expect, but I know it wasn't this." She waved her hand and sighed again. "Look, I've gotta go. You enjoy the rest of your evening," she said and quickly turned away from him. She felt her eyes beginning to water and the last thing she wanted was for him to see how upset she was over him.

Dumbfounded, Stefan stood rooted in confusion. A sick feeling seeped through his pores as he watched Charisse walk to her car, get in and drive away without another word or glance in his direction. His heart filled with the fear of a dreadful reality—he had lost her even before he'd had the chance to really get to know her.

CHAPTER 11
A SECOND CHANCE

The silence was deafening during the funereal ride home.

Knowing Charisse was upset about the woman who had assaulted Stefàn, and despite his apparent vexation regarding her brazen behavior, Myra noticed that he still gave her his number. She didn't want to tell Charisse, "I told you so," but that thought echoed in her brain like the incessant ticking of the second hand on a clock. Stefàn was no good for her. Hopefully, it was now obvious to Charisse that he was a womanizer and nothing but bad news. Besides that, he wasn't saved. *How could Charisse even fall for someone like him?* She really wanted to tell her that, but her dear friend was hurting right now and Myra knew anything she said about him would only serve to make her feel worse.

Going directly to her bedroom when they got back to her house, Myra followed her. "Are you okay?"

Charisse muttered, "Yeah. Are you spending the night or do you want me to take you home?"

"No, I'll stay."

The girls were silent for the next few minutes. Charisse had flopped down on her bed and Myra had taken a seat on her chaise. "Charisse, you know how he is," Myra finally said.

"Myra, please, I don't want to hear it."

"But Risi..."

"Myra!"

Throwing her hands up, she conceded. "Okay. I'm going to watch a movie. Do you want to watch with me?"

"No, you go ahead. I want to chill for a while."

"All right." Myra turned and went downstairs to the den.

After a while, Charisse decided to take a shower. As soon as she entered her bathroom, however, she changed her mind and figured a nice, hot bubble bath would actually do her more good.

As she lounged in the warm water and tried to soak the pain in her heart away, she prayed. "Father, is there a lesson here You want me to learn? Why do I feel so strongly for this man? He seems so wrong for me. What is it about him that makes me care for him so much? I don't understand. Sometimes when we least expect it, blessings can come from places we would never think to look for them. Could this man be in my life because of something You want me to see? Is there something You want me to do? What role is he to play in my life? You didn't give me a spirit of jealousy, Father. Please take these feelings off my heart," she pleaded as tears spilled from her eyes.

When Charisse emerged from her bathroom thirty minutes later she felt more refreshed, but was still down in the dumps.

As she lounged on her brocade chaise in a T-shirt and leggings, her bedside phone suddenly rang and startled her out of her maudlin mood. Automatically moving to get up and answer it, she quickly changed her mind. Feeling sorry for herself, she had no desire to put on a happy face for anybody, nor was she in the mood to explain her melancholy.

After three rings, Myra called up from downstairs, "Do you want me to get that?"

"I don't care," Charisse called back.

Myra picked up the extension in the den. "Hello."

"Myra?"

"Yes."

"This is Stefan. May I speak to Charisse, please?"

Pausing momentarily before she removed the receiver from her ear, Myra didn't bother to cover the phone when she called out, "It's him."

Unable to resist the need to hear his voice, Charisse slowly rose from her seat to pick up the extension. "I have it, Myra." It was still a few seconds before she put the receiver to her ear. "Hello," she said cheerlessly.

"Charisse, are you okay?"

"I'm fine."

"Can I talk to you?"

"I'm on the phone, aren't I?"

"Can I come over?"

"For what?"

"Because I need to talk to you."

"Why can't you say what you have to say on the phone?"

"Because I need to see you to say what I have to say."

She huffed loudly.

"Please?"

"I don't care," she said in resignation.

"What's your address?"

She gave it to him.

"I'll be there in ten minutes." The line went dead in her ear.

When Charisse hung up the phone, she returned to her chaise. *Why'd I do that? Why'd I tell him he could come over? Because you want to see him.*

Less than ten minutes passed before her doorbell rang. Charisse had not moved from her bedside haven. Myra, who was still downstairs, answered the door. She was surprised to see Stefan and was so disappointed in Charisse she couldn't even say anything.

"What's up, Myra?" he said after an uncomfortably long silence.

"Hello."

She made no move to let him in.

"Charisse is expecting me."

Finally, she stepped back so he could enter.

"I'll get her," she grumbled, not bothering to offer him a seat.

"Thank you."

She climbed the stairs and entered Charisse's bedroom. "Your friend is here." She made no attempt to hide her disapproval.

Charisse chose to ignore Myra's scowl, and rising slowly, dragged herself from her bedroom. She could see him from the top of the stairs and was affected the same way she always was upon seeing him—with nervous excitement. Stefàn had obviously gone home because he was now wearing jeans.

"Hey, Charisse," he said softly as she descended.

"Hi." Moving toward her living room, she said, "Come on in here."

Charisse took a seat on the sofa. Stefàn sat beside her.

"So what is it you wanted to talk to me about?"

"I wanted to apologize to you."

"For what? You don't have to apologize for anything. You said it yourself, you didn't do anything wrong. It's not like you're my man. I don't even know why I acted like that. I'm the one who should be apologizing to you." She rambled as if she was afraid she would lose him if she didn't explain her actions.

"Charisse, she wants to buy a house."

"Whatever," she said flippantly with an off-handed wave. "I had no reason to walk out without saying anything to you. It's not like you promised me anything. I wasn't expecting to see so many of your women there, I guess."

"I'm not involved with anyone who was at the house, Charisse. I swear."

"It doesn't matter anyway."

"Yes, it does. Look—"

She cut him off. "No, it was stupid of me to think you wouldn't know anyone there. Those were your friends and you told me you've been going to their parties for years, so, of course, you're going to know people there. I can't believe I was actually jealous. Why should I be? I have no right to be."

Reaching over, Stefan took her hand. "Charisse, please let me say something." He paused a moment while she calmed down. "Listen, whether you believe it or not, I am sorry for what happened. That woman, Jeannette.... I was as shocked as you were by the way she assaulted me. I don't know her, but she wants me to show her some houses. That's why I gave her my card. But aside from that, I owe you an apology for the way I behaved. I invited you there and I should have been more attentive to you. No, I'm not your man, but you're my friend and that means a lot to me. *You* mean a lot to me, Charisse."

Staring straight ahead, Charisse gave away no trace of what she was feeling.

Pausing briefly to gather his thoughts, he continued. "Yes, I knew several women there, but I swear, I wasn't trying to get with any of them. I realize I should've been less selfish and probably should've checked a few situations that I didn't. I'm sorry for making you feel uncomfortable because of my actions or... inaction." He paused again and took a deep breath.

Charisse's hand was still resting easily in his.

After a few uncomfortable seconds, Stefan continued. "Risi, next to my sister and my Mom, you're the only woman I know that I don't have to front with. I can be myself around you and whether it means anything to you or not, that means the world to me. You're special to me and I don't want to lose your friendship, especially over nonsense like this. I'm truly sorry and I hope you can forgive me. I promise you, nothing like that will ever happen again."

With Stefan's last apology, Charisse finally turned to face him. She could see he was sincere and was relieved. After a thoughtful moment, she softly said, "I have to forgive you. I can't expect God to forgive me if I can't forgive you."

A tentative smile crossed his face. "Well, I thank you and I thank God you feel the way you do." Then teasingly, he asked, "Do you still love me?"

"I can't stand you," she quipped as she rolled her eyes at him in mock disdain.

Stefan laughed, "Good, 'cause I can't stand you either."

Against her will, Charisse chuckled.

"There it is," he said.

"There what is?"

He gently caressed her cheek. "Your beautiful smile." Charisse blushed, and realizing that he'd embarrassed her, he said, "I'm gonna leave before I wear out my welcome."

He stood and made his way to the door.

"You're showing that woman a house tomorrow?" Charisse asked as she walked him out.

"Yeah."

"I know it's not Christ-like to be spiteful, but make sure you take her to the biggest, most expensive ones you can find." Then, looking up, she murmured, "Forgive me, Lord."

He laughed again. "Oh, no doubt; she made the mistake of telling me price is no object."

"You realize she wants more than a house, don't you?"

"Yeah, but I'm not interested."

Charisse believed him but added, "She doesn't seem the type to take 'no' for an answer."

"I run my show, Charisse. No one runs it for me unless I give them permission. And believe me, if there was no commission in this for me, I'd quickly hand her off to one of the other agents in my office."

She chuckled at his dilemma.

He leaned in and softly kissed the side of her mouth. "I'll talk to you soon."

Electric charges raced through her with his gentle buss and garnered a shy smile. "Be careful."

He winked. "Always."

When she closed the door, Myra was standing behind her. "So what's he got to say for himself now?"

"Look, Myra, I understand how you feel about Stefàn, but I don't feel the same way. I care about him. And whether you believe it or not, I don't believe he's ever lied to me. I'm not trying to get him to fall in love with me or anything like that. We're just friends, so I would appreciate it if you would keep any negative comments you have to say about him to yourself because, just like I would never sit by and let anyone trash you, I won't listen to you trashing him either. Okay?"

Myra sighed. "Okay."

"Thank you. Are you coming with me to church tomorrow?"

"Yes."

"Good." Turning toward the den and linking her arm with her best friend's, Charisse asked, "What were you watching?"

CHAPTER 12

AIN'T UNDERSTANDING MELLOW?

"Myra, aside from the fact that you believe Stefan is a player, what is it about him you dislike so much?" Charisse asked.

They were in Charisse's Corvette with the top down, on the way to Myra's apartment in Brooklyn. It was ten minutes past eleven on Sunday morning and they had just left Charisse's church. The sun was shining brightly and the day promised to be as warm and beautiful as the preceding days had been.

After Stefan left last night, Charisse and Myra had watched a movie. They'd steered clear of talking about Stefan or the pool party, so the night had been pretty enjoyable. Still, Charisse had gone to bed with troubled thoughts of Stefan and her best friend's strong aversion to him. She sensed the influence of her upbringing was playing a large role in Myra's cynicism but that did nothing to dispel her discomfort.

Upon awakening that morning, Charisse had initially decided not to ask Myra about the basis of her feelings for her new friend. As they ate breakfast and prepared to leave for church, however, Charisse felt their conversation was stilted and forced. She was sure the reason for this had everything to do with Stefan. That being the case, she put aside her earlier decision because she needed to know why Myra felt the way she did. It mattered what her best friend thought, especially about someone who, it seemed, would have an apparent impact on her life one way or another.

"I don't like the way he disrespected you yesterday."

"He didn't disrespect me."

Myra looked askance at Charisse as she said, "The way he was flirting with all those women?"

"Okay, he was flirting, but how was that disrespectful to me?"

"He invited you there."

"But I'm not his woman, Myra, and I'm not trying to be. We hardly know each other."

"And you're going to tell me his flirting didn't bother you?"

"Yeah, it did, a little," Charisse admitted sheepishly.

"More than a little. You had an attitude for most of the time we were there."

"But that wasn't his fault. That was my own jealousy, which I had no right or reason to feel. Stefan has never implied or suggested we be anything other than what we are."

"Yeah, but you've already been out with him four times," Myra pointed out.

"What four times? I went riding with him. He went riding with me, which, by the way, wasn't a date, and yesterday."

"He brought you dinner at your job."

"But that wasn't a date, either. In fact, the only time that could even be considered a date was maybe last Sunday, but even that was—"

"Well, Thursday when you got your car—" Myra interrupted.

"I told you, that wasn't a date. I picked him up to ride with me and we happened to have dinner together, which I paid for."

"Why would you buy him dinner?" Myra asked in astonishment.

"Because I wanted to."

"You can't tell me you don't like him, Charisse."

"Of course, I like him, but we're just friends, Myra. I like you, too."

Myra rolled her eyes at Charisse as she muttered, "Please."

Laughing, Charisse continued, "Look, I know who Stefan is and I have no intentions of being added to his harem. He knows what I'm about, how I'm living. I've even talked to him about my faith. And I don't see anything wrong with us being friends."

"Yeah, but we both know you'd like to be more than that. I know you, Charisse. You like this guy more than you're letting on," Myra insisted.

"I've never denied that I like him. He's really a very decent guy."

Myra looked over at Charisse in disbelief. "You call the way he behaved yesterday, decent?"

"He didn't do anything wrong yesterday," Charisse insisted. "He knew a lot of people there. A lot of them were women," Charisse stated directly, "but so what? He's an exceptionally good looking man and he's very charming. Women are drawn to him and he plays on that. Most intelligent people draw on their strengths. But he wasn't trying to get with any of them."

"How do you know?"

"Because he told me he wasn't."

Myra shook her head. "I can't understand how you can be so gullible."

"I'm not being gullible, Myra," Charisse agitatedly decried. "Stefan promised he wouldn't lie to me. He's never given me any reason to believe he has or does. I talk to him every day. You don't. You don't know anything about him except what I tell you."

"I know what I see," she insinuated.

"Do you really believe you can know everything about a person from seeing him two times?" Charisse asked sarcastically.

"He acted just like he did at Jewel's wedding."

"Maybe, but he's a single man. He's not committed to anyone."

"He invited you there," she repeated.

"He invited you there, too."

"You invited me."

"Only after he suggested it. Myra, he's not my man. He's my friend. That's it. We've never kissed or anything. He's never even *tried* to kiss me. I talk to him like I talk to you and we talk about everything. I'm learning about Stefàn, the man, not the myth, because he wants me to know him and I want to know him. You call it gullible but I think he wants me to know the man apart from his reputation. We all have two sides—the public and the private. Stefàn is showing me his private side. We talk about our childhoods, our weaknesses, our fears. And I told you, we even talk about Christ. He's trying to understand what motivates my faith and I want to teach him. For all you know, my relationship with him could lead him to Christ."

Myra huffed in disbelief.

"Why is that so hard for you to believe? No one is beyond for-giveness and God's grace, Myra, not you for being so judgmental, nor Stefàn." Charisse could feel herself becoming very defensive, so she took a deep breath and tried to rein in her emotions. "Listen, we have a real friendship growing and that's what I like. He respects how I feel. That's why he came by last night. He knew I was upset even if I had no right to be and he cares enough about me to try and fix what was wrong. That's what friends do. That's what we do, Myra. He really is a very sweet man. And yeah, I want to get to know that man. I'm not setting my hopes on him. I have no ill-conceived notions that he'll suddenly become the perfect man to settle down with. But I like hanging out with him. I have a good time with him. He's a lot of fun and much more interesting than you could probably imagine."

"I don't want to see you get hurt," Myra said softly.

"I don't want to get hurt either, Myra, and believe me, if I ever start to feel like I'm getting too…enamored of him, I will drop him like a hot potato."

CHARISSE WAS BACK AT HER HOUSE BY THREE O'CLOCK that afternoon. She was there for all of ten minutes when her telephone rang.

"Hello."

"Hey, Charisse. How you doin' today?"

"I'm good, Stefàn. How're you?"

"Pretty good. I'm getting ready to get out of here."

"You're at work?"

"Yeah."

"I just got back in from taking Myra home."

"Did you go to church today?"

"Absolutely."

"Did you enjoy it?"

"Yes, I did, but I always do."

"I'm glad to hear that. What do you have planned for the rest of your day?" he asked.

"Nothing."

"Have dinner with me?"

Smiling, she replied, "Okay."

"Feel like taking a ride on the bike?"

"Ooh, yeah," she said excitedly.

He laughed. "Cool. Listen, I'll come and get you at about five o'clock, okay?"

"Okay."

"Looking forward to it," he said softly. "See you then."

When Stefàn pulled up in front of her house, promptly at five o'clock, Charisse was sitting on her front steps. Having changed from her church clothes, she had put on a pair of pale pink jeans since they would be on the motorcycle. Under the matching jacket thrown over her shoulders, she wore a sleeveless white T-shirt.

"Hi," she called to him.

He pulled into her driveway and immediately turned off the bike's engine. *Wow, she's sitting there waiting for me. Does that mean she's as eager to see me as I am to see her?* Deliberately removing his helmet as he tried to staunch his excitement at the possibility of his thought being the truth, he said, "Hey, gorgeous. You look pretty in pink."

"Thanks. Let me go get my helmet. Would you like something to drink before we go?" she asked as she held the door open.

"Sure; I'll take a glass of ice water."

"Come on in."

Following her into the house, Stefan pulled off his driving gloves as he walked in, and unzipped his jacket.

"What time did you go to work this morning?"

"I was there at eight."

"Yeah, that's about the time we left this morning. It was a little tough getting up 'cause we were up late watching a movie."

"When I left here last night, I went home and crashed."

"Did you show that woman any houses today?"

"Yeah, she was my first appointment."

"Any luck?"

"Not yet, but I didn't expect much the first time out. I've got a few properties to show her, though. She was a royal pain, too."

Charisse laughed. "Trying to get more than a house, huh?"

Sighing, he said, "I don't have a problem with a woman who makes it clear what she wants…as far as…."

"Sex?" Charisse offered since he appeared to be struggling with the word.

Stefan actually blushed before he continued. "Yeah. But, this woman…. She's like an octopus. I swear she's got eight arms," he said with a frown.

Laughing animatedly, Charisse asked, "What did you say to her?"

"I told her I've got a woman and I don't mess around."

She was shocked. "No, you didn't."

"Yes, I did. It didn't matter to her, though. She said, 'I won't tell her if you don't.'"

Charisse shook her head as she handed him a tall glass of ice water. He drank it in one long gulp.

"Thirsty, huh?"

"Yeah. I meant to grab a bottle of water before I left but walked out without it."

"That's a very nice jacket," she commented.

"Thanks. I had it made when I first got my bike."

She reached out to touch the leather. "It's really soft."

"Like butter." The jacket was simply tailored with a zip front closure, a barely visible breast pocket, side slits, and zippers on the cuffs of the sleeves. It was unlined, with a straight, upstanding collar, and besides the zippers, the only other noticeable detail was the name, Coop, embroidered over the pocket in red.

"Do you ride all year round?"

"No. During the spring and summer, mostly. Or in the fall, if it's warm enough. Once the weather breaks, I break out the wheels."

"Let me go get my helmet so we can go." As she walked out of the kitchen, Charisse put her arms in the jacket on her shoulders. Seconds later, she returned with her helmet in hand. "Ready when you are."

"I'm ready," he said with a smile.

"So, where are we going to eat?" Charisse asked him.

"I've got something special in mind. You'll see," he told her as they walked out of her front door.

Charisse hopped up on Stefan's bike like an old pro. He was tickled by the change in her attitude from just a week ago, but was happy she felt so comfortable riding with him because he enjoyed having her on his bike.

Taking off immediately, they only rode for about twenty minutes to a small park a few towns away. When Stefan pulled into the parking lot and turned off the engine, Charisse was puzzled. Once she had removed her helmet, she asked, "Is there a restaurant in this park?"

He was climbing off the bike when he answered, "Nope. I made dinner. I thought we could dine alfresco."

Charisse looked at him with a questioning smile. "Alfresco?"

"Yeah, you know, out in the open, unless you want to go to a restaurant."

"No. Alfresco is fine." She proceeded to climb off the bike.

"Good. I have everything we need right here," he said as he unpacked the storage containers that flanked his rear tire.

Charisse was surprised at how much he had actually packed in the containers. They were a lot bigger and deeper than they appeared from the outside. From one he pulled a bottle of red wine, napkins, cups and small paper plates, and from the other he pulled various plastic containers and utensils which he promptly placed in a thermal sac he had removed, as well. Removing his jacket, he neatly folded it and stashed it in the container he'd just emptied. Charisse also removed her jacket and handed it to him. After securing the box, Stefan unfastened the blanket that was rolled and tied behind the seat of the bike.

"So what's on the menu?" she asked.

"You'll see." He smiled. "Come on, let's walk down by the lake. We can probably find a nice spot down there."

"Can I help you carry some of that?" she asked.

"No, thanks. I've got it."

"At least give me your helmet," she directed.

Conceding, he handed it to her. As she closely followed where he led, Charisse had to struggle to contain the smile she felt coming from her heart.

This man is full of surprises.

About five minutes later, they came to a rise. On the other side was a pond that was set in the center of a lush stand of trees and flowering shrubs. Quite a few of the park's patrons opted to enjoy the atmosphere in this area but it was by no means crowded. A rich, vibrant green carpet of grass immediately made her feel like kicking off her shoes and running her toes through it. Suddenly, a light breeze blew and Charisse's nostrils were pleasantly assailed by the sweet fragrance of the beautifully colored blossoms near the lake.

"Here's a good spot," Stefan said from a few feet ahead of her.

He had stopped near a large elm tree. As he put his bag down and removed the bottle of wine, Charisse cooed, "This is really nice, Stefan."

Smiling sheepishly, he said, "I thought you might like a little.... Well, I figured this would be better than sitting in a stuffy restaurant. It's such a beautiful day."

"Yes, I have to admit this is better." Reaching for the other end of the blanket, she helped him spread it under the tree.

Minutes later, they were each barefoot and seated on the covering. Unbelievably nervous, Stefan tried hard not to let it show as he removed the containers from the sack.

"I hope you like fried chicken."

"Yes, I do," she said. "Did you fry this yourself?"

"Of course. Do you think I'd serve you some Popeyes or Kentucky Fried Chicken?"

Subduing the chuckle she felt in her gut, Charisse smiled and said, "I really like Popeyes chicken."

"Well, Miss Ellison, I'll have you know that Popeyes doesn't have anything on me. My fried chicken is the bomb. As a matter of fact, it's one of my best dishes," he intoned with mock offense.

"I didn't say it wasn't," she said, defending herself.

"Well, I'm just letting you know."

This time she didn't try to contain her laughter. "So what else is on the menu?"

"Tossed salad, some cheese and crackers, and grapes. You know, just a little light fare." His face suddenly taking on a boyish quality, Stefan was worried she might be displeased by his choice of foods.

"I like cheese and crackers and grapes and salad," she told him reassuringly.

Smiling affectionately, he chose not to reply. For the next few seconds, they gazed at one another in a manner that displayed their mutual fondness.

"Do you want to eat now?" he asked aloud but he was thinking, *stay cool, Coop.*

"Okay, but can we say grace first?" she asked.

"Oh, sure. Do you want to or do you want me to?"

"Would you?"

"Sure."

Charisse watched as Stefan lowered his head and in a soft but clear voice blessed the food. As he recited his prayer, she added her own silent word of thanks for more than just their meal. When she heard him say, "Amen," she looked up at him and the smile she felt in her heart appeared on her face.

He began to lay out plates and utensils on the blanket so she asked, "Do you have a corkscrew for the wine?"

"Yup." On his a key ring, aside from numerous keys, was a combination bottle opener/corkscrew attachment, which he promptly pulled off.

As he reached for the bottle of wine, she said, "I'll make our plates."

"Okay."

Shifting her position on the blanket, Charisse sat with her legs folded Indian-style. She reached for the container with the salad and began to dish some out on their plates.

"I hope you don't mind, but I put a little oil and vinegar on it so I wouldn't have to carry dressing, too," Stefan informed her.

"No, that's fine."

"You're so easy to please," he said lovingly.

Blushing, she shrugged.

When he had uncorked the bottle, he poured a little into each of their cups, then set the bottle near the tree so as not to accidentally knock it over. Reaching next for the foil-wrapped bundle of chicken, he asked, "Do you like light or dark meat?"

"Dark."

He placed a couple of legs on her plate and a breast on his own.

"Thank you. You didn't by any chance bring any bread, did you?" she asked.

Frowning in dismay, he said, "No, sorry, but there's the crackers."

"Oh yeah. I need to lay off the bread, anyway."

"I'll remember next time," he promised.

"I'm sure you will."

As she sampled the chicken, he watched her closely, awaiting her judgment.

Her immediate, involuntary reaction speaking louder than any words, he didn't miss when her eyebrows rose slightly and her mouth twisted in amazement.

Knowing he was waiting to hear what she thought of his cooking, she purposely remained silent.

"So?"

"So, what?" she asked teasingly.

"What do you think?"

"Oh, of the chicken?"

"Yes, of the chicken."

"Oh. It's good."

He smirked. "Just good, huh?"

She laughed. "No, it's very good, Stefàn." Proceeding to lick the digits on her right hand, she added, "Finger lickin' good."

"Told you," he said with a satisfied grin.

Laughing again, she said, "You're just like a little boy looking for approval."

"I'll be that."

When they had finished eating the chicken and salad and had their fill of cheese and crackers, they both stretched out, Stefàn on his back and Charisse on her stomach.

"This is a nice little park. It's not as big as the one we went to last week, is it?"

"Oh no. You could put this one inside that one."

"Have you been to all the parks in Bergen County?" Charisse asked him.

He laughed and said, "No. Actually, Julian put me on to this one. He brings his little boy up here. There's a really cool playground on the other side of the pond."

"Julian has a son?"

"Yeah, he's seven years old. L'il Jay. He's my godson."

"Do you come here often?"

"No. I've actually only been here a couple of times. Once with Julian and L'il Jay and once when I was babysitting, I brought him up here."

"You, babysitting? I can't picture you doing that."

"Yeah, as long as the kid is walking and talking, we can hang. I've got three nieces and three nephews and although I don't do it very often, every now and then, I'll go get them and take them out. We always have a ball, too. Little babies scare me, though," he admitted.

"So, I guess you don't have any kids of your own?"

"Oh, no. No baby's mama drama here."

Charisse laughed. "Why are you so afraid of babies?"

"They look so fragile. I'm scared I might break the kid if I hold it."

Smiling, she said, "They're stronger than you think. You have to make sure you hold them right."

"That's why I don't bother."

"So, you don't ever plan to have any kids of your own, huh?"

"Oh, yeah. I love kids."

"I'm sure your wife will expect you to hold your son or daughter before they actually learn to walk."

In a caressing manner, Stefan said, "Well, you'll have to show me the right way to hold him or her."

Charisse wasn't completely sure she'd heard him correctly, so to avoid possible embarrassment she decided not to ask for clarification of his statement. But Stefan watched her closely for a reaction to his comment. He smiled when he realized that she wasn't going to entertain his statement.

Instead, she said, "Every time I talk to you, you surprise me."

"Why is that?"

"I don't know. I had a picture of you in my mind and I'm finding out that you're not really what I had pictured at all."

"Is that good or bad?" he wanted to know.

Smiling shyly, she said, "So far, it's been good."

"Well, I'm glad to hear that. I have to admit, though, I've pretty much pictured you just as you are."

"Is that good or bad?"

"It's all good," he said softly.

After a few minutes of thoughtful silence, Charisse said, "I really appreciate you coming by last night."

"I need to apologize to you again for the way I behaved."

"No, you don't," she insisted.

"Yeah, I do." Stefàn rolled onto his side and propped himself up on his elbow so he was facing her. "I was thinking about it last night after I left you and I realized I acted like a jerk. I don't know if you've noticed, but I like you, Charisse. I like you a lot. Considering we only met a week ago, the way I've been feeling… the strength of my feelings for you scared the hell out of me, so I was purposely avoiding you yesterday."

Simultaneously surprised and a little bruised by his admittance, Charisse turned her face away with his revelation.

"You probably think I'm… I've never felt like this before. I've never known anyone who got under my skin so quickly and so completely. Then when I saw you get in the pool…." Stefàn huffed almost as if he couldn't believe he was actually telling her this. "I saw the way several of the men there were looking at you and I got jealous. Pitiful, right?" he said to her.

Charisse smiled sympathetically and uttered a tender, "No."

"I enjoy spending time with you and want to spend more time with you. I want to get to know you, Charisse, and I want you to get to know the real me."

"Can I ask you something?" she said before he could say anything more.

"Sure."

"You date a lot of women, right?"

"Not like you probably think. I don't run around with a different woman every night. I've never done that. There were a couple of women I'd occasionally go out with, but never anything serious. It's only been a week but I haven't seen any of them since we met and I've only spoken to one and told her I couldn't see her, and that's pretty unusual."

"Why did you tell her that?"

"Because I don't want to see her, or anyone else for that matter. I've become...." He took a deep, resigning breath before continuing. "You've monopolized all of my free time, whether we're together or not. I can't seem to get you off my mind. I realize you're not looking to get involved with anyone who doesn't share the same beliefs as you, but I want to learn what makes you feel the way you do. I'm willing to do whatever I have to do to prove that I'm serious about what I'm saying to you."

"I like you, too, Stefan, and it kinda scares me, too, how I feel about you. I've been wondering if God is testing me or something to see what I would do. I told you, I've taken a vow of abstinence."

"I understand and what I'm feeling is not about getting physical with you," he sincerely stated, but felt he needed to explain fully. "I'd be lying, though, if I said I haven't thought about you that way but I know where your head is and where your heart is, and I'm not trying to do anything to make your life difficult. Not by any means. I want you to trust me."

"I do," she said with a nod.

"Thank you for that," he said as he reached out and gently touched her hand.

Charisse turned her palm up and curled her fingers around his large mitt.

"Can I share something with you?" he asked.

"Sure."

"I couldn't help noticing last night when I got to your house, your friend didn't seem too pleased to see me. She doesn't like me much, does she?"

Surprised by Stefan's frank comment, Charisse asked, "Why do you say that?"

"Well, yesterday at Dre's, I jokingly made a remark about your bathing suit and she pretty much bit my head off when she informed me that you were grown and single and could do what you want, just like me. Then last night when I called and came by, she didn't ask me in until I told her that you were expecting me."

Charisse sighed. "She's worried about me; that's all."

"Worried about what?"

"That you're going to hurt me. She thinks you only want to take advantage of me."

He was silent as he considered what she revealed.

Wanting to assure him that she didn't feel the same, she added, "Myra's only seen you twice and both times you were…well… you were seemingly doing the playboy thing. She thinks you were disrespectful to me yesterday and that I'm being gullible for trusting you."

"Wow," he said in a near whisper.

"I told her we were just friends, but she thinks you have a secret agenda."

"In some respects, she's right. I do have an agenda, but it's no secret. I want to be with you, Charisse."

She was unable to respond to his bold declaration.

"I hope you realize, I would never consciously do anything to hurt you."

"I wouldn't be here, Stefàn, if I thought I had to worry about that."

"I'm sorry she feels that way."

"Me, too."

"I'm glad it doesn't affect how you feel."

"Well, I know you a little better than she does. There's a lot I don't know, but what you've shown me, what I've learned about you so far… You've given me no reason to mistrust you. The only promise you've ever made to me was that you wouldn't lie to me and I don't believe you have."

"I haven't and I won't," he assured her.

Softly, she replied, "I don't think you would."

"Will you give me a chance to show you who I really am?"

"Yes. Will you accept who I really am and what I believe?" she asked him in return.

"I already have," he softly replied with a gentle smile.

AFTER DROPPING CHARISSE OFF, Stefàn rode by Julian's house. Although it was nearly dark outside, Julian was in his driveway washing his car.

When Stefàn turned off his bike's engine and pulled off his helmet, he snickered as he called to Julian, "You're the only man I know who waits until it's dark outside to wash his car."

"Hey, well, I can't be like everybody else."

"No doubt." Stefàn laughed. He climbed off his bike and stepped over to his friend. The men touched fists.

"What's up, man? Where you comin' from? I called your house a little while ago," Julian said.

"I just dropped Charisse off."

"Charisse, huh?"

"Yeah. Charisse."

"So, what was up yesterday? She got bent about that chick stepping to you like she did, huh?"

"Yeah, that and a few other things, but I can't really blame her. I invited her there and I should have been more attentive," Stefàn admitted.

"So you're serious about her?"

"Yeah, Dub. I told her, too."

"How'd she take it?"

"She's open," he said with a smile.

CHAPTER 13
AND SO IT BEGINS...

"Province Realty. This is Stefàn Cooper. How may I help you?"

With her heart beating like a bass drum, she replied, "Good evening, Stefàn."

A broad smile lit his face and a warm sensation permeated his body as he pleasantly replied, "Charisse. Good evening to you. How are you this fine evening?"

Stefàn had called her that afternoon at work, but she hadn't had an opportunity to get back to him. When Charisse finally made it home that evening, she had barely put down her pocketbook before she picked up the telephone and dialed his office number, which she had memorized. It was just after six thirty.

"I'm very well, thank you, and yourself?"

"I'm doing better now that I'm talking to you."

"Flattery will get you almost anywhere."

Stefàn laughed. The sound was contagious so she joined him.

"Are you still at work?" he asked.

"No, I'm home. I'm sorry I didn't get a chance to call you back before I left."

"Oh, that's okay. Got out early today, huh?"

"No, just on time," she replied.

"I heard that."

"Are you going to be there much longer?" she then asked.

"No, actually I was about to lock up. I was hoping this wasn't a client when I answered your call."

"Do you have plans for the rest of the evening?"

His heart skipped a beat in anticipation of her next words when he answered, "No."

"At lunchtime today, I was given a couple of passes to the pre-screening of a new Denzel Washington movie at the theater in Ridgefield Park. They said it's a romantic comedy. I was wondering if you'd be interested in seeing it with me?"

"Denzel, huh?"

"Yes."

"I guess you're a fan?" he asked with a smile in his voice.

"Yeah, he's okay," she facetiously answered.

Stefan laughed. "As long as I don't have to compete with him, I'd love to go, Charisse."

She was thinking, *you don't have to compete with anyone.*

"What time does the show start?"

"Seven-thirty."

He glanced at the watch on his wrist. "All right. I'll lock up here and head right over to you. I should be there in about twenty-five minutes. Is that cool?"

"That's fine. I'll see you then."

Stefan wasted no time setting everything in order at his office, expediting his departure so he could get to Charisse. He couldn't help but smile as he took the fifteen-minute drive from his job to her house.

Charisse smiled in surprise when her doorbell rang at a couple of minutes past seven.

Wow, that was quick. Is he as eager to see me as I am to see him?

She was still dressed in the sand-colored silk suit she'd worn to work, and had only removed her pantyhose and changed her shoes, putting on a pair of low-heeled mules. As soon as Charisse opened the door and got a look at him, she was glad she hadn't changed because Stefan was decked out in a beige suit and his brown hued multi-colored tie was still tightly knotted at his neck. Since he had been casually attired the last few times she'd seen him, she'd forgotten how resplendent he looked dressed in business apparel.

She warmly uttered, "Hi."

"Hi, gorgeous," he softly replied. As he stepped into her house, appreciative eyes took in her form from head to toe and were pleased by what they saw.

"You must have been walking out the door when I called you," she said.

"Just about. I didn't want to have you waiting for me too long."

Looking up into dark orbs that adored her, she told him, "That's okay; I wouldn't have minded."

A playful smile crossed his face, highlighting his solitary dimple and causing a shiver to race up her spine.

"Do you want to take my car or yours?" he then asked.

"You can drive."

The theater was a fifteen-minute ride from Charisse's house but when they arrived, there were only a few seats left in the crowded auditorium.

"There are two seats down front," Charisse said in a soft voice, just as Stefan took her hand and led her in the opposite direction.

"I see two seats back there," he told her.

The vacancies were in the center of the very last row of the hall. Once they had squeezed their way past the people already seated, Stefan leaned close to her and asked, "Is this okay for you?"

"Yeah, this is good. I didn't even see these seats."

"Would you like anything from the concession stand?"

"No, that's okay. I don't want you to have climb over these people again."

"Would you like something from the concession stand?" he repeated, disregarding her concerns.

She smiled at him and meekly replied, "Some popcorn."

"Butter?"

"A little, and a 7-Up or Sprite."

"Okay. I'll be right back."

About ten minutes later, Stefan made his way up the aisle and through their row back to his seat.

"Did I miss anything?" he asked as soon as he sat down.

"Just a couple of previews. I was beginning to worry about you," Charisse stated good-naturedly.

"I figured I might as well use the facilities while I was out there. The brother on the end didn't look too happy to see me when I came back through. I'm not trying to get into anything in here," he told her in a whisper. "I hope you don't mind that I got a large popcorn and soda for us to share."

"Of course I don't mind. I figured you would."

Moving his mouth close to her ear, he said, "You know, you make it very easy to like you."

Charisse could only blush. Inhaling the exotic fragrance of his cologne, her heart beat so loudly in her ears she wondered if he could hear it. She couldn't believe how nervous she felt sitting so close to him. It wasn't as if she'd never been to the movies with a man before. For some strange reason, the darkness of the auditorium and the closeness of their seats, in addition to sharing popcorn and a soda with him, made the whole affair seem so much more intimate.

Suddenly, to her chagrin, she realized that she had actually asked him out on a date. There was no mistaking it. Unlike their previous meetings, there was no other way to look at this. It was date. *God, what is he thinking of me? He must think I'm one of those fast women who sees a man she wants and makes no bones about going after him. Oh, no. That's not the impression I want him to have of me.* At that very moment, without looking, she reached over to dip her hand in the popcorn bucket. Stefan did the same.

"Sorry," she muttered, pulling her hand away as if she'd been burned.

"No apology necessary," he told her softly, lifting the bucket to make it easier for her to take what she wanted.

With a deep sigh, she said, "Thank you."

"Charisse, would you do me a favor?" he whispered.

Turning her face toward him, she answered, "What?"

"Relax," he gently urged.

She nodded as she faced forward.

"Charisse."

"Yes?"

"As much as I'd like to, I won't bite you."

Looking over at him in surprise, she saw the glint in his eye through the darkness of the theater and his playful smile and couldn't help but return it. A chuckle escaped her lips as she thought about what he'd said.

Stefan's teasing had broken the ice and she was eventually able to relax and enjoy the movie, his company and his closeness.

Afterward, he suggested they have dinner. Stefan drove them to a quaint Spanish restaurant not far from the movie house.

They ordered a carafe of sangria and Charisse allowed Stefan to order her meal. He informed her that he frequented this particular restaurant quite often and knew the owner personally. As they awaited their meals and sipped their wine, Stefan continued with his teasing.

"So, Charisse, should I be worried?"

"About what?"

"About you taking advantage of me?"

"What do you mean?" She hadn't yet caught on to him.

"I mean, the other day you told me I didn't have to worry about you trying to take advantage of me, and now you're asking me out on dates," he nonchalantly stated.

Mortified, her face took on a look of distress so prominent that he quickly reached across the table for her hand and said, "I'm just playing with you."

When she didn't recover quickly enough from his dig, he moved to the chair next to her from his position across the table. "Sweetheart, please don't take what I said to heart. I was only teasing."

"Yes, but you put voice to my fears. When we were in the movie theater I was thinking that."

"And what's so wrong with you asking me out on a date?" he asked.

"I just don't want you to get the wrong idea about me, Stefàn."

Affectionately caressing her digits, tenderness filled his tone as he spoke. "I don't have any wrong ideas about you."

She sighed.

"Can I ask you something?" When she nodded he continued. "Why do I make you so nervous?"

"I don't know," she whispered with her head bowed.

"Charisse, look at me." Aligning his earnestness with her trepidation, he dialed up the candor when he touched her chin and reminded her, "You promised you wouldn't lie to me."

"I know."

"Then tell me why you're so nervous around me?"

"Because I like you."

A warm smile played on his lips when he said, "I like you, too. More than a little bit."

"It just seems…we're so far apart in…how we live," she tried to explain.

"We don't have to be."

"Stefàn, I'm trying to live a life that's completely different from the way I used to live. I don't party like I once did, I don't drink like I used to. I don't even…." She sighed.

"I don't want to corrupt you, Charisse. I want to see you. I want to spend time with you. But I want you to be comfortable around me."

Absently pulling her hand from his and nervously fidgeting with her utensils, she admitted, "It's not that I'm uncomfortable around you, it's more like...I'm too comfortable around you. You make me...." She sighed loudly. "I want to spend time with you, too."

"Your birthday's next week, right?"

"The Saturday after next," she answered.

"Do you have any plans?"

"No. I already bought my birthday present," she told him with a smile.

"Let me take you out for your birthday. I want to do something special for you. Will you let me do that?"

"You know what you can do for my birthday that would be very special?" she asked instead of answering his question.

"What?"

"Come to church with me."

"Okay," he easily replied.

"You will?"

"Sure. Now will you let me take you out for your birthday?" he asked, looking at her through inquisitive eyes.

"You don't have to."

"I want to. Are you going to deny me that?"

"No."

"Good. Now do me one more favor."

"What?"

He reclaimed her hand and clasped it between both of his. "Be yourself around me. I want you to be as comfortable as you please. I respect you, Charisse. I respect how you're living and I promise

I will never do anything to compromise you or your beliefs. Can you trust my word?"

"Yes." She nodded.

Stefàn brought her hand to his lips and placed a tender kiss on her palm. "You are very special to me. More than you probably know, and I just want to be with you, be around you." Suddenly, he took the hand he still held and placed it against his chest. "Can you feel my heart beating?"

"Yes." It was racing.

"That's you. You excite me on a level so deep…" He chuckled lightly. "It's scary. I'm not talking about physical excitement either. I feel…I feel like there's permanence between us. Like there's some greater destiny in store for us. Together. I've never felt that with anyone, but that's how I feel with you."

Charisse was speechless. Like wildfire, an overwhelming feeling of joy spread through her.

Stefàn smiled that crooked smile he had and said, "You don't have to say anything. It's blowing my mind, too."

She couldn't help but laugh with him. "I'm glad you feel that way. I would let you feel my heart, but you already know."

"I can feel your pulse." Stefàn leaned in closer and placed a soft kiss on her cheek. "I'll save the real one for another time."

Charisse could only blush.

Tenderly caressing her hand as he held it, he asked, "What size do you wear?"

"What size clothes?"

"Yes."

"Six."

"What size shoe?"

"Eight."

"Do you like to go the theater?"

"Yes."

"What about concerts?"

"I like old school groups; the ones that sing those sweet love songs."

"Yeah, I know what you mean. What's your favorite color?"

"Orange. Bright orange."

"Yeah? What's your favorite thing to do on a rainy day?"

She giggled. "Stay at home and watch movies."

"Alone?"

"Well, I don't really have a choice there. I live by myself and I don't have a boyfriend."

"Well, the first part of that's true," he casually stated.

She smiled.

"Do you like the beach?"

"Yes, but I really like sitting on the beach more than I like swimming in the ocean. I love to swim, but I prefer pools. I like picnics. Like yesterday. I really liked that."

"You like walks in the park?" he asked.

"Yes, and rides on motorcycles," she told him with a big smile.

He laughed. "Okay."

At that point their food was served, breaking into their shared peace. Stefàn offered to say a blessing over the meal, causing Charisse's already growing ardor to soar.

DURING THE FOLLOWING WEEK, Charisse and Stefàn got together, if only for a little while, each day. Tuesday and Thursday they shared late dinners at restaurants in neighboring towns and Wednesday they double-dated with Julian and his friend, Robin.

Stefàn, who had already made up his mind that he wanted Charisse to be the lady in his life, found with each day, his affection grew stronger and stronger. Still, he had made no attempts—upon greeting or leaving her—to kiss her more intimately than the pecks they shared on each other's cheeks. Several times when he was alone, he found himself daydreaming about her, about making love with her but he immediately suppressed those urges. That was a dream that would only be fulfilled if they walked down the aisle together.

He often found it funny that only weeks ago, if someone had suggested anything in the neighborhood of commitment or marriage, he would have loudly balked at the thought. Now, he looked forward to Charisse one day becoming his wife. Stefan wanted to take care of her. Materially, she was fully self-sufficient; after all, she had a great career, her own home, car and probably a pretty good bit of money in the bank, considering the field she was in. But he wanted to be the man who supported her in any way she wanted or needed. He wanted her to be his family, the mother of his children, his life mate. She was everything—his sun, moon and stars. The love he felt for her was so strange to him; he'd never known a feeling this engrossing. He had been in love before, but his selfish nature had ruined the relationship he had with Janine Taylor, his first real love. Never fully recovering from her rejection, Stefan had made the decision to let no other woman get close to him. He had lived for so long in his protective cocoon, a self-imposed state of emotional exile, that it had become a way of life. Then Charisse came along, and like a tornado, blew all of his defenses down. In truth, he had to admit, he had never felt better. Like he'd told Julian, he felt as if he was high all the time. Charisse had him flying; she made him feel as if he could do anything and he was looking forward to doing it all with her at his side.

CHAPTER 14

FAMILY AND FRIENDS

The following Friday, Stefan left his office at seven-thirty. Heading straight home, he quickly showered and changed since he had managed to visit his barber earlier in the day to freshen up his haircut. A friend from his childhood was getting married on Sunday and was having a bachelor party that evening at a club in his old neighborhood in Queens. Despite not really wanting to attend, Stefan felt obligated to make an appearance, at least for a couple of hours.

He had spoken to Charisse earlier in the day and invited her for dinner at his house on Saturday evening. When Stefan was active on the dating scene, he took pleasure in wining and dining his lady friends. However, that usually entailed taking them out to a restaurant or some other venue. For Charisse, he wanted to do something special; something he'd never done for anyone else.

When they'd gone riding this past Sunday, he had personally fried the chicken and made the salad they'd eaten. That was no big deal for him; he'd been frying chicken since he was fifteen years old. Now he wanted to prepare a romantic, candlelight dinner for Charisse so she would know, beyond a shadow of a doubt, the depth of his feelings for her.

The bachelor party wasn't scheduled to begin until ten o'clock, but Stefan hadn't seen his parents in a few weeks, so he decided to pay them a visit before heading to the club. The elder Coopers lived in a two-story Colonial-style house in Baldwin, Long Island, twenty minutes past the location of the party.

Stefan's parents had been married for thirty-five years. His father, Michael, or Mike, as everyone called him, was a licensed electrical engineer who had retired from Con Edison two years earlier at the age of fifty-six and gone into business for himself. An inch or so shorter than Stefan, he was just as handsome, if not more so. Accentuated by a silver shock of thick, wavy hair, Mike Cooper's features reflected what Stefan would most likely look like when he reached his late-fifties. Despite the twenty-five-year difference in their ages, Mike's physique was as toned as his eldest son's because he was nearly as vain as Stefan and just as dedicated to physical fitness.

Stefan's mother, Damaris, was the principal of the public elementary school Stefan and his siblings had attended when they were children. A statuesque beauty, Damaris stood five feet, eleven inches in her stockinged feet and had a figure women half her age envied. Older than her husband by two years, Stefan thought his mother was the epitome of the black woman. Wearing her salt and pepper, naturally curly hair cut short and close to her scalp, Stefan had inherited his sense of style from his mother. Some people might classify Damaris as snooty since she was never seen in public without makeup and her bearing and style of dress was very classy, but in truth, her personality was warm, welcoming and she was much beloved by the students, parents and school faculty, as well as by the community at large.

Mike and Damaris lived a very active lifestyle and traveled often, actually at every opportunity that came their way. They had been all over the world on numerous cruises and excursions of all sorts. Since their children were grown and living their own lives, the couple took full advantage of their "childless" status and viewed the second half of their marriage as a rebirth in which they often behaved as newlyweds.

When Stefan arrived, he noticed the lights were on in his parents' backyard, so after parking, he headed back there. The house had a screened-in deck and since the night was warm, Mike had a couple of steaks on the grill. Damaris was setting the table on the deck for a late-night supper for her and Mike.

"Oh, I'm just in time to eat," Stefan called as he walked toward them.

"Sorry, buddy, this is a table set for two," Mike called back when he noticed his son.

"That's all right; treat me like a stepchild," Stefan playfully moaned.

"Hi, baby. We weren't expecting you. We would have put a steak on for you, too," Damaris said as he approached.

Kissing his mother and giving her a big hug, he told her, "It's cool, Mom. I'm not staying anyway. I came by to say hi. I'm on my way to a bachelor's party at Skip's."

Walking over to his father, the two men embraced and Stefan kissed his father's cheek. "Who's getting married?" Mike asked.

"I don't know if you know Greg Baker. He lived a couple of blocks from us in Queens but we didn't really hang out much until we got to high school. He's getting married in Montego Bay, Jamaica on Sunday."

"That sounds nice," Damaris said.

"Yeah, right?"

"So how are you, baby?" she asked her son.

Taking a seat on one of the stools at the bar on the deck, he said, "I'm good, Mom. How you doin'?"

"Great. You look sharp."

He was dressed in black pants, shirt and shoes topped by a red sport jacket. "Thanks."

"Hope you're not going to be acting a fool at this bachelor party," Damaris said with a sideways glance.

Stefan quietly laughed, "No, Mom. I'm really not even in the mood to go but...you know. We're pretty cool so I want to at least show my face for a couple hours."

"Since when are you not in the mood for barely-clad women shaking their behinds?" Mike asked, knowing what a ladies' man his son had always been.

Stefan smiled. "Mom, you're going to be happy to hear this, but I've met someone who...well, she...she's given me a new outlook on a lot of things."

"And who is this?" Damaris asked.

"Her name is Charisse Ellison. We met at my friend, Terry Wilson's, wedding two weeks ago."

"Just two weeks and you've already got a new outlook on life?" Mike questioned. "She must be some woman."

"She is, Dad. She's pretty amazing."

Damaris and Mike exchanged a look of pleasant surprise.

"Y'all are probably like, 'is he for real?' Well, I am." Stefan lowered his head briefly and a jocund sound escaped his lips. "She's going to be your daughter-in-law one day."

"What!" Damaris made no effort to hide her astonishment at this admission.

"You've known her two weeks and you're already planning to marry her, huh?" Mike said.

"Daddy, when did you know Mommy was the woman for you?" Stefan challenged.

Mike looked fondly at his wife and smiled. "The first time I asked her out and she turned me down."

Damaris grinned at the memory.

"She turned you down?" Stefan asked, looking from his mother to his father.

"Four times," Mike admitted.

"He wouldn't take no for an answer. I went out with him to get him to stop asking me out," Damaris revealed.

Stefan laughed. "So how'd y'all end up married?"

"She had the time of her life, like I told her she would if she went out with me," Mike bragged.

Still laughing, Stefan asked, "Is that true, Mom?"

"Yes. He was everything I didn't expect him to be. Your father was something of a playboy and I'd heard about his reputation. See, I had just moved into the neighborhood a month before. It was my first apartment and my first full-time teaching job. My next door neighbor had warned me about him. He lived with your grandparents in the building across the street from me. I thought he was arrogant and full of you-know-what. He was gorgeous, though," Damaris added with a nod of her head.

"So he wore you down, huh?"

"I guess."

"Persistence pays off, son," Mike said with a knowing smile.

"But you changed your mind about him after one date?"

"As much as I struggled not to, yes, I did. He was the perfect gentleman and he somehow learned that I loved the Temptations. He took me to dinner in the city, then to my surprise, we went to the Apollo. I had wanted to get tickets to this show but after I paid my rent and my other bills, I couldn't afford it. We had seats in the first row, dead center, and he didn't even mind that I acted a fool when Eddie Kendricks singled me out in the audience while he was singing, 'You're My Everything.' I acted a pure fool, but he was really sweet about it," she said as she looked lovingly at her husband.

"Well, see, Dad, you realized Mommy was the woman you wanted to spend the rest of your life with before you'd even gone out with her. I've spent the last ten days with this young lady and every day I'm with her, my feelings get stronger and stronger," Stefan explained. "She's different. She's not like any of the women I usually fool around with. She's in the church for one, but she's not a holy roller, if you know what I mean. She's new to her faith, but she's really serious about it and she talks to me about what she feels about that and, come to think of it, she, uh, she put me off at first, too."

"What do you mean?" Damaris asked.

Stefan proceeded to tell his parents about his first encounter with Charisse. "My feelings were really hurt when she told me she didn't want to get involved with anyone like me."

"And you didn't take offense to that?" Mike asked.

"Yeah, I hung up on her."

"So how'd y'all end up going out?" Mike asked as he got up to turn the steaks on the grill.

"She called me back and apologized. The rest, is history."

"It's not a problem for her that you're not in the church?" Damaris asked.

"I'm going to church with her on Sunday. Her birthday is next week and I asked her if I could take her out and do something special for her birthday. She asked me to come to church with her. So I am."

"Are you really serious about her, honey?" Damaris asked. Although she and Mike did not regularly attend church, Damaris didn't take anyone's faith lightly and she hoped Stefan wasn't doing so either.

"Yes, Mom. I love her. I'm in love with her. It's not infatuation, either."

"How do you know?" Mike asked.

"I've been infatuated before. This is so much more than that. She's abstaining from sex. She made a vow to not be intimate with any man who was not her husband and I'm all right with that. I'm more than willing to wait for her. I've never even kissed her. Well, at least…not a real kiss."

Mike and Damaris looked at their son in silence for a long moment. Damaris could see in his eyes the seriousness of his confession and was overjoyed. She often worried about Stefan, more so than her other two children. Devin and Nikki were both married with children and had settled into their lives with their families and were doing well. She had often wondered if Stefan would ever settle down. Too many times to count, she'd questioned him about that and he'd usually become irritated whenever she'd bring the subject up. To hear him admit he had met someone who had inspired such growth in him gave her a new appreciation for her oldest child. She knew Stefan well enough to know that when he set his mind to something, there was no stopping him, and he appeared very determined with regard to his relationship with this young lady.

"So when are we going to meet her?" Mike asked.

"Soon."

"What does she do?" Damaris asked.

"She's an accountant, a CPA."

"Is she pretty?"

Curving his lips upward to create a picture-perfect smile, Stefan boldly declared, "No, she's beautiful, inside and out."

"Our son is in love, baby," Mike said matter-of-factly.

"I see."

"I never thought I could feel so strongly about anyone, especially someone so different from me. She's quick to admit she was no saint before she was saved, but her conviction is so strong now that it makes me curious to learn what it is that motivates her. I believe in God, in Jesus Christ and everything, but, I don't really understand Christianity the way she does. She wears her faith proudly but she doesn't condemn you if you don't feel the same way she does. I feel an uncommon sense of peace and joy whenever I'm around her. She really makes my whole... She makes me feel good all over," Stefan reverently admitted.

"You're sure what you're feeling isn't motivated by lust, son?" Mike asked.

"No, it's not that. No doubt she's beautiful, very sexy, very appealing, but going there with her is so unimportant, Dad. I'm not going to lie and say I've never imagined what that would be like, but she's so awesome that if she says we have to wait until we're married, I'm more than willing to wait. She's worth it."

"Does she know how you feel, Stevie?" Damaris asked, using the nickname she'd given him as a child.

"About wanting to marry her? Not yet."

"What if she doesn't feel the same?"

"Mommy, she has feelings for me. It's funny, but we connected immediately. When I first saw her at that wedding.... Actually, we saw each other at the same time. When her eyes locked on mine, there was something there that drew me like a magnet. That's part of the reason she put me off at first." Stefan paused momentarily. "This woman makes my heart race whenever I'm near her. I want to take care of her. I want to do everything and anything I can to make her happy."

"Wow," Mike whispered, impressed by the depth of feeling he could hear in his son's tone. He was happy, despite how genuinely surprised he was at the change in Stefan. He had never heard his son express such heartfelt emotion when speaking of any woman.

"Well, you've definitely got to bring her around so we can meet her," Damaris told him.

"I will, Mom. You're gonna love her, too."

"YOU'RE REALLY SERIOUS ABOUT HIM, HUH?" MYRA ASKED.

It was Saturday morning and she and Charisse were on their way to the Garden State Plaza mall for their monthly shopping trip. This was an outing they had been taking together for the past three years, ever since Charisse bought her townhouse in Englewood. She would drive to the Bronx to pick Myra up from one of her shops and they would spend about four or five hours going from store to store, trying on clothes, shoes and the like. When they were each satisfied that they'd found everything they wanted, they would then decide on a restaurant to eat lunch or dinner, depending on the time, before Charisse drove Myra back to her shop.

"Yes, Myra. And the feeling is mutual. The way we connected from the start and the way we feel about each other is no mistake."

"What about all that stuff you said about cutting him off if you felt like you were getting too deep?"

"That was before I knew him. All the things we thought about him being a player and everything were true. He's a single man and he was enjoying his bachelorhood. And there's nothing wrong with that. But he's serious about us being together, Myra, as a couple. He's already told me he feels like there's some greater destiny in store for us, together. He said he feels a permanence about our relationship."

"So what about your promise not to have sex before you get married? You really think he's going to go along with that?" Myra skeptically questioned.

"He knows about that and he said he would never do anything to compromise that and I believe him."

Myra had nothing to say to that, but she still could not quell the doubt she felt about Charisse's relationship with Stefan. Could he have really changed so quickly from the flirtatious Casanova he had shown himself to be at Jewel and Terry's wedding, then again at the barbecue they'd all attended, to this attentive, caring being Charisse was espousing?

"I can tell from your silence, you still don't believe me. Once you get to know him, you'll see what I'm talking about. And you will get to know him, Myra, because he's already declared himself my boyfriend, which is fine by me, by the way. He's making dinner for me tonight, and he promised to go to church with me, too."

"You're sure he's not doing all of this to soften you up?"

"What do you mean?"

"When he thinks he's got you where he wants you, his true colors are going to come out and you'll see that he's as much a player as you first thought he was."

"I don't think that will happen, Myra, but if it does...." Charisse shrugged. In a low tone, she said, "I have faith in him. I don't believe he's playing with me at all. God brought Stefan and I together for a reason. With me being new in my faith and his wanting to understand what motivates me, we are in a position to learn a lot about each other, about Christ and grow together. Granted, up until we met, we were living very different lives, but deep down, we're not really all that different. He wants to spend time with me, quality time, so we can get to know each other. I wouldn't even be surprised if we got married one day," she said with a smile.

"Married?"

"Yes, married. I love him, Myra. It's only been two weeks, but I can't deny what I feel in my heart for him."

Reiterating her constant concern, Myra said, "I don't want you to get hurt, Risi."

"He won't hurt me."

"PROVINCE REALTY, STEFÀN COOPER SPEAKING. How can I help you?"

"What's up, Coop?"

"Hey, Dub. What's good, man?"

"You feel like taking a ride over to East Orange to play some three on three with Joe and them when you get off?"

"Can't tonight, man. I've got a date."

"How late you working? We're looking at going over there at about five," Julian countered.

"I'm out of here at four o'clock but I have to do some food shopping. I'm making dinner for Charisse."

The disbelief was evident when Julian asked, "You're making dinner?"

Stefàn had to laugh at his friend's reaction. "Yeah, man. I'm making jambalaya."

"Have you ever cooked jambalaya before?"

"No, but I've got a great recipe that Margie gave me. And I've tasted it. It's off the hook," Stefàn told Julian.

"Yeah, but that doesn't mean it's going to come out the way it did when Margie cooked it, man. Why would you want to do that to Charisse?"

"What? Man, I'm a very good cook, Dub," Stefàn indignantly announced. "Just 'cause I don't do it often doesn't mean I can't. I can follow a recipe. It's not that complicated. I've already got most of the stuff I need; I just need to pick up a couple of lobster tails."

Julian was silent on the line for the next few seconds.

"You still there?" Stefàn asked after a while.

"Yeah, I'm just... I'm trippin', man. You must really have it bad for this lady, you're cooking dinner for her. That's my thing."

"Julian, I'm in love with her."

"Really? Are you sure?"

"I've never been more certain of anything in my life, man. I'm going to marry her."

"You said that before."

"I mean it, Dub. I want her to be my wife. I want her in my life for the rest of my life. This is no mistake, the way we feel about each other. We haven't known each other for any length of time, but she's feeling what I'm feeling, Dub. I know it. I'm going to church with her tomorrow."

"Well, that's good. Listen, man, I hope everything you want your relationship with her to be comes to pass. You're my man and if Charisse makes you happy, makes you feel like—"

"She makes me feel like I can fly," Stefan reverently whispered.

Julian smiled. "That's great. Hold on to that. It's not often you meet a woman who makes the kind of impression she has obviously made on you. If you believe she's the woman you're supposed to spend the rest of your life with, she probably is. Are you prepared to give up the life you've been living to be with her, Stefan?"

"I've already done that. I don't want anyone else. I don't need anyone else. She's all the woman I need."

"Didn't you say she's abstaining from sex?"

"Yes, but I'm cool with that. I don't have a problem waiting until she's my wife to make love with her." He huffed. "I haven't even kissed her, man. Not a real kiss."

"What are you waiting for?" Julian asked.

"The right time. I don't want her to have any misconceptions about my intentions. I want her to realize she's more important to me that any physical gratification we could share. This is real, Dub. This so real for me."

"I'm happy for you, Coop. I knew it would happen one day, I just wasn't expecting it this soon," Julian said with a chuckle.

"Neither was I, but I'm glad I realized how I could have messed this whole thing up before it was too late. I'd be miserable if I couldn't be with her."

"Are you going to tell her how you feel?"

"Yeah, but I'm going to wait until her birthday. I'm taking her on the World Yacht for dinner. I'm going to tell her everything then."

CHAPTER 15
HAPPY BIRTHDAY, MY LOVE

E agerly anticipating the night ahead, Stefan was on his way to pick Charisse up for her birthday dinner an hour and a half after he'd left work Saturday evening. When he left his office, he stopped to buy the gift he'd seen earlier in the day, then rushed home to shower and change.

Deciding that tonight would be the night he would tell her the true extent of his feelings, he planned to leave nothing to chance. He wanted her to know his intentions, and if she allowed him, his kiss would give her a taste of forever.

It had been a struggle to suppress the urge up until now, especially after last weekend when he'd made dinner for her. His jambalaya had turned out perfect and Charisse had enjoyed it so much, she'd eaten two helpings and taken a container of it home. She had brought over a couple of DVDs so after dinner, they'd sat snuggled together and watched her favorite movie, *You've Got Mail*. He had never seen it before and wasn't particularly in-terested in seeing it that night, but she wanted to watch it so he humored her. Surprisingly, it turned out to be a pretty good story and he was moved by Charisse's tears when the movie came to a happy ending.

She was surprised when he drove her home late that night and asked what time she wanted him there the next morning for church. "I thought you were going to come with me for my birthday," she'd said.

"I am, but I'd like to go with you tomorrow, too, unless you don't want me to," had been his reply.

The desire to take her in his arms and kiss her sweet lips peaked when she told him, "I would love for you to come with me tomorrow, Stefán. That would really make my day."

When she opened the door to his ringing at six thirty-five, her beauty stole his breath, solidifying his decision to truly make her his woman. Dressed in a sleeveless orange silk sheath that stopped just above her knee and contoured the lines of her hourglass figure, Charisse was a picture of sophisticated elegance.

"Hi, Stefán," she sweetly cooed with a bashful smile.

"Good evening, Charisse," he reverently whispered. "You look amazing."

Blushing, she replied, "Thank you."

Her face was lightly made up with a hint of natural tones high-lighting her eyes, cheeks and lips, and her short stylish haircut sweetly accentuated the lines of her comely face. When he noticed that she was wearing a pearl necklace and earrings he thought, *perfect*. Unable to refrain from perusing the complete canvass before him, he saw that her flawlessly pedicured feet were nestled in muted gold strappy sandals. She looked downright delicious to him.

Awestruck by her appearance like never before, Stefán made no move to enter the house, although she held the door wide for his access. "You coming in?" she finally asked.

"Oh, yeah," he said with a chuckle as he was brought back to the present and entered her home.

"You look very handsome," she told him.

"Thank you," he said with a warm smile.

As usual, whenever Stefán put on a suit and tie, his clothing laid on his lean, athletic frame as if it had been tailored to his exact specifications. Tonight he sported a navy-on-navy striped three-button suit with a baby blue shirt. His silk jacquard tie and pocket square were the same hue as his shirt and his highly polished black shoes completed his *GQ* cover model look exquisitely.

"Have a seat. I need to get my top, then we can leave," Charisse said as she turned to leave the room.

"Before you do that, I have something for you," he told her as he reached into the inner pocket of his jacket and produced a long, slim velvet-covered case.

When he handed her the box, she asked, "What is this?"

"Open it."

With trembling fingers, Charisse lifted the cover and gasped in shock. Looking up at him with wide eyes, she murmured, "Oh my goodness, Stefan. This is beautiful."

Taking a step to close the distance between them, he softly said, "Happy birthday, Risi."

"Thank you!" Staring in amazement at the expensive bauble, Charisse sighed, "Why did you do this?"

"When I saw it, you immediately came to mind. I thought you might like it," he tenderly stated.

"I love it," she said as she gazed at him through watery eyes.

Inside the case was a double-strand cultured pearl necklace with a pearl and diamond encrusted clasp. As Charisse eyed the breathtaking adornment, her heart raced with the implications his gift signified. *Is he trying to tell me something by buying me something so extravagant?*

"Would you wear it tonight?" he asked.

"Of course," she softly muttered.

"Turn around," he directed.

Following his instruction, Charisse turned her back to him. Seconds later, she felt his fingers gently unfastening the clasp on her necklace. He lovingly reached around her, removed the necklace, and placed it in the opened box she still held. Removing his gift, he positioned it on her slender neck and secured it.

Standing behind her, Stefàn could smell the light citrusy scent he had come to identify with her and love. The urge to kiss her on the nape of her neck rose quickly in his chest, but he stifled his desire and gently turned her to face him.

A slow smile formed on his face as he appreciatively murmured, "Beautiful."

The necklace felt warm against her skin but she wasn't sure if the heat radiated from the stones or his gaze. Raising her hand to touch the stones, she nervously sighed, "Thank you."

They stood for seconds that seemed to go on forever before Stefàn said, "We'd probably better get going."

"Yes," she said, snapping out of her trance. "I'll be right back."

When Charisse got to her bedroom, she went straight to her dresser mirror and stared in awe at the exquisite necklace. He had positioned it so the elegant clasp was visible from the front. "God, what do You have in store for me?" she whispered at her reflection. "You've got plans for me; let me know what they are, please?"

Knowing she didn't have time to stand there questioning God's purpose for her life or Stefàn's role in it, Charisse stepped to her closet and retrieved the orange silk over-blouse of her dress. Donning it quickly, she checked her appearance in the full-length mirror near her closet and smiled. Snatching her gold clutch purse from atop her dresser, she headed back downstairs to her waiting escort.

The couple arrived at Pier 81 on the West Side Highway in New York City at seven-twenty. Charisse turned to him as he pulled into the parking lot for the World Yacht. Before she could utter a word, however, he asked, "You don't get seasick, do you?"

"No," she answered with a smile.

"I thought we might take a dinner cruise. Do a little dancing, enjoy the sights from the water," he said, sounding almost insecure.

"That sounds wonderful. I've always wanted to take this cruise," she assured him.

"Well, I'm glad you'll be experiencing it for the first time with me."

"I am, too."

Upon boarding, they were shown to a table in the main dining area. The World Yacht set sail promptly at eight p.m. Seated on the starboard side of the ship near a window, Charisse and Stefàn had an unobstructed view of the waterway and the New York City skyline.

A waiter came to take their dinner orders only moments after they were seated. Once they had placed their order for a bottle of Shiraz and had made their appetizer and main course selections, Stefàn turned his attention to Charisse. "Our food won't be ready for a while. Why don't we take a walk out on deck."

"Okay."

Rising, he stepped over and helped her from her chair. Taking her hand, he brought it to his lips and gently kissed it. "Sweet," he simply murmured.

Although the sun had not yet set, it was beginning its downward slide past the horizon. A warm breeze rose off the water, serenely fanning the couple as they moved to the stern of the vessel and stood near the deck railing.

"Did I tell you my parents are having a backyard barbecue tomorrow in my honor?" Charisse asked.

"No, you didn't. Sounds like it should be nice," Stefàn commented.

"You're going to come with me, right?"

"Would you like me to?

"Of course. That'll give you a chance to meet my family. They're all eager to meet you."

"What have you told them about me?" he skeptically questioned.

"I haven't really told them a lot. Myra's volunteered information about you to my mother, but she doesn't know you like I do, so there's not a lot of factual information she can give them."

"So, tell me something. What is it with Myra? I haven't seen her since that time two weeks ago at your house after Marsha and Dre's cookout, but she was pretty hostile toward me. You said she's trying to look out for you and all, but her attitude was a bit intense."

Charisse went on to explain a little about Myra's upbringing and the reasons for her strong distrust of men, in general. She told Stefan, "Don't take it personal. It's not really you."

"I take it she doesn't have a man?"

"No."

"It's no wonder with that attitude," Stefan said with a frown.

"She's really not so bad. She's more afraid of letting down her barriers than anything else. You have to get to know her," Charisse said, defending her friend.

"Well, I guess that'll happen with time." Changing the subject quickly, he said, "Julian wanted me to invite you to church with him and his ex-wife tomorrow. I told him we were going to your church."

"Oh, does he go to church regularly?" Charisse asked.

"Not really. He goes with Michele and L'il Jay from time to time, but not every Sunday."

"Do they go in Teaneck?"

"Yeah. First Baptist. It's the church they got married in."

"Do they date?" Charisse questioned.

Stefan chuckled. "I don't know what's up with them. I tell Dub all the time he and Michele should just get married again. They act like they're married anyway. They do everything with their son together. They're like this," he said, holding up two fingers in close ranks with one another.

Charisse smiled. "Why'd they break up?"

Stefan shook his head. "I don't know. They were both young when they got married and really, they only did it because she was pregnant. He said they were never really in love but they've always gotten along great. I don't know, Charisse. Julian and Michele are a mystery I can't explain."

"So, he's not serious about that girl, Robin, huh?" she asked.

"No, but they've been hanging out for a while. She's always been the sure bet if he wanted a date, but he's never gotten serious with her. Robin's like one of the guys."

Charisse laughed and added, "Well, I'd like to go with Julian and Michele tomorrow."

"You would?"

"Yes. They can come with us to the barbecue, too, if they want."

Injected with a sudden warmth, Stefan felt a surge of electricity in his heart at her thoughtful offer. As he gazed into her eyes, he felt his love for her swell to new proportions.

Charisse saw the intensity in his stare and shyly turned away to look off toward the horizon. "It's such a beautiful night," she softly uttered.

Not interested in viewing anything but her, he replied, "You told me orange was your favorite color but you didn't tell me how amazing it looks on you."

Charisse blushed. "You didn't tell me you were such a romantic."

"You inspire me, Charisse, in ways no woman ever has."

"Why?"

"Well, let's see. You're as smart as you are beautiful, as adventurous as you are spiritual, as crazy as you are serious." She frowned comically with this comparison but he continued. "And as sweet as maple syrup."

"That's all?" A mischievous smile played about her mouth.

Stefan laughed out loud. "No, that's not all. You, Miss Ellison, have caused me to look at myself and think about my life in a way I haven't in a very long time. You make me see that—although I can't really complain about the way my life's been going—I've been missing something."

"What do you think that is?" she asked, seriously wanting to know.

Stefan was slow to answer. Under his intense scrutinization, Charisse felt her body temperature begin to rise before he softly stated, "You."

Charisse didn't know how to respond verbally, but the power of that one word had her already rapidly beating heart, skipping.

Moving closer to bridge the tiny gap between them, Stefan whispered, "May I kiss you?"

Looking up into his eyes, she smiled. "I was wondering when you were going to get around to that."

His own smile lit his face. "I promise not to keep you waiting any longer."

Placing his hand under her chin, he gently raised her head and slowly lowered his until their mouths came together. Although already in four-inch heels, Charisse went up on her toes to afford him an easier time of reaching her eager lips. Fireworks exploded in her brain the instant their oral connection was made for his kiss was as sweet as honey. Pulling her closer until she was wrapped in his tender embrace, she felt him push his warm tongue into her mouth, devouring her completely, urgently, leaving no misconception about his yearning for her. Stefan's kiss, though gentle, was voracious and filled with passion; a raging inferno inside of him that burned for no one but Charisse. Her arms went around him and before she could even think about it, she was holding him as if her life depended on it. The feel of his strong, hard body pressed against hers set embers burning within her.

Seconds later, Stefan reluctantly pulled his head back, but kept his arms securely around her. Charisse's eyes were still closed, her lips slightly parted as though awaiting the continuation of their shared intimacy. When her lids slowly opened, he could see the mirror of his feelings in them.

The transformation from mere friends to soul-mates was now complete.

"Do you understand now why I waited so long to do that?" he gently asked.

"Yes," she breathlessly replied. She still hadn't recovered from his heady kiss.

"Do you believe in love at first sight, Charisse?"

"I do now," she sighed.

"Can you feel how my heart beats for you?" he warmly murmured.

"Yes."

"I love you, Charisse. I love everything about you. Will you let me show you?"

"Yes."

"I'm not the type of man you probably pictured yourself with, but…I need you to know I will do whatever it takes to prove to you I'm sincere. I feel like, in you, I've met the woman I'm supposed to spend the rest of my life with. No, that's not right. I know I have. I want to marry you, Charisse."

Her eyes widened in surprise at his declaration.

Before she could respond, he continued, "We've only known each other for three weeks, and you probably think I'm putting the cart before the horse, but I know what I feel and I've never felt this way before."

"I've never felt this way either, and that's what scares me about you sometimes," she admitted.

"Don't be afraid of me or of what you feel. I won't hurt you. I just want to love you."

"I want to be loved by you," she softly murmured. Returning her heels to the deck floor, Charisse rested her head against his beating heart. In a voice tinged with sadness, she whispered, "I knew it would be hard."

Stefan instinctively knew what she was referring to. His own desire for her flared red hot in his loins. If she hadn't already told him about her vow of abstinence, he would otherwise try to convince her to spend the night with him. But he loved and respected her far too much to ever try to sway her from her moral convictions simply to appease his own selfish nature— regardless of how recently she may have adopted them.

Again placing his hand under her chin, he raised her head and said, "Charisse, I'm not going to make it hard for you to sustain your promise. There is so much more that I love about you than what we could share physically," he said and lightly brushed his lips across hers. "I don't have a problem waiting until we're married, because we *will* be married and when I make love to you, it will be forever."

"Do you really want us to get married?" she asked.

"Absolutely. If you'll have me."

She felt tears coming to her eyes. "I will. I mean, I do. I mean, I want to be your wife."

Their lips came together again, though briefly. "I love you, Stefan," she breathed.

"And I, you, Charisse." Placing a tender kiss on her forehead, he reluctantly released her.

Noticing that their server had delivered the wine they'd ordered, Stefan took her hand as he said, "Let's have a toast to celebrate our love."

August 6th

All praises to my Lord and Savior, Jesus Christ.

Thank You. Thank You. Thank You, Father, for the best birthday I have ever had. You have blessed me in so many ways I cannot even count them all, and You keep blessing me. I just spent the most amazing evening with Stefan. You put us together for a reason, Lord, and I believe I know what that reason is. I have prayed many times for someone to love and for someone to love me. He wants to marry me. He's willing to wait for me. He promised he would never try to compromise me or make me forsake my vow of abstinence. He loves me more than that, he says. I can feel his love when he looks at me, when he touches my hand, when he puts his arms around me and when he kisses me. I knew when I made the vow that the true test would come when I met someone I care deeply for and was faced with their willingness to respect my position. Thank You, Father, for sending me Stefan. Also, because he has been away from the church for so long, but has now willingly returned with me and is trying to learn more about You and about all You do for all of us. I've only recently returned and am beginning to understand and live for Christ, but with Stefan I think we can grow in Christ together. What I know, I can teach him. He wants to understand. What I don't know, we can learn together. Thank You, Father. Thank You for blessing me with this wonderful man.

CHAPTER 16
MEET THE PARENTS

Once they had all gone home and changed from their church clothes to more casual attire, Julian and Michele met up with Stefan and Charisse and followed them to her parents' home in Springfield Gardens, Queens. It was almost two p.m. when they walked into the spacious backyard of the elder Ellisons. Already in attendance and scattered around the yard were Charisse's older brothers, David and Johnny and their families, Star and her daughters, Christina and Candice, Myra (who had been picked up by David), her cousin, Jewel with Terry, and several other of her relatives.

John Ellison was at the grill, turning a slab of ribs when Charisse walked up and hugged him from behind. "Hi, Daddy."

"Hey, baby girl! Happy birthday! I was wondering when you were going to get here." Putting down the fork he'd been using, he turned and gave her a big hug, lifting her off her feet, and kissed her cheek.

Charisse giggled as she always did when her father gave her one of his bear hugs. "Thanks, Daddy." She turned to Stefan then and said, "You remember Stefan, right? From Jewel's wedding."

"Of course, I do. How are you, son?" John asked with a genuine smile as he reached out to shake Stefan's hand.

"I'm good, Mr. Ellison. How've you been?" Stefan asked.

"Can't complain. I knew I'd see you again."

Stefan smiled and looked to Charisse for her reaction. She merely blushed.

"Mr. Ellison, these are our friends, Julian and Michele and their son, L'il Jay," Stefàn stated, making the introductions.

"Hello." John greeted them cheerfully, shaking Julian's, Michele's and L'il Jay's hands in turn. "Welcome. Make yourselves at home. There's plenty to eat and drink."

"We have a case of sodas and Coronas in my trunk," Julian said. "I'll run and get them real quick."

"Thank you, Julian, but you didn't have to do that," John said.

Julian shrugged. "No big deal, Mr. Ellison. That's how we do it." He turned to start back to his car.

"Listen, you all call me John or Johnny. Except you, little man," he said, addressing L'il Jay. "You call me Uncle Johnny, okay?"

"Okay," L'il Jay said with a bashful smile.

"Where's Mommy?" Charisse asked.

"Inside. She's putting the finishing touches on the potato salad," her father answered.

Grabbing Stefàn's hand, Charisse said, "Come on. I want you to meet my mother. C'mon, Michele. I'll introduce y'all to everybody else, later."

Stepping through the back door of the house, Charisse and company came directly into the dining room. Moving immediately to her right and into the kitchen, she found her mother and her maternal grandmother. Both women were steadily working on their respective dishes.

"Granny Nan! Hi!" Charisse called as she hurried over to her grandmother and gave her a big kiss. "How you doin'?"

"Hi, sweetie pie. I'm good. How are you?"

"Fine."

"Happy birthday."

"Thank you. Hi, Mommy."

"Hi. Happy birthday," Mrs. Ellison said as she reached out to hug her daughter.

"Thank you. Mommy, Granny, this is Stefan and Michele and L'il Jay."

Stefan reached out to shake Mrs. Ellison's hand first and also leaned in and kissed her cheek. "Hello, Mrs. Ellison, it's a pleasure to finally meet you."

"Likewise, Stefan. I've heard a lot about you."

"I hope some of it was good," he stated.

"Most of it," she said with a mischievous grin.

"Hello…" Stefan paused, unsure of how to address Charisse's grandmother.

She immediately answered his concern. "You can call me Granny Nan, just like everybody else, hon."

He smiled at the handsome elderly woman as he extended his hand. When she took it, he leaned in and kissed her cheek, as well. "It is a pleasure to meet you, Granny Nan."

After greeting Michele and her son, Granny Nan turned her attention back to Stefan. "So you're my granddaughter's young man, eh?"

"Yes, ma'am," he said as he smiled over at Charisse.

"He's a looker, Risi," she said.

"I know." She laughed along with Michele and Barbara.

"Thank you."

"We're gonna have to have a talk later," she told him.

"Yes, ma'am. Whenever you're ready."

"Mrs. Ellison, can I help you do anything?" Michele asked.

"Oh, no, thank you, sweetheart. And, please, call me Barbara. You take your son outside and relax. We'll be out in a minute. Charisse take Jay outside and introduce him to your nieces and nephews. There's plenty of children here for you to play with, honey."

"Okay," he shyly replied.

IT WAS CLOSE TO SIX O'CLOCK WHEN STEFÀN DECIDED it was time for him and Myra to have a heart-to-heart talk about Charisse. He had already encountered Charisse's brothers, having played a few games of bid whist with them, during which time they'd tried their best to intimidate him. Soon seeing that their attempts were fruitless, they conceded that maybe this fellow wasn't so bad for their younger sister after all.

Stefàn had also had a very intense conversation with Granny Nan and decided right after their conversation began that he was crazy about her. She had a wonderful sense of humor, while simultaneously letting him know that Charisse was not to be toyed with. "She's my youngest grandchild, although I have several great-grands who are younger than her. But from my own children, she's the youngest and has always been—don't tell anybody this—my favorite. She's always had a heart of gold, and has made some bad decisions with regards to the men in her life because she can sometimes be naïve. But she's not stupid—not by a long shot—and I won't stand for you taking advantage of her now that she's given her heart to God."

"Granny Nan," Stefàn assured her, "I will never take advantage of her. Charisse means more to me than I can explain. She has impacted my life in a way no one ever has, and I plan to make her my wife. I have to. I know how precious she is, and I'd be a fool to let so beautiful a woman get away. And one thing I've never been is a fool. You won't ever have to worry about her as long as she's with me. I'd give my life to keep her safe and happy."

Since he and Myra had history through Charisse, although they'd only seen each other twice, he had no misconceptions about what she thought of him. Despite Charisse's explanations for her cool demeanor, Stefàn felt a need to explain himself to Myra. He understood her skepticism regarding his association with her best friend. Unwittingly shielding his heart from a love structured in truth, prior to meeting Charisse he had been out there taking full advantage of all the opportunities thrown his way by the women he met. His only concern had been his own pleasure and happiness. But Charisse had changed all of that without even trying. Stefan he had made a one hundred and eighty degree turn in his life. Anyone who knew him and knew the way he used to live would likely be skeptical, too. If he were on the outside looking in at someone else, he would have his own doubts about their sincerity in light of such a drastic change.

Knowing how close the women were, and that with Charisse in his life, he would regularly have contact with Myra, he didn't want there to be any friction between them. He wanted her to know his intentions toward Charisse were genuine. Stefan wanted them to be friends, at least as much as she would allow them to be, but he wanted to be the one to offer the olive branch so she would know his heart was true.

Charisse's sister-in-law had been sitting with Myra, but when she walked away, Stefan took the opportunity to approach.

Coming from her rear, he said, "Hey, Myra. Mind if I join you?"

Looking up at Stefan, she shrugged indifferently and said, "No, help yourself."

Taking the seat Suzette had just vacated, Stefan pulled it a little closer to Myra and asked, "Are you enjoying yourself?"

"Yes. Are you?"

"Oh yeah. Charisse's family is great. I think they like me."

"So you've managed to pull the wool over their eyes, too, huh?"

"Now, see, that wasn't nice," he said, looking squarely into her eyes.

Unable to hold his gaze, she looked away in embarrassment. "You're right, that wasn't very nice. I apologize."

"Apology accepted."

They sat silently for the next minute or so until Stefan said, "I really do love her, Myra."

"You don't even know her."

Leaning forward to emphasize his point, he told her, "I know her well enough to know that I want to learn everything there is to know about her and do whatever I have to do to be in her life and to have her in mine. I also know enough about her to know that she loves you and that she'd be happy if we tried to be friends." When Myra didn't respond, he continued, "Can we be friends, Myra?"

"Will you tell me something?"

"Anything."

"What's up with that woman at your friend's cookout? The one who stuck her tongue in your ear?"

Stefan reared back and frowned as if in pain. "Nothing! The only thing that woman can do for me is let me sell her a house. There was never anything between us. I only met her that day. Even if I wasn't in love with Charisse, I wouldn't pursue her. She's too old."

"You were flirting with a lot of women that day. Charisse was very upset with you."

He hung his head and softly stated, "I was a jerk that day. I explained to Charisse that the only reason I was acting out like that was because I was afraid of her."

Myra looked skeptically out of the corner of her eye at him.

Stefan smiled. "I know how that sounds, but it's the truth. Charisse had had such an impact on me that she scared the devil out of me. I needed to…. I couldn't let her see that she had me so shook up."

"So what's changed?"

"I realized how ridiculous I was acting and that if I didn't check myself, I'd lose any opportunity I might have to get to know her."

"She's very sensitive, Stefàn, and doesn't know how to love half-way. When she gives herself, she gives her whole self, so when her heart is broken, she's devastated," Myra felt the need to tell him.

"I won't break her heart, Myra. I'll protect it. I love her with every ounce of my being. She's the most important person in my life and all I want to do is spend every day proving that to her."

Myra stared into Stefàn's unwavering eyes for the next few seconds with neither of them uttering a word. Folding her arms across her chest, she very quietly stated, "You know, Charisse has always been more of a sister to me than my natural sisters have ever been and I worry about her. She believes God put you in her life for a reason, and while I have my own issues with God, I know how happy she seems to be now that you're together."

"She makes me feel like… I feel like I can do anything because she loves me," he said in tone filled with wonder.

"I believe you," Myra admitted.

Feeling as though the thick block of ice that had been separating them since they'd met was beginning to melt, Stefàn took a chance and broached a subject he figured would probably be more uncomfortable than Myra would admit. "Why are you so angry, Myra?"

Caught off guard by his question, Myra jerked her head and shot a venomous look his way. "What?"

"I didn't stutter," he calmly replied.

Indignation colored her face, but she was unable to hide the fact that he'd broken through her previously impenetrable barricade of protective self-righteousness. Nevertheless, she was determined not to answer his question. As far as she was concerned, it was none of his business.

CHERYL FAYE

The two sat in silence for the next several minutes until Stefan compassionately asked, "Who hurt you?"

"What makes you think anyone hurt me?" she agitatedly responded.

"Because you're too beautiful a woman to be so cynical about men. And it's just about men because I've seen how you interact with women. You're protecting yourself, and the way you were coming at me was to protect Charisse. That fierce protectiveness comes from being a victim; from being hurt. Take my word for it; I've been there. Charisse is the one who freed me."

"What do you mean?" Myra asked, her curiosity piqued by his seeming transparency.

Despite knowing the root of her temperament due to Charisse's confiding the truth to him yesterday, Stefan didn't expect that Myra would open up to him if he didn't first expose himself to her. That being the case, he told her about Janine.

Listening as Stefan explained how he was ultimately responsible for the heartbreak he endured by the first woman he had ever loved, and how he had built a wall around his heart to prevent anyone else from ever having the opportunity to break it again, moved Myra to tears.

"I grew up in a family full of men who use women at their whim. My father did it to my mother, my brothers do it to their women, and they did it to our mother before she died, too. All of the men who've ever been close to me have hurt me, so forgive me if I have a hard time when I see a man trying to grin up in my face or hear him throwing meaningless compliments in the hopes of getting in my pants, or my friends' pants, for that matter," she testily stated.

Sympathetic to her feelings, Stefan tenderly remarked, "I'm sorry that's how you grew up, but all men aren't like that, Myra."

"You were."

"I was, but I'm not representative of all men. Don't judge the whole barrel by a few bad apples. I know plenty of good men who know how to treat a woman to make her feel like she's the most important thing in their world. Believe me, I've done plenty of women wrong because of my own issues, but even I'm not that man anymore thanks to Charisse. Don't let what your father and brothers did to your mother or you color your view about all men. You'll miss the man God created for you."

"God?" she questioned in puzzlement.

Stefan chuckled. "Yeah, God, 'cause it could've only been Him who gave Charisse to me."

"Hey, what are you two talking about?" Charisse asked as she approached them from behind.

Stefan smiled and looked up at her as he reached for her hand. "You."

"I hope it was good," she said, looking at Myra.

Pulling Charisse down on his lap, he told her, "How could it be anything but?" Kissing her softly on her ear, he said, "Right, Myra?"

"It was all right," she said with a mischievous grin.

"So, you mean you two weren't fighting over me?" Charisse asked teasingly.

Stefan laughed and Myra couldn't help but chuckle. "No, we've put down our guns."

"Hey, I was never armed. I was ambushed," Stefan stated with a smile in Myra's direction.

"Touché."

CHAPTER 17
TIMES MARCHES ON

Over the course of the next several months, Stefan's and Charisse's love for one another grew without bounds.

Having decided there was nothing he wouldn't do to prove his love for Charisse was true, Stefan made a conscious effort to understand the root of her faith. In so doing, he experienced an awakening of his own.

He and Charisse began attending services every week at First Baptist Church after their initial visit with Julian and Michele. Several weeks later, Charisse made the decision to transfer her membership from New Covenant Baptist Church in New York to First Baptist for several reasons. Primarily, because she felt a stronger connection to the pastor and congregation there. The fact that it was closer to home played a major role in her decision, too, but she was largely influenced by how much Stefan enjoyed attending services there.

During that time, he came to know Christ for himself. After three months of attending Sunday services and weekly Bible study with Charisse, Stefan made the decision to give his life to Christ.

The Sunday before Thanksgiving, he picked her up at the usual time but she noticed that he seemed quite pensive from the moment he greeted her.

Inquiring about his uncharacteristic silence, Stefan simply responded, "I'm okay, Risi. I've got some stuff on my mind that I'm trying to work out."

Concerned about his demeanor, since she felt no tension from him directed at her, she decided not to push him. She figured if he wanted to discuss what was on his mind, he would.

The sermon that Pastor Young brought that morning was entitled, *When God Calls, Do You Answer?*

Stefan listened intently as the speaker outlined the diverse ways God speaks to His people. Pastor Young also made plain the multitudinous manners of avoidance we use to bypass God's explicit commands.

When his sermon was over, Charisse noticed that there were tears streaming down Stefan's face. She reached over and took his hand, then bowed her head and silently prayed that he might be comforted in the knowledge that whatever load was laying heavy on his heart, God could lighten it.

When Pastor Young offered the congregants an opportunity to answer God's call and become a part of the fellowship of First Baptist, Charisse felt Stefan pull his hand from her grasp. Opening her eyes, she found his gaze fixed on her.

"He's calling me, Risi." With that, he rose from his seat and made his way down the aisle to the waiting deacons.

When he rose during that Sunday's invitational, her resounding joy was second only to what she felt by knowing Christ for herself. His baptism took place two weeks before Christmas.

Having developed a relationship with Charisse's family from the start through his honesty, sense of humor, and devotion to Charisse, Stefan was always very relaxed in their presence. As was his way, Stefan had easily charmed Barbara Ellison, but when he learned that she frequently baked his favorite dessert, German chocolate cake, he was smitten.

When Charisse met Stefan's parents and siblings, she was welcomed into his family with open arms. It had been so long since Stefàn had brought a woman home for his parents to meet that they knew, despite his having already told them, that Charisse was "the one." Damaris Cooper noted the way Stefàn gazed at Charisse when she wasn't looking or when she was in conversation with someone else. Mike noticed the way his son spoke her name. Devin teased Stefàn mercilessly. "Whatever happened to, 'I ain't never gettin' married! I got too many females wanna sample this.' I remember you saying that to me; wasn't that long ago either."

Stefàn's response was a shrug. "Yeah, but I hadn't met Charisse yet."

Nikki and Charisse hit it off right away. After realizing they had very similar taste in clothing, they made plans to go shopping together.

Upon becoming a member of the church, Stefàn became active in the church's ministries. Two that he immediately joined were the Junior Basketball League and Upward and Onward, a ministry dedicated to preparing young people for corporate America. Being the avid sports enthusiast he was, as well as an excellent basketball player, Stefàn was eager to participate in the League. Although, ideally, he would have preferred coaching the boys, he was assigned as assistant coach to the girls' team. They took to him right away, too. Aside from all of the girls feeling he was the finest coach they'd ever had, he was extremely patient with them, and brought out talents in them they were not even aware they had.

As a part of Upward and Onward, Stefàn brought his knowledge of business and real estate to the fold. Owning real estate, both as a resident and as a landlord, he was able to offer precious insight on the same. He also encouraged Charisse to participate in the ministry as her accounting skills would be invaluable in giving these young people a leg up on the business world.

Following a conversation with one of the deacons where Stefàn had divulged his expertise in the martial arts, he was asked to lead a self-defense seminar that the church had been considering for some time.

Outside of the church, Stefan and Charisse spent countless hours together. Charisse began working out with Stefan on a regular basis, whether it was at the health club they learned they were both members of, or in the alternative, Stefan's makeshift workout room. He taught her how to use free weights in her training and soon, visible signs of her efforts were evident. Already possessing a shapely physique, Charisse's body now exhibited muscular definition not previously obvious.

They both enjoyed the theater and eating out, so at every opportunity, they indulged their passion. Another activity they shared was shopping. Each of them loved fine clothing and spared no expense when purchasing their attire. Once they had learned each other's clothing sizes, they never hesitated to buy a garment or accessory they admired for the other. They were essentially inseparable.

True to his word, too, Stefan never pressured Charisse to become intimate with him, regardless of how much he wanted to make love to her. On one occasion, however, Charisse had succumbed to her own physical yearnings.

It was right after their first argument. When they had cleared the air and each had expressed what their respective issues had been during their somewhat heated exchange—looking to the Bible for guidance—they both acknowledged that in a different time in their lives, they would have handled it all very differently.

After making up, they'd snuggled on Charisse's sofa to watch a movie. Before long, they were kissing. Sensuous, singsong moans harmonized with spellbinding shivers of anticipation, as their kisses became deeper and hands began to roam and explore each other's bodies. Soon, they were horizontal, with Charisse on top. Stefan's arousal was evident and Charisse could not pull herself away from the feeling of his hard body beneath hers. Quickly realizing that things were getting out of control as they neared a pleasurable brink they both wanted to cross, Stefan pushed her away.

"What's wrong?" she asked.

"Sweetie, you have to get up."

Charisse groaned. "No, please, Stefan."

"Honey, if you don't get up, we might end up doing something you'll regret later and I don't want you to do that."

"But I want you," she heatedly sighed and attempted to kiss him again.

Turning away, he said, "I know, Risi, and I want you, too. You have no idea how much so. But not like this. We agreed we would wait, right?"

She looked away from him and didn't respond.

"Right?" he repeated.

"Right," she grumbled.

Assisting her, then sitting himself up in an uncompromising position, Stefan placed his arm around her shoulder and pulled her close. "I love you, Charisse, and I so want to love you like that but think of how much better it will be if we wait. I know with everything that's just happened…." Pausing briefly, he kissed her temple then continued. "I want our first time together to be as husband and wife. You mean that much to me." Chuckling, he stated, "A few months ago, I would have been all for us getting busy, but I realize how very special making love with you will be and I can't do it like I have in the past. Not with you, baby."

"I'm sorry," she mumbled sadly, feeling as if she had broken her vow.

"Oh, sweetie, don't apologize. I know how you feel; I feel the same way. The physical attraction between us has always been there, right from the start. But this is me, you don't ever have to apologize for feeling the way you do. Believe me, I understand and God does, too."

"I love you so much, Stefân."

Again, he softly kissed her temple and whispered, "And I love you, too, Risi, more than I've ever loved anyone."

"Thank you for being so strong when I'm not."

"That's what we have to be for each other. When I'm weak, you're strong and you pull me through. It's only fair that I should do the same for you."

That night, Charisse got on her knees and prayed for forgiveness, but she also thanked God for all that Stefân had become in his life and hers.

IN THE MONTHS PRECEDING THE HOLIDAY SEASON, several changes took place in the lives of Julian and Myra, as well.

Julian ended his association with Robin for good when she betrayed his trust in an inexcusable manner.

She had spent a particular Friday night in late September with Julian and they had tickets to see a play the following Saturday evening. Julian had earlier made plans to meet Stefân and a couple of their friends at a nearby basketball court Saturday morning to play ball for a couple of hours. He had known Robin for so long that he trusted her to stay alone in his home until he returned.

Whenever Julian went to the courts, he always carried a towel and a dry shirt to change into because he didn't like sitting on the leather seats of his car in wet, sweaty clothing. He left his house that morning and had driven a third of the way to the park when he realized that he'd forgotten his towel and shirt. As such, he'd turned the car around and headed back. Opening the door to his house, he hadn't bothered to close it since he would be turning around and leaving immediately. He could hear that the Bose radio in the living room was still tuned to the same station he'd been listening to in his car. Hurrying up the stairs to his bedroom, he'd been appalled to find Robin going through his dresser drawers, specifically one where he kept his financial records. She'd been so engrossed in reading his private papers that she hadn't even heard him come in.

"Find what you were looking for?" Julian quietly asked, despite the fact that he was seething at being violated in this manner.

Startled beyond compare, Robin's hands flew up and the papers she had been reading left her hands and fluttered to the floor. "Julian—" she began to explain.

"Get out of my house," Julian demanded in the same calm manner.

"But, I was just—" she tried to tell him.

"I don't want to hear it. Just leave. Get your things and get out of my house. Don't bother calling me either, 'cause there's nothing you could ever tell me to explain this."

"But how am I supposed to get home?" Robin had asked.

"You should have thought about that before you started rifling through my drawers."

With Robin completely out of the picture, Julian began devoting all of his time to Michele and L'il Jay. Instead of the occasional occurrence of attending Sunday services with Michele and their son, Julian began accompanying them each week. Often while L'il Jay was in the children's Sunday school class, Julian and Michele would sit with Charisse and Stefàn during the service in the sanctuary.

Always possessing an endless affection for Michele, Julian found himself really falling in love with her for the first time. He began to court her much like in the days before they were married. Julian, although having always been the more serious of the two when it came to love and relationships, admired Stefân's commitment to Charisse. While proud of the growth Stefân had experienced in the past months and grateful to Charisse for inspiring it, Julian realized something more important. His own God-chosen woman had been in his life for years and he had not recognized it, nor was he doing what he should to insure she stayed there. That being the case, he set out to rectify that situation.

Also during this time, Julian took a chance he had been dreaming about for several years and purchased a McDonald's franchise in Piscataway, New Jersey. He had always wanted to go into business for himself and with encouragement from his best friend and hope-fully future wife, Michele, he stepped out on faith and did it.

FOR MYRA, ROMANCE CAME IN THE FORM of a "knight-in-shining-armor."

One Tuesday evening in October, as she walked from her salon on One Hundred and Eighty-third Street to the subway that would take her to Brooklyn and home, Myra was the victim of a purse snatcher.

She seldom took the four-block walk to the subway by herself, especially after dark. She would usually take a cab or one of her workers would drop her off. Although the neighborhood was not one of the best in The Bronx, it would never be considered one of the worst either. On this particular night, Myra was the last to leave the salon because she had stayed behind to reconcile her books. She was meeting with Charisse, her accountant, the very next day; it was time to pay her quarterly taxes on her business.

At a few minutes before ten, she started her walk and never considered that she might be in any danger. She'd grown up in this neighborhood, after all. Many of the residents were familiar to her from her childhood.

Myra was a block and a half from the train station when she realized that she was being followed. She didn't know where the person trailing her had come from and initially paid them little attention until she realized the distance between them had shortened. As her heart began to race with anxiety, Myra picked up her pace. When she passed in front of a large apartment building she briefly considered detouring into it, but was afraid she'd get caught without a way inside. Cursing her decision to wear a dress and heels to the salon that day, she longed for her sneakers and jeans.

Deciding to cross the street despite the entrance to the subway being only a few yards ahead of her, as she moved to the curb, the thief ran up behind her, knocked her off balance, snatched her pocketbook and took off running. Falling hard, Myra skinned her knee and the heel of her left hand as she reached out to prevent any major damage. She cried out in anger and pain and struggled to control the tears she felt coming to her eyes.

It seemed as if only seconds had passed before the man reached for her and asked, "Miss, are you all right?"

Frightened by his sudden appearance, Myra recoiled in fear and cried, "Leave me alone!"

"No, it's okay. I got him. Here's your purse." Sure enough, in his hand was her pocketbook. She saw that the strap had been cut.

It was then that she looked up into the man's face. He was gorgeous. Suddenly, she was embarrassed. Instead of reaching for her pocketbook that he still held out to her, she tried to smooth her dress and get to her feet. He immediately offered his assistance.

"Are you okay?"

She nodded quickly and tried to stand before she realized that the heel of one of her shoes had broken off. Completely mortified, she began to cry.

The man put his arms around her and tried to calm her. His touch was gentle and although he was a total stranger, Myra felt safe in his arms.

"Where is he?" she moaned against his strong chest.

"He's not going anywhere. I saw him when he hit you, but he didn't see me. He's laid out. The cops are on their way."

Reluctantly pulling away from him, Myra noticed his jacket. "I got blood on you. I'm sorry."

Remembering her slight injuries, she looked first at her hand, then down at her knee; the pain began with her realization.

"Don't worry about it. Let me see." He reached for her hand. Moving under the street light for a better view, he examined her wound. "It's not too bad. Looks like it stings a bit though, huh?"

She nodded.

"You live around here?"

"No, I live in Brooklyn. I was on my way to the train station."

"You're a long way from home. What are you doing around here? I mean, if I'm not being too personal."

He again handed her pocketbook to her and this time she took it as she answered, "I own a hair salon a few blocks from here. I was on my way home."

Suddenly lights were flashing and the burp of a siren sounded as two police cars pulled up near where they were standing.

The man she was standing with immediately presented a badge and called out, "He's laid out between the van and the Lexus over there."

One officer came over to them and the three others headed in the direction he'd pointed. "What happened?" the officer asked.

"He knocked her down and grabbed her purse," he explained.

"Who are you?"

"Barretto Martinez, New York State Court Officer. I live up the street."

"Your name, Miss?"

"Myra Lopez," she shakily answered. "I have a salon a few blocks from here and was walking to the subway when he ran up behind me."

"Are you okay?" the officer asked.

"Yeah, I guess," she answered as she once again examined her hand.

"We'll need you to come to the station to give a statement."

"Okay."

"She needs some first aid," Barretto firmly stated. "Do you have a kit in your car?"

The cop looked as if he was offended by Barretto's tone, but shrugged. "Yeah. Come have a seat in the squad car."

When she started limping toward the car, Barretto asked, "Do you have another pair of shoes in your shop?"

"Yeah, but it's three blocks away," she moaned.

"We'll have them take you by there before we go to the station."

"You're coming, too?"

"Of course. They're going to need a statement from me, too, since I knocked him out."

"What did you hit him with?"

"I gave him a chop at his throat. Took the wind right out of him."

They were at the squad car and Barretto helped her into the back seat, although she sat with her legs out of the car. The policeman had a first aid kit in his hand, which Barretto promptly relieved him of. Without hesitation, he removed the needed equipment, squatted before her and skillfully began to clean the wound on Myra's knee.

"I never thanked you for what you did," she suddenly said to him.

He looked up at her with a smile. When he tenderly said, "De nada, preciosa," Myra noticed for the first time, the deep, melodious timbre of his voice.

She fell under his spell in that moment. He was the most beautiful creature she had ever seen. His golden-honey beige face was without blemish and his kissable lips were surrounded by a soft peach-fuzz mustache and goatee. She guessed he stood about six feet tall and probably weighed about two hundred pounds. As he squatted before her, she could see the outline of his muscular thighs. His hands were large and strong, but gentle as he tended to her sore knee. His jet black hair was cut close but was naturally wavy. Deep set, chocolate brown eyes were hooded by thick, dark eyebrows and projected his strength and his tenderness.

Barretto rode with her in the back of the police squad car, but sensing her nervousness refrained from conversation. However, he asked the officer driving to stop by her salon so she could change her shoes. When the officer started to balk, Barretto stated, "Come on, guy. Would you have your sister hobbling around with a broken shoe for the next couple of hours when she doesn't have to? Her store is only a block or so out of the way."

Myra could tell the cop was tired of Barretto. His commanding personality, while irritating the officer, endeared her to him even more. The policeman made the requested detour. "Gracias," Myra sweetly whispered to Barretto. His response was a wink.

Although the ride from her salon to the police station was a short one, she felt his eyes on her the entire time. *If only I had met him under some other circumstance*, she thought.

It was almost two hours later when Myra was finally able to leave the police station. The detective she had given her statement to offered her a ride to Brooklyn but she declined. She called a taxi service. Barretto walked her outside and waited until her car came.

"You gonna be all right making it home by yourself?" he asked as they waited.

"Yes." There were so many other things she wanted to say to him, but having him stand so close made her heart race. Finally, she gathered her courage and told him, "I don't know what I would have done if you hadn't come along. My keys to my shop and everything else is in this bag."

"I happened to be in the right place at the right time. I'm glad I was able to be of assistance," he humbly stated.

"You were a life saver," she said.

A dark blue Lincoln Continental pulled up alongside of them. The passenger side front window slid down and the driver leaned over. "Somebody going to Brooklyn?"

"I am," Myra replied.

Barretto stepped in front of her and opened the rear passenger door for her. "I'm sorry we didn't meet under better circumstances," he said, voicing her earlier thought.

"Me, too." Myra then asked, "How are you getting home? We can drop you off."

"It's not that far. I can walk it."

"No. Come on, we'll drop you off," she said and reached for his hand, refusing to take no for an answer.

Barretto smiled and acquiesced.

When the car pulled up in front of his building, he said to the driver, "My man, get this lady home safely. She's had enough excitement for one day."

"No problem," the guy answered.

He then offered his hand to Myra, "Buenas noches, bonita."

"Gracias." Myra blushed but leaned over and kissed his cheek. "Usted es mi caballero en armadura brillante."

Barretto smiled and exited the car.

As it drove away, Myra looked out the rear window. Barretto waved at her and for the first time in many years, Myra said a heartfelt prayer. "El Dios, déjame por favor verlo otra vez."

In the days immediately following her ordeal, Myra could do nothing but think of Barretto Martinez. No man had ever occupied her mind with such undeniable persistence. When she met with Charisse the next day and recounted everything that had happened, she excitedly told of how she boldly kissed him when he left her, stunning Charisse as never before.

"You kissed him?"

"I had to. Risi, you had to be there. He was wonderful. I could tell the cop was getting sick of Barretto giving him orders, like when he told him to take me to change my shoes. He was so commanding, but when he looked at me and talked to me, he was so gentle."

"So did you give him your number?" Charisse eagerly asked.

"No. He didn't ask for it," Myra said with a tinge of sadness.

"You should have slipped it in his pocket or something."

"He knows where the shop is. Maybe he'll come by there. Or maybe he didn't ask for it because he's married."

"Did you see a ring?"

"No, but that doesn't mean anything," Myra said. "Lots of married men don't wear rings." After a few seconds of silence, Myra lamented, "I'll probably never see him again."

"I'll say a prayer that you do," Charisse told her cheerfully.

The following Saturday, Myra's and Charisse's prayers were answered.

Unable to get the beautiful chica he had assisted off his mind,

Barretto decided to take a walk up to her salon. Although he'd been by there with her that night and saw that the salon was fairly large, he was altogether stunned when he saw the place bustling with activity. Hesitating briefly before entering, he eventually did so and walked up to the reception desk. A cheerful young Latina wearing too much makeup immediately greeted him.

"Buenos dias, señor. May I help you?"

"Si. I was wondering if the owner is in?"

"Oh, Myra? She's in her office. ¿Su nombre?"

"Diga su Barry."

"Uno momento," the girl said and instantly reached for the telephone on her desk. Seconds later, she announced, "Alguien Barry nombrado está aquí para usted, Myra." Pause. "No sé, él no dijo." Pause. "Muy bien, uno momento." Turning her attention to him, she asked, "Barry, who?"

"Barretto Martinez. We met a few days ago."

Into the receiver, she said, "Barretto…. Muy bien." She hung up the phone and said, "She'll be right out."

"Gracias." Barretto turned away from the desk and looked into the shop. Every chair was filled with women either getting their hair or nails done. There were even a few chairs in the back where women were having work done on their feet. The waiting area was packed, too, and the noise of women's voices speaking in both English and Spanish clashed with the reggaeton song coming from a hidden source. He noticed that numerous pairs of eyes seemed to covertly study him and he briefly felt as if he was under inspection.

Then he saw her coming from the back of the salon in his direction. Quickly surveying her beauty, her long brown hair was out, falling freely over her shoulders. She was wearing a pair of faded blue jeans that were molded to her small but shapely bottom.

A t-shirt with the very fitting words, "Latin Beauty," spelled out in rhinestones across her voluptuous breasts, was tucked smoothly into the waistband of her jeans and outlined her hourglass physique. Barretto felt an involuntary tightness in his chest at the sight of her.

"Hi!" She greeted him cheerily and reached out to hug him. "I'm sorry I didn't realize who you were right away."

Welcoming and returning her embrace, he answered, "That's okay. How are you?"

"I'm great! How are you?"

Smiling, he replied, "Pretty good. I thought I'd come by and see how you were. You've got quite a busy place here." He was genuinely impressed.

"Thanks. I have another salon across town. My cousin runs it for me. I don't know nothing about doing hair," Myra flippantly stated with a wave of her hand. "I just handle the money."

Barretto laughed. "Well, hey, that's what it's all about, right?"

"Yeah."

They stood awkwardly silent for the next few seconds.

"So, what's up?" Myra finally asked.

"Oh, I was wondering if you'd like to go out sometime? You know, to dinner or a movie or something?" Barretto asked, feeling suddenly tentative.

"I'd love to," Myra answered immediately.

"You would?"

"Yes. Actually, you should let me take you to dinner since you rescued me," Myra added.

He chuckled. "Oh, no, I couldn't let you do that."

"What? Take you to dinner?"

"Yeah. Especially as payback," he said.

"Well, I figured, it's the least I could do."

"You don't owe me anything for that. I couldn't stand there and watch what that guy did to you and do nothing."

"Well, I really appreciate you being there for me. I'll never forget it," she said as she smiled up at him.

Barretto fell under her spell at that moment.

During their first date later that very day, they each revealed more about themselves to one another than they ever would have in the past. She talked about her family and her upbringing, being completely honest about her cynicism and fear with regard to men. He revealed how only months earlier he had caught the woman he had been engaged to marry cheating in his own apartment and how he'd sworn never to give his heart again. Making it clear that neither of them was in any hurry to get into anything heavy, they decided to take things slow and let nature take its course.

MYRA AND BARRETTO HAD BEEN DATING for a little over a month when they were invited to Charisse's house for a dinner party. To everyone's surprise, Barretto, Stefan and Devin knew one another. Barretto and Stefan had competed against each other in several martial arts tournaments during their late-teens. Neither could say one had bested the other because they'd each been victorious during their various competitions. There was a mutual respect that was evident when they were reacquainted and they spent much of the evening talking about the early days of competing.

With Myra's new relationship, Charisse noticed a positive change in her friend. Aside from the welcomed reduction in her usual cynicism toward men, she became more free-spirited. Barretto taught Myra how to drive and with her newfound knowledge, she wasted no time getting her driver's license and buying herself a car. Conveniently, there was a garage a block away from her salon on Tremont Avenue, where she immediately reserved a monthly space so she could drive back and forth from Brooklyn to her shops. Getting from one salon to the other, she simply hailed a cab or used the cross-town bus. Her involvement with Barretto opened up a whole new world to Myra and the glow of her happiness showed on her face, in the way she carried herself and the way she related to people, in general.

B y the Advent season, Charisse and Stefan had been dating steadily for almost five months. On several occasions before then, they had discussed their future together, specifically, the type of marriage ceremony they wanted, where they would like to spend their honeymoon, how many children, and so forth. They even talked about going into business together—literally, becoming their own bosses. Stefan reasoned that with his real estate acumen and her accounting knowledge, they could invest in the real estate market and make a killing.

On Christmas, however, Stefan planned to put into action all they had talked about in the past.

It had been Stefan's idea for them to host Christmas dinner at his house since it was the larger of their two homes. Although they had spent the Thanksgiving holiday between each of their families, they didn't want to have to rush from one to the other so no one would be slighted. To Stefan's thinking, this would afford everyone the opportunity to be together on Christmas day, as well as be witnesses to his surprise.

Their parents had met earlier when Stefan threw a barbecue over the Labor Day weekend, and had hit it off immediately. Barbara and Damaris assisted Charisse in preparing the dinner menu for Christmas.

Between both families, there were over twenty people in attendance, including nieces and nephews. Myra and Barretto were also present. The only immediate family member not there was Charisse's brother, Johnny, who was in California with his wife's family.

The menu consisted of the traditional roast turkey with stuffing—Charisse's first; baked ham; roast beef and gravy; collard greens and string beans, both seasoned with pork neck bones; macaroni and cheese, which Damaris made and everyone raved about; mashed turnips; candied yams topped with marshmallows; cranberry sauce—jellied and whole berries; and homemade dinner rolls; aside from an array of desserts. Barbara had even made Stefan his own personal German chocolate cake, which he promptly put away to save for another day.

Everyone exchanged gifts, but the children were the stars of the day and all went away with big smiles and full bellies.

After dinner, while the ladies put the remaining food away and cleaned up, the guys gathered downstairs in Stefan's family room to watch football on his wide screen television.

The conversation in the kitchen soon turned to the men.

"So, Myra, how're things going with you and Barry?" Barbara asked, knowing Myra's history and her cynical view of relationships.

With a shy smile, she replied, "It's going very well. He's a really great guy."

"What did you get for Christmas?" Star asked.

"A pair of gold earrings and a matching chain and pendant."

"Why didn't you wear them?" Charisse asked.

"I always wear my mother's cross on Christmas," she explained.

"Oh, yeah, that's right."

"What did you get from Stefan?" Star then asked.

Charisse smiled. "A mink jacket. I'll bring it out and show y'all after we finish up in here."

"What did you get him?" Barbara then asked.

"A Rolex watch and—

"And?" his sister questioned. "That wasn't enough? I know you spent a pretty penny on that."

"I don't mind spending money on Stefàn, Nikki, because he appreciates everything I give him. That's just how we do," Charisse stated in a matter-of-fact tone. "I also got him a new helmet for his bike."

"I wish he would get rid of that bike," Damaris said with a frown.

"Oh, I hope not. I love riding that bike."

"Y'all are both out of your minds," Myra said.

"Stefàn's no daredevil. He's a very safe driver; otherwise I wouldn't ride with him. We're not trying to get ourselves killed."

"I was kind of hoping he would give you an engagement ring," Charisse's sister-in-law, Suzette, said.

"Yeah, right," Star agreed.

"When the time is right, he will," Charisse calmly stated. "It really doesn't matter anyway because we're going to get married."

"We all know that," Barbara said, "but it would've been nice."

"Maybe he'll surprise you for the new year," Nikki added.

"Maybe. Whenever he does it will be all right with me, so...," she smiled and shrugged.

"Can you believe he's even talking about *getting* married, Mommy?" Nikki said to Damaris.

"That's a huge step in Stefàn's world, but Charisse, you've inspired quite a bit of change in him."

"I don't think it was me. I'm pretty sure it was God," she responded.

"You're probably right," Damaris answered. "Whatever the catalyst, he's a better person—a better man, for it."

"I always thought Stefàn would be the one to never get married," Nikki said.

"They say there's someone for everyone," Barbara chimed in.

"Obviously, Stefan hadn't found what he needed until he and Charisse met. No one, I don't care what they might tell you, wants to grow old by themselves. God didn't make men and women for them to live apart, he made us to live together."

"In marriage," Charisse added.

"Yes, in marriage."

"I'm glad you two never moved in together," Damaris said.

"There would be too much temptation if we did that," Charisse said.

"What do you mean?" Star asked.

"Too much temptation to have sex."

The room suddenly grew quiet.

"You make it sound like y'all have never done it before," Suzette said, breaking the silence.

"We haven't."

The women looked from one to another, perplexed by Charisse's statement.

"Y'all have never had sex?" Star asked.

"No."

"Why not?" she wanted to know.

"Because I made a vow that I wouldn't until I was married, and Stefan respects that."

"My brother, Stefan?" Nikki questioned with wide eyes and a chuckle.

Charisse smiled. "Yes, your brother, Stefan."

"How long have y'all been dating?" Suzette asked.

"About five months."

"But you're going to marry him, so that shouldn't count," Star said.

"Our plan is to get married, yes, but tomorrow is not promised to any of us and there's no telling what might happen from one day to the next. I promised God that I would not lay with another man unless he was my husband and as yet, Stefàn is not my husband; regardless of what we have planned. Besides, we're not even engaged yet, remember?"

"Yeah, but—"

"There are no buts. We talked about this before we got together. He knew how I felt from the very start and cares enough about me that it didn't make a difference to him. That is very special to me. No one has ever shown me that kind of love."

"But don't you get…horny, sometimes?" Star asked.

"Yeah. I didn't say I was dead," Charisse said with a chuckle.

The women all laughed.

"But we don't act on it. There are so many things that Stefàn and I do together and we love each other more than just for the way we feel physically."

"Did I hear my name?" Stefàn called as he walked into the kitchen.

"Wasn't nobody talking about you," Nikki teasingly fibbed.

He walked over to Charisse and put his arms around her as he nuzzled her neck. "Hey, baby. You miss me?"

She smiled up at him and wrapped her arms around his waist. "Of course, I do."

They shared a soft kiss on the lips.

"It must be half-time," Barbara said when John walked into the kitchen, followed by Mike, Devin, Barry and David. Nikki's husband, Tony, soon followed with their son, Anton, in tow.

Packed into Stefàn's large kitchen, there were soon several conversations going on at once. Some of the guys were there to get snacks—a slice of one of the many cakes or pies Damaris, Barbara or Charisse had baked; others wanted something to drink. Stefàn and Charisse had pretty much tuned everyone out and were still standing in a loving embrace near the sink.

Suddenly, Stefàn went down on one knee. Initially, Charisse

thought he had dropped something, until she noticed that he was holding an open box with a diamond ring inside. Her mouth fell open and her eyes widened at the sight.

John Ellison noticed right away what was happening and nudged Barbara and Mike, who were standing on each side of him. The others then took notice and the room immediately became deafeningly still.

"We've talked about it many times, Risi, but I want to make it official. Charisse Marie Ellison, would you do me the honor of becoming my wife?"

Tears formed in her eyes and her vision became a blur, but a huge smile covered her face as she screamed, "Of course I will!"

Removing the bauble from its bed, Stefan placed it on her left ring finger. He then stood before her and wrapped her in a tight embrace as they shared a passionate kiss. All around them, however, there was clapping and laughing and shouts of "It's about time," "Congratulations," and "I had a feeling he was going to do it today."

Damaris and Barbara were both in tears as they embraced one another. John and Mike shook hands and embraced, each very happy with what had transpired between their children. In the next seconds, Stefan and Charisse were surrounded by their families and overwhelmed with hugs, kisses and heartfelt best wishes.

The date was set for April 28th, three weeks after Stefân's thirty-fourth birthday. The wedding would have taken place sooner if they hadn't been required to attend pre-marital counseling at the church, and if Pastor Young's schedule had permitted. Charisse and Stefân were eager to wed. As it was, they decided on a small ceremony, attended only by family and their closest friends. The entire wedding party numbered eight with Myra as Charisse's maid of honor, and Julian, as Stefân's best man. Charisse's sister, Star, and Stefân's sister, Nikki, served as bridesmaids, while Stefân's brother, Devin, and their paternal uncle, Angelo, who was just seven years Stefân's senior, stood as groomsmen. Star's six year old daughter, Candice, was the flower girl, while Julian's son, L'il Jay, was a junior groomsman.

Myra, with the help of Star and Nikki, threw a bridal shower for Charisse the night before the wedding at the Teaneck Marriott at Glenpointe, where the reception was also going to take place. Barbara and Damaris were both in attendance, along with Stefân's and Charisse's grandmothers, aunts and other relatives from both families. To Charisse's embarrassment, and at Star's suggestion, a male stripper was hired to perform for the guests. Although every attempt was made to make her the center of attention during his commanding performance, Charisse politely, albeit adamantly, refused. Several other women present, however, were more than happy to vie for the man's attention and assist him in his routine. Even one of Charisse's older aunts made it very obvious how much she was enjoying his show.

Stefan's bachelor party was held the same night at a club in Hackensack. Julian was responsible for setting everything up and the event was enjoyed by all, including John, Mike and Stefan's paternal grandfather. Although Stefan's lifestyle had changed dramatically since he and Charisse had gotten together, he still could not deny how much he enjoyed the raucousness of the party held to celebrate the end of his bachelorhood. In truth, he was much more reserved than he might have been in the past because he loved Charisse with all his heart and couldn't, in good conscience, do anything that would cast any doubt about his devotion to her. When the party ended, his guests raved about what a great time they all had.

The following morning, Julian was at Stefan's house by eight-thirty with a garment bag and duffel bag containing everything he would need to prepare for the wedding. The ceremony was scheduled to begin at one p.m.

When he rang Stefan's door, he expected a groggy greeting.

"Hey, dude, come on in," Stefan cheerfully offered.

"I didn't wake you, huh?" Julian asked as he followed Stefan into his kitchen.

"No, I've been up for a couple of hours. I just finished working out and I'm getting ready to make something to eat. You hungry?"

"Sure, I can eat. So, you couldn't sleep?" Julian asked.

"I slept okay, but I am a little restless."

"You nervous?"

"No." He moved to the refrigerator and as he reached for the carton of eggs and other fixings, asked, "You want an omelet?"

"That'll work."

"I forgot to give you her wedding band yesterday. Do me a

favor and go look on my dresser. It's right there in the front."

"Have you spoken to Risi this morning?" Julian asked as he rose from his seat.

"Yeah, about an hour ago."

Julian left the kitchen and Stefan continued preparing their breakfast.

When he returned, he was openly admiring the bauble. "This is a beautiful ring, man," Julian reverently uttered.

"Thanks. I hope she likes it," Stefan said.

Looking up at him in surprise, he asked, "Are you serious? Man, she's gonna love this."

Stefan chuckled lightly. "Yeah, I guess."

"Coop, what's up?"

Stopping what he was doing, Stefan looked over at his child-hood friend and said, "I don't want to disappoint her."

"Why do you think you would?"

"I don't know." He sighed. "This is the most important thing I've ever done in my life. This is for real. This is forever, man." Shaking his head, he continued, "I can't mess this up."

"You won't. I know how much you love this woman, Coop, but I know how much she loves you, too. As long as you stay centered in Christ… As long as you keep your marriage centered in Christ, y'all can't fail."

"Yeah, you're right. So, Dub, tell me something. What are you gonna do about Michele?"

Julian lowered his head for a brief moment before he looked into Stefan's eyes and said, "I'm going to ask her to marry me again tomorrow night."

Stefan smiled. "Good." Shaking his head in agreement, he repeated, "Good. I'm very glad to hear that. What's happening tomorrow?"

"Nothing special. I'm going to take her out to her favorite restaurant and just do it."

"I'm really glad to hear that, man. I never did understand why y'all broke up in the first place."

"We did it for the wrong reasons. Yeah, she was pregnant, but then when she lost the baby… I don't know. I wanted to do the right thing by her."

"Do you love her?"

"I've always loved her," Julian told him.

"Are you in love with her?" Stefan then asked.

"Yes. Unlike before, I know this is where I'm supposed to be. No one has ever been in my corner like Shelly is. She's had my back through it all."

"Yeah, I know." Stefan chuckled. "Bet you'd have never guessed you'd be standing here with me on my wedding day, huh?"

Julian chuckled, too. "Not until I saw you with Charisse. I always knew she was the one."

ACROSS TOWN AT CHARISSE'S HOUSE, Barbara, Myra, Star and her daughters, Granny Nan and the bride sat around Charisse's dining room table munching on a continental breakfast of mini croissants and danish, various melons, berries and the like, while sipping tea, coffee and/or juice.

Myra's cousin, Connie, was due to arrive at approximately ten a.m. to tighten up Charisse's newly cut hairstyle and do her makeup, as well as Myra's, Star's and Barbara's.

As Charisse spread a generous dollop of cream cheese on a croissant, her sister scolded, "You'd better cool it with that cream cheese or you won't be able to get into your gown."

"I have plenty of room in my gown, thank you very much," Charisse said flippantly, as she took a healthy bite of the treat.

"You nervous?" Myra asked.

"Nope. I've been waiting for this for too long to be nervous," Charisse replied.

"Yeah, right," said Star. "Tonight's the big night."

"What do you mean by that?" Granny Nan inquired.

"Charisse and Stefan have never done it before," Star said with a wink at her grandmother. Since her daughters were present, she didn't want to go into any more detail than that, but Granny Nan caught her meaning immediately.

"Oh no? Well, this is a special day for you, isn't it?" she said with a mischievous smile at Charisse. "I didn't think anyone waited anymore these days. I'm glad to know you did. Especially with such a good lookin' man as yours."

"It's not like she's a virgin," Star clarified.

"Excuse me, Star," Charisse said, slightly chagrined. "Who asked you?"

"Well, you're not!"

"So, what? We all have pasts. That doesn't mean we have to live the rest of our lives making the same mistakes we once did. I made a vow not to go there again with any man who was not my husband, and Stefan and I kept that vow. Our waiting and his decision to respect my vow will only make our experiences together that much more enjoyable."

"Like I said, tonight's the big night. Make sure you come up for air every couple of hours. I'd hate for you to miss your flight in the morning," Star teased.

"Mommy, is Auntie going swimming tonight, too?" six year old Candace innocently asked.

"You could say that, baby," Star laughed. The others joined her.

Charisse blushed and said with a wave of her hand, "I ain't thinkin' about y'all."

CHARISSE MADE A BREATHTAKINGLY BEAUTIFUL BRIDE in a strapless satin A-line gown with cascading side drape and sweep train. Stefan, decked out in a white tuxedo with satin appointments, was equally grand to behold. Standing together at the altar as they exchanged the vows they'd written for one another, it was evident to everyone in attendance that they were made for each other. Their mutual love and adoration was clear to see and was a light around them the entire day.

Damaris and Mike had never seen Stefan so at peace and the joy that emanated from him was almost tangible. John and Barbara were totally pleased with their youngest daughter's choice for a husband. They had no doubts that Stefan would love, cherish and provide for Charisse until he took his last breath.

For the couple, getting through the reception—although a truly magnificent event—was a chore. Their thoughts ran along the same lines and they had confided their deepest desires to one another in the limousine from the church to the banquet hall. While wrapped in Stefan's tender embrace, Charisse gazed into his eyes and murmured, "I want to be alone with you."

Smiling, Stefan could only concur. "I second that emotion. Do you think they'd miss us if we didn't come to the reception?"

"Probably. I don't know why, though. That party's not really for us. It's for them. Let them enjoy it. They can tell us about it later," she said with a mischievous grin. "Let's go home. I want to make love with my husband."

Stefan chuckled. "Don't tempt me, Mrs. Cooper. There's nothing I'd rather do more than take you home and show you how much I've craved you. But maybe it's better we wait."

"Better for who?" Charisse grumbled.

"I'm too excited right now. I'd be a disappointment to you."

"That's something you could never be," she assured him as she pressed her mouth to his and savored his sweet kiss.

As he drowned in Charisse's affection, Stefan thanked God that she was finally his. He thanked God that Charisse had inspired such change in his life. He thanked God that Charisse had shown him, through her love and her life, that he, too, was a child of God, and that every good thing in his life was of God. He thanked God for showing him how to love the incredible woman who now bore his name and prayed God's continued grace and strength that he would always be as much a blessing in her life, as she was in his.

When Charisse and Stefan returned from their ten-day honeymoon to Italy—Rome, Vatican City, Tuscany, Positano and the Almafi Coast—they immediately resumed their search for a new home. Charisse was more than happy to leave it to Stefan to find houses for them to consider. She never even glanced at a real estate ad. In the meantime, she had moved into his split-level home, and at Stefan's suggestion, instead of selling her townhouse, they decided to rent it.

After looking at several different houses in the Teaneck/Englewood/Tenafly area, they decided on a young, four-bedroom, three-bathroom colonial in a cul-de-sac in Englewood, about two miles from Charisse's townhouse. The fifteen-year-old house, which had only one previous owner, was one in which they planned to set down roots, and that would accommodate their growing family once they started having children. An expansive backyard—accessible from the formal dining room as well as the kitchen—boasted a brick patio and a built-in grill. There was also a large two-room, partially finished basement. The unfinished portion was a laundry room. A two-car, attached garage and fireplaces in the living room, family room, and master bedroom were major selling points. The master bedroom suite also featured a private deck and panoramic windows that overlooked the yard and their wooded acreage behind it. The master bath had a separate glass-enclosed shower stall, a spa tub, double sinks and a sequestered commode. The spacious kitchen featured an island and a breakfast nook. Charisse fell in love with the house at first sight, as Stefân had known she would.

Incorporating the furniture from both residences for the family room, kitchen, basement, and spare bedrooms, they opted to buy new furniture for their living room, dining room and master suite. Charisse thoroughly enjoyed the task of interior designing with Stefân. Their respective tastes in home décor were quite similar, so they seldom squabbled over what to buy.

They were completely moved into their new home by July and wasted no time having the families over for a Fourth of July barbecue, which also gave everyone a chance to tour their new digs.

It was also the perfect opportunity to celebrate Julian and Michele's reunion. As Julian had shared on Stefân's wedding day, he'd taken her to dinner at her favorite restaurant and popped the question all over again. Unlike the first time, however, Julian was doing it for all the right reasons, and to his delight, Michele's love for him was reciprocated.

They were married in a private ceremony at First Baptist Church, attended only by their parents and son, Michele's sisters, Stefân, Charisse and Michele's best friend and her husband. Instead of a reception and honeymoon, they invested their money in a new home and L'il Jay's private school tuition. For that reason, Stefân and Charisse used their July fourth barbecue to honor their friends.

Myra and Barretto were still going strong as well. Although Myra had never fully given her trust to any man before, Barretto had been able to break down all of her defenses and she was enjoying a relationship with him, the likes of which she had never experienced. She had even spoken to Charisse on several occasions about her desire to marry him and bear his children, something she had previously sworn that she would never do.

By the time September rolled around, their real estate investments were really paying off. That being the case, in addition to their home, the six-unit apartment building in Queens that Stefan already owned, and Charisse's townhouse, they were looking into buying a dilapidated brownstone in Brooklyn. Stefan had all the connections needed to have the work done on renovating the place. They decided they would wait until the renovations were completed to determine whether they would lease the units or sell the building outright.

Stefan, being the sharp-minded businessman he was, and trusting Charisse implicitly, severed his relationship with the accountant he'd been working with for years and turned all of his financial records over to her. He also asked her to take charge of their overall household finances since that was her forte.

By combining their knowledge and working together, Stefan eventually left the employ of the realty office he'd been with for several years and branched out on his own. Encouraging him when he exhibited the slightest trepidation or reservation about making the move, Charisse knew how much he'd been wanting to do this and reminded him at every opportunity that God had not brought him this far so that he could fall short of His promise.

By Thanksgiving, they had been married for seven months. Everything they touched together turned to gold. Stefan's business was doing well; Charisse had been promoted to an officer position at her firm, but she was also doing a good deal of freelance work, too. Stefan thought it would be a great idea for her to go into business for herself, too, but she thought it would be better to wait until she was home after the birth of their first child.

Eager to expand their family beyond the two of them, when Charisse awoke the morning before Thanksgiving to find that her cycle had begun again, she could not contain her tears.

Stefan was still asleep and she didn't want to wake him, but she was thoroughly distraught. *Something must be wrong with me.* Their love life was healthy and active and their appetites for one another were never easily satisfied. Despite the fact that they had been able to take advantage of the unexpected wait by achieving several goals, by now Charisse wanted to have a baby more than anything.

She had expressed her concern about not becoming pregnant to Stefan on other occasions and he was always very empathic, but fervently believed and assured her that when God was ready for them to conceive, He would make it happen. And although Charisse's faith in God was strong, she couldn't help wondering why He hadn't yet blessed them with conception.

After showering and trying hard to hide any signs of her unhappiness, Charisse emerged from the bathroom to find Stefan in the midst of his regimental push-ups.

"Good morning, baby," he called as she moved across the room.

"G'mornin'," she mumbled in return.

Being acutely tuned in to her moods, Stefan immediately picked up on Charisse's melancholy. Rising from the floor, he turned to face her. "What's the matter, baby?"

Charisse had sat on the cushioned stool at the foot of the bed so her sad face was not visible to him. She didn't utter a word, but shook her head to indicate nothing was wrong.

Stefan took a few steps in her direction and sat next to her. Taking her hand, he at once noticed her sadness. Putting his arm around her and pulling her closer, he expressed his genuine concern when he asked, "What's wrong, Risi?"

"I just got my period again."

Stefan embraced her fully then and kissed her gently on her temple. Feeling her pain as if it was his own, he desperately wanted to have children with Charisse, yet cherished the time they now had to themselves because he knew with children things would inevitably be different.

Trying to reassure her, he softly intoned, "It'll happen, baby. Maybe God wants us to get a little more settled before He blesses us with kids. With me going out on my own and the new building and everything, we've got a lot on our plates right now."

"Don't you want us to have a baby?" she tearfully inquired as she looked into his eyes.

"Of course I do. I want us to have several babies, but I'm in no rush. We've got our whole lives ahead of us, sweetheart. We're still young and…" he kissed her sensuously, "I kind of like having you all to myself."

That was not what she wanted to hear. Charisse rose and started to move away from him. "Something's wrong. I just know it."

Remaining seated, he reached out to her. "Honey, come here." Reluctantly, she allowed him to pull her back to him. "I'm sure you're fine."

"No! Stefan, something's wrong. I can feel it," she insisted as she wrapped her arms around her middle.

"Do you have pain or something?"

"No, but… I should've gotten pregnant by now. It's been seven months. We've never used anything. We do it all the time. I should be pregnant. There's got to be something wrong!"

To calm her, he conceded, "Okay, honey, listen. We'll make an appointment and go check it out. I'm sure they'll tell you it's nothing."

Sighing as she stood between his legs and wrapped her arms tightly around him, she lamented, "I want to have a baby."

"I know, Risi, and we will." He coaxed her onto his lap. Charisse allowed him to comfort her. "I love you, sweetheart. God's gonna bless us with kids. I know He will. We don't always know why He does things the way He does, but we know His will is perfect, right?"

She nodded.

"He knows how much we love each other, and how much we're going to love the children He blesses us with. We have to be patient and accept that His time doesn't always jibe with our time."

"I know," Charisse mumbled.

"Kiss me."

He turned his head up to her and she lowered her lips to his. "I love you so much," she said through the tears that remained.

"I know. I love you; more than you could possibly know," he emotionally asserted.

They sat that way for the next few minutes until Stefan asked, "You gonna be okay?"

"Yeah."

Patting her backside gently, he said, "Let me jump in the shower. I'm only going to be at the office for a couple of hours today. I'll meet you back here. You think you can be back here around two o'clock?"

"Yeah."

"Good, then we can get to the store and get the rest of the stuff we need for tomorrow."

"Okay."

"I figure if we get started early enough, we'll have the rest of the evening to get everything together for this brood." They were hosting Thanksgiving dinner for both families the next day.

Before rising from his lap, Charisse told him, "Thank you."

"For what?"

"For being such a wonderful husband."

He smiled as he said, "It's only fair, having a wife as incredible as you are."

"I love being your wife."

"I love being your husband."

She kissed him once more and said, "Okay, time to go to work."

Despite Stefàn's confidence that they would conceive a child in due course, in her heart, Charisse could not be convinced.

Barbara Ellison called her daughter at her office that morning. Charisse's day was unusually slow, affording her entirely too much time to dwell on what she perceived to be her problem. Barbara picked up on Charisse's sadness immediately.

"What wrong?" she asked when Charisse answered the call without her typically cheerful greeting.

"Hi, Mommy."

"Why do you sound so blue this morning?"

"I think something's wrong with me."

"What do you mean?" Barbara asked with concern.

"I got my period again today. There must be a reason I'm not getting pregnant."

"Maybe it's just not your time, honey."

"No, Mommy, something's wrong. I can feel it."

"Are you in pain?" Barbara asked, echoing Stefàn's concern of that morning at Charisse's insistence.

"No, that's not what I mean. I can feel it in my heart that something is wrong."

"You've never had any gynecological problems, have you?"

"No, but—

"Honey, you're worrying about this too much. Stressing over it can cause all kinds of problems. Why don't you relax and let nature take its course. You and Stefàn have plenty of time for children. Besides, once they start coming, the two of you won't have any more time for yourselves. You should enjoy this time you have."

"I want to have a baby, Mommy."

"I understand that, Charisse, but just because you haven't conceived yet doesn't necessarily mean there's something wrong."

"Mommy, Stefan and I do it all the time."

"I'm sure you do. You're newlyweds who waited until you were married to even go there. I'm sure you've been making up for lost time. Nevertheless, don't presume the worst because you got your period again. As wonderful as motherhood is, take the time to enjoy your husband and your new life together."

As much as Barbara's words were meant to give Charisse comfort, they provided none.

She spoke to Myra that day as well, and heard more of the same.

"Risi, I'm sure you're fine. Maybe God isn't ready to bless you with children yet."

Myra had, in the months since she'd been dating Barretto, started attending church more regularly, and although she had not yet joined a congregation, she was vigilant about attending Bible study once a week.

"Why not? Why do you assume that God doesn't want me to have any kids?" Charisse said, taking Myra's comment completely out of context.

"I didn't say that, Risi."

"Stefan and I have been faithful and prayerful. We work hard and freely give to the church as well as to other people or organizations in need. God promised that if we did as He told us, He would bless us with the desires of our heart. My desire is to have a child. If it's not happening, it must be because something is wrong!"

Nothing anyone said could change her mind. Charisse insisted on making an appointment with her gynecologist at the earliest possible time. Knowing how stressed she was over their unsuccessful attempts, Stefan agreed to accompany her. Even he tried to convince her that as long as she continued to stress over the situation the more likely their chances of conceiving would be reduced, but his words, too, fell on deaf ears.

Two weeks after Thanksgiving, was the earliest appointment they could get with Charisse's doctor. After explaining their situation, Dr. Chase informed them that a couple was not considered infertile until a year had passed of unprotected sex without conception. He tried to assure Charisse that the case was the same for many couples and that any number of circumstances could be attributed to them having not conceived yet.

Charisse could not accept even his expert opinion. She insisted on being tested. When Dr. Chase saw how upset she was, he agreed to administer the fertility tests simply to calm her. While they were preparing, Stefan asked Dr. Chase if he should be tested as well, just to save time. The doctor felt that was a good idea.

Ten days later, Charisse received a telephone call at home from Dr. Chase, asking that she and Stefan come in to see him the very next day. She assumed the worst when he told her that he would not give her any information over the telephone, but would rather wait until they were both together in his office.

When Stefan arrived home that evening, Charisse was a nervous wreck when she told him about Dr. Chase's call. Without hesitation, Stefan grabbed her and held her close. Trying to comfort her, he whispered, "It's going to be all right. Don't worry, Risi, everything's going to be all right."

"No, it won't. Doctors don't call unless something's wrong. I know it, Stefan. I just know it."

"Sweetheart, we can't assume anything. Let's wait and see what he says, okay? I don't want you getting yourself all worked up and we don't even know what he's going to tell us. Let's just wait and see."

"But, Stefân—"

"No, buts. Listen, God has already blessed us in so many ways, right?"

"Yes," she said between sniffles.

"He's not going to stop now, baby. We're living right. We're praising Him every day. Let's not forget to give Him thanks for what He's already given us. We need to pray on this, Risi. We need to give this whole situation over to God and let Him work it out for us. We can't let go of our faith, honey. Now's the time to hold on tighter than ever."

"I know."

The next morning, just before they started downstairs from their bedroom to leave for Dr. Chase's office, Stefân reached for Charisse's hand.

"Honey, let's say a prayer before we go."

Stefân and Charisse knelt beside their bed and Stefân began by saying, "O God our help in ages past. Our hope for years to come. Our shelter from the stormy blast and our eternal home. Father God, we come today, first, to say thank You for another day of Your amazing grace and Your tender mercy. Thank You for the many, many blessings You have already given us. We thank You for the love we share that is made whole through Your love for us. We thank You for the gift of prosperity which has allowed us to purchase our home and live comfortably in it. We thank You for all of our material possessions, but know that they are nothing in the grand scheme of things. Father, we thank You for our health and happiness and the joy which You have planted in our hearts. We thank You for Your precious son, Jesus Christ, who died for us while we were still lost. Thank You, Jesus, for your sacrifice. Heavenly Father, we ask your forgiveness of our sins. Father, forgive us for anything we may have said, done or thought that dishonors Your Holy Name. And we thank You for being a forgiving God, for we know that Your grace and mercy are sufficient for us today and every day. God, You know the concerns of our hearts. We're going to see this doctor today to hear his report to find out whether our desire to have a child will be hindered in any way. Father, I ask You to grant us the strength to accept whatever report we are given with courage and the assurance that despite what he may tell us, all things are possible for You. We know that if it is Your will, no matter what, You will bless us with children, and if it is not Your will that we become natural parents, You will continue to bless us in ways too numerous to count. And God, I pray You give us the vision and wisdom to recognize your blessing if it doesn't come the way we expect. You are our sacred and sovereign Lord, and we give You all honor and glory and praise, Father. We love You and in all things we magnify Your Holy Name. And we ask that the words of our mouths and the meditations of our hearts will be acceptable in Your sight, O Lord, our strength and our Redeemer. In the mighty and matchless name of our Lord and Savior, Jesus Christ, Amen, Amen."

By the end of Stefan's prayer, Charisse was in tears. She reached over to hold him and he embraced her warmly, placing a tender kiss on her forehead. They remained in that position for the next few minutes until Charisse murmured, "Okay, I'm ready."

CHAPTER 21

WHO SAID IT WOULD BE EASY?

A lthough he tried to put up a brave front, Stefan was numb as he and Charisse left Dr. Chase's office. Like a prophet foresees the future, Charisse had called it: there was something wrong. Never in a million years would he have entertained the notion that they might never be able to have children. Assuming that with everything they had going on, God was giving them time to get settled in their marriage, the worst possible scenario became his reality; his truth.

Venturing out on his own only four months ago—leaving the real estate office he had worked at for the last seven years—he had already received commissions on two sales. With the rents from the apartment building in Queens and Charisse's townhouse, plus her salary and the money they had in the bank from combining their assets, they were well in the black. The purchase of the Brooklyn brownstone had gone through and the renovations would be completed in a couple of weeks if everything continued to go as smoothly as it had been. They had made the decision to sell that property outright as opposed to renting it. Once that sale was finalized, they expected to recoup every cent they'd put into it, and turn a nice profit at the same time.

It had seemed to him that with his marriage to Charisse, their blessings had begun pouring in with abundance, just like it says in Psalm 23: "My cup runneth over." They paid tithes to their church on everything they received and offerings over and above their tithes because there was no doubt from Whom their blessings came. They were faithful, active members of the congregation of First Baptist. Stefan had often spoken to Charisse about how much his life had changed for the better since he had come to Christ, and he always thanked her for showing him the Way.

He remembered when they met, she told him there were aspects of her Walk that weren't easy, but that at those times she would cling all the more to her faith in God to get her through. He knew that was what they had to do now but he had never been tested before, not like this. Ever since he had accepted Christ as his Savior, his life had been filled with good times, laughter and blessings galore.

Why now? Why this?

"Honey, you okay?" Charisse asked as they made their way through the parking lot to their car.

"Yeah, I'm fine," he insisted with a smile that deceived no one.

"You wanna get something to eat?" she asked.

"No, I've gotta get to work."

"Oh. I thought maybe you'd want to take the rest of the day off."

"I've got too much to do. Besides, it's too early in the game to start taking time off."

"Yeah, I guess so," she solemnly replied. "Do you want to eat out tonight or should I cook?"

"You don't have to cook. We can order in. I should be home by seven. You're going in, right?"

Charisse sighed. "Yeah. I would've taken the day if you weren't going in, but I might as well."

Stefan opened the passenger door of their car for her but before she got in she hugged him. "Things that are impossible for man are possible for God. I believe that with my whole heart," she whispered.

Feeling a lump in his throat, Stefan choked it back as he returned her embrace. "I know, sweetie."

"I love you, Stefan," she said as she looked up at him with watery eyes.

"I love you, too." Brushing his lips across hers, his hold tightened for a brief moment.

"We'll get through this."

"I know."

He released her in the next seconds and started around to the driver's side. "Do you want me to run you by the house so you can get the other car, or should I take you to the bus stop?"

"I'll take the bus," she replied before ducking into the car.

The drive to the bus stop was made in silence. Stefan could feel Charisse's eyes on him but he never turned to her—he stayed focused on the road in front of him. When they arrived at the stop, he pulled to the curb to wait with her.

She glanced at her watch and said, "It should be here in the next few minutes."

It was the first time they had ever been together with palpable tension between them.

"Do me a favor, Risi," Stefan suddenly said, breaking the thick silence. "Let's keep this between us for now, okay. I don't want to hear everybody's opinion of what we should do, what's going to happen, or none of that."

"Of course, baby."

"Here comes your bus."

Charisse turned and looked out the rear window. Leaning over, she offered her lips to her husband. Gently caressing her face, he kissed her tenderly. "I'll see you tonight."

"I'll be home early."

"Okay."

Through the rear-view mirror, Stefàn watched as Charisse boarded the bus that would take her to New York. When the bus pulled around him and continued on its route, Stefàn restarted the car and headed to his office.

HIS CELL PHONE VIBRATED YET AGAIN. He didn't even have to check. It was the fifth time Charisse had called but he wasn't planning to answer this time either. He couldn't talk to her. As numb as he was feeling, he couldn't do much of anything except nurse his fourth double shot of vodka as the world turned, business as usual.

It was nine-thirty and he'd been at The Den for the last two hours. When he left his office after a totally wasted day, his intention had been to go straight home. When he thought about Charisse and the look he knew she would give him—not one of disappointment, as would be expected, but one of sympathy—he couldn't face her. After the way she'd carried on, certain that she had some kind of physical dysfunction which was preventing them from having a baby, only to find out that *he* was the dysfunctional one…. The last thing he wanted was her sympathy.

All these years, he'd been so sure it was his diligence in protecting himself that had kept him from having to deal with "baby's mama drama." *Ha, you wish! All this time, you've been shooting blanks.* So much for his machismo. The unconscionable truth fused his mind, body and soul in a foreign uncertainty and the rhythm that had heretofore produced harmony in his life was now off-key. What a devastating blow to his ego. As soon as they'd walked into Dr. Chase's office, he'd known it was him. He'd sensed it when the doctor looked everywhere around that room except into his eyes. "Low motility," he'd said. Weak sperm is what he meant, Stefàn knew. He'd wanted to scream at him, "Why don't you just tell it like it is? I've got weak sperm!"

Stefan was angry. He never bothered to ask Dr. Chase if there was anything that could be done to cure him. As a matter of fact, after the doctor explained exactly what low motility meant, Stefan had pretty much tuned him out. He couldn't repeat anything the doctor had said after he heard, "your sperm does not have enough strength to swim through the cervical mucus to penetrate your wife's egg." Venturing into a fog, everything after that was blurred; his words a bunch of mumbo-jumbo. Charisse proceeded to grill Dr. Chase; he was aware of that, but he couldn't even remember what she had asked. He had made an appointment, at Charisse's urging, to go back for a follow-up exam and testing, but he didn't even know when that was to take place.

How could you do this to me, God? You know how much Charisse wants to have a baby but You gave me weak sperm. I can't even give her a child. She's been faithful to You. She's changed her life for You and so have I, and this is the thanks we get? I haven't known You long, and was probably one of the biggest sinners out there, but I've changed. Is this my punishment? If so, fine, but why punish Charisse? She doesn't deserve this. You know how important this is to her.

Rooted in a pain he could not unravel, Stefan was so anesthetized by his agony that he didn't even realize he was crying. Tears were streaming down his cheeks as he lifted the glass to his lips and finished off the contents. "She doesn't deserve this," he drunkenly mumbled as he lowered his head to the table.

IT WAS AFTER TEN AND CHARISSE WAS DESPERATE WITH WORRY. Stefan hadn't answered any of her calls, not at his office nor on his cell. *Where could he be?* Although he had put up a good front when Dr. Chase dropped the bomb about his condition, Charisse knew Stefan well enough to realize how shaken he had been at the news. He had asked that she not tell anyone about the doctor's report, but how could she ask anyone for help without explaining what had happened?

Julian will probably know where he is if he's not with him. She would be highly surprised if Stefan hadn't confided in Julian what had been going on with them. Suspecting he felt this was an assault on his manhood, Charisse knew the men's bond was such that even this was something Stefan would most likely share with his closest friend, so she called him.

Michele answered the call after two rings.

"Hi, Shelly, it's Charisse."

"Hey, girl. What's up?"

"Is Stefan there?"

"No, he hasn't been by tonight. Is everything okay?"

Charisse could hear the immediate concern in her tone. "No," she shakily replied. "Is Julian there?"

"Yeah, hold on a minute. I'll get him."

"Thanks."

Charisse could hear in the background, "Honey, come get the phone. Risi's looking for Stefan."

Seconds later, Julian came to the phone. "Hey, Risi. What's up?"

"Julian, Stefan hasn't come home and I've been calling him and he won't answer his phone. Do you know where he might be?"

"What happened?" he asked instead of answering her query.

"I don't know if he told you that we were seeing a doctor today 'cause we were having trouble getting pregnant."

"Yeah, he told me."

"Well, we found out today that something's wrong with him. When we left the doctor's office, he insisted that he was fine and that he was going to work. He said he would be straight home afterward, but I haven't been able to reach him. I knew he wasn't fine, but he wouldn't tell me how he was really feeling." She was crying openly now. "I'm worried about him, Dub. I want him to come home."

"Risi, don't worry. I don't know where he is right now, but I'll find him and bring him home, okay?" Julian assured her. "You stay by the phone. I'll call you as soon as I know something."

"Thank you, Julian. I love him so much. Tell him that I love him when you find him, please."

"I will, baby. Don't worry. I'm sure he's all right. He probably just needed some time to process what's happening, that's all. I'll find him."

When Julian hung up the telephone, he turned to Michele and said, "I've got to go out for a minute, baby, see if I can find Coop."

"What's the matter?" she asked.

"Stefan hasn't come home and he's not answering her calls. She said he got some pretty bad news this morning that's got his head messed up," Julian answered.

"Do you think you know where he is?"

"Well, I know where he used to hang. I'm going to try those spots first."

"Be careful, okay? And call me as soon as you find out anything. Should I wake Jay and go over and stay with her?"

"No, she'll be all right. I probably won't be gone that long. Just pray for them."

"I will."

Julian hit three spots in the surrounding neighborhood that he and Stefan used to frequent regularly before he stepped into The Den. Although they had occasionally darkened this particular bar's doors in the past, it was not one of their regular haunts. The Den's usual clientele was a little below the standards of the folks they used to run with. Besides, neither of them hung out like they once had since they both had families to care for now.

Despite the irregularity of their visits, they were known by the owner, Jerry, who was at the register behind the bar when Julian entered. The man called to him, "Hey, Dub, your boy's in a bad way back there."

"Thanks, man. I was looking for him."

Stefan was seated at the rearmost table with his back to the door. His head was down, as if he had fallen asleep. The jacket of his suit was carelessly thrown across the back of the chair facing him, and an empty glass rested on the table before him.

Julian placed his hand on Stefan's shoulder when he reached the table. Stefan's head jerked up and he bellowed, "Let me get another one, Jerry!" Blinking to clear his vision, his upper body swayed as he recognized Julian. "Dub! Whassup...my brotha? Wa'chu doin' in here?"

Julian picked up Stefan's jacket and carefully draped it across the back of the chair next to him as he took the seat across from his friend. "I came to get you."

Frowning as though Julian's words had not immediately registered, after a prolonged moment he rubbed his temple and voiced, "You... came ta...get me? Why?"

"Because Charisse is worried about you. How come you haven't answered any of her calls?"

"Cha...risse," he slurred and his lips curled into a crooked smile. "You know...Dub ...my wife is a...helluffa woman."

"I know, she is."

Stefan's head dropped suddenly as if his neck had broken. Seconds later, he slowly lifted it and looked at his best friend. "Know what?"

"What?"

"I'm shootin'...blanks."

Julian's heart lurched in his chest.

"I can't make no babies, Dub." Stefan sighed. "She wants …a baby an I…can't…make none."

"More than that, she wants you to come home," Julian gently stated.

Shaking his head, he murmured, "Can't go home." Stefan's eyes began to water. "How c'n I look at her? I love her…so…much and I…can't…even give her the…one…thing she wants."

"The only thing she wants, Coop, is for you to come home. She's worried about you."

"But…what c'n I say ta her?"

"Tell her you love her, like you just told me. She loves you, man. She told me to tell you that. Charisse wants you to come home. All that other stuff, she doesn't care about. She just wants you," Julian assured him.

"Dub, am I…so bad that God…had to pun…ish me like…this? I know I messed…up b'fore, but I'm not that bad…am I?"

Julian's eyes became watery. He empathized with his dear friend's pain. "God's not punishing you, Stefan. Just 'cause the doctors say one thing, don't make it the final word. Besides, that was only one doctor's opinion. You need to get a second opinion. That guy could be wrong."

"No…he's not wrong. I can…feel it," Stefan said, giving in to his grief.

Julian refused to allow him to sink any lower into his depression. He grabbed Stefan's jacket up and rose to his feet. Grasping his friend's arm, he said, "Come on, let's get out of here. You don't need to be in this place. I'm taking you home."

"Can't go home," he groaned.

"Yes, you can. Your wife is worried sick about you and I'm not going to let you sit here feeling sorry for yourself and get more wasted than you already are. Now, come on, get up."

Stefàn rose shakily to his feet with Julian's help. As soon as he moved to take a step, he stumbled, but Julian caught him and kept him upright. "I'm a little toasted," he slurred with a chuckle.

"You're more than a little toasted. You stink of vodka."

"Well, it's not like...I wanna kiss...you either," Stefàn indignantly replied and snickered.

Julian couldn't help but chuckle himself. Reaching into his pocket, he removed a roll of Breath Savers. "Open your mouth."

"Why?"

"Open your mouth, man!"

Stefàn did as he was told and Julian pushed three mints into it.

"You tryin' ta say...my...breath stinks?"

Julian simply shook his head. "Man, if I didn't love you so much, I would kick your butt."

"As if...you could," he slurred.

"In the condition you're in, L'il Jay could kick your butt."

Stefàn thought that comment was extremely funny.

Practically carrying him, Julian guided Stefàn to the front of the bar and toward the exit. "How much does he owe you, Jerry?"

"Is he all right?" the owner called back.

"Nah, man, but I'm taking him home."

"Don't worry about it," Jerry said with a shrug. "I figured it was something serious 'cause I ain't never seen him like that."

"Thanks, man. Can I come back and get his car in the morning?" Julian asked.

"Yeah, just make sure it's locked up."

"A'ight. Thanks."

"Later, Jerry!" Stefàn bellowed drunkenly as they exited the bar. He then said, "Dub, you gonna come with me?"

"Come with you where?"

"Home. Risi gonna be...mad at me," he said, sounding quite childlike.

"How do you think you're getting home, man?"

"I'ma drive. How else?"

"You're in no condition to be driving anything. We'll come back for your car in the morning. I'm driving."

"I can make it home," Stefan argued and immediately misstepped, practically falling to the ground.

"Yeah, you're in great shape," Julian said as he held him up and led him to his car.

Julian leaned Stefan against the car as he opened the passenger door.

"Dub, you think ... she gonna be mad at me?"

"She's not mad at you. She's just worried about you."

"No. I mean, 'cause…I'm shooting…blanks."

"She don't care about that."

"But she wanna have a baby."

"Come on, get in," Julian said as he tried to physically coax Stefan into the car.

"Wa'chu think, Dub? I…can't make a baby."

"You don't know that for sure. That was just one guy's opinion. Besides, God's the one who makes the final decision when it comes to that. Just pray on it, man."

Stefan huffed in disgust. "He don't wanna hear nothin' I gotta say."

"Come on, man, get in the car."

"You think she…still love me?"

"Of course she does. Why do you think she called me and asked me to find you and bring you home?"

"I love her so much." Stefan suddenly began to sob. "I love her so much, Dub."

Julian wrapped his arms around Stefan and said, "I know you do. It's gonna be all right, Coop. I promise, everything's gonna be all right."

CHAPTER 22
A TEST OF FAITH

C harisse was waiting at the door when Julian pulled up. She was so happy when he called to tell her he was bringing Stefan home, but he'd warned her about his condition. She had never seen Stefan drunk and she didn't know what to expect, but she thanked God that he was home and he was safe.

It was freezing outside and she only had on her pajamas and robe, but she stood with the door open. It looked to her as if Stefan was asleep. His head was back against the headrest and he gave no indication that he knew where he was.

"Thank you, Julian," she called.

"Don't worry about it, Risi."

Julian crouched and reached into the car to pull Stefan out, who looked as if he was unconscious.

"Is he okay?" Charisse worriedly asked.

"Yeah, but he passed out on the drive over here. I'll take him upstairs."

Julian lifted Stefan and tossed him over his shoulder as if he weighed nothing. He walked past Charisse into the house and straight up the stairs to their bedroom. Dropping him on the bed as gently as he could, he removed Stefan's shoes and placed them at the foot of the bed.

Hearing Charisse behind him, he turned to her. "He's gonna have a monster of a headache in the morning, but he'll be fine."

"Did he tell you what Dr. Chase said?"

"Yeah. Take care of him, Risi. This is really messing with him."

"I will, Julian, and thank you again for bringing him home," she said as she started to well up.

Julian reached out and hugged her. "He loves you so much, but he's scared right now. You're going to have to be strong for the both of you for a while, Charisse. Don't give up on him, okay?"

"I won't. I never will."

Julian kissed her temple and said, "I know you won't."

AFTER LOCKING THE DOOR BEHIND JULIAN, Charisse returned to their bedroom. Stefan was still flat on his back, and from what she could tell, still unconscious.

Moving to stand beside him, she leaned over and caressed his face. "My sweet man."

Suddenly, he turned his head toward her and opened his eyes. "Risi?"

"I'm here, baby."

As he attempted to turn toward her, Stefan groaned. "I'm sorry, Risi. Don't be mad at me."

Throwing her arm across his prone form, she said, "Shh, honey, I'm not mad at you."

"But I can't give you no babies," he said and tears began to flow from his eyes.

"I don't care, Stefan. As long as I have you, I have everything I need." As she gazed at him through the moisture in her own eyes, she continued, "Besides, Dr. Chase doesn't have the final say in whether we have a baby or not. Only God can determine that, and I believe that He's going to bless us in due season. Remember what you said, with everything we've got going on He's probably giving us a chance to get settled? I'm sure that's what's happening. But even if it's His will that we never conceive a child of our own, we could still adopt."

He reached up and hugged her with all the strength he had, unable to control the sorrow he felt any longer. They cried in each other arms until they had both exhausted all of their tears.

"I'm sorry I made you worry," he mumbled.

"That's okay. I'm sorry that…this is happening to us. But one thing I want you to know, Stefàn, and never forget. I love you. I will always love you, no matter what. You're my husband and we're going to get through this. Together. Okay?"

Unable to say anything due to the emotions that were overtaking him, he simply nodded.

AWAKENING THE NEXT MORNING, Stefàn wanted to die. His head felt as if it were filled with concrete. Unable to rise, but knowing he needed to, he went up on his knees in a feeble attempt to remove himself from the bed. With every part of his body except his knees and his head lifted from the mattress, he groaned.

Charisse was nowhere to be found and he needed her desperately. "Risi." It was barely a mumble.

His stomach was churning uncontrollably and his head was spinning. *Stop! Stop turning the bed!* He wanted to yell at the unseen forces that were making his world spin out of control, but he didn't even have the strength to utter those few simple words.

Seconds later, he collapsed back on to the bed. Like a paraplegic with no control over his limbs, Stefàn attempted to worm his way off the mattress. After what seemed to him like an hour, but was merely five minutes, he was on the floor. Seated with his back against the wooden frame, his head lolled as though his neck muscles had been snapped.

"Risi," he groaned once again in a volume no louder than a dying man's final utterance.

Without warning, however, in the next seconds, he felt the bile coming up his throat.

Grateful for the wastebasket beside the bed, he grabbed it, stuffing his face almost entirely inside as he threw up.

Charisse, at that very moment, was entering the room.

"Stefan!" In alarm, she ran to his side, dropping down beside him and wrapping her arms around his heaving shoulders as he retched repeatedly. Ignoring the horrific odor of his vomit, Charisse held on to him, rubbing his back and trying to soothe not only his debilitated body, but his aching heart as well.

When his regurgitating ceased, Stefan slowly raised his head and groaned in pain.

Charisse reached past him and moved the wastebasket as far away as she could from her vantage point. Placing one of his arms around her neck, she tried to help him up from the floor, but found that to be an impossible task.

"Honey, try to get up."

"I'm sick, Charisse," he moaned.

"I know, but you don't want to stay down here. Come on, let's get you up and back in bed."

"My head…"

"Your head must be killing you. I'll get you some aspirin, okay?"

Leaving him momentarily, she took the basket with her to the bathroom. She dumped the offending contents in the toilet and quickly flushed, then placed the basket on the floor of the water closet and closed the door behind her, shutting in the foul stench until she would deal with it later.

Washing her hands at the double sink vanity, she then reached into the medicine cabinet and removed the aspirin bottle. Taking the rinse cup from the counter top, she filled it with water and returned to Stefan's side.

"Here, baby," she said as she squatted next to him.

Placing the cup on the floor beside her, she opened the aspirin bottle and removed three. "Take these."

Still feeling the effects of his binge, Stefan's movements were slow. Finally, reaching for the tablets she had in her hand, he put them all in his mouth at once.

"Here."

She handed him the cup of water and he emptied it. Dropping the cup unceremoniously onto the floor, he leaned his head against the mattress and closed his eyes.

"Baby, don't you want to get back in bed?" Charisse asked.

"I wanna die," he lamented without opening his eyes.

"I don't want you to die. What would I do if you died?"

He opened his eyes and looked at her.

"I'm damaged goods, Risi."

"No you're not. You're my husband and I love you."

"Why? I can't give you the babies you want. I'll never—"

"I don't care about that," she cut him off. "What's important to me is you. Us. Don't you know that you're all I need? We're gonna be all right, honey. Don't you know how blessed we are to have each other?"

"But I know how much you wanted—"

"There are many things I've wanted in my life but haven't always gotten and I'm still okay. Look at me. I'm still okay. I've got what's important." Cradling his face in her hands, she continued. "I've got my husband, my family, my friends… We have a beautiful home. We've got each other. I'm not going anywhere and I'm not going to let you go either. We're going to get past this. We've got so much to be thankful for, don't you see?"

Stefan stared at her, trying to figure out if she was for real or just a figment of his imagination. His mind still foggy from his alcoholic haze, he wasn't sure if she was speaking from the heart or simply to cheer him up.

"Come on, baby. Get up off this floor. I'll call Carrie and let her know you won't be in today. I'm going to stay here, too, and make sure you're okay."

With her help, they were able to get him back onto the bed.

Pulling the covers up to his chin, Charisse sat down beside him and kissed his forehead. "I love you," she tenderly stated.

"I love you, Risi," he reciprocated as his eyes filled.

"Get some sleep, baby. When you wake up, I'll run you a nice bath and you can sit in the Jacuzzi and soak for a while. Then I'll fix you something light to eat, okay?"

He nodded.

When she rose to leave the room, he reached for her hand. "Risi."

"Yes, baby?"

"I'm sorry."

She shook her head and smiled sadly. "No. You have nothing to be sorry for."

"I'M ANGRY WITH YOU RIGHT NOW, GOD. I don't know if I have any right to be, but I am. There are so many things I want to say to You but I don't even know where to start. Where's Your grace now? Where's Your mercy? Is it because of all those years I was so careless about other people's feelings? Other women's feelings? I know I've used so many women for my personal satisfaction. I realize how selfish I was. If I never asked Your forgiveness before, I'm asking for it now. Please. Please, Lord."

Tears streamed down Stefan's face as he knelt by the side of his bed and pleaded to God.

The effects of his previous night's binge had been slept off. No longer sick to the stomach from alcohol or struggling with a pounding head, now he warred with emptiness, as though the most important part of his soul had been wrenched from his body.

"What kind of man can I be if I can't even give my wife a child? I can give her anything except the one thing she wants most. I love her, God, so much. How can I look into her beautiful eyes, knowing how disappointed she must be with me? I know You can do anything, God. I know You can..." His sobs broke free from his breaking heart. "God, I know nothing is too hard for You. Please, fix me. Fix me, God."

Charisse stood silently outside the door of their bedroom, tearfully listening to her husband's heartfelt entreaty. She sent up her own silent prayer. *I love him so much, Lord. Please take his hurt away. Please wrap your comforting arms around him. Please bless him with Your peace, Lord. Let him see how much I need him and love him. I don't care if we never have a child. I just don't him to hurt anymore.*

Not wanting Stefan to see how upset she was, and even more, not wanting to interrupt his very personal moment with God, she turned and went back downstairs to the kitchen.

Since he was awake, she decided that she'd make him a fruit smoothie instead of anything too heavy just yet since she was unsure how his stomach might feel. This time when she started back up the stairs, she purposely tried to make as much noise as possible so he'd know she was coming.

Entering the bedroom, she found him standing at his bureau.

"Hi, baby. I was hoping you'd be up. I made you a banana smoothie. They say they're the perfect remedy for a hangover. How do you feel?" she asked.

"Hi, honey. I'm okay."

Placing the glass on the side table, she moved in front of him and wrapped him in a tender embrace.

Stefan eagerly reciprocated her hug, kissing her atop her head.

Looking up at him, she asked, "Want to share a bubble bath?"

He smiled sadly but replied, "That would be nice."

"Julian brought your car back a couple of hours ago."

"Where was it?"

"At the bar where he found you last night," she told him.

Stefan shook his head in disgust. "I'm sorry, baby. I must've really showed out last night, huh?"

"No, actually, you were pretty docile." She smiled up at him and added, "You shouldn't drink, though."

Unable to stifle his chuckle, "Don't worry. I won't be doing that again. What time is it anyway?"

"Six-forty."

"P.M.?"

When she nodded in the affirmative, he mused, "I slept the whole day away."

"You needed it." She moved out of his embrace and reached for the smoothie, picking it up from the side table. "Here, baby, drink this. I'll go run the tub. If you want, I'll order something in when we get out."

Minutes later, Charisse reclined comfortably against Stefan's form in their oversized whirlpool tub.

"Do you think I should get a second opinion, Risi?" he asked.

"Yes."

"And if I get the same report?"

"We'll just... We'll just give it to God and leave it there."

"I think He's punishing me for the way I used to live. It's not fair that you have to suffer for what I might have done, though."

"The only suffering I feel is because of how this has affected you." Charisse repositioned herself in the tub so she could face him. "Honey, it's so important to me that you know I am not disappointed in you. If it turns out that we never have a child, I'll be okay with that as long as we're together. As long as it doesn't affect the way we love each other. I still believe, no matter what the doctors say, that God is going to bless us with a child. We can't always figure out why He does what He does. And like you said the other day, our time is not the same as His time. Maybe there's something He wants us to learn before He makes us parents. I don't know. I don't even think we should be trying to speculate on why He does what He does the way He does it. We're just not that smart," she said with a slight laugh. Placing a sudsy hand on his face, she lovingly leaned in and kissed him. "You are the man God selected for me to spend the rest of my life with and I love you so much. I believe as long as we don't turn our backs on Him, He will bless us with the desires of our hearts."

"I'm a little angry with Him, right now, Risi," Stefan admitted.

"I think He can handle it. Just don't stay angry, baby. We need to stay in prayer about this, but we need to never stop thanking Him for the ways He has blessed us already. He's given us so much. His Word promises that anything we ask for in His name will be given to us. I believe that."

"I want to believe that, too. Pray for me, Risi. I need all the prayers I can get right now," Stefan said.

"I will never stop praying for you, my sweet man."

Pulling her into his arms, Stefan kissed his wife as though his life depended on it.

THEY BROKE THE NEWS TO THEIR PARENTS ON CHRISTMAS DAY. Damaris cried. Mike asked Stefan, "How are *you* doing, son?"

Looking over at Charisse before answering, he reached for her. Pressing his lips to the back of her hand, he answered, "We're dealing with it. Not really much else we can do."

"Have you considered adoption at all?" Mike then asked.

Shaking his head, Stefàn replied, "We're going to wait on God. If He leads us in that direction, we'll talk about that then. Right now, we're just trying to get past this present reality."

Seeing how upset his mother was, Stefàn moved over to her and wrapped his arms around her. "Mom, I know you must be disappointed."

"Oh, baby, it's not that. Of course I would love to have grand-children from you and Risi, but I'm more concerned about you. Are you sure you're okay?"

"Yeah. I'm okay, Mom."

"We could use your prayers, though," Charisse added with a smile.

Her parents were equally saddened by the news.

When they were alone, Barbara asked Charisse, "How's he handling this, baby?"

"He was devastated at first, but he's getting better. We're going to another doctor after the first of the year for a second opinion, but if we get the same diagnosis, we're just going to wait and see. Dr. Chase didn't say it was impossible for us to conceive, just that it was highly unlikely."

"Would you ever consider adoption?" her mother asked.

"I don't know. I mean I know there are hundreds of children out there who need good homes, but we haven't thought that far into the future yet. We're just going to take it one day at a time and stay in prayer about it."

"I'll pray for you, too."

"Thanks, Mommy. We can never have too many people praying for us."

AFTER RECEIVING THE SAME REPORT upon seeking a second opinion, Stefàn tried to do as Charisse suggested. *Give it to God and leave it there.* Wishing he were as faithful as she was, he, nevertheless, struggled with trying to figure out why this was happening to them.

Although he tried to put up a good front for Charisse's sake, she saw right through his charade.

He came home from work one evening to find her waiting for him on the living room sofa. The house was dark, except for one lamp on the end table near her.

"Hey baby, why you sitting in the dark?" he asked as he walked over to kiss her.

Leaning up to receive his buss, she said, "We need to talk, Stefan."

"What's up?" he asked, taking a seat next to her.

"I thought we agreed that we would let God work this out for us?"

"What do you mean?"

"You've been putting on a good show for the last few weeks, but I want you to stop worrying about this."

"I'm not," he lied.

Seeing through his deception, her look was scolding and penetrating.

She knows me too well. "I've tried, baby."

"Do you realize this is affecting your sleep? You've been tossing and turning, talking in your sleep and you wake up exhausted every morning. It's beginning to show on your face, baby. I can't have you walking around looking all busted, now," she said good-naturedly.

"I've been keeping you awake, too, huh?"

"Yeah. Besides, do you know it's been almost three weeks since we've made love. I miss you."

"I'm sorry. I know it's selfish to think of this as a personal assault against my manhood, but that's how I feel. I can't help it. I feel less than—"

"You're not and I don't think of you that way," she interrupted before he could finish his statement. "Sweetheart, you're the only one who thinks that. You have the power to believe that God is punishing you for something you've done in the past or preparing you for something really great in your future. Nothing I can say or do will ever convince you otherwise. You have always been—since we first met—the most confident person I've ever known. You've always been sure of yourself in everything you do. You've never let anyone tell you that you couldn't be something or do something that you have your heart set on. This is no different. If you believe that you…that we will never have a child…we won't. You have to believe it right here," she said as she pressed her hand against his heart. "Hebrews 11:1 says, 'Faith is the substance of things hoped for, the evidence of things not seen.' If you don't have faith that God can open doors that no man can, it won't happen."

Stefan pondered Charisse's words, taking them to heart. Staring into her eyes, he saw the love he had come to depend on radiating out to him and he clung to it. "You're right. I've let this whole thing knock the wind out of me and I've been struggling to catch my breath ever since." He reached out and pulled her into a tight embrace. "You are so good for me. I don't know what I would do without you, Risi. And you're right. I need to stop feeling sorry for myself and get busy living the life He's blessed me with. I'm sorry for neglecting you, baby."

"You don't have to apologize to me, honey. I just need my man back."

He rose suddenly from the sofa, but leaned down and swept her into in his arms.

"What are you doing?" she asked with a giggle.

"I've got some catching up to do. I hope you're ready."

"Well, if I'm not, I'd better get ready, huh?"

"I know that's right." Before heading toward the stairs, he kissed her softly and said, "Thank you for reminding me of who I am."

CHAPTER 23

BACK TO LIFE

T he self-defense seminar that Stefan taught last year at the church was so well-received by the members that he was asked to repeat it twice a year. Being the expert martial artist that he was, and remembering what an impact the training had on his life as a youngster, Stefan asked Pastor Young if it would be possible to begin a regular training program for the youth ministry. Not only would it be a useful skill that the children could carry with them for the remainder of their lives if they chose to stick with it, but the discipline required and gained by the study was invaluable.

Pastor Young, though agreeable to implementing the program, was concerned about the funds needed to be successful with it. Stefan assured him that cost would not be an issue. Recruiting Julian, his brother, Devin, and Barretto as volunteer teachers, by the end of July they were given access to the fellowship hall on Tuesday and Thursday evenings to hold classes.

Initially, only ten students ranging in age from seven to twelve enrolled, but when the other kids learned how much fun the ten pioneers were having, they asked to join the class. Ultimately, they ended up with twenty-eight students ranging in age from seven to seventeen. That being the case, Stefan broke the training up into three groups by age—seven to ten years old; eleven to fourteen years old; and fifteen to seventeen years old—and implemented six-week sessions. At the completion of two sessions the children were then tested and ranked. Stefan taught the youngest group with Devin overseeing the mid-aged kids and Julian and Barretto pairing up for the oldest kids since they were the largest group. Noticing how dedicated the children were to the martial arts training, Stefan donated uniforms to each one on the condition that if they decided to drop out of the program, they would return it so someone else could use it.

One of Stefan's students was a boy by the name of Jared Malik Mills. Jared was a high-spirited seven-year-old with an eagerness to learn *and* play. Jared lived with his grandmother, Mrs. Mills, a widow in her mid-seventies. Jared was the child of Mrs. Mills' only daughter, Margaret, who'd died when Jared was two years old. The boy had no real memory of his mother; he knew only what his grandmother told him about her. Jared's father had never been a part of his life.

Loving the child's energy and enthusiasm, Stefan took a quick liking to Jared when he began the martial arts lessons because his rambunctious personality reminded him of himself when he was a child. The boy was small for his size, but he was smart and quick-witted, and always respectful. Whenever Stefan saw him on Sundays at church, Jared greeted him vociferously.

By Charisse's and Stefan's second wedding anniversary, the martial arts program had been up and running for nine months and each of the students enrolled in this current session were doing well.

One Sunday in early May, Stefan approached Mrs. Mills after service. Jared had missed the preceding week's lessons.

"Mrs. Mills," he greeted her cheerfully and with a warm embrace. "How are you?"

"Oh, hello, Stefan. I'm doing pretty well. How are you, son?"

"I'm well. Is everything okay? I missed Jared last week at class."

"I know. I'm sorry. He was upset with me, too. It's just that sometimes I'm so tired by the time I get through with him with his homework and everything, I don't always have the energy to bring him out. That boy wears me out sometimes," she confessed.

"Oh, you should have called me. I'd have come and picked him up. As a matter a fact, why don't I do that? I'll come get him and bring him to class. He can bring his books and I'll make sure he gets his homework done and gets something to eat. That way you can get a break in the evenings. By the time I bring him home, he'll be ready to take a bath and get in bed," Stefán suggested.

Finding the idea appealing and intrusive all at once, Mrs. Mills shrugged, "I couldn't have you go to that trouble."

"Mrs. Mills, it would be no trouble at all. It would be my pleasure. I know he's a handful and God bless you for everything that you do for him. If I can do anything to lighten your load, I'm more than happy to. I'm kinda fond of the little guy anyway," Stefán said with a sincere smile.

"You sure you wouldn't mind?"

"Absolutely."

She smiled in relief. "That would be such a big help to me. I don't have nobody to help me with him and sometimes I feel so bad 'cause I can't do all the things with him that he'd like to do. I'll give you a little something for your trouble."

"You'll do no such thing," he adamantly refuted. "I told you, it's no trouble and I've got nothing but time. Maybe on the weekends I can come and get him and take him out. I have nieces and nephews his age and he'd be right at home with them."

"I'm sure he'd like that. I don't always feel comfortable letting him go outside by himself, you know, with all these sick people snatching kids up and all," she said with a frown.

"I completely understand that. You wouldn't have to worry

about him with me. I'll make sure he's fed and exhausted by the time he comes back home," Stefan assured her.

"Mr. Cooper! Hi!"

Stefan turned at the loud greeting as Mrs. Mills scolded her grandson, "Jared, stop yellin' in this church."

"Sorry, Grandma. Hi, Mr. Cooper."

The youthful smile greeting Stefan was genuine and bright and warmed his heart immediately. The curly haired, dark-skinned child who stared up at him with "hero-worship" adoration was oblivious to the fact that his white shirt was pulled halfway out of the waist of his pants or that his clip-on bow-tie was askew.

"What's up, little man?" Stefan asked as he held his hand out, palm up.

Jared slapped his palm with his own and answered, "Nothing much."

As he adjusted the boy's bow-tie, Stefan said, "I was just talking to your grandma about picking you up for your lessons from now on."

"For real?" he asked excitedly.

"Yeah, for real." Stefan was tickled by his reaction.

"Good, that way I won't miss no more classes," he said as a frown flickered across his face.

"Tuck in your shirt, Jared," his grandmother chimed in.

He started to do as his grandmother directed, but when Stefan added that he'd have to bring his school books and couldn't take any lessons until his homework was done, Jared halted his movements and cried, "Aw, man."

"Aw, man, nothing. That's the deal. Are you with it or not?" Stefan asked.

Jared shrugged in concession, "I'm with it."

"All right, let's shake on it," Stefan said, offering his hand.

Jared took the large appendage and shook it robustly.

"My man." Giving his attention back to Jared's grandmother, Stefan said, "Mrs. Mills, do you need a ride home?"

"That would be nice, if you don't mind," she answered with a smile.

"I don't mind at all."

"Where's Charisse?"

"She's got a meeting with the Women's Ministry and won't be home until later. You wait here, I'll bring the car to the door," Stefan offered.

"Okay. Thank you, sweetheart."

"Can I come with you? Can I go with him, Grandma?"

"Sure, come on, man."

"Go on," Mrs. Mills said, shaking her head.

She smiled as Jared took Stefan's hand and walked away with him. "Thank you, God, for that sweet man," she whispered.

BY THE MIDDLE OF JUNE, Jared Mills was a fixture in the Cooper household. Most Friday evenings, Stefan picked him up when he got off of work and returned him to Mrs. Mills on Sunday after church.

Jared was now also involved in the little league baseball team that Julian's son, L'il Jay had been playing with for a couple of years. He had taken to addressing them as Uncle Coop—as L'il Jay did—and Aunt Risi.

Stefan loved having him around and Charisse was tickled and more than a little overjoyed that Jared so occupied Stefan's mind that he had no time to think about their still childless status. In actuality, they hadn't talked about it now for several months. There were even times when Charisse wondered if he had completely given up hope that they'd ever have a child. Although it had been over a year since the diagnosis, she still prayed every night for God to bless them with a child of their own.

The Thursday before Fathers' Day, however, sparked a series of events that Charisse would never have predicted.

As usual, Stefàn left his office and headed straight to Mrs. Mills house to pick up Jared for their martial arts class.

Greeting her with a kiss on the cheek, Stefàn asked, "How're you doing today, Mrs. Mills?"

"I'm pretty good, Stefàn. How you doin'?"

"I'm great. Where's my man? I'm surprised he's not waiting for me at the door like he usually does."

With a frown, she answered, "He's up in his room. He's upset about something that happened at school today. He's been in there all afternoon."

"What happened?" Stefàn asked with genuine concern.

"I'll let him tell you. You go on up."

When Stefàn opened the door to Jared's room after lightly tapping and getting no answer, he found the boy stretched out on his bed with his face turned away from the door.

"Jared? Hey, buddy, what's going on?"

Jared didn't reply, but Stefàn noticed his body quake as though he were crying.

Moving to the bed and sitting next to his prone form, Stefàn reached for the youngster and lightly brushed his hand across his head. "What's the matter, J? Come on, turn over and talk to me."

Jared turned and looked up at Stefàn with tear-filled eyes.

"Hey, what happened?" Stefàn pressed as his heart ached at the sadness he witnessed in his little friend's eyes.

Sniffling and suddenly dragging his sleeve across his face to wipe his runny nose, Jared began. "Grandma won't let me stay home from school tomorrow."

"Why don't you want to go to school?"

"'Cause tomorrow is 'bring your fathers to school day' and everybody's got a daddy 'cept me," the child groaned.

Stefan's heart lurched in his chest. He reached for Jared and lifted him onto his lap and enclosed him in a tight hug. "Hey, that's all right. Don't cry, Jared. I'll go with you tomorrow."

"But you're not my daddy."

"Yeah, but I could be your godfather. Do you know what that is?" Jared shook his head.

"A godfather is someone who takes over the job of a father when the real father is not around. So you'd be my godson."

Jared looked up into Stefan's eyes with a hint of confusion. "But it won't be… You won't be my real father, though."

"That's all right. Ask your grandmother. A godfather is very important. He's supposed to take care of you like your father would."

"I wish you could be my real father," Jared moaned.

Stefan had to close his eyes and bite his tongue because his impulse was to respond, "I wish I was your real father, too." Instead, he squeezed Jared a little tighter. "So what d'ya think of my idea?"

Jared peered hopefully into Stefan's eyes. "You would really come with me?"

"Of course, I would. You're my man, right?" He put out his open palm and Jared slapped it hard.

"Right."

"All right. See, that was an easy problem to solve. Get your stuff together. We're already late and everybody's gonna be asking, 'where's Mr. Cooper?'" Stefan said in a comical tone.

Jared laughed and jumped down off of Stefan's lap.

As he proceeded to retrieve what he needed to take with him, Stefan asked, "Did you do your homework?"

"We didn't have any," Jared eagerly answered.

"Okay. I'll be downstairs."

"Okay!"

When Stefan got home that night after returning Jared to Mrs. Mills, he was a little disheartened. He recounted to Charisse the conversation he'd had with Jared and how heart-broken he was about his situation.

"That boy needs a full-time dad, Risi."

"I know, baby, but you're doing a wonderful thing by going to school with him tomorrow and by spending time with him on such a regular basis," she assured him.

"Yeah, but that's no real fix for him. I mean, the weekends when I have to work, he's just stuck. Mrs. Mills can't keep up with him. And truthfully, at her age, she shouldn't have to. She should be enjoying her golden years without having to run behind an energetic seven year old like Jared. You think I don't notice how relieved she looks every time I pick him up?"

"I'm sure she is. But what more can you do for him than what you're doing?"

Stefan chose not to voice what he was really feeling. Instead, he said a silent prayer that God would give him a clear signal to proceed in what he was thinking.

The weather was warm and sunny that Fathers' Day weekend, so Stefan hosted an impromptu cookout after church, inviting his and Charisse's parents and siblings, Julian's small family and Myra and Barretto. Although, he and Charisse had invited Mrs. Mills to come home with them after church, she opted to spend the afternoon with her best friend, Eva Chambers, at the senior citizens home where she resided. As such, Jared was present at the cookout as well.

Everyone in both families had already met Jared and had fallen under his spell. He was considered by all to be another one of the kids in the Cooper/Ellison clan.

As they lounged around the backyard that afternoon, Myra, Charisse and Michele watched as Stefan wrestled with Jared, L'il Jay and his nephews, Michael and Sean.

"Stefan acts just as bad as those kids," Michele said, with a chuckle and a shake of her head.

"Who you tellin'?" Charisse replied with a smirk.

"He's really crazy about that little boy, Jared, huh?" Myra suddenly asked.

"You have no idea."

"Where are his parents?"

"His mother passed away when he was just two years old and according to Mrs. Mills, his father's never been around," Charisse replied.

"How old do you think Mrs. Mills is, Risi?" Michele asked.

"She's got to be at least in her seventies, I would think."

"And she's taking care of him by herself?" Myra asked incredulously.

"She's trying."

"He looks like a handful."

Michele and Charisse chorused, "He is."

The women laughed.

"I guess Stefan's been a real blessing to her, then," Myra added.

Charisse nodded pensively and sighed. "Jared's been a blessing to us, as well. Stefan devotes so much of his time to him that I don't think he's really even thought about our situation."

"I didn't think so," Myra said.

"Have you guys thought about alternatives at all?" Michele asked.

"Not really. I still believe God's going to bless us with our own child one day. I'm not giving up on that hope."

"That's good, but what if that doesn't happen, Risi?" Myra

asked. "I know how much you've always wanted kids. Maybe adoption is something you should at least consider."

"I'm still not ready to think about that. Besides, Stefàn has been happier in these last few months than he's been in a long while, and I don't want to mess with that."

"I don't want to think too negatively, and God forbid this should happen, but what would happen to Jared if Mrs. Mills passed away?" Michele asked.

"I don't know, Shelly. I *really* don't want to think about that."

AT STEFÀN'S SUGGESTION, Mrs. Mills registered Jared in the summer day camp program L'il Jay had been going to for the past few years so he was out of her hair during the day. The martial arts lessons were on hold during July and August, but Stefàn still trained Jared when they got together.

He was becoming more and more attached to the child with each passing day.

Jared's eighth birthday was July twelfth so Stefàn and Charisse threw him a birthday party and invited all of their nieces and nephews, as well as several of the children that went to Sunday school with him. He had a wonderful time, it being the first birthday party that he'd ever had, and he was delighted with all of the new toys and video games he received as gifts. Mrs. Mills told Stefàn at the end of the party, "You and your wife are the best thing that's ever happened to that boy. I only wish he had full-time parents like the two of you. You're going to be a wonderful father and mother when you have your own children."

On a Wednesday night in August, just after Charisse's thirty-second birthday, Stefàn surprised her as they sat on the swing in their backyard.

"Honey, how would you feel about adopting a child?"

"I don't know. I wouldn't mind, if that was what you wanted to do. I still think we're going to have a baby of our own one day, though," she answered truthfully.

"Yeah, we might."

She had been leaning against him but sensing something was on his mind, she sat up to take in his countenance. "Is adoption what you really want to do?"

Stefan studied her face for a long moment before he replied, "I want to adopt Jared."

Initially surprised by his statement, Charisse quickly surmised that she shouldn't have been. Knowing how strong the bond of love and adoration between the two was, she had to admit that over the course of the last few months, she had gotten quite used to having him around and he had become very dear to her as well.

"Did Mrs. Mills say something to you about this?"

"Not really. I told you what she said after his party, but even before that... I've been thinking and praying on it for a while. Risi, he needs permanence. Mrs. Mills loves him and does the best she can for him, but he needs a man in his life on a full-time basis, not just on the weekends."

When she didn't respond, Stefan continued, "There's a reason Jared and I met; why we hit it off so well, right from the start. I've always wanted a son and with me being... Well, with my problem, I may not ever...I may not ever be able to have one naturally. I've accepted that, Risi. You said it yourself, that God gives us the desires of our hearts if we follow Him. I've prayed and prayed that He would bless us with a child, baby, but I realize, too, that the answers to our prayers don't always come packaged the way we'd like them to. We have a tendency to put God in a box, thinking if He doesn't do it like this or like that, He's not going to do it. But the more I think about it, the more I believe that's what He was doing when He brought Jared and I together. He needs a father and I want a son. This is a lot to ask of you, but please think about it, baby. This is so important to me. I feel like this...like Jared is God's way of fulfilling the desire of my heart."

Recognizing the sincerity of his plea in his piercing brown eyes, Charisse smiled. She reached for his hand and simply said, "If that's what you want, Stefan, and if Mrs. Mills has no objection, then that's what we'll do."

Stefan stared at her for a long moment as his eyes welled with tears. "Are you sure, Risi?"

She moved closer to him and wrapped her arms around him. "Yes, I'm sure. I love that little guy, too, you know."

Charisse and Stefan decided to wait until Sunday after church to speak to Mrs. Mills about their proposal. The remainder of that evening was spent discussing Jared and his grandmother. They considered everything, including letting Mrs. Mills move in with them so she'd still be with Jared.

"We certainly have the room, if she wants to stay here," Charisse said.

"You wouldn't have a problem with another woman in your kitchen?"

"I don't anticipate that there would be any problems," she replied.

"I can't imagine she'd want to stay in that big house by herself," Stefan pointed out.

"Do you really think she'll let us do this, baby?"

"I don't know, Risi. But if she honestly considers what's in Jared's best interest, she'll go along with it. She knows how much we love him, and I'm sure she knows he'll be in good hands.

Besides, she'll be able to see him whenever she wants. She'll still be a part of his life."

"And hopefully she'll rest easy, knowing he's loved and being cared for."

"Right."

The following Saturday afternoon, Charisse was in their backyard tending to her small flower garden when the phone rang. Stefan had been at work since nine-thirty that morning and she wasn't really expecting him until close to seven that night. This was one of those rare weekends when Jared was not with them, so for most of the day she had been absorbed in minor projects around the house.

Removing her gardening gloves as she rose from her knees, she moved to the patio table where she'd placed the cordless extension when she came out of the house an hour earlier. Wiping the sheen of perspiration from her forehead with the sleeve of her shirt, she picked up the receiver with her other hand.

"Hello," she cheerily answered.

"May I speak with Stefan Cooper?"

"He's not in right now. Can I take a message?"

The male caller asked, "May I ask who I'm speaking to?"

"This is his wife. Who is this?"

"My name is Doctor Anthony Mazzarelli of Hackensack Medical Center. I'm calling with regard to Edna Mills. She had her nephew listed as her emergency contact."

"What happened? Is she all right?" Charisse anxiously inquired as the pace of her heartbeat quickened in fearful anticipation of the caller's next words.

"I'm afraid not. She's suffered a massive coronary."

"Oh, no. Where's Jared?"

"You're referring to her grandson? He's with a representative from the Department of Children and Families. That young man may have saved her life. He called 9-1-1."

"Are they still at the hospital?"

"Yes. Will you please contact your husband and ask him to come as quickly as possible?"

"We'll be there in thirty minutes."

True to her word, Charisse and Stefan rushed into the emergency room of Hackensack Medical Center a half hour later.

Immediately upon hanging up from the doctor, she'd dialed Stefan's office as she hurried into the house and up to their bedroom to clean herself up and change. She'd caught him as he was walking back in from a showing.

Heading directly to the information desk, Stefan addressed the nurse, "I'm here for Edna Mills. Dr...." He paused, not remembering the physician's name.

"Dr. Mazzarelli," Charisse chimed in as soon as she heard him hesitate.

"Are you a relative?" the nurse/clerk asked.

"I'm her nephew," he lied, before truthfully stating, "and her emergency contact."

"One moment, please." The hospital employee picked up the telephone and punched in three digits. She spoke softly into the receiver, then waited for a reply. As she hung up the phone she said, "Dr. Mazzarelli has her in surgery."

"Where's Jared?" Stefan urgently asked.

"Who's Jared?"

"Her grandson. My nephew," he quickly added.

"Oh, the little boy. He's in the lounge with someone from DCF. That's right around the corner on your left."

Charisse called back, "Thank you," as they immediately started away from the desk.

Upon entering the lounge, they heard, "Uncle Coop! Auntie Risi!" Jared came barreling toward them with his arms outstretched.

Stefan scooped him up and into a tight embrace. "Hey, man. You okay?"

Jared nodded but tears welled in his eyes as he stated, "Grandma fell down on the floor and I called 9-1-1."

Charisse reached out to stroke his head as Stefan replied, "I know. They told us. That was very smart thinking, what you did. I'm proud of you."

"Is Grandma gonna be okay?" he asked in a worried tone.

"I hope so. The doctors are operating on her to make her better," Stefan answered.

"Let's say a prayer for her, okay?" Charisse suggested.

"Okay."

The three of them embraced and before Charisse or Stefan could utter a word, Jared began, "Dear God. Please make Grandma better. Please don't let her die 'cause I don't want her to die. She's a good Grandma and I love her. But if you make her die, please let her go to be with my Mommy so she won't be alone no more. Amen."

Charisse was in tears by the time Jared closed his prayer; the innocent request made with the sincerity that could only come from a child's heart.

"That was a beautiful prayer, Jared," Stefan told him.

"It certainly was," Charisse said.

"How come you're crying, Auntie Risi?"

She smiled and answered, "Because I'm so proud of you."

"But why would that make you cry?"

"Well, when I get very emotional, like now, the tears come on their own."

"That's 'cause she's a girl, right?" he asked, addressing Stefan.

"Yeah, but it sometimes happens to us fellas, too," he explained. "Just not as much."

Across the room, Angela Robinson watched the touching scene. In the ninety minutes since she had arrived at Hackensack Medical Center, she'd developed a fondness for the boy, Jared Mills. Quite a talkative little fellow, he'd already told her all about his Uncle Coop and Aunt Risi, as well as how he'd called the ambulance when his grandmother collapsed on the living room floor. He'd given her the impression that he was a fearless young man, but she didn't miss the relief he displayed at the sight of his aunt and uncle.

She hated to break up their reunion, but she had a job to do. "Excuse me. I'm Angela Robinson from the Department of Children and Families. Are you related to Mrs. Mills?"

Stefan and Charisse stole a quick glance at one another before answering. Stefan started to lie and tell the woman he was a member of Mrs. Mills' family, but quickly decided that he would tell the truth and trust that God would work everything out.

"Not by blood, no. Mrs. Mills is a very close family friend, and Jared is my godson."

"Can I have your names, please?"

"I'm Stefan Cooper and this is my wife, Charisse. We'll be able to take Jared home with us, won't we?"

"I would have to have permission from his grandmother for that," Miss Robinson stated as she wrote their names on a form on the clipboard she was holding.

"But she might be incapacitated for days," Charisse interjected.

"I'm sorry."

"But she had the hospital call me. I know it was so that we could take care of Jared. He's a part of our family. Mrs. Mills would want him to be with us," Stefan insisted.

"Mr. Cooper, I don't make the rules. Unless I have written approval, Jared is going to have to come with me."

"No!" Jared yelled. "I wanna go with Uncle Coop!"

"Where will you take him?" Charisse wanted to know.

"He'll be placed with a foster family—"

"That he doesn't know and who doesn't give a damn about him," Stefan raged.

"What kind of sense does that make?" Charisse wanted to know. "He knows us. Mrs. Mills knows us. We love him and he knows that. His grandmother knows that."

Stefan reached out and caressed Charisse's face reassuringly and winked at Jared before taking the woman's arm and moving her out of their earshot.

He tried to appeal to her sense of decency. "Miss Robinson, you can't do this to him. Don't you think he's got enough to deal with, with his grandmother being sick and all. He needs stability right now. He needs to feel safe. He's safe with me and Charisse. As a matter of fact, if it weren't for the fact that Mrs. Mills took him to the dentist this morning, he would have been at my house, where he spends most of his weekends."

"Mr. Cooper, the hospital called us. With that call, a file is opened. I can't walk back into my office and tell them that I released the child to a non-family member."

"The hospital's records list me as Mrs. Mills' nephew. I could have told you the same thing when you asked me, but I didn't want to start this whole process with a lie."

When Miss Robinson didn't immediately respond, Stefan asked her, "Do you believe in Christ?"

She was taken aback. "My religious beliefs are not at issue here, Mr. Cooper."

"I know that, but would you just tell me. Do you believe in Him?"

"Yes, I do," she answered with a challenge in her tone and glare.

"What do you think He would do in this situation?"

"That's not fair. I'm pretty sure He wouldn't want me to lie or put my job at risk."

"Miss Robinson, I'm not trying to put your job at risk either. I want you to think about Jared. He's like a son to me." Stefan paused momentarily, then added, "Truth be told, my wife and I were going to talk to Mrs. Mills tomorrow after church about the possibility of adopting Jared. At her age, she's really too old to care for him the way he needs. He's a handful and I don't mean because he's a bad kid or anything like that, 'cause he isn't. He's a great kid, but he's a kid; full of life and energy and he wants to rip and run and do all the things that kids his age should do. She can't keep up with him. The reason he spends so much time with me and my family now is so that he can be a kid in every sense of the word and to give Mrs. Mills a break. He spends time with my nieces and nephews, who are his age, and my wife and I have the stamina to keep up with him. Mrs. Mills should be enjoying her golden years, but with his mother gone and his real father having never been in his life, she's all he's got, except for us. We love him and he loves us. If Mrs. Mills could, she would tell you that Jared should be with us." Sighing, heavily he asked, "Isn't there anything you can do?"

Angela Robinson stared up into the piercing brown eyes of this handsome stranger and was torn between her duty as a representative of the state and a child of the King. *He had to go and play the Christ card*, she thought. Sensing his sincerity, she'd witnessed the genuine love shared between he, his wife and Jared. DCF's first duty and concern was for the welfare of the children who came through the system, she reasoned. It was hard not to let her emotions get the best of her in her work, but common sense suggested that these people were safe. She didn't know Mrs. Mills, but she had them listed as her emergency notification. There had to be a reason for that. *Trust and believe*, a soft voice spoke to her heart.

Her own life flashing before her in seconds, Angela, as a product of the system, had vowed to do everything in her power to see that other children were spared her pain. Having been bounced from family to family, she had never felt the love directed to her that was exhibited by this couple for this little boy; something she had always wished for.

Sighing in submission, she whispered, "I'll list you as the boy's uncle since Mrs. Mills has already listed you as her nephew and I'll put that you were already here when I arrived. But, I'll need to visit your home and still get permission from Mrs. Mills when she gets out of surgery."

Stefan's reaction shocked her. He hugged her and kissed her cheek. "Thank you. Thank you so much. God bless you."

Angela blushed as she glanced over at his wife for her reaction. She was smiling as she moved over to them and like her husband, embraced her. "Thank you, Miss Robinson."

"You're welcome."

It wasn't until Sunday afternoon that they were able to see Mrs. Mills. Charisse had arose that morning and began getting herself and Jared ready for church, but Stefan was of a mind to forego the Sunday service and head straight to the hospital. Charisse insisted that they needed to inform Pastor Young and the congregation so that they could all pray for Mrs. Mills' quick and total recovery.

When they entered her room, Mrs. Mills was sitting up, but her eyes were closed and initially, they thought she was sleeping. The moment she heard Jared's voice, however, she opened her eyes and gave them all a weak smile.

Stefan lifted the boy so that he could kiss her cheek. "How you feelin', Grandma?"

"I feel better now that I know you're all right."

Charisse moved around to the other side of her bed and bent over, placing a soft peck on her forehead. "We're glad to see you're all right, too."

"You gave us quite a scare," Stefan good-naturedly added. "Everyone's praying for you at church."

"Thank you, baby. Thank you both," she said as she looked from Stefan to Charisse with a grateful sigh. "I'm so glad you came. I don't want Jared to end up with no strangers."

"Don't worry. God is doing His thing and the caseworker who came to the hospital yesterday is a sister in Christ. She's going to do what she can to make sure he stays with us until you come home," Stefan assured her.

Mrs. Mills didn't respond and the look that filled her eyes was one of sadness. "I need to speak to you, Stefan. Do you think you could come by tomorrow sometime?"

Stefan looked questioningly at Charisse before he replied, "Sure. But you can talk to me now, if you need to."

She reached up and took Charisse's hand and said, "No, I'll wait until we can talk in private."

Charisse and Stefan knew instinctively, she didn't want to speak in front of Jared.

"It's okay, Mrs. Mills. He'll be by tomorrow," Charisse answered. "Won't you, honey?"

"Yes. I'll come on my lunch break."

"Did they give you my things? My house keys and purse?" she then asked.

"No, but they may be here in this closet," Charisse said as she moved to the cabinet in the adjacent corner. Opening it, she found a clear plastic bag with clothing, a smaller clear plastic bag that contained a watch and other pieces of jewelry and a woman's purse. She held it up for Mrs. Mills' inspection. "Is this yours?"

"Yes," she nodded. "Would you reach into my purse and get my house keys?" she directed Charisse.

Doing as she asked, Charisse held them out to her.

"Stefàn, before you come tomorrow, I need you to stop by my house and bring me something. In my bedroom closet, on the upper shelf, there's a lock box. The key to it is in my right night table drawer. Get that and bring them both to me when you come tomorrow, sweetheart."

"All right, Mrs. Mills."

"Grandma, I could show Uncle Coop where it is and I could come with him."

"That's okay, Jared. He'll be able to find it by himself. And besides, I need to talk to Stefàn alone."

"I'm not gonna have to go with that lady, am I?" Jared asked, close to tears.

"What lady you talking about?" she asked him, then looked from Stefàn to Charisse for clarity.

"The woman from DCF," Stefàn answered.

"Oh no, baby. That was taken care of, right?" she said, again looking to Charisse and Stefàn for verification.

"I think so," Stefàn replied.

"Well, after tomorrow, we'll know for certain. I'm gonna make sure of that," Mrs. Mills said with finality.

Stefàn was at Mrs. Mills' bedside at twelve fifteen Monday afternoon. When he arrived there was an older white gentleman seated at her bedside. A folder with various official-looking documents was open and spread out on top of her bedcovers.

"Stefàn. Your timing is perfect," Mrs. Mills greeted him cheerily.

She was sitting up in the bed, a tray of food that didn't look the least bit appetizing was on the movable table in front of her.

"How are you feeling today?" he asked as he leaned over and kissed her cheek.

"I'm coming along. I'll be better when they stop sticking me. I feel like a pin cushion, all these blood tests they keep taking," she griped.

He smiled in response. Turning his gaze to her other guest, he introduced himself. "I'm Stefan Cooper." He extended his hand over the bed.

The man rose from his chair to a height matching Stefan's and smiled warmly as he accepted his hand. "Art Rosen. I'm Edna's attorney. I've heard a lot of good things about you and your wife. Charisse, right?"

"Yes. It's good to meet you."

"Likewise," Art said.

He was a slender man, although he had a bit of a paunch at the middle and his gray pinstriped suit looked as though it had seen many years of wear. His white shirt was dingy, as though it had never been washed with bleach, and combined with the stained blue tie he wore made him look somewhat shabby, but his eyes gleamed with a friendliness only someone truly comfortable with themselves could display.

"How's Jared," Art then asked Stefan.

"He's great. He's at day camp, right now."

"Stefan's gotten him involved in quite a few extracurricular activities in addition to the martial arts lessons he gives him and the other children at church," Mrs. Mills told Art as she reached for Stefan's hand. "He's been a God-send to me."

At that moment, another visitor entered the room.

"Mrs. Edna Mills?"

Stefan turned and recognized the woman from DCF he and Charisse had spoken with on Saturday.

"Yes."

"Hi," she said to Stefan with a shy smile before addressing Mrs. Mills. "I'm Angela Robinson from the Department of Children and Families. How are you feeling?"

"I'm doing much better, thank you," Mrs. Mills answered. "This is my attorney, Mr. Arthur Rosen."

"Hello," she said.

Becoming completely professional, Art replied, "Good afternoon, Miss Robinson. Do you have some papers that you need Mrs. Mills to sign, specifically, related to the guardianship of her grandson, Jared?"

"Yes. Um, Mr. Cooper told me on Saturday that you would sign over custodial rights for Jared's care while you were hospitalized," she said addressing Mrs. Mills.

"That's right."

"I have the papers here for you. I was supposed to take him into custody on Saturday, but I could see that Mr. Cooper and his wife have a relationship with Jared, and since you had listed Mr. Cooper as your emergency contact, I made a judgment call and let them take him. Once you sign, if you're ever hospitalized again, we can avoid going through this."

"Thank you."

"After today, that won't be an issue, anyway," Art added.

Mrs. Mills then asked, "Stefan, did you bring that box?"

"Yes, it's right here," he said, reaching down and removing it from the shopping bag he had placed on the floor near the wall. After he handed it to her, he reached into his pants pocket and stated, "Here's the key."

Taking the box and key, she opened it. "I have all of my important papers in here. Jared's birth certificate, my insurance papers, my will, everything."

"CHARISSE, YOU'RE NEVER GOING TO BELIEVE what happened, baby," Stefan said excitedly into the telephone.

It was two-thirty that same afternoon, and he was on his way back to his office.

"What?"

"I just left the hospital. Mrs. Mills is doing much better. She was sitting up talking with her lawyer when I got there. That girl from DCF came by, too."

"Okay, but what happened?"

"Mrs. Mills' attorney had guardianship papers with him. He said he has to file them with the courts, but that's just a formality. She signed over custodial rights for Jared to us and asked me to speak with you about us adopting him."

"You're kidding."

"I kid you not, baby. See how God works?"

"Did you tell her we were going to ask her about adopting him?"

"I sure did. She had me crying up in there," he said with a laugh.

"We're going to take Jared by there tonight, right?"

"Yeah. What time are you getting off?"

"I'll leave here at four and meet you at the house. What time are you picking him up?"

"Around five. Why don't I pick you up and then we'll go get him and head straight to the hospital. We'll tell him when we're all together."

"Okay. Wow, can you believe how this all worked out?" Charisse asked in awe.

"Honey, I've come to realize that we should never be amazed at the movement of God. We need to learn how to expect a miracle," Stefan said.

CHAPTER 24
EXPECTING MIRACLES

It was January twenty-third and the preceding five months had been rife with highs and lows. Charisse and Stefàn each prayed that with the new year, things would calm down and they would be able to get back to life in the slow lane.

The adoption of Jared Malik Mills-Cooper was finalized near the end of September, although he had been living with them since Mrs. Mills' hospitalization. Jared had been so excited about officially becoming Stefàn's son that during that first week he introduced just about everyone he encountered to his "new dad," regardless of whether they knew Stefàn or not.

Mrs. Mills was in the hospital for two weeks after her heart attack and was sent to a nursing home upon her release, much to her chagrin. Charisse and Stefàn tried to convince her to come and stay with them, but she wouldn't hear of it. Knowing that she would need around-the-clock care—which they had been willing to pay for—and not wanting to be a burden to them, her logic was that with their marriage being just two years young, the last thing they needed was an old woman under foot. She told them time and again that she planned to move into the senior citizens' development her friend, Eva, lived in.

Sadly, a week before Thanksgiving, Mrs. Mills suffered a fatal heart attack and never got to realize that dream. Jared took his grandmother's passing very hard but Stefàn and Charisse did everything they could to assure him that they would be there for him for many years to come.

In October, they learned that Julian and Michele were going to have another child. Michele had been skeptical about sharing the news with them because she realized, despite the adoption of Jared, how Charisse still clung to the hope that she and Stefân would conceive their own child. Julian insisted that they would be happy for them regardless.

Michele and L'il Jay were visiting at the Cooper home one Saturday afternoon. The boys were in the family room playing video games. Charisse and Michele were chatting in the kitchen. When Michele rose from her seat to place a cup and saucer in the sink, Charisse asked, "Shelly, are you pregnant?"

Michele was slow to face her. In fact, Charisse noticed that she'd lowered her head as though she dreaded having to break the news to her. When she finally turned around, her face was sad, but she answered, "Yeah, I am."

"Why do you look so sad?" Charisse wanted to know.

"I know how hard you and Coop have been trying...."

"Oh, no, Michele. Did you think we wouldn't be happy for you?" Charisse rose from her seat and embraced her. "Girl. If you weren't pregnant, I'd hit you, but I don't want to hurt the baby. I'm delighted for you. I think it's wonderful."

Michele's eyes watered and she returned Charisse's embrace. "Julian told me I was being silly, but I didn't want to make you feel bad."

"Oh, so what'd you think, that you'd hide out for the next six or seven months and then when the baby came, tell us a stork dropped it on your doorstep?"

They both laughed.

"I don't know. I hadn't thought that far ahead," Michele admitted.

"When are you due?" Charisse asked.

"Around the middle of March."

"Girl, I really need to hit you. You been pregnant all this time and didn't tell us?"

"I'm sorry for underestimating your friendship. I promise it'll never happen again.

"It better not," Charisse warned.

Myra, too, learned that she was with child during those months and she and Barretto became engaged. They set a wedding date for after the baby's expected arrival in July. Unlike Michele, however, Myra told Charisse the moment she found out, even before she told Barretto.

"Can you believe it, Risi? I'm going to have a baby. Would you have ever imagined?"

"Honestly, Myra, no, I don't think I would have. But I'm happy for you," Charisse truthfully replied. "With you and Shelly both expecting now, mine must be right around the corner."

Myra was silent on the line for the next few seconds.

"You think I'm being overly optimistic, don't you?" Charisse stated after the inflated pause.

"No. I'm sorry, honey. I should have thought twice before I called you," Myra sadly commented.

"Why? I'm happy for you, Myra. For you and Michele. It's been two years since we found out and since we've adopted Jared. Stefan seems pretty content about the whole situation because he has his son, but I still believe, and I'm not going to stop believing, that God is going to bless us with a child of our own. I don't care how long I have to wait. I'm not going to stop believing that. I'm expecting my miracle. I won't ever let that go."

"I love you, Risi. Your faith is such an inspiration to me," Myra told her.

"I have to hold on to my faith in God, Myra. I'd be a nutcase without it."

And although Charisse was truly happy for her and Stefân's friends' blessings, she did find herself a little melancholy at times, wondering, if indeed, she would ever experience the joy of giving birth to Stefân's child.

A few days before Christmas Stefân had been working late because he'd had to go out to the Queens building to meet with his superintendent regarding a tenant they were trying to evict for non-payment of rent. Arriving home at almost nine-thirty, Jared had already been put to bed since it was a school night.

He found Charisse lounging on the chaise in their bedroom. The lights were low and the house was utterly quiet. At first he thought she might have fallen asleep since she didn't stir upon his entrance, but then he stepped in front of her and noticed her tear-stained face.

Reaching out to caress her cheek, he murmured as he knelt beside her, "Risi, honey, what's wrong?"

She opened her eyes and looked at him with the saddest expression he had ever seen. Feeling her pain, his heart broke into a thousand little pieces.

Immediately folding her into his arms as one might a wounded bird, her barely audible sobs were as torturous for him as open-heart surgery without anesthesia. Instinctively, in the next seconds, he knew the cause and his own failure once again loomed large in his mind.

His dream of being a father had been fulfilled when they adopted Jared. As far as Stefân was concerned, he was his son and that was all there was to it. And although he knew that Charisse's love for the boy was genuine, her longing for the joy of carrying a child to term and bringing it into the world was left unfulfilled. With Michele and Myra both expecting, and despite her true happiness for them, he was fairly certain that for her, their conception issues were maximized.

Knowing there were no words he could say that could adequately address what he knew she was feeling, he just held her in silence. After a while, when he noticed that her sobbing had ceased, he lifted her into his arms and carried her across the room to their bed. Laying her gently on the sheets, he stood and began to undress, letting his clothes fall at his feet. Once completely disrobed, he moved onto the bed and pulled her into his arms. Charisse clung to him in desperation and Stefan knew that the only comfort he could give her on this night was the most natural expression of love God had ever created.

ON THIS PARTICULAR JANUARY MORNING, Charisse was in the kitchen making pancakes and bacon for breakfast. The previous night, eight inches of snow had fallen on their town and Stefan and Jared had just come back inside from shoveling. At least, Stefan had been shoveling—Jared had been making snowballs for the fight Stefan promised they could have after they'd eaten breakfast.

Charisse was at the stove when Stefan entered the kitchen. Coming up behind her, he wrapped his arms around her waist and nuzzled her neck. "Smells good in here."

"You must be starving after all that. Did Jared help you at all?"

"Not a whole lot, no," he said with a chuckle.

As if on cue, their son entered the kitchen and said, "Mommy, you should see all the snowballs I made."

"Is that what you were doing out there? I thought you were going to help Daddy shovel."

"Well, I got some of the snow out of the way, right, Dad?"

"Yeah, I guess you could say that. How many did you make?"

"About thirty or something."

"Wow! That many?" Charisse asked. "Are you going to share them?"

As he took a seat at the table, he casually responded, "Nope."

"No?" Stefan asked, feigning insult. "You mean, you're going to make me go out there and make my own snowballs after all the hard work I did shoveling the driveway?"

Jared grimaced. "Okay. You can have some, but not too many. You're bigger than me so you could probably make them faster than me anyway."

"How many pancakes do you want, Jared?" Charisse asked.

"Can I have three?"

"Why don't you start with two?" Stefan suggested. "If you finish those, you can have a third one, okay?"

"Okay. Can I have two pieces of bacon, please?"

"Sure," Charisse said as she placed a plate in front of him on the kitchen table.

"Is it very cold outside?' Charisse asked.

"No, surprisingly, it isn't," Stefan answered. "Baby, you sit down. Let me fix your plate."

"No, it's okay. I've got it."

"Sit down. Relax. Let your man wait on you for a change."

She couldn't refuse him that. "Yes, sir."

After breakfast, the three of them went out in the backyard and had a snowball fight. After that, they took turns making snow angels. Charisse and Stefan were having as much fun, if not more, than Jared. Neither had done anything so carefree since they'd been kids, but with Jared as a part of their lives now, they found themselves more and more often reverting back to activities they'd enjoyed as children just to keep him entertained.

Later that night, as Charisse and Stefan lay snuggled in their bed, she said to him, "I'm really glad we adopted Jared. I love having him here."

Stefan smiled and answered, "I'm glad you feel that way, sweetie. He's a great kid, isn't he?"

"Yeah, he is. He'll probably be a great big brother, too," Charisse added.

Stefan was taken aback by her comment and asked, "Are you pregnant?"

She chuckled softly, "I wish. Just wishful thinking, that's all."

The telephone rang. Stefan looked at the digital clock on the night stand as he reached out to answer it. "Who'd be calling here at eleven o'clock on a Saturday night, knowing we've got to get up in the morning for church? Hello," he said into the receiver.

"Stefan, this is Johnny. Is Charisse there with you?"

He picked up immediately on the urgent tone of Charisse's father's voice. "Yeah. Is everything okay?"

"No, Barb's mom had a heart attack. We're on our way to the hospital."

"Oh, man. Where is she?"

"Columbia Presbyterian."

"We'll be there."

"No. Don't come yet. Jared's probably asleep. I'll call you again when we get there. Star's there with her right now and David and Jonathan are on their way. I'll keep you posted."

"All right."

When he hung up the phone, Charisse asked, "Who was that?"

Stefan turned to her and pulled her into his arms. "Granny Nan had a heart attack, baby."

"What? No!"

"That was your dad. He said they're on their way to the hospital. He said he'd call as soon as they get there."

"We have to go," she insisted as she pulled away from him and threw the covers off. Rising from the bed, she insisted, "I have to go see her. Where is she?"

"She's at Columbia Presbyterian. But, honey, Jared's asleep."

"Then you stay here with him. I have to go."

Stefan rose from the bed and hurriedly moved to her. She had begun to remove her bed clothes but he grabbed her. "All right, baby. We'll go. But I'm not letting you go by yourself. We'll take Jared over to Dub's, okay?"

"Fine." Unable to maintain her composure, she broke down. "Oh Stefan, please let her be okay. I don't want to lose her."

"We'll leave it in God's hands, baby. That's all we can do."

It was a few minutes after midnight when they arrived at the hospital. Charisse's parents, sister and brothers were all there.

"Where is she?" Charisse asked as she rushed to her father's side.

John embraced his youngest daughter, "She's right in there. Mommy's in with her."

Charisse moved away from him without hesitation and went to her grandmother's bedside.

Stefan told her father, "She insisted on coming."

"I had a feeling she would. Where's Jared?"

"He's with Julian. How's she doing?"

John shook his head. "It doesn't look good."

Stefan sighed.

Meanwhile, Barbara, Star, David and Jonathan. stood nearby as Charisse embraced her grandmother's prone body. Granny Nan looked weaker than Charisse had ever seen her and it frightened her. "Granny Nan, I love you," Charisse cried in her ear. "Please wake up. I don't want to lose you. Please wake up."

Stefan entered the room then, going straight to Barbara. He embraced her and gently inquired, "How are you, Mom?"

"I'm scared."

He reached for Star's hand and pulled her into their embrace.

Through the fog caused by the medicine she'd been given, Granny Nan opened her eyes and saw her family standing around. She felt

Charisse's tears on her cheek and reached a weakened hand up to caress her head.

"Granny," Charisse hopefully uttered.

"Don't cry, baby girl. Your granny's tired," she softly stated. She smiled at Charisse and told her, "I'm proud of you, girl. I'm so proud of you." She paused and closed her eyes, causing everyone to hold their breath in dread. Seconds later, however, she opened them and asked, "Is that Stefan?"

He released Barbara and Star and moved to her bedside, "Yes, Granny, I'm here."

She reached out to him. "Come here, baby."

Stefan took the frail appendage and leaned in close to hear her speak.

"You take care of my girl. You hear me?"

He smiled, though tears formed immediately in his eyes. "I will. Always."

"And you take care of those babies." With the little bit of strength she had, she squeezed his hand and urged him, "You take care of them."

He looked questioningly at Charisse, but her attention was focused on her grandmother. Granny Nan closed her eyes again and sighed. Then she was gone.

The funeral for Nannette "Granny Nan" Billings was six days later. By the time they'd left the Ellison's home that evening after the repast and returned to New Jersey, Charisse was mentally and physically exhausted.

Going straight up to her bedroom, she disrobed without ceremony and climbed right into bed.

"Daddy, is Mommy all right?" Jared asked as Stefan helped him prepare for bed.

"She will be. She's just a little sad right now."

"How come everybody's dying?"

Stefàn smiled and said, "Not everyone's dying, J. It may seem like it with your grandma and now Granny Nan, but we're still here, right?"

He shrugged, "Yeah."

"Besides, both of them lived to a good old age and they enjoyed their lives with their families, but God wanted them to be with Him now."

"Is Grandma and Granny Nan angels now?"

"I think they are."

"Can I go and give Mommy a good night kiss?"

"Yeah, I'm sure she'd like that."

Stefàn followed Jared into their bedroom but stood leaning against the door frame as their son moved to the side of the bed.

"Mommy?"

Charisse slowly turned to him.

"I wanted to give you a good night kiss."

She reached for him and he climbed up onto the bed. Hugging him close, Charisse was unable to stifle the tears that came to her eyes.

"Daddy said that Granny Nan is an angel now, so you don't have to be sad anymore. She's with God."

"I know, baby, but I miss her. I'll be okay, though, so don't you worry about me."

"I love you, Mommy."

"I love you, too, Jared."

He kissed her cheek and said, "Sleep tight. Don't let the bed bugs bite," before jumping down from the bed and running back to his room.

When Stefàn returned to Jared's room to tuck him in, he told him, "That was a nice thing you said to Mommy. That'll make her feel better."

"I hope so." Jared knelt beside his bed and said a quick prayer as Stefan watched. He then climbed into his bed.

Stefan kissed him on his forehead. "Good night, son."

"Good night, Daddy. I love you."

"I love you, too."

A WEEK LATER, CHARISSE AWOKE FEELING NAUSEOUS. As she rose from the bed, a wave of dizziness hit her like a brick, causing her to swoon. Stefan was just coming back into the room after taking a shower and noticed her unsteadiness.

"You okay, baby?"

"I just felt so dizzy all of a sudden," she told him as she placed a hand on her forehead.

"Sit down," he said as he reached for her. "Maybe you got up too fast."

"I don't know. I don't feel that good. I feel like…" Suddenly, she wretched and, unable to contain it, threw up on the floor.

"Whoa!" Stefan gasped as he jumped out of the way of the trajectory.

"Oh no," she cried as she dabbed her mouth with the back of her hand. "I'm sorry. I don't know what happened."

"It's all right, baby. Come on, let's get you in the bathroom, just in case you're not done."

She wasn't. By the time she was, she felt like all of her energy was sapped. Stefan helped her wash her face and brush her teeth, then he carried her back to bed.

Jared came barreling into the room just then, but Stefan called out, "Watch your step, J. Mommy had an accident."

Stopping in his tracks, Jared moaned, "Yuk. Mommy threw up!"

"Yes, we know. Go on back to your room while I clean this up."

"Pew, it stinks!"

"Go to your room," Stefan warned.

"I'm sorry, Stefan. I don't know what's the matter with me."

"It's okay, honey. Lay there for a minute until you feel better." As he went about cleaning up the mess, he asked, "Do you think maybe you should stay home today?"

"I don't know."

Suddenly, it dawned on him. "Risi, did you get your period this month?"

"I have to check my calendar, but I think it's due any day now."

Taking the last of the soiled paper towels he'd used to clean up Charisse's regurgitation into the bathroom, he came back into the room and sat beside her on the bed.

"I have to tell you something that's been on my mind since Granny Nan died. That night in the hospital she said something to me that I thought was really strange."

"What?"

"You didn't hear her?"

"No. What did she say?"

"She told me to take care of you, then she told me to take care of those babies."

"Take care of *those* babies?"

"Yeah."

"What babies?" Charisse asked.

"I don't know. I've been trying to figure that out. I think if she was talking about Jared, she would have said so, but then she wouldn't have said, 'babies,' plural."

They stared at one another for a long moment in silence, each pondering Stefan's words. Finally, he asked, "Is there any chance that you might be pregnant?"

A chill ran down her spine and a sudden nervousness filled her. *Could it be?* In a barely audible voice she murmured, "I don't know."

"You said you were feeling dizzy, right? And nauseous. Well—" He shrugged. "This sounds like morning sickness."

Charisse looked over at him but couldn't find the words to comment.

"How do you feel? Do you still feel dizzy?"

"No."

"What about your stomach? You still nauseous?"

She shook her head.

"Why would Granny Nan say that?" he suddenly questioned.

"I don't know. I—"

"I've heard it said that people, just before they die, sometimes have premonitions. Maybe she saw something," he pondered. Then, as if certain and broaching no argument, he said, "You have to take a pregnancy test. Call Dr. Chase."

"Stefan, I don't want to call him and he tells us it's a false alarm. I couldn't bear it. Not now."

"Don't you want to know?" he asked.

"Only if it's positive," she honestly replied.

Jared entered the room then. "Can I come in now?"

They both turned to him, as if they were surprised to see him standing there.

Stefan recovered and said to Charisse, "Relax, baby." He glanced back over at Jared, "Come on, guy. Let's get you some breakfast and get you off to school."

"Can I have a piggyback ride, Dad?"

"A piggyback ride?"

"Yeah." Jared smiled up at him.

"You're too big for a piggyback ride."

"Unh-unh. Pleeeasse?"

"Okay, okay, stop begging." Stefan turned his back and squatted. "Climb on up."

As Jared attempted to do so, Stefan grabbed him around the

waist and turned him upside down. A gleeful scream issued from Jared's mouth, followed by uncontrollable giggles as Stefan tromped out of the room with him.

"Be careful with him, Stefan!" Charisse yelled behind them.

Twenty minutes later, Stefan returned to their bedroom. "I'm just going to run him to school and come right back. You rest until then."

"I need to start getting ready for work," she said.

"No, we're going to take a day off today. Both of us." He snatched his keys and cell phone out of the box in his armoire. Stepping over to the bed, he leaned over and kissed her quickly on the mouth. "I'll be right back."

When Stefan returned thirty minutes later, Charisse was stepping out of the shower.

"Hi, what took you so long?" she asked as he entered the bathroom to find her wrapped in a towel.

"I stopped at the pharmacy and bought you a pregnancy test." With that revelation, her heart began to race.

Stefan noticed the agonizing look she tried to hide and moved to embrace her. "Honey," he gently urged, "wouldn't it be better to find out now, than us losing our hair worrying or wondering?"

"I'm not worried."

"Risi—"

"What if it's negative?" she asked with tears brimming in her eyes.

"Then we keep trying," he reasoned.

She closed her eyes and buried her head in his chest. "I don't want to be disappointed."

"Honey, this is really the first time it's ever seemed like a possibility, right?"

"Yeah, but—"

"Don't you see? I have a feeling. Granny Nan saw something. God whispered something in her ear before He took her, baby, and she whispered it in mine. I was flaking before and I had my doubts that we'd ever even be having this conversation, but, Risi, I believe God is going to do this for us. I believe He wants to give us—give you—what you've prayed for. You've been so faithful to Him, even when I wasn't. You've rejoiced over the way he's blessed Shelly and Myra... You've given so much love to Jared." His own eyes began to water as he thought about how strong she'd been when he should have been. "You kept it all together when I literally fell apart. I believe this is our time."

Charisse looked up into his eyes through her tear-filled ones. "I'm scared."

"Don't be, sweetie. I'm here and we're going to make it through this together, like we have been, no matter what the outcome. I believe you are blessed and highly favored of the Lord. He won't let you down."

Her hold on him tightened. "I love you, Stefan.

He placed a tender kiss on her lips, adding, "I love you, too, sweetie."

"I did tell Myra I was expecting my own miracle."

"And what did Pastor say? He said we should pray with expectation and not be surprised when God shows up and shows out."

"Okay, give me the test."

After reading the instructions and following them to the letter, Charisse and Stefan returned to their bedroom to wait. Although the results would be revealed in sixty seconds, they took that time and prayed silently together.

More than a minute had passed when Stefan said, "We should check now."

"You do it."

He leaned over and gave her a lingering kiss of assurance before rising and moving to the bathroom. It seemed to Charisse like forever before he returned. The look on his face was unreadable.

"What is it?" she anxiously asked as he steadily moved closer to her.

A tear fell from his eye as he knelt before her and showed her the display on the meter. "We're pregnant."

CHAPTER 25

START SPREADING THE NEWS

Needless to say, the Cooper and Ellison clans were thrilled about the news of the impending birth of Charisse and Stefan's first biological child. Barbara and Damaris began planning the baby shower almost immediately, regardless that it would not take place for another seven months, at least.

Myra was overjoyed for Charisse, not only because she would finally have her heart's desire with the birth of Stefan's child, but because their children would actually grow up together.

After a thorough examination by Dr. Chase's partner in practice, Dr. Judith Talbot, who would oversee Charisse's obstetrical care, it was determined that her due date was approximately September 20th.

Stefan was euphoric and couldn't sing God's praises enough upon learning that He had proven the doctors wrong. "Ain't nothing too hard for my God," became his catch phrase. And despite how happy she was that she would finally come to know personally what it was to carry a child to term and bring it into the world, Charisse was happier that Stefan's confidence in himself through God had been restored.

Their only disappointment had been when they first told Jared. His reaction had been totally unexpected.

The rest of the day after they found out had been purely perfect. It seemed as if they had cried tears of joy for the rest of the morning. Between shared kisses, whispered promises, passionate coupling and prayers of thanksgiving, the couple reveled in their oneness like never before. They were excited about sharing the news with Jared. As Charisse had mentioned just days before, she thought he would be a wonderful big brother. His easy demeanor and naturally loving spirit made him the ideal nurturing type of older sibling.

They picked him up from school together. Jared was surprised to see them. Normally, he went to an after-school program at the church and was picked up by one of the program's counselors.

"Hi, Mommy and Daddy. What are you doing here?" he happily questioned as he ran to them.

"Hi, baby," Charisse replied as she hugged him. "We took the day off from work today."

"Are you still feeling sick?" he asked, remembering her earlier excitement.

"No, thank goodness. I feel much better."

"Hi, Daddy." He then turned to Stefan and embraced him.

"Hey, dude. How was school today?"

"It was good. I got a hundred on my spelling test."

"Excellent," Stefan cheered.

"That's wonderful, Jared."

"Thanks, Mom. Miss Abelman put my paper up on the bulletin board with a gold star again."

"Very nice," she said.

"It's the fifth one this year!"

"Way to go, champ. I'm proud of you," Stefan told him.

"Thanks, Dad. Can we go to Pizza Hut for dinner tonight?"

As he held the car door open for Jared to climb into the backseat, Stefan looked over at Charisse and said, "Well, you know what? This is a special day so we should celebrate. Sure, let's go to Pizza Hut. How much homework do you have?"

"Just two things. My math and vocabulary words. I have to write sentences for every word."

"All right, we'll go home and you can knock that out. Then we'll go to Pizza Hut, okay?"

"Okay."

Once seated behind the wheel, he turned back to Jared and said, "Mommy and I have some news to tell you, anyway."

"What?"

"You ever think about what it'd be like to have a little brother or sister?" Stefan asked.

"No."

He looked over at Charisse and smiled. "Don't you think it would be cool, though, to be a big brother?"

"Yeah, probably, but where would they sleep? In my room?"

Charisse and Stefan laughed out loud at that query. "No, you'd have your own room and he or she would have their own room."

"Okay."

"Jared, aren't you curious as to why we're asking you this?"

"Are you going to get another kid so I have somebody to play with?"

"Well, sort of. Mommy's going to have a baby."

Jared turned his focus to Charisse. "A real baby?"

"Yes, sweetheart. A real baby. That's why I was sick this morning. Sometimes when women first get pregnant, they get an upset stomach and that's what happened to me."

"Oh," he remarked with downcast eyes.

A puzzled looked passed between Charisse and Stefan. "What do you think about that?" Stefan asked.

Jared shrugged. "I dunno." He then began fidgeting with his knapsack, and purposely looked everywhere but at Charisse or Stefan.

Charisse was heartbroken. She thought he would be happy that their little family would be growing. Uncertain of whether it was due to a heightened sensitivity caused by her condition or something else, her eyes began to water so she faced forward so he wouldn't see. Stefan did, however, and reached over and took her hand. He mouthed, "It's all right."

When they arrived at the house, Jared headed straight for the stairs, taking them at a run.

"Where you rushing off to?" Stefan called behind him.

"Gotta do my homework," he answered without slowing his pace.

"He doesn't seem very happy about it," Charisse said.

"Maybe he's in shock. I'm really surprised by his reaction, too. Let's give him some time. I'll go talk to him; see what's on his mind."

"I want him to be happy, too."

"I know, honey, but don't you go worrying yourself, okay? He'll come around." Stefan wrapped her in a warm embrace, and kissed her tenderly on her forehead.

Stefan waited about twenty minutes before he went to Jared's room to try and find out what was on his mind.

His bedroom door was closed, which was unusual, so he tapped three times before opening it. "Hey, buddy. How's it going?"

"Okay." Jared was stretched out on his bed and instead of doing his homework, he was aimlessly playing with a pencil.

"How come you're not doing your homework? We're not going to Pizza Hut until you're finished."

"I don't wanna go."

"Why not?"

He just shrugged.

"You still have to do your homework."

"I will."

"What's the matter?" Stefan asked.

"Nothing."

"Jared, look at me."

Jared had yet to make eye contact with Stefan.

"Jared."

When the boy turned to meet Stefan's gaze, there were tears pooling in his eyes.

Seeing this, Stefan sat on the bed beside him and reached out to touch him. "What's wrong, J?"

"I thought you and Mommy liked me."

"What? What d'you mean? We love you."

"But if Mommy's gonna have a baby, then you're gonna send me away," he cried.

"What? Jared." Stefan reached over and pulled him into his arms. The boy's cries were heart wrenching. "Why would you think that? We're not going to send you anywhere. You're our son."

"But I remember when this boy at school said that when his mother died and he went to live with somebody else, that they sent him away when they had a baby of their own. They told him that they couldn't keep him anymore."

Stefan leaned away from him so he could look him squarely in the eye as he assured him, "Jared. I don't know what happened with that boy, but that's not going to happen with us. You are our son. Don't you remember? I told you that once we adopted you, we would be your real parents. We're not only part-time foster parents. You are our son, just as sure as the baby that Mommy has will be ours. The only difference is your natural mother gave birth to you. That's all. That's the only difference. We love you. We're not sending you anywhere. We're a family. This baby is going to be an addition to our family, not a replacement for you. Oh, son, don't ever think, not for a minute or even a second that we don't love you or that you're not important to us. You're our son. Our first son and you'll always be that, okay?"

"For real?" His sobs had decreased to mere sniffles.

"Cross my heart. For real, for real."

"I don't want to live with nobody else, Daddy."

"You won't, not until you're old enough to move out on your own and start your own family, and that's a long time away."

Charisse was at the door in the next second. "Can I come in?"

Turning slightly, Stefan said, "Come on in, baby."

"Jared, you okay?"

He'd been leaning against Stefan so he sat up and nodded that he was.

"What's the matter?" she asked when she noticed that he'd been crying.

"I thought you were going to send me away now that you're having a baby."

She came and knelt on the floor in front of him and asked, "Why would we do that?"

"A kid at school was sent away when his foster parents had a baby."

Charisse cupped his sweet face in her hands and kissed him on his forehead as she told him, "But you're our son, just as if you were our own flesh and blood. Besides, we can't have a baby without you. We'll need you to help us teach him or her how to walk and talk and all kinds of big brother stuff."

"For real?"

"Absolutely. You'll be the only big brother our baby will have. And when I say our baby, I mean mine, Daddy's and yours, too."

A tentative smiled began to show. "It's gonna be my baby, too?"

"It sure is," added Stefan.

"When's it gonna come?" Jared asked.

"Not until September so we have plenty of time to get ready."

"It's gonna be in here?" he asked as he pointed to her belly.

"Yup. You'll even get to feel it kick when it gets bigger."

Jared reached for Charisse and wrapped his arms around her neck in a tight embrace. "I love you, Mommy."

"I love you, too, sweetheart. Always and forever."

CHAPTER 26
SEEING DOUBLE

Once Jared got it fully in his mind that he was not going to be replaced by the baby that Charisse was having, he became quite excited about the impending birth and becoming a big brother. Having always been an inquisitive young fellow, his questions now came nonstop. "Mommy, how did the baby get in there?" "Daddy, how did you put the baby in there?" "Mommy, how's the baby gonna come out?" "Daddy, when the baby comes out, can I teach him how to do karate?"

Stefan told Jared that with Charisse's condition, she would have to be very careful what she did and that the two of them, being the men in the family, would have to take care of her and keep her safe. That being the case, whenever Jared was at home with Charisse, especially if Stefan was not there, he followed her around, making sure she didn't do anything to overexert herself. If he thought she was doing something too strenuous, like lifting a grocery bag—he was right there to help her. Charisse was tickled by his helpfulness sometimes. Other times she would tell him, "Jared, if you don't sit down and leave me alone, I'm going to take away your Xbox."

Stefan attended all of Charisse's appointments with her. He, much like Jared, sometimes annoyed her with his constant coddling and fawning. Upon complaining to her mother about their new habit, Barbara told her, "Once that baby gets here and starts taking up all of your time and attention, you're going to beg for some of that coddling from your husband, so enjoy it while you can."

The Tuesday after Mother's Day, Charisse was scheduled for her monthly check-up and was slated to have her first sonogram. She and Stefan still hadn't made up their minds about whether they wanted to know the sex of the baby beforehand. They had been discussing names since the day she'd taken the home pregnancy test. Jonathan Michael—after their fathers—or Stefani Marie were the front-runners.

She had taken the day off from work, but after breakfast, while she was getting dressed to take Jared to school, she told Stefan, "You know, I think it's time we sold the Corvette."

He looked stricken. A little over a year ago, he had reluctantly sold his motorcycle. "Why?"

She chuckled when she replied, "Honey, don't be upset. It's not that serious."

"But why do we have to get rid of the 'Vette?"

"Well, for one, it doesn't really suit our lifestyle anymore. We can't fit Jared and the baby in it."

"Yeah, but that could still be our play car. You know, for when we go out—just the two of us," he reasoned.

She laughed. "You're ambitious 'cause I can't see that happening once the baby gets here for quite some time afterward."

Moving nearer to her at her dresser, Stefan wrapped Charisse in a soft embrace. "Just because you're having a baby doesn't mean we won't have any more alone time. I still plan to date you like I've been doing all along." Every two weeks, they made time for dinner out, a movie or some other such shared time sans Jared.

"Yeah, but we won't really be able to do that until the baby's a few months old. Besides, I'm not sure I'll even want to be apart from him or her until a few months after the birth."

Stefàn reminded her with a laugh, "Honey, we'll probably have to fight our mothers just to spend some time with our baby."

"Yeah, you're probably right about that."

"But seriously, I don't think you need to sell the 'Vette. At least not yet."

"We need another car. The Beemer is fine, but we should probably get an SUV or a minivan."

"Okay, so we'll go look at cars this weekend. Does that work for you?"

"All right."

Kissing her lightly on the side of her head, he released her and continued preparing himself for work. "Your appointment is at eleven-thirty?"

"Yes. Will you be able to get away?" she asked.

"Absolutely. You're getting the sonogram today, right?"

"Supposed to be."

"Yeah, I wouldn't miss that for anything. What do you think it is?" he smiled and asked.

Charisse shrugged. "I don't know. Sometimes I'm certain it's a boy, but other times, I feel like it's a girl."

"Maybe it's one of each."

She cut her eyes at him. "Don't even joke like that."

STEFÀN MET CHARISSE IN THE PARKING LOT of the medical complex that housed Dr. Talbot's offices later that morning. It was an unseasonably warm day with the temperature already in the upper eighties.

"Hi, baby." He greeted her with a kiss on her mouth and a quick embrace. "It think it's going to be a scorcher today. What do you think?"

With her arm around his waist, she replied as they entered the building, "Yeah, this sun is no joke. What's this summer going to be like if it's this hot already? I'm certainly not looking forward to carrying around all this baby weight in ninety-degree heat."

"You feeling okay?"

"Just hot."

Dr. Talbot was ready for them fifteen minutes after they arrived. Her nurse ran Charisse through all of the preliminary procedures—getting her changed, taking her blood pressure, pulse, and weight—then left her and Stefan to wait for the doctor.

As they waited, Stefan said, "Baby, you look like all of a sudden you've put on a bit of weight. Just in the last couple of days."

"I've gained five pounds from last month. That's too much. I have to watch what I eat. I'm not trying to blow up like Shelly did."

Julian's wife, who had given birth to a daughter in late March, had gained nearly forty pounds during her pregnancy. Little Nia Juliana Walker had weighed in at nine pounds and four ounces.

"Yeah, Shelly did put on quite a bit of weight, but Nia was quite a big baby. Hopefully, you won't have to push out a nine pounder," he said with a chuckle.

"You hope? You and Jared have to stop giving in to my cravings and start telling me 'no!'"

He laughed outright. "One thing I can't see myself ever doing is refusing a pregnant woman her food cravings. But don't worry, Risi. If you do put on a lot of weight, I'll have you in the gym every day working it off. When I'm done with you, you'll be as fly as you were the first time I laid eyes on you."

"Are you implying I'm not that fly now?" she teased.

"Oh no. You're still fly," he flirtatiously stated. "It's just a different size plane."

Charisse playfully swatted him after that remark, but she was laughing right along with him when Dr. Talbot entered the room.

"Well, I'm glad to see you both in such high spirits. I take it you're feeling pretty good, Charisse," she commented.

"Hi, Dr. Talbot. Yes, everything is fine. Stefàn was teasing me about my weight."

"How are you, Stefàn?" the doctor asked.

"I'm good, Doc. How are you?"

"Well, thanks. Charisse, you've put on five pounds since last month."

"I'm not happy about that."

"Well, we're going to do a sonogram today, so we should be able to determine if that's baby weight or if we should put you on a diet. Sometimes, during the middle trimester, the baby can grow pretty quickly in spurts. That might be the case here."

"I hope so."

Pulling the extending leaf from under the exam table, Dr. Talbot said, "Why don't you stretch out and we'll get started."

Following the doctor's instructions, Charisse lay back and watched as Dr. Talbot went about preparing the sonogram machine. Stefàn held Charisse's hand and followed the doctor's every move as well.

"This gel will be a bit cool on your stomach," Dr. Talbot warned.

When the gel was squeezed onto her abdomen and the wand used to spread it around, Charisse couldn't help but react to the coldness. "Woo, 'cool' is an understatement."

Dr. Talbot turned on the machine and immediately an image appeared on the screen. At first, neither Charisse nor Stefàn were able to make out the form they were seeing. Then suddenly, Stefàn said, "That looks like two babies."

Dr. Talbot's response was, "It is."

"Two?" Charisse murmured.

"Yes. It looks like you're having fraternal twins, Charisse." Pointing at the monitor, Dr. Talbot explained, "Can you see? This is where the sacs are separated. You're having twins."

"Oh my God," Stefàn sighed.

Charisse was speechless at first. She turned to Stefàn, but his eyes were fixed on the image in front of them. Tears were streaming from his eyes. Charisse reached out and wiped at one of the streams.

"Look at God," she finally said. "Look at God!"

She reached for him and he moved closer and laid his head on her breast and wept. To Dr. Talbot, she said, "Fraternal means two eggs and two sperm, right?"

"That's right."

Charisse just shook her head and again intoned, "Look at God."

UPON LEAVING DR. TALBOT'S OFFICE, Charisse followed Stefàn to his office. Second order of business, tell their parents. The first order of business was to thank God.

When Dr. Talbot left them after the examination, Stefàn and Charisse immediately offered up a prayer of thanksgiving to God. Sitting face to face with their hands clasped, Stefàn led with the words, "Father God, how excellent is Your name in all the earth. O Father, please forgive me. How could I have ever doubted Your miracle-working power? But thank You, God, for showing me in the most amazing and gracious manner how truly awesome You are. Lord, You haven't failed to bless us continually in so many ways we can't even begin to recall, but to give us not one baby, but two...O Lord, O Lord, how excellent is Your name!!"

Charisse picked up there. "Most gracious God, we thank You for Your perfect love. We thank You for entrusting the care of Your son, Jared, to us. God, we thank You for blessing us with the ability to conceive two children in love. Oh, Father, thank

You for Your grace and Your mercy, God. If we had ten thousand tongues, God, we could never thank You enough. We promise God to never take these gifts You've given us…these lives You've put in our care…for granted. We promise to always look to You for guidance in raising Your children, Lord. Oh, God, how we love You. How we praise Your Holy Name, Father. Thank You, thank You, thank You. In Jesus' mighty name, Amen!!

Tears streamed from their eyes as they stood together. Stefan gazed lovingly into her beautiful brown orbs and softly spoke. "You are a gift from God, Risi. My life has only gotten better and better since you walked into it. Now you're about to be the mother of not just one of my children, but two. They said it most likely wouldn't happen, but look what God has given us. You never doubted. I love that about you."

Holding her in a passionate embrace, he tenderly kissed her. Stefan, at that moment, was soaring through the clouds. Feeling as if there was nothing in the world he couldn't accomplish with God at the center and Charisse by his side, he was more certain than ever that from here on out, whatever came their way—be it good or bad—they would be okay; they would make it through. What more proof did he need that his God *was* God?

Arriving at his office, Charisse greeted his assistant Carrie with a bright smile. She was itching to tell someone—anyone—their big news but before she could utter a word, Stefan said, "Carrie, I'm not taking any calls for the next hour."

"Okay."

When he closed the door behind them, he turned to Charisse and said, "You were about to tell her, weren't you?"

"I'm about to bust, Stefan. I have to tell somebody."

"We'll call your folks, then conference in mine and tell them all at the same time, right now. How about that?"

"Okay. Do you want me to dial?"

"I've got it, baby. You sit down and relax. You look like you're about to hit the ceiling."

Needless to say, their parents were ecstatic. When they ended their twenty minute conference call with them, Stefan dialed Julian to tell him the news, then Charisse called Myra, who was due to deliver her baby in two months.

"What do you think Jared's going to say when we tell him?" Charisse asked.

"I have a feeling he'll be pretty psyched about it."

"We have to come up with two more names, just in case it's two boys or two girls. We can still go with Jonathan Michael and Stefâni Marie if it's a boy and a girl, but otherwise…."

"We'll figure something out, baby. We've got time."

Charisse sat across from him and shook her head. "Can you believe it? We're actually having twins. How am I going to do this? I don't know the first thing about raising one baby and now we're going to have two?"

Rising from his seat, Stefan same around the desk and knelt in front of her, "Don't get yourself all worked up, Risi. My mom and yours will both be there to help us out. We'll be fine."

"Yeah, but—"

"There are no buts, honey. God would never give us more than we could bear. I know you believe that. We'll be fine."

CHAPTER 27

A MATTER OF LIFE AND....

Charisse and Myra's cousins, Connie and Carmen, had planned a surprise baby shower for Myra in the middle of June to be held at a catering hall in Englewood. Connie and Carmen over-saw the food preparation while Charisse and Star, along with her daughters, took care of the decorations. The guest list numbered in the low seventies.

As had been their habit for several years, Charisse and Myra were getting together for their monthly shopping outing. Knowing that Myra would be none the wiser, the shower was scheduled for that Saturday. That being the case, Charisse used the pretense of taking a gift to the birthday party of one of Jared's friends as the means for getting Myra there.

Since Charisse was only six months pregnant, although seemingly getting larger by the day, she still drove so she picked Myra up from Barretto's apartment late that morning.

"I've told you this before, but you really look cute pregnant, Myra," she told her as she struggled to climb into the new SUV Charisse and Stefan had purchased.

Grumbling, Myra responded, "Girl, I'll be so happy to have this baby. I can't take it anymore. I feel like a house."

Charisse laughed. "Can you imagine what I'll look like in another month or so, with double the cargo?"

"God bless you, Risi, 'cause I'd lose my mind if I found out I was having twins."

Nodding her understanding, Charisse admitted, "To be perfectly honest with you, I'm still a little nervous about it. I can't imagine having two babies crying at the same time, both wanting to be changed, fed, held... I'm almost dreading the first time I'll be home alone with them."

"I guess the doctors don't know everything, huh?" Myra said, referring to their diagnosis that Stefan would most likely never father a child.

"I always told Stefan that God had the final say in these matters. But the fact that in light of their premature conclusion, two of my honey's little swimmers hit the mark... Unh! To God be the glory!" Charisse exclaimed joyfully.

"Amen to that."

"It would be great if one was a boy and the other a girl."

"Yeah, that would be cool."

"Do you think you and Barry will have more kids after you get married?"

Unconsciously rubbing her stomach, Myra replied, "Well, I would love to have a daughter and even though Barretto's ecstatic that this is a boy, he wants a girl, too."

Several hours later, after they'd completed their shopping and before heading to what Myra thought would be dinner, Charisse told her, "I'm going to swing by and drop off this gift before we go eat, okay?"

"That's fine."

Upon arrival, Charisse asked, "You want to come in with me to get something to drink, or use the bathroom?"

"Ooh, yeah. Bathroom."

Upon entering the catering hall, they headed straight to the ladies' room. As they were washing their hands, Myra asked, "Now, whose birthday party is this?"

"One of Jared's friends. He went to the office with Stefân this morning, but they walked out without the boy's gift. So instead of them having to go all the way back home, I told him I'd bring it by since I'd be out anyway."

Myra smiled. "That was nice of you."

"Well, you know, I can't help myself," she replied in a teasing manner. Picking up the shopping bag which held the gift, Charisse said, "This shouldn't take too long, then we can go eat."

"Bueno. Yo y mi bebé tienen hambre."

"Okay, cool it with the Español."

"We're hungry! I naturally slip into my native tongue in times of stress," Myra cracked.

Holding the door as Myra exited the restroom, Charisse laughed and said, "Don't worry, I'll make sure you get fed, even if I have to snatch something from right here."

At that moment, Charisse's cell phone rang. Unbeknownst to Myra, the call was right on schedule. "Hi, honey." Whispering to Myra, "It's Stefân."

"I gathered," Myra whispered back.

"Yeah, we're here. We stopped in the ladies' room first. Are you still here?"

Listening to his response, she then answered, "Okay. I'll be in in a minute."

"Stefân's here?" Myra asked when Charisse ended the call.

"Yeah. The boy is one of his students. I hope they're not expecting me to stay, too." Moving down the corridor, she added, "I think they're back here."

Music could be heard coming from one of the rooms they passed, prompting Myra to comment, "Sounds like there's a couple of parties going on in here."

"Probably. I think they have rooms upstairs as well."

Reaching for the door at the end of the hallway, Charisse said, "I think they're in here."

She eased it open and stuck her head in. "Yup. In here."

Holding the door open, she let Myra enter first.

"SURPRISE!!!"

BY SEPTEMBER FIRST, CHARISSE WAS READY for her babies to be born. Although, her expected due date was the twentieth, she had already put on twenty-seven pounds and was quite uncomfortable most of the time. She stopped working at the beginning of August, taking her maternity leave a few weeks earlier than originally planned, but it was doubtful that she would return to the accounting firm. She intended to take the opportunity of being at home—albeit with the babies—to try and get her own accounting business off the ground.

On July fourteenth, Angelo Miguel Martinez, a beautiful baby boy who weighed in at six pounds and four ounces, was welcomed into the world by beaming parents, Myra and Barretto. Charisse was overjoyed for her friend and thanked God for blessing Myra with a joy and peace she had been lacking in her life for so many of the years they had known one another.

Myra and Barretto were married two weeks later in a private ceremony attended only by their closest friends and family. In August, they moved into their first house—a three-bedroom, split-level ranch located in Peekskill, New York.

For Julian, the cycle of life was also at a peak. The McDonald's franchise in Piscataway was doing so well, he purchased a second one in Montclair, New Jersey. Since his law practice was still thriving—he had been offered a partnership at his firm just after Nia was born—and the franchises were growing, Michele was able to quit her job as an executive assistant and become a stay-at-home Mom. Her experience, however, allowed her to step into the full-time role of handling all administrative aspects of their businesses.

In the Cooper household, Jared was flourishing under Stefan's and Charisse's guidance and he had experienced a growth spurt in the last year. For the longest time, he came up to Charisse's shoulder in height. Now he stood almost face-to-face with her, giving them the impression that he was going to be quite tall when he reached his full size. He was also doing well in school. On his final report card before the summer break, his teacher had recommended that he be placed in an advanced fourth grade class. Jared was already reading well above the fourth grade level and mathematics happened to be one of his favorite subjects.

He was also very excited about the impending birth of his first siblings. Bounding with an overzealous joy, Jared made all kinds of promises to Charisse and Stefan about how he would help with the feedings, diaper changing, etc., but Charisse didn't really expect that would last past the first month, if that long. Despite how quickly he was growing and maturing, Jared was still a very active young boy who loved most sports, the martial arts and playing video games, and unless he was watching a movie, never sat idly long enough for grass to grow beneath his feet.

Saturday during Labor Day weekend, Damaris and Barbara hosted a baby shower for Charisse at the Ellison's home in Queens. Although it wasn't a surprise to Charisse, she was taken aback by the unexpectedly large turnout. The gathering was attended by members of her large family, including several from out of town, and also by relatives of Stefan that he hadn't seen in quite some time. Additionally, friends from their congregation and co-workers of Charisse and Stefan and their parents came out to celebrate the impending birth of the twins.

By the time all of the gifts were opened, there wasn't a single item that the couple needed to purchase in the way of welcoming their new infants. It took Stefan, Julian, Devin and John Ellison— all driving SUVs or minivans—to transport all of their shower gifts to their house.

On Sunday evening, after the dishes had been washed and Jared was in bed, Charisse and Stefan were lounging comfortably on the plush leather cuddler sofa in their den and listening to a classic Grover Washington, Jr. CD.

Tenderly kissing her on the side of her head, he murmured, "This has been some weekend, hasn't it?"

"To say the least." Basking in their mutual love, Charisse snuggled closer in Stefan's embrace. "Can you believe all the gifts we got yesterday? We've got everything."

"Yeah, how 'bout that? All we have to do is wait for them to make an appearance." Placing one of his large hands tenderly on her rounded abdomen, he asked, "How are you feeling, honey?"

At that moment, one of the babies moved in such a manner that a knot formed beneath Stefan's hand. "I feel like somebody is shifting position in there," she responded with a chuckle.

"Does that hurt when your stomach tightens up like that?"

"No. It's a little uncomfortable but that's about it."

"Are you sorry we didn't find out what we're having before-hand?"

"No. We're having a boy and a girl, though. I'm pretty certain of that now."

"Why so?"

"I don't know. It's just a feeling. I was praying the other day and I felt like God confirmed my sense that we have one of each. I felt this warmth flow all over me and a peace that...well, that passes understanding."

"It would be great if you have a boy and a girl. I have a feeling these will be the only children we ever have naturally," Stefan admitted.

"Would it bother you if that was the case?"

"No. Not at all. These two are more of a blessing than I could have ever hoped for. I'm satisfied."

"I am, too."

Five days later, when Charisse went in for her weekly doctor appointment, their faith in God was truly put to the test.

"Charisse, one of the babies has turned and is in position for natural birth. The other isn't and I don't like what I'm hearing," Dr. Talbot said with a grim countenance.

"What are you hearing?" Stefan questioned before Charisse could.

"One heart rhythm has slowed dramatically. It's a good thing you had to come to the hospital today because I'm going to admit you, Charisse, and we're going to deliver these babies by C-section today."

Truly terrified for the first time since she was informed that she was having twins, Charisse asked, "Are they going to be all right?"

"That's what we're going to try and insure. Stefan, if you want to stay with her during the birth, you'll need to put on some scrubs. I'll have one of the nurses bring you a pair."

Seeing the look of worry on his face, she said, "Try and stay calm. You're going to have to be strong for all of you over the next few hours." Reaching for his hand, she added, "I'm praying for you, too."

Two and a half hours later, Charisse was in the delivery room with Stefan by her side. Trying to remain composed and keep Charisse calm was very difficult in light of all of the activity going on around them.

When they had asked Dr. Talbot earlier what could be the cause of the problem, especially considering that up until then, everything had been going so well, she explained, "Sometimes the baby can become entangled in the umbilical cord and circulation or oxygen can be compromised."

"What does that mean for the baby?" Stefan asked.

"If it's not caught in time, a loss of oxygen could cause brain damage or even death. That's why I want to get Charisse ready to go as quickly as possible."

Now, watching and listening to the delivery room doctors, nurses and attendants as each went about their respective duties, Charisse looked to her husband. "It's going to be all right, isn't it?"

Leaning close and kissing her on her forehead, he camouflaged his own fears with calm. "Yes, baby. God wouldn't have brought us this far to take one of our babies, I don't think."

"Remember Abraham?" she couldn't help responding.

"Yes, but remember, God didn't take Isaac. He wanted to see if Abraham loved Isaac more than he loved Him."

"What if something's wrong with the baby, Stefan?" Charisse worriedly asked.

"Whatever happens, Risi, our babies will be perfect in God's eyes and we will love them exactly as they are. Won't we?"

"Yes," she whimpered. "I'm afraid."

"So am I, but God's got this and He's got us. We'll all be fine. I'm believing that with all my heart and you should, too."

At that moment, Charisse saw a strength emanating from her man that was almost palpable and she believed every word he said. "I love you."

He pressed his lips to hers for a long moment. "I love you."

Charisse had been given an epidural anesthetic, and Dr. Talbot told her unless there was a need for her to be put under, she would remain awake for the entire procedure.

"Okay, Charisse, I'm going to make the first incision now," Dr. Talbot stated, breaking into their private moment.

She had been explaining everything as it happened but suddenly became uncharacteristically silent.

Sensing something wasn't right, Charisse asked, "What's wrong?"

"It's what I expected," she solemnly stated. "The cord's around his neck."

Charisse immediately heard the sound of bustling and was anxious because she couldn't see what was happening, but Stefan noticed that the tiny infant was blue and his frail body was limp. Dr. Talbot quickly handed the baby off to another doctor in the room.

God, please don't take our baby, he silently pled so as to not worry Charisse any more than she already was. The intense pounding of his heart threatened to burst through his chest.

"Stefan? What's wrong? How come he's not crying?"

"They're working on him, baby," he softly replied, as he looked across the room to where little Jonathan Michael Cooper was hidden from his view as the attending physicians cared for his first-born child.

Within the next few minutes, amidst what seemed like chaotic activity, Stefan heard someone say, "He's not responding." He knew it was not meant for his ears, but his auditory nerves were hypersensitive at that moment, attuned to everything that was being said regarding the health of his newborn.

"Stefan, what's happening?" Charisse asked nervously. When he didn't answer her right away, Charisse agonized, "What's happening?"

Stefan reached for her hand and reluctantly turned his eyes away from his child. Unable to restrain the tears that welled, he solemnly told her, "He's not doing too good."

"What do you mean?" she asked in a panic.

Dr. Talbot, knowing the situation looked grim for their new-born boy, tried to assuage the tremendous rush of anxiety by directing her patient's focus to the other infant waiting to be born. Moving quickly, she reached into the incision in Charisse's abdomen and removed a seemingly healthy baby girl. As she cleared the mucus out of the infant's mouth and from her face, Dr. Talbot proclaimed, "You've got a daughter." With that pronouncement, the girl began to wail angrily as if she was highly perturbed about being removed from her warm, comfortable cocoon and thrust into the cold, sterility of the delivery room.

Torn between rejoicing at the sound of their daughter's cry and the silence that was suddenly deafening from across the room, Charisse and Stefân wept in anguish and relief.

Instead of handing little Stefâni Marie Cooper to one of the nurses, as was standard practice, Dr. Talbot immediately placed the child on her mother's breast.

Tearfully looking into her eyes, Charisse asked, "Where's my other baby?"

Dr. Talbot looked across the room to the station where the other doctors had been feverishly trying to save the other infant. Stefân followed her eyes and saw when the physician shook his head sadly. Unable to stifle the sound, he let out a cry of disbelief, "NO!"

Immediately rising from the stool where he'd been sitting beside Charisse's prone form on the delivery table, he moved across the room as if he'd forgotten she and their daughter were there. The doctors and nurses moved aside to allow him a view of the lifeless body of his first-born son. Staring in disbelief, his body trembled uncontrollably and the sound of devastation in the pit of his stomach had no choice but to be expelled from his throat and out his mouth.

"Stefan? Stefan? What's happening?" Charisse cried in terror at the sound. Unable to move from where she lay, not only because of the infant lying on her breast, but because her body was still torn open from the caesarean section, a defenseless fear and rage swept through her because no one was telling her what was going on.

Overwhelmed with sadness, but knowing she still had a job to finish, Dr. Talbot sympathetically stated, "He didn't make it, Charisse. I'm so sorry, but I've got to get you closed up. I'm going to give you a sedative so that we can take care of you and we'll get your little girl cleaned up, too."

"No," Charisse moaned, as a nurse gently removed her daughter from her chest and an anesthesiologist covered her mouth with a plastic mask. In seconds, she was unconscious.

CHAPTER 28
...WHERE THE GRACE OF GOD CAN'T KEEP YOU

When Stefan learned that his chances of fathering a child with Charisse were slim to none, he'd experienced a devastating blow to his ego. As a self-proclaimed embodiment of the quintessential man, the knowledge that his capacity to reproduce was less than normal had shattered his sensibilities. And despite the admittedly prosperous path his life had taken since that unwelcome fact had been revealed, up until the moment Charisse had actually become pregnant, he'd never fully exorcised the mental anguish brought on by that knowledge, despite his semblance of acceptance.

But now, with the death of his son—his first natural-born son—he was experiencing an emptiness he couldn't describe and an anger that burned in his heart toward God that was so consuming he couldn't even find the words to express it.

When the hospital staff wheeled Charisse out of the delivery room and into recovery, they explained to him that she would be out for a few hours. The anesthetic that Dr. Talbot had the anesthesiologist administer was a powerful one. She knew when Charisse awoke, she would be torn between the desire to hold and care for their newborn daughter and grieving for the loss of their son. Encouraging Stefan to try to maintain an appearance of strength for her, he wondered how he was supposed to do that. He didn't feel as if he could call on God for the support he needed. He didn't want to know anything from a god who would offer him and Charisse such profound hope only to snatch it away from them before they could even hold it in their hands.

But he needed to be there for Charisse when she came to. After they'd taken little Jonathan's lifeless body from the room, they handed him his daughter, Stefàni. Through his tears he could see how beautiful she was and he was grateful for the gift of her life, but he couldn't quell the pain of losing his son, even as the joy of her life pulsed in his hands.

She was a perfect little baby, too. Her head was covered with thick, dark curls and she already possessed eyelashes that women spend hundreds of dollars on cosmetics to have. Her lips, a shade or two darker than the complexion of her face, were curved in what seemed to be a smile as she slept peacefully in his arms.

Tears slid down his face as he studied her flawless form and countenance. Baby Stefàni was strong like his wife; a point he realized when he put his index finger in the curve of her minuscule fist and she promptly gripped it possessively. Awash with joy at the fact that she was his own beautiful little angel, his soul simultaneously ached for his son.

A matronly-looking nurse who could have been his grandmother stood nearby trying to appear occupied with some important task. Knowing she was studying him, Stefàn also knew she was waiting for him to turn Stefàni over to her so he could do what no parent wanted to after losing a child—get on with life.

That painful process would begin with calls to his folks and Charisse's. They'd spread the word throughout the rest of the family, but he also had to reach out to Myra and Julian, their best friends, both of whom had just welcomed new life into their growing families.

Then there was Jared. How would he tell their oldest son? Although he was not a child of his loins, Stefàn loved him as if he was and knew how much he eagerly looked forward to walking in his new status as a big brother. Jared had already been touched by the death of so many in his young life that Stefan was unsure how he'd take one more.

Innately sensing his need, the woman turned to face him at the same instant he looked to her. Her face was a picture of sadness, but she tried to smile at him as she reached for Stefani. "I'll take good care of her," she gently assured him.

He didn't bother to wipe the tears from his face but stared helplessly into her eyes, silently pleading for her to tell him his present nightmare was just a terrible mistake and that his son was alive and waiting in the next room to be cradled in his arms as he'd done his twin sister. Instead, she said, "I'm so sorry about your boy. The doctors did everything they could to save him. I guess God had other plans for that little one."

God? God? He wanted to scream, "There is no God!" How could God do this to them? What had they done to deserve such excruciating pain?

The nurse, who he suddenly noticed wore a nametag that read *Mary de Jesus*, saw the rage that flared in his eyes at her mention of God. By the Spirit, she was prompted to tell him, "We will never be able to fully understand the movement of God. And despite how painful His moves can sometimes be, we have to never forget that He doesn't make mistakes. His ways are not our ways and His thoughts are not our thoughts. Your son is resting in the Master's hands and free from all hurt, harm and danger. Be comforted knowing that you have been blessed with a beautiful angel in your daughter who will be a constant reminder of God's grace and goodness."

Her words had their desired effect because he immediately refocused on Stefani. She was alive and he was her father and would do everything in his power to love and protect her. He was her father and she needed him. He was Jared's father and Charisse's husband and they needed him. And regardless of the fact that he would never have the opportunity to bounce his newborn son on his knee, teach him to how to tie his shoes or dribble a basketball, he was Jonathan Michael's father, as well, and he still needed him, too.

BARBARA AND JOHN ELLISON WERE WITH STEFÀN at Charisse's bedside when she awakened. Once the fog from the anesthesia had fully lifted, she remembered the events of the day and immediately reacted.

"Where's Jonathan?" she cried as she attempted to sit up, only to be stopped by the sharp pain that shot through her abdomen where she'd been stitched up.

Stefàn rose from where he was seated on the right side of her bed and reached for her hand as he leaned over her. "He's gone, baby. He didn't make it." The moisture that returned to his reddened eyes confirmed for Charisse that it was all real.

"I thought I was dreaming," she cried. "I thought it was a dream."

He gently embraced her from one side as her mother stood and caressed her from her left.

"Why, Stefàn? Why would God take him from us? Why would He do that?"

Stefàn, possessing nary a comforting word to offer, struggled to quell the anger that threatened to boil over just at the mere thought of God.

Her mother felt helpless as she watched her youngest child grieve the loss of her firstborn. She didn't know how to comfort her because this was something she had never experienced. As a mother, one could often count on one's own experiences to help a daughter when she is gifted with the blessing of motherhood, but here Barbara had nothing to draw from. She looked to her husband who had always been able to read her, and he immediately moved to embrace and comfort both his wife and child.

"Where's Stefàni?" Charisse asked through her tears.

"She's in the nursery," Stefàn answered.

"I want her. I want my baby," she adamantly demanded.

"I'll get her," Barbara immediately replied and turned to leave the room.

If she couldn't do anything else for her daughter, she reasoned, she could at least do this.

"Did you see him?" Charisse asked her husband.

He slowly nodded as a tear spilled over his lid and slid down his cheek.

"I want to see him," she lamented.

"No, baby, you don't."

"I want to hold him," she argued.

Remembering the coldness of his skin as he held his son, Stefàn knew that if Charisse felt him like that, her pain would only be magnified, and he had to protect her in any way he could. "Honey, you don't want to feel him like that."

At that moment, Stefàn unwittingly sent up a silent thank you when he saw his mother-in-law enter the room, holding their daughter. "Here's Stefàni, baby."

Barbara moved next to her daughter and handed the newborn over. "The nurse said she's hungry." Producing a bottle from the pocket of her jacket, she removed the covering from the nipple before handing it to Charisse.

Studying her precious daughter closely, watching every movement and facial expression as if she might never see her again,

Charisse's vision began to blur as she thought about her other child; the one she'd never hold, the one she would never get to feed, change or whisper to. Pulling her closer to her breast, she cradled Stefani against her heart, yearning to feel a wisp of what she may have felt in the nine months she'd shared with her brother in the womb. Longing to feel that closeness they'd experienced despite their separate nests of development, she wondered, too, if Stefani could sense that he was no longer with her. He would have been her older brother and Charisse was certain he would have always looked out for his younger twin sister, had he been given the opportunity.

"I miss him, even though I never got to hold him," Charisse lamented.

Sitting on the edge of the bed next to her, Stefan gently brushed her hair back. "I know, sweetie." Touching his chest, he continued, "I have an ache right here for him."

Stefani began to whimper, so Charisse put the bottle to her mouth. She couldn't help but marvel at the way the infant lunged for the nipple, instinctively knowing that there was life-sustaining nourishment for her there.

Taking her eyes off of Stefani for just a moment, she asked Stefan, "Does Jared know?"

"Not yet. I asked Julian to pick him up from school, but I told him not to even tell him that you'd given birth. I don't know how I'm going to tell him."

"God will give you the words, son," John said softly.

Stefan looked over at his father-in-law and coldly stated, "I don't want anything from God. He's given me enough already, don't you think?"

John didn't comment, but was sympathetic to Stefan's anger. He had never walked in this young man's shoes so he couldn't discount what he was feeling as unreasonable.

Charisse, however, was saddened by Stefàn's outburst. She wanted to be angry with God for taking their son, too, but gazing down at their beautiful little girl made her anger and even her hurt, wane ever so slightly. For so long they had held little hope that they'd ever have a child of their own, and while for four months they'd believed they would be blessed with two, they still had the perfect little girl God had so graciously given to them. Did she want her son? Absolutely. Did she mourn the life of the child she'd carried to term but never had an opportunity to hold or even gaze upon? Without a doubt. But Charisse could not so easily lambaste God for taking their little boy. She couldn't help but consider that maybe God had spared them a greater agony by taking him now. Was there a health issue he might have been subjected to that could have made it difficult not only for Jonathan, but also for them to cope with? They would never know. All she knew was the soft, warm feel of her daughter in her arms. All she could cling to was the love she already felt for this little one and the joy she had already become in her life. Charisse would always wonder why she was not given the opportunity to cradle her son against her bosom the way she did Stefàni, but she knew that God's embrace was even more comforting than hers could ever be.

She didn't say anything to her parents, or even to Stefàn, but she knew when they were alone, she would have to help him understand that they could not give up on God. She had to make him recognize that God's sovereignty was unquestionable.

JARED WAS ASLEEP BY THE TIME STEFÀN LEFT THE HOSPITAL and finally made it to Julian and Michele's house. His friends were cautious about saying too much, but made it clear that they were just a phone call away if he or Charisse needed anything.

When Stefàn called him earlier and told him the awful news,

Julian was immediately reminded of his and Michele's first pregnancy. Unlike Charisse, Michele hadn't carried their child to full term. She had miscarried at five months, but it was a devastating blow for them regardless.

Stefan didn't want to wake Jared so he merely carried him to the truck and laid him across the back seat. He drove them home in silence, opting not to turn on the car stereo because he was still trying to think of how to break the news to him.

When they arrived home, Stefan pulled the SUV into the garage and shut the car off. Sitting motionless behind the wheel for a few minutes and wanting to pray to God for the words to explain what had happened, his wrath toward Him was unyielding.

"Daddy?" Jared sleepily called from behind him.

Stefan turned in the seat and forced a smile. "Hey, buddy."

"Where are we?"

"Home." He pulled the key from the ignition and pushed his door opened. Stepping out of the vehicle, he immediately opened the back door and reached for his son. "Come on, guy. Let's get you to bed."

Normally considering himself too old to be carried, Jared was so tired and sleepy at that moment that he didn't even fuss. In the same sleep-laden voice he asked, "Where's Mommy?"

"She's at the hospital."

Stefan was carrying him through the door into the kitchen when Jared inquired, "Did she have the babies?"

"Yes."

The affirmative answer sparked a bit of excitement in him and brought him fully awake. "Did she have a boy and a girl like she said?"

Stefan stood Jared in front of him and flipped on the ceiling light before he answered, "Yes, Jared, but there was a problem."

"What kind of problem? Is Mommy okay?" he asked with a worried expression.

Stefan reached out and ran his hand across Jared's soft curls. "Come over here and sit down with me, son." He guided Jared to the breakfast nook where they ate every morning.

Jared was quite astute for one so young and immediately sensed that his father was about to give him some bad news. "Daddy, what happened to Mommy? Is she okay?" he repeated.

"Mommy's fine, son." Stefan sighed deeply. "The doctor was worried when we went for Mommy's check-up because she noticed that one of the heartbeats had slowed down, so they had to operate to get the babies out. Little Jonathan was strangled by the umbilical cord. That's what connects him to Mommy and that's how babies are fed and nourished while they're in their mother's tummy. They tried to save him but...he...." Stefan faltered and tears came to his eyes.

"He died, Daddy?"

Stefan couldn't speak, but he nodded affirmatively.

Jared lowered his head and sat silently beside his father. After several minutes, he timidly asked, "Is baby Stefani alright?"

Reaching for a napkin from the holder in the middle of the table, Stefan wiped his eyes and blew his nose before he answered. "Yes. She's fine." He tried to smile when he told Jared, "She's a beautiful little girl, too."

Jared noticed that his father was having a difficult time trying not to break down in front of him so he reached up and put his arms around Stefan's neck. "I'm sorry, Daddy, that baby Jonathan died, but he'll be okay. My first Mom and Grandma and Granny Nan will take care of him in heaven. He's gonna be an angel just like them."

Against this innocent child's unflinching assurance, Stefan had no defense. He fell against Jared's shoulder and let his oldest son's embrace be the comforter he so desperately needed.

Nearly five minutes later when his tears had finally ceased, Stefan straightened himself on the bench of the nook and told his son, "I'm sorry, Jared." He pulled another napkin from the holder and again wiped his face and blew his nose.

Jared, continuing in a demeanor of wisdom well beyond his nine years, reached up and touched Stefan's shoulder as he said, "You don't have to be sorry, Daddy. Remember you told me that it's okay for boys to cry when they're hurt? And even though you didn't hurt yourself on the outside, I think probably when your insides hurt, it's even worse, right?"

Stefan looked into the face of the child seated next to him. Marveling at how appropriate his words were for the situation, a sad smile appeared as he pulled Jared into his arms.

Enclosing his son in a hug that he hoped expressed his gratitude, pride and love, Stefan, nevertheless, wanted to be sure he knew. "I love you so much, Jared, and I'm so proud of you. I was so angry with God for taking Jonathan from me that I forgot to remember everything He's given me. I am so glad you're my son. You are a blessing that could never be replaced. He gave me a beautiful little girl in Stefani. Wait 'til you see your little sister. You're going to love her right away. I have so much to be thankful for. Thank you, Jared, for reminding me of that."

"You're welcome, Daddy. Can I go see Stefani and Mommy tomorrow?"

"Absolutely. Mommy's going to be glad to see you, too, but right now, we both need to go to bed. I'm exhausted."

They rose from the nook and started out of the kitchen and toward their bedrooms upstairs.

With his foot on the first step, Jared asked, "Daddy, can I sleep in your room tonight?"

"Sure, buddy. Put on your pajamas and come on in."

Jared rushed to the task, hurrying up the stairs ahead of Stefan. It wasn't often that he got to sleep in the king-sized bed his parents shared, but was excited whenever he could.

It was only a few minutes later when he came barreling into the room. Stefan was seated on the edge of the bed in his pajama pants.

"You get Mommy's whole side tonight, J," Stefan told him. "Climb on up."

"Aren't we gonna say our prayers first?"

Ironically, Stefan hadn't even thought of that, even though he and Charisse had continued the practice Jared's grandmother taught him by praying with him every night before he went to sleep.

"Yeah. I forgot," he embarrassedly stated.

"Want me to do it?" Jared eagerly offered.

"No, son, this is something I have to do."

The father and child knelt next to one another beside the bed. Jared lowered his head in anticipation of his father's prayer, but it was not so readily forthcoming. Stefan pondered what he would say for well over a minute before he began.

"Heavenly Father, this has been the hardest day of my life." Stefan paused right there because he felt his hurt and pain begin to well up in his spirit and he wanted to be strong for his son beside him. But the memory of the day's events overwhelmed him when he recalled the image of his dead infant son lying on the cold examination table once the doctors had given up any chance of reviving him. He couldn't contain his emotions. With a sadness he had never known or hoped to experience again, he tearfully continued, "I'm sorry, God, for being so angry with You. I forgot to remember that even though You took Jonathan, You've given me so much. You blessed me with an amazing son when You gave me Jared. You trusted me to bring him up right, to be the man we both know he can and will be. You blessed me with Charisse. When my heart was closed and afraid to love, You sent her to me, knowing that she was everything I needed to help me draw closer to You. You proved the doctors wrong. Risi always believed that You would bless us with a child, but I took them at their word, even though I knew in my heart there's nothing too hard for You to do. I'm sorry," he cried. "You gave me the most beautiful daughter, Stefâni. She is perfect, God. More than I could have ever hoped for. And I almost forgot because I kept looking at what I'd lost. But I know now, God. I know for certain that Jonathan is with You. That You love him more than I ever could and that he was Yours before he was ever mine. Forgive me, please. I love you, Father. Please continue to watch over my family, to protect them and strengthen them. This has been the hardest day of my life, Lord, but it's also been the best day. You showed me that You love me in spite of my faults. Help me to be everything my family needs, through the hard times and through the good times, God. Help me to be the best father my children could ever have. I promise to always look to You first for guidance and strength in raising them. Help me to be the husband Charisse deserves, God. She is such a precious gift and I will love her and thank You for her until I take my last breath. Thank You, God, for being God. Thank You for Your unfailing grace and Your goodness. In the Name above every name—Jesus. Amen."

DAMARIS COOPER WAS AT THE HOSPITAL at nine a.m. Saturday morning, before visiting hours officially began. When she told the security guard that her daughter was a patient, she was given access to the maternity ward without question.

She struggled to control her displeasure at Stefan's insistence yesterday that she wait a day before coming. If for no other reason, she wanted to be there for Charisse. Having lost a child just hours after its birth, she felt she was able to identify with what Charisse must have been feeling.

When she entered Charisse's room that morning, she was delighted to find her new granddaughter asleep on her daughter-in-law's chest. She wasn't sure if Charisse was sleeping as well, or if she merely had her eyes closed, but Damaris was glad to see she was in better shape than she expected.

"Risi," she softly called as she moved closer to the head of the bed.

Charisse opened her eyes upon hearing her nickname and smiled upon seeing Damaris there. She reached up to take her hand.

Damaris kissed her gently on her forehead and tenderly asked, "How are you, honey?"

Charisse just shrugged as her eyes immediately began to water. Damaris understood.

Taking a closer look at little Stefani, she murmured, "She's adorable."

"Thank you."

Damaris sat on the edge of the bed and wiped the tear that began to slide down Charisse's cheek. "I'm so sorry about Jonathan. I know how hard it is to lose your baby like that. It happened to me before Stefan was born."

Charisse was surprised and although she didn't say anything, it showed on her face.

Damaris continued, "Stefan doesn't know. None of the kids do. Mike and I never told them. He was our first-born. His name was Michael, after his father. He was born with a birth defect called anencephaly. They told me right after I delivered that he probably wouldn't live out the day. He died about five hours after he was born."

"Did you get to hold him?"

"Yes. He died in my arms. I thought I would die right along with him," Damaris admitted.

"I didn't get to hold Jonathan. I wanted to but they gave me an anesthetic after Stefàni was born and it wasn't until several hours later that I came to. I thought I'd had a bad dream," she shakily told her mother-in-law.

Damaris nodded her understanding.

"I'm worried about Stefàn. He's so angry with God. I think he hates Him because He took Jonathan," Charisse stated sadly.

"I could hear it when I spoke to him yesterday."

"I can understand his anger, but I can't overlook what He gave us with Stefàni." With those words, Charisse adjusted her daughter so she could gaze down at her angelic countenance.

"He won't hold on to it. That little girl is going to melt his heart, I just know it," Damaris said with a smile.

"Would you like to hold her?" Charisse offered.

"Oh, please, could I?"

Taking the child in her arms, Damaris cooed and sang to her newest grandchild. "She looks like Stefàn did when he was born. He had a head full of curly hair like this and those thick lashes. She's so beautiful."

"Where's Mike?" Charisse asked.

"He had to take his car in to the shop. I didn't have the patience to wait for him so I drove myself. He's going to meet me here. Has Stefàn told Jared yet?"

"He was going to tell him last night. I haven't tried calling him this morning so I don't know how he took it."

As if the very mention of Stefàn and Jared was enough to conjure them up, the two of them strolled into the room in the next seconds.

"Mommy!"

"Hi!"

Jared rushed to her side and stretched over the bed rail to hug her. Charisse was so happy to see him and returned his embrace with as much effort as she could muster. Looking to Stefan, and seeing a peace that wasn't there the day before, she smiled lovingly at him. Before she could say anything, though, Jared called out, "Hi, Granma Dee. Is that Stefani?"

Damaris was tickled by the look of wonder on Jared's face and answered, "It sure is. You want to hold her?"

"Ooh, can I?" Turning quickly to Charisse, he asked, "Can I, Mommy?"

"Yes, you can. Sit down in that chair and Granma will show you how to hold her."

Jared didn't hesitate to do as he was told and as Damaris passed Stefani to her older brother, Stefan sat beside Charisse on the bed. Leaning over, he sensuously kissed her.

"You okay, baby?" she asked him.

"Yeah. Are you?"

She took a deep breath and after careful consideration replied, "I think so. You told Jared?"

"Yeah. That's an amazing kid we've got. He was the man of the house last night," Stefan admitted with that wry smile. Kissing her once more, he whispered, "We're so blessed."

By three o'clock that afternoon, every member of the Cooper and Ellison families had either been to the hospital or was still in attendance. Myra, Barretto, Julian and Michele were also there. Everyone was sympathetic to Charisse, Stefan and Jared's plight, but thankfully, no one was morbid and the mood in her room throughout the day was fairly upbeat. They all fawned over Stefani, and Charisse and Stefan knew that she was going to be the darling of both clans before all was said and done.

Charisse was grateful to them all for the love and support they were showing but by this time, she'd been up since Damaris' arrival that morning and was beginning to feel the strain of keeping them all entertained.

Barbara and Damaris noticed that Charisse had become very quiet and seemed to be trying to stay awake.

"We've got to get everyone out of here," Damaris said to her counterpart.

"Yeah, I was thinking that, too," Barbara agreed.

"Okay, everybody, listen up," Damaris suddenly announced, getting everyone's attention. "We need to let Charisse rest. She's been through enough for one day and needs to get some sleep. So, let's go. Everybody out!"

As they all began to leave, the families offered up their love and encouragement, promising to pray for them and give any assistance they might need.

Stefan, who had been seated beside her on the bed, told her, "I'll be right back, sweetie. I want to say good-bye to everyone, okay?"

"Okay."

Charisse smiled in relief at her mother-in-law and shrugged as her mother came and stood beside her. Barbara leaned over and kissed her forehead. "I love you, sweetheart. You get some rest. I'll be back tomorrow morning, okay?"

"Okay, Mommy. I love you."

Damaris was right behind Barbara when she said, "Your mom and I are going back to your house. We'll take Jared with us, so don't you worry about anything, all right? You get some sleep." She leaned over and kissed Charisse's cheek.

"Thank you, Damaris. I love you, too."

When they joined Stefan and the rest of the family in the waiting room, he was telling them, "We really appreciate you all being here for us. It's been kind of crazy. Half the time we're crying about Jonathan and the other half rejoicing about Stefani. So thanks for being so patient with us."

"Come on, Coop, you know how we do," Charisse's brother, David, stated. Everyone murmured their accord.

"I know. And I can't tell you how grateful we are to be a part of this family. When Risi gets out of here, which we're expecting will probably be Monday or Tuesday, we're going to have a simple memorial service for Jonathan, just for the family. Dub, Myra, y'all know that includes you, too."

"We know," Myra stated, speaking for her husband, Barretto, Julian and Michele.

"So, listen, I've got to get back in there to my girls. Are any of you going back to my house besides the grandparents?"

"We are," his sister commented regarding she and her husband, "and Devin, you're coming back, too, right?"

"Yeah," his brother agreed.

Charisse's sister and brothers all stated they would be, as well.

"Okay, so I'll see y'all a little later then. Mom, you have the key, right?"

Damaris answered, "Yes, baby. Don't worry about us. Barb and I will put something together for everyone to eat and we've got Jared. You worry about Risi and Stefani, and we'll see you when you get there."

Returning to Charisse's bedside moments later, Stefan found her already asleep. Stretching out beside her, he cradled her in his arms and tenderly kissed her temple. She groaned slightly and moved deeper into his embrace. "I love you," she sleepily mumbled.

"I love you."

"God loves us, too," she said as she opened her eyes and looked up at him.

Smiling, he told her, "More than I could have ever imagined."

"Mommy, do I look okay?" Jared asked as he stepped into their bedroom. The eleven-year-old was wearing a navy blue suit with a white shirt and blue and red striped tie.

"You look better than okay," Charisse told him as she straightened his tie. "You look quite handsome, young man."

Jared blushed and said, "You always say that."

"Because it's always true."

At that moment, Stefàn entered the room carrying Stefàni. "You almost ready to go, baby?" he asked her.

"Yup. Here, I'll take her."

The instant Charisse uttered the words, Stefàni reached for her and cooed, "Mommy!"

"Come here, girlie. How's my girl, huh?" she asked and gave her daughter a kiss on the cheek.

Stefàni immediately reached for one of the hoops in Charisse's ears. "Oh, no, you don't," she said, tilting her head away from the toddler's reach.

Stefàni laughed, thinking her Mommy was playing a game.

Moving nearer to her, Stefàn said, "I like that dress, baby."

"Thank you."

"Mommy, can I hold Stefàni?" Jared asked.

She handed her off to their son. Jared moved to the stool at the foot of Charisse's and Stefàn's bed and sat with his little sister on his lap. In the next instant, Stefàni began to squirm so Jared lowered her to the floor. She headed straight back to Charisse. They had just celebrated her second birthday two days ago.

"Come here, Stefani," Jared called to his baby sister as she stood between her brother and parents, seemingly trying to determine which way she wanted to go.

After a few seconds of indecision, she laughingly responded to Jared's beckoning and clumsily scampered back to him. She was crazy about her big brother and the feeling was mutual.

It was Sunday morning and the family was preparing to leave for church.

While Jared was occupied with Stefàni, Stefàn took the opportunity to embrace his wife. "He's amazing with her, isn't he?" Stefàn said.

"Yes, he is," Charisse contended with a smile as she lovingly gazed at their children.

Placing his hand on her rounded belly and gently caressing it, he murmured, "You are absolutely beautiful. Have I ever told you that?"

Looking up into eyes that adored her and that she adored, she said, "I think a time or two, you have. But you're no slouch yourself, you know?"

Stefàn lowered his head and she didn't hesitate to go up on her toes to receive the kiss he was offering. "I love you, Charisse, and I thank God for you and our children and our life. You are the best thing that has ever happened to me and I will spend the rest of my life loving you and making sure you know how much I love and need you."

At six months pregnant, Charisse was at a place in her life she could have never even dreamed. Recalling the scripture, *it has not yet appeared what you shall be*, she told her husband, "God has given me everything I have ever wanted and needed in you, Stefàn Michael Cooper, and I will never ever take you or your love for granted. I love you, my beautiful man."

Their lips came together again, albeit more passionately, but they were soon called to task when they heard Jared say, "Okay, Stefani, go get Mommy and Daddy so they can stop smooching all over the place and we can go to church."

CHARISSE AND STEFÀN WERE STANDING just outside the sanctuary after service waiting where Jared usually met them when he got out of Sunday school. Stefàn was holding Stefàni in his arms but she was busily squirming, wanting to get down and run as any healthy two-year-old was wont to do.

"Hi, Mom. Hi, Daddy," Jared boisterously called as he approached them.

"Hey, dude. How was Sunday school?" Stefàn asked.

"It was great! We're going to do a play about David and Goliath for Homecoming Sunday and I'm gonna be David!"

"Wow, that's exciting," Charisse encouragingly cheered. "Were you rehearsing today?"

"Yup. We have to have rehearsal on Wednesday, too. I have a note right here," Jared said, as he held a piece of paper out to her.

Charisse took the paper from his hand and quickly perused it. Putting it in her pocketbook, she told him, "Okay. I'll sign this when we get home and you can turn it in when we come for rehearsal on Wednesday."

"Okay."

"You ready to go?" Stefàn then asked Charisse.

"Uh-huh. Jared, do you need to use the restroom?"

"No, Mommy. I went before I came out here."

Leading the way, Stefàn turned and headed toward the exit. Charisse and Jared were right behind him.

"Stefàn?"

The entire family turned to the left at the sound of the woman's voice. Charisse recognized the strikingly beautiful sister from the sanctuary. She'd noticed her when she walked in because she'd been admiring the orange print dress she was wearing.

Stefan frowned briefly at first, realizing that the face was familiar to him. It took a moment before he remembered where he knew her from. "Janine?"

She nodded slowly as a tentative smile crossed her face. "Hi."

"Janine. Wow," he reverently uttered. "Janine."

Then, to her and Charisse's surprise, Stefan shifted Stefani on his hip and reached out to embrace her.

"How are you?" he exuberantly asked.

"I'm great. How are you?"

"Excellent. Wow, it is great to see you. You look amazing," he said.

Janine's eyes shifted to see the reaction of the woman standing behind Stefan as it was obvious they were together.

"Thank you. Who is this beautiful little girl you're holding? Hi, sweetheart," she said as she reached out and touched Stefani's little hand.

"This is my daughter, Stefani." Then turning to Charisse, he said, "And this is my wife, Charisse, and our son, Jared." He placed his hand on Jared's head with the introduction.

"Hello," Charisse amicably greeted her.

"Hi. Nice to meet you," Janine said.

"What are you doing here?" Stefan then asked Janine. "Do you live nearby?"

"No. I'm waiting for my husband. He went to the men's room. We're here with friends."

"Okay. Good. Do you have any kids?" he asked her.

"Yes, we have four children. The oldest is thirteen and our baby is eight. They're at home with my mother."

"How is your mother?"

"She's good."

"Give her my regards, will you?"

"Sure."

Turning again to Charisse, he said, "Honey, this is Janine."

"I know, you just introduced us," Charisse said with a comedic grin.

"No, this is Janine. I told you about her remember? Janine."

Understanding dawned on her and Charisse replied, "Oh, Janine."

"Yeah." While they were on their honeymoon, Stefan had shared with Charisse the story of his first love and the way he had mistreated her and how she had broken his heart by not forgiving him. Turning back to Janine, who was looking at both of them strangely, he told her, "You don't know how glad I am to see you. I never really apologized to you for what I did. For the way I behaved. I was so busy blaming you for the way you reacted, that I never took the time to understand the reasons why you had to do what you did. I never wanted to admit how much I didn't deserve you, and I took my pain out on so many unsuspecting women." He sighed and shook his head in shame. "I never considered how much I'd hurt you and how precious a gift I had squandered until I met Charisse some ten or eleven years later. You were right not to give me another chance to hurt you. And I don't blame you anymore for not forgiving me."

"I did forgive you, Stefan. If I hadn't, I wouldn't have been able to move on."

"Well, Janine, it's because of you that I was able to recognize what a really good woman looked like and what she was worth. God used you and your tough love to teach me a lesson in humility. Of course, with my hard head, I didn't get it right away," he admitted with a shrug, "but I finally got it. I bet you didn't know that."

Janine didn't comment but the look on her face was one of affectionate appreciation.

Stefan reached out and took her hand. "Thank you, Janine. Thank you."

She smiled brightly. "Don't thank me, Stefan. Thank God."

ABOUT THE AUTHOR

Cheryl Faye recently returned as a resident to Harlem, New York, where she was born and raised and is an active member of First Corinthian Baptist Church. A legal secretary by profession, Cheryl is the proud mother of two sons, Michael and Douglas, and grandmother to Mikayla. Cheryl has five previously released novels; *Be Careful What You Wish For*, released in Spring 2005 for Strebor Books International, *First Love* and *A Test Of Time* for BET Books, and *A Time For Us* and *At First Sight* for Pinnacle Books, an imprint of Kensington Publishing. Her short story, *A Second Chance At Love*, was included in a Mothers' Day anthology *Mama Dear*, for Pinnacle Books. *Who Said It Would Be Easy?* is her first foray into the Christian fiction genre, but Cheryl believes she has definitely found her niche.

Cheryl can be reached at MsCherylFaye@gmail.com or on Facebook. Please include a subject matter in your message. No attachments, please.

IF YOU ENJOYED
"WHO SAID IT WOULD BE EASY?,"
PLEASE CHECK OUT CHERYL FAYE'S

BE CAREFUL WHAT YOU
Wish For
A NOVEL

AVAILABLE FROM STREBOR BOOKS

Chapter 1

Sitting comfortably on the plush gray leather living room sofa with her stockinged feet tucked under her ample bottom and wearing an old pair of sweatpants with a hole in the knee and a paint-splattered sweatshirt, Jamilah Parsons cradled a bowl of her favorite ice cream, Häagen-Dazs® Vanilla Swiss Almond, in her lap, despite the chill in the apartment on that cold February night.

Jamilah's roommate and childhood friend, Sabrina Richardson, accompanied by her latest conquest, Darius Thornton, had just entered the apartment that Friday evening looking glamorous as always.

Wearing a full-length fox coat which draped her long, slender frame as if she had been born in it, Sabrina's long, luxurious black hair fell down her back and, combined with the fur, gave her a regal air she carried all too well. Jamilah had always believed Sabrina could have been a high-paid super-model who traveled the globe showcasing world-renowned designers' clothing while her picture graced fashion magazine covers worldwide. Possessing stunning looks with a figure to match, in addition to the exaggerated air of sophistication she had learned from her mother, Sabrina, nevertheless, was determined to fulfill her childhood dream of marrying a wealthy man so she would not have to work for a living.

"Hey, J," Sabrina chirped.

"Hi."

Immediately noticing what Jamilah was watching on television, Sabrina frowned. "Not again, Jamilah."

Ignoring Sabrina's comment, Jamilah continued watching Robert Townsend's *The Five Heartbeats*, one of her all-time favorite movies. Since there was no special man in her life right now, and being the movie buff she was, Jamilah frequently passed her time in front of the television or at the theater, if she was not curled up with a good book or working.

"You remember Darius, don't you?" Sabrina inquired.

"Yeah. Hi."

Believing him to be one of the most handsome men Sabrina had ever brought home, Darius reminded Jamilah of Denzel Washington, although she thought he was much better looking. Wearing his dark brown hair in a stylish fade, his smooth, cocoa-brown face was clean shaven, allowing his true masculine allure to shine. Although not unbecoming, his nose was somewhat flat, but his lips looked soft, sensuous and ripe for kissing. Despite his finely polished *GQ* cover model look, Darius' warm, welcoming personality shone through as did his sincerity when he smiled at Jamilah and greeted her in that smooth baritone voice she remembered. "Hello, Jamilah. How are you?"

"Fine, thanks."

Having a substantial title or position as a prerequisite to dating Sabrina, Darius was a senior associate at a major New York City law firm. She had been seeing him for a little over a month and often bragged that he would bend over backwards to do anything she asked. Beauty aside, Sabrina was quite pretentious, and it amazed Jamilah somewhat that Darius, who exuded humility, would be so taken with her. The old adage "opposites attract" sprang to mind whenever Jamilah thought of the obvious contrasts in their personalities, but truth be told, the same could be said of her and Sabrina's friendship.

Peeling off her fur coat and tossing it carelessly across the arm of their rose-floral silk upholstered easy-chair, Sabrina said, "Sit down, Darius. I'll be right back."

Beneath the luxurious coat, Sabrina wore an ecru angora turtleneck sweater over ecru wool gabardine slacks. High-heeled leather boots of the same hue completed her ensemble. Standing five feet, eight inches in her stocking feet, even in her four-inch heels she was still dwarfed by her handsome friend who stood close to six inches taller.

Giving further direction as Darius took a seat at the opposite end of the sofa, Sabrina intoned, "Jamilah, keep Darius company for me while I go change."

Sarcastically, Jamilah responded, "Yes, ma'am." Smiling apologetically at Darius when she realized that Sabrina had not even taken his coat, she added, "Let me hang up your coat, Darius."

"Oh, thank you." Rising to remove his tan cashmere overcoat, he handed the garment to Jamilah, who immediately noticed how elegantly his brown tweed suit covered his tall frame. When he unbuttoned his suit jacket, she could see that his white shirt was crisp, as if freshly ironed. A beige and brown "power" tie was knotted expertly at his neck.

After hanging his coat in the closet near the front door, Jamilah then picked up Sabrina's fur coat from the chair and hung it up, as well. Before taking her seat again, Jamilah asked, "Can I get you anything? Something to drink? Some ice cream maybe?"

"Oh, no, thank you, Jamilah. I'm fine," was his reply.

You most certainly are, you gorgeous hunk of... Secretly ashamed of her lustful thoughts, she asked, "Is it really very cold out?"

"Yeah, the hawk is out in full effect tonight."

Chivalrously, he waited for her to sit back down before he did the same. *Mmm, Mama raised him right*, she thought. Seated again, Jamilah picked up her bowl of ice cream, assumed her former position and resumed eating. Silence ensued for the next few minutes until she spoke.

"Do you want to watch something else? I've already seen it a dozen times, as I'm sure you've guessed from Brie's remark. I can turn this off."

"No. Actually, this is one of my favorite movies," Darius commented.

"Really?"

"Yeah. I've seen it about five times myself. It kind of takes me back. Me and a couple of my college buddies used to sing together. We did a few talent shows while we were in school," Darius admitted.

"Really?" Sitting up straight on the couch, she placed her bowl on the glass-topped coffee table and turned toward him. "You know, I used to sing with my cousins when we were little. We never did any talent shows, but we put on plenty of shows at family gatherings."

Laughing, Darius guessed, "The Supremes, huh?"

"The Parsonettes."

Puzzlement covered his face.

"Our last name is Parsons."

Nodding with understanding, he responded, "Oh."

"Hey, what are you two talking about?" Sabrina inquired as she returned to the living room. Dressed now in red silk lounging pajamas, wearing red satin stiletto mules with her hair pulled over one shoulder and fresh make-up, Sabrina looked stunning.

Jamilah noticed that Darius was immediately taken in by her friend's appearance.

Sitting next to him and draping one of her long slender legs across his lap, Sabrina listened as Jamilah said, "Darius was just telling me that he used to be in a singing group when he was in college."

Cooing in his ear with slight envy, she remarked, "Is that right? You've never sung for me."

Jamilah blushed, but not as deeply as Darius did, she noticed. Suddenly feeling like a third wheel, she grabbed the remote control and turned off the television before picking up her bowl and heading out of the room.

No one noticed her departure.

Entering her spacious bedroom and turning on her bedside lamp, Jamilah sat on top of the multicolored goose-down comforter that covered her queen-sized bed and finished what was left of her ice cream.

"How come I can't meet a man as fine as that," she murmured in her solitude.

Placing the bowl on the nightstand and rising from the bed, she walked over to the full-length mirror that hung on the closet door and gazed at her reflection. *I'm no beauty like Sabrina, but I look good enough*.

Two inches taller than Sabrina and full-figured, Jamilah, however, was by no means fat. *Healthy*, that's what her mother called her. Her size sixteen hips had turned plenty of men's heads and her ample bosom had captured many men's undivided attention. Beautiful, blemish-free, pumpernickel brown skin was her covering. Her nose and mouth were small and more European-looking than African in their structure. Many times had she been told that the slant of her eyes was very sexy. Shoulder-length culture locks were worn like an Afrocentric crown.

Maybe if I was a little slimmer… She suddenly frowned. "What am I thinking about? There is nothing wrong with me." Turning in a huff and walking back to her bed, Jamilah picked up the book she was currently reading from the nightstand and propped herself up against her fluffy throw pillows to read.